Christmas
at Fox
Farm

BOOKS BY HELEN POLLARD

helen pollard

Christmas at Fox Farm

Bookouture

Published by Bookouture in 2021

An imprint of Storyfire Ltd.
Carmelite House
50 Victoria Embankment
London EC4Y 0DZ

www.bookouture.com

ISBN: 978-1-80019-954-5
eBook ISBN: 978-1-80019-953-8

To my mother's love of the Yorkshire Dales – I couldn't have written this book without it.

Chapter One

'I hope you brought your sharpest knives,' Jean said as everyone arrived at her little cottage.

Now there's something you don't hear every day, Daisy thought. But tonight was pumpkin-carving night, so it was a case of all hands – and knives – on deck.

Jean greeted them all with a cheerful smile, and her kitchen greeted them with the delicious smell of cinnamon toast and spiced tea.

'Sorry about the lack of alcohol,' Jean said as she handed them mugs. 'I didn't think it mixed with sharp implements!'

Daisy stared at the pumpkins of all sizes lined up on the long, scarred table. 'Are you sure you have enough, Jean?'

Her wry comment was met with Jean's customary twinkle from pale-blue eyes, her face wrinkling along with her smile. 'You can never have enough pumpkins. Halloween wasn't a thing when I was a girl, back in the Dark Ages.' Her broad Yorkshire accent was friendly and down-to-earth. 'Reckon I missed out, so I'm making up for it now. Besides, think how big the yard is.' She swept her grey hair up and tied it with a band. 'How are your carving skills? As good as your art?'

'I don't know. I've never carved a pumpkin.'

'Sorry, Daisy. Me and my big mouth. Well, there's a first time for everything, and simple designs can be effective. Leave the fancy stuff to the café crew, eh?' She jerked a thumb at Angie and Sue, who were already getting started.

As the kitchen filled with chatter and laughter and pumpkin pulp and advice-giving, Daisy watched how everyone set about their task and tried her best with hers.

Angie, Fox Farm's café manager, wielded her knife with remarkable capability as she created a complicated design involving bats swooping from a tree branch.

How does she do that without the whole thing collapsing? Daisy wondered.

'The Halloween Trail's looking great,' Jamie enthused. Only eighteen, he'd joined as a summer sales assistant in the gallery, but he was so personable that Jean had kept him on for his gap year. This week, he'd put an orange streak in his hair, and his nails were painted alternate black and purple.

Daisy thought about the bright scarecrows they had spent Fox Farm's closing day setting up; and then there were the witches in black cloaks and hats, the ghosts (white sheets over balloons, suspended from trees), and the large rubber spiders and bats they had hung.

'The pumpkins will make the trail even better. Except mine.' Daisy turned her pumpkin's wonky frown and angry eyes to face the others. 'Can't believe I call myself an artist.'

'Every skill's different,' Jean said. 'I may be a good potter, but I couldn't paint a beautiful picture like you do in a million years. Anyway, practice makes perfect. Plenty more to do. Would a slice of carrot cake keep you all going?'

'Mmmm, Jean, this is the best,' Sue, Angie's café assistant, mumbled as she ate.

'Thank you, but flattery won't get you out of more work,' Jean said, laughing. 'One more pumpkin each.'

'I hope I won't get too many small children in the gallery this week, all sugared up and with sticky fingers,' Lisa said as she concentrated, her tongue poking from the corner of her mouth. 'What specials have you got on at the café, Angie?'

'White-iced ghost ginger biscuits, black-iced bat shortbread, orange and purple cupcakes, and healthy pumpkin soup to offset the sugar rush.' Angie winked at them all.

Daisy smiled at the chatter. Good food, good company, friendly noise… Daisy had been used to plenty of noise in the past, but this was a different kind. A *good* kind.

By the end of the evening, her arm ached as she waved goodbye to everyone.

'I'll pop round early in the morning, Jean, to place the pumpkins around the trail for you,' she offered. 'Seven thirty?'

'That's grand, Daisy. You know me – I'll be up long before then.'

Daisy shivered against the night chill as she crossed the cobbled farmyard to her studio and hurried inside, straight through to her living space… if you could call it that. Situated at one end of the long, low building, there was only room enough for a bed, an armchair, a cupboard and a tiny kitchenette, with a small shower room attached.

Previous artists-in-residence had only used the studio as somewhere to work, display and sell. Nobody had actually *lived* there before. But since the only place Daisy could call home when Jean offered the residency to her last spring was a dilapidated caravan on a local farm,

Daisy had been happy to spruce it up. Seven months on, she was perfectly content in her cosy little den. It was yet another temporary living arrangement, but then, Daisy's whole life had been defined by temporary arrangements. Fox Farm was a particularly *nice* one.

*

Daisy wasn't one to lie in. During her childhood, getting up early was often the only peace she might get in the day.

With a mug of tea in hand, she entered her studio, switched on the lights and checked that everything was ready for Fox Farm's Halloween week. She'd put a few decorations up – mock cobwebs and strings of cardboard pumpkins – but she hadn't gone mad. She didn't want them to detract from her work.

Daisy had chosen the prints and canvases currently on display for their autumn colours – greens, purples, oranges, browns – in anticipation of this week's extra footfall, although she suspected that harassed parents trying to corral their offspring around the Halloween Trail would be more interested in bribery at the café than purchasing art.

Ah well. Time to sort the pumpkins out.

Scraping her hair into an untidy ponytail, she pulled on jeans, an old sweatshirt, wellies and a cagoule, then stepped outside, enjoying the stillness for a moment.

Oh, Fox Farm is so perfect!

Her studio, converted from a cattle byre, lined the side of the square opposite the entranceway to Fox Farm. To her left was the half-converted barn, never completed and currently used for storage. To her right stood the large grey-stone building that housed the café and gallery, once the main farmhouse, with Jean's little cottage and garden at its side. Jean's was the original farmhouse, dating back to the late 1700s, around the same time Daisy's cattle byre was built. The larger farmhouse had been built later, in the mid-1800s, as the farm prospered. All the buildings were of wonderful old Yorkshire stone, their history steeped into their frontages.

It's such a shame that Jean changes her studio artist every year. Only five months left for me. What I'd give to stay... Still, I'm a part of it for now, and that's all that matters.

Daisy crossed the still-dark yard to Jean's cottage, frowning as she noticed there was no light on downstairs; no clattering coming from the kitchen. Her gaze drifted upwards. No smoke from the chimney, either, although there was a light on in the bedroom.

A sense of unease unfurled in her belly.

She's had a lie-in, Daisy. It was a long, busy evening, and the woman's in her seventies, for goodness' sake.

Daisy tried Jean's door. It wasn't locked. *Typical Jean. Old country ways.*

She stepped into the familiar kitchen with its pinewood table and dresser, cream walls and pleasant clutter, dominated by the large cooking range. Daisy had enjoyed many mugs of strong tea sitting in this kitchen these past few months, chatting with Jean.

But there was no sign of morning activity. The kettle was cold; no smell of toast. The carved pumpkins sat waiting on the table.

She could get on with placing them along the trail. But she didn't like this quiet. If Jean were getting dressed, she would hear *something*, surely?

Daisy almost called out, but she didn't want to wake Jean. Instead, she kicked off her wellies and crept upstairs. If Jean *was* still asleep,

Daisy would creep right back down again and feel awful for intruding, but her gut demanded that she should check. She pushed open the door to Jean's bedroom, wincing as it creaked.

Jean was in her armchair, fully clothed, slumped and unresponsive.

Daisy rushed to her side. 'Jean?'

Jean didn't seem to be unconscious… but she didn't seem to see Daisy, either. Her face looked lopsided.

'Oh, no. Please, no.' Grabbing the phone from Jean's bedside, Daisy dialled with shaking fingers. 'Ambulance, please. I think someone's had a stroke.'

Chapter Two

Daisy gripped Jean's hand. The downside of being so far out in the countryside meant the paramedics would take some time. Fox Farm was only a mile from the nearest village, Winterbridge, but the nearest ambulance station was much further.

Daisy's mind raced. None of the staff were due for at least an hour. She should phone someone. Angie? Lisa?

Jean's nephew. Alex.

Jean never had children of her own, but Alex was her favourite nephew. He lived in Winterbridge, though Daisy barely knew him. He came to Fox Farm every Tuesday on its closing day to help Jean with jobs that needed doing, but that was when Daisy was out and about, taking a breather and seeking inspiration, or painting in her studio. They occasionally crossed paths, nodding hello or exchanging a polite comment about the weather, both too preoccupied with their days for anything more. Once, he'd come to fix the heater in her studio and taken time to study her art. Another occasion, they had coincided over a cuppa at Jean's, but he'd seemed intent on getting back to his chores rather than idling away the time in gossip and chatter. Even so, he was pleasant enough, and attractive in an outdoorsy way.

Daisy didn't know his phone number, though. Glancing at the bedside table, she spotted Jean's mobile. Was it passworded? *Of course not. Jean didn't bother with such things.* With relief, Daisy got into the contacts list and clicked on the first entry.

'Aunt Jean. This is early. What's up?' Alex's deep voice sounded puzzled but upbeat.

Daisy took a breath. 'This isn't Jean. It's Daisy.' When he didn't reply, she added, 'At Fox Farm. I live in the cattle byre.'

That hadn't come out right, but it hardly mattered.

'Daisy. Yes. Hi. And you're using Aunt Jean's phone because…?' His tone changed. 'Is something wrong? Is she okay?'

'No.' Daisy fought back tears. 'I've called an ambulance. I found her in the cottage. She looks as if she hasn't been to bed all night.' A sob escaped. 'I think she might have had a stroke.'

'I'm on my way. I'm on my way. You'll stay with her?'

'Yes. Of course.' But he had already ended the call.

*

Alex stared at the phone in his shaking hand, trying but failing to control the adrenalin rush.

Aunt Jean. The one stable, stalwart influence in his life since… Since forever.

'Don't you do this to me, Aunt Jean! You'd better be alright, do you hear me?'

It was early, but he was already at Riverside, resealing a pane of glass in one of the greenhouses that had felt draughty the day before. Mornings were the best time of day, Alex reckoned. Peace and quiet before the rest of the world intruded.

Yanking his keys from his pocket, he weaved through the maze of outbuildings and greenhouses to his truck, dialling Jules, his manager, on the way. It went to voicemail.

'Jules, there's an emergency at Fox Farm. Don't expect to see me today. Sorry.'

Starting the truck's engine, he glanced over at the plant nursery, his pride and joy, forlorn in the early-morning light. 'Sorry, guys. This comes first.'

And then the tyres ground into the gravel as he backed out and pulled onto the road that ran alongside the river towards Winterbridge.

Narrow country lanes lined with solid drystone walls were not ideal for a rushed journey, but Alex knew them like the back of his hand, so he took risks. Anyone else out and about at this time was probably local. Tourists, day trippers and hikers wouldn't get started till it was properly light.

As he drove, he panicked about his aunt and mulled over Daisy. He hoped he hadn't been too curt with her on the phone, but surely she would understand. He didn't know her well, but Aunt Jean spoke fondly of her, and Alex got the impression the two of them had become close since Daisy had moved into the studio.

Thank goodness for that, he thought as he reached Winterbridge and turned up the hill for the mile to Fox Farm, swerving to avoid a rabbit taking its own sweet time to cross the road. For whatever reason, Daisy had been up early, found Aunt Jean and called for help. Otherwise, it might have been another couple of hours before Fox Farm's staff noticed his aunt wasn't around and decided to find out if there was a problem.

And so it was with a sense of deep gratitude towards this near-stranger that Alex ignored the parking spaces along the roadside and drove all the way into the farmyard, screeching to a halt outside the cottage. He stormed up the stairs to the bedroom where his beloved aunt was slumped in her chair, dazed and oddly lopsided.

She looked at him, but he wasn't sure she saw him.

Daisy was kneeling on the floor beside Aunt Jean's chair, patting her hand and murmuring reassurances.

Alex briefly took in the younger woman's bedraggled early-morning appearance. It touched him that she had concentrated solely on his aunt and not worried about that.

'Daisy. Thanks for calling me.' He bent to kiss his aunt's cheek and squeezed her shoulders. When she didn't respond, he fought back a tear. 'Any idea how long the paramedics will be?'

'They were out on another call. They said maybe thirty minutes. Anytime now, I reckon.'

Daisy tried a wobbly smile, her brown eyes troubled, and Alex's heart went out to her. This must have been an awful ordeal for her.

'I'm sorry for not finding her sooner,' Daisy mumbled.

'Please don't be sorry. If it wasn't for you, it could've been much longer.' He hesitated. 'Will you and the others manage today? It'll be busy, with it being half-term and Halloween week.'

'I don't see why not,' Daisy reassured him. 'Don't worry.'

The sound of a siren cut in, and they both sighed with relief.

'I'll show them upstairs,' Daisy offered, leaving him to take her place.

Alex watched her go, her oversized wellie socks flapping, her shapeless sweatshirt doing her no favours at all, and wasn't at all surprised that Aunt Jean liked her so much.

*

Daisy made tea for Alex, adding two spoons of sugar for shock. He took it gratefully. While the paramedics attended his aunt, she helped him pack a bag with a few of Jean's things. Once the paramedics were ready to carry their patient downstairs, Daisy took her leave.

'Will you call me later?' she asked Alex. 'My number's on Jean's mobile.'

He nodded. 'You'll explain to everyone?'

'Of course.'

'Thank you, Daisy. For everything.'

Back at the byre, Daisy only had time to take a quick shower and pull on smarter jeans and her knitted pumpkin sweater before the others began to arrive.

'I passed an ambulance near the village,' Angie announced as she unlocked the café. 'Hope it's nobody around here.'

And so it began – Daisy catching each person as they arrived, explaining about Jean and watching their upset, then soothing and reassuring, even though she had no idea whether there was any reassurance to be had. Jean wasn't just an employer to them – she was much loved.

'What'll happen?' Lisa wondered. 'Who'll run Fox Farm now?'

'I've been managing that café for donkey's years,' Angie said decisively. 'We'll manage for now, won't we, Sue? And you've been at the gallery a long time, Lisa. We all need to muck in, that's all. Alex is a capable lad. When he's got over the shock, he'll sort it out, I'm sure.' She glanced at her watch. 'Nearly nine. We'd better get a shift on.'

'The pumpkins!' Daisy remembered. 'They're still in Jean's kitchen.'

'I'll do them,' Jamie offered. 'Surely nobody'll be here dead on nine.'

Fox Farm was barely organised when the first visitors arrived.

It was a busy day for midweek, with local parents happy to have somewhere to keep their children occupied for an hour or so. Daisy could see from her studio that the café was packed. Besides the Halloween revellers, there would be the usual walkers, day trippers and people bringing an elderly relative out for lunch and a mooch around the gallery.

Fox Farm's situation, on a crossroads where three country lanes joined, meant there was always trade. Tourists might spot it on a drive and be tempted to stop. The surrounding countryside, criss-crossed with public footpaths, provided a ready supply of ramblers, keen to refuel with a hot drink and cake or lunch. Locals loved it as a place to meet up, too.

As she'd expected, Daisy's studio was only moderately busy, although her distinctive style – acrylics in gentle colours, based on the Yorkshire Dales countryside and villages, with quirky additions like crooked barns and farmhouses, comical sheep, cheeky sheepdogs – generally did well here. For Halloween, she had painted a couple of new pieces – one of a ramshackle farmhouse with a ghost hovering over the rooftop and a cauldron bubbling in the kitchen window, and the other of a herd of sheep chasing a scarecrow across a field. Guessing they might have limited appeal, she had only had a few prints made for now, but she'd enjoyed creating something fun and different, and both were admired by her browsing customers.

In an effort to distract herself from thinking about Jean, Daisy got on with painting at the work end of her studio. That was another reason she'd snapped up Jean's offer for the year – a space to create. Potential customers loved to watch her work and ask questions, although that sometimes meant she didn't get as much done as she'd like.

It was midday before her mobile rang.

'How is she?' she asked as soon as she heard Alex's voice.

'Stable, but she's in intensive care.'

Daisy's heart sank. 'Is it that bad?'

'It'll take a while to tell,' Alex said, his voice breaking a little. 'They've been doing tests. If the stroke happened late last night like we think, then she didn't get the immediate treatment they'd usually give. That's detrimental, apparently.'

When a sob escaped from Daisy's throat, Alex said gently, 'Don't feel guilty about that, Daisy. Jean lives alone. It's lucky that you live on site and found her when you did.'

'How long will she be in hospital?'

'That depends on how much damage was done and what treatment she'll need. But it is serious, so she'll be in for a good long while.' He sighed. 'Look, I know this is a hectic week for Fox Farm…'

'Don't worry about it,' Daisy said immediately. 'Angie and Lisa can cope. It won't be the same without Jean around to step in where she's needed, cover at busy times and so on, but they'll manage.' It occurred to her that Alex was neglecting his own business. 'What about Riverside?'

'They'll get by without me. My manager, Jules, is the most capable woman I know.' He chuckled. 'Apart from Aunt Jean, that is. Look, I'm sorry, but I need to go. Give my regards to everyone and update them, will you? I haven't time to call them, too.'

'No problem.' Daisy clicked off and stared through her window, oblivious to the sound of excitable children in the cobbled yard. Jean's stroke sounded serious. If only Daisy had realised yesterday evening when she'd left Jean that something like this would happen.

You're not psychic, Daisy. Like Alex said, she's lucky you were around when you were.

Alex had sounded so upset, and his love for his aunt was plain. The fact that he spent Riverside's closing days helping out at Fox Farm, doing everything from fixing fencing to caring for Jean's cottage garden, showed how much he cared. Jean had told Daisy that Alex had spent most of his school holidays with her and her late husband, William, hinting that he'd had an unhappy childhood. She'd often said how proud she was of him for making a success of his business, but she hadn't mentioned a wife or partner. Daisy assumed she would have, if there was anyone. Beyond that, Daisy knew very little about him.

What she *did* know was that Alex was more attractive than she'd realised. Their occasional, brief encounters hadn't given her time to assess, although she had to confess to noticing broad shoulders and a muscled physique in the summer months when he wore a T-shirt. But the time they had spent waiting for the ambulance together that morning had given her the opportunity to take in his hazel eyes, and the overlong brown hair and day-old stubble that gave him an appealingly dishevelled look.

Daisy winced. Goodness knew what he'd thought of *her* this morning! She could only hope he'd been too intent on his aunt to notice. She had dressed for dragging a load of pumpkins around the Halloween Trail, not attending a fashion parade.

Not that it made much difference. Daisy never dressed fancy. When she was working, she was bound to get paint somewhere, so she favoured jeans or dungarees and a jumper or T-shirt. She figured it helped her image in the studio, anyway – people expected artists to look messy and untidy. Today's knitted pumpkin sweater was an exception, donated for seasonal purposes by Jean, who was a prolific knitter. When she was out hiking, Daisy was no more fashionable, inevitably in jeans or walking trousers and a cagoule. As for her hair, it had always been limited – straight and boring brown. Daisy found it easiest to keep it long so she could tie it up, out of the way.

Even if she wanted to dress up, do her hair, slap on make-up (*Make-up? What's that again?*) Daisy doubted it would make much difference. On a day when she was being kind to herself, she knew she wasn't glamorous. On a less kind day, she reckoned she was verging on plain. She'd decided a long time ago not to let it worry her.

Too distracted to work, Daisy gazed through the window at harassed mothers pulling scarves tighter around children's necks and hats down over ears against the afternoon cold. She couldn't bear the idea of Jean lying in hospital, attached to tubes and drips and machines, helpless. Jean was a force of nature; indomitable.

Over one of their many cuppas together, Jean had told Daisy how she and her husband William had inherited the farm from his side of the family, but neither of them were farmers. The little cottage was big enough for the two of them, so over the years, William had converted the other buildings. First, they had opened up a downstairs room of the main house to sell Jean's pottery, with only a handmade sign to attract customers. Then, recognising the potential for catching passing ramblers, they had started a little café in the room next to it. Local artists and craftspeople began to ask if she would take their work, so they had opened up one of the 'bedrooms' upstairs, then the second and third. Jean would only take Yorkshire artists, at a wide range of prices to suit all pockets, and she still stuck to that.

'This is a Yorkshire farm in the Yorkshire Dales,' she'd told Daisy. 'Let others sort themselves out!'

Finally, about ten years ago, Jean had got William to turn the old cattle byre into a studio, her idea being to host a different artist there each year to keep things fresh. Daisy was lucky to have been offered it this year... not least because Jean had made an exception for her and wasn't charging rent.

Daisy was in awe at what Jean had achieved over the years. Jean *was* Fox Farm. What on earth would they do without her while she recovered? *If* she recovered?

A tear ran down her cheek. *Don't think that way, Daisy!*

Chapter Three

It had been one of the worst days of Alex's life. Seeing Aunt Jean slumped in her chair; the ambulance ride; the starkness of Accident & Emergency; the blood tests and swallow test and brain scan and drip attachments and oxygen mask; the wait for a bed… All had taken their toll.

Alex knew his aunt wouldn't live forever, although sometimes he wished she could. But at only seventy-two, bird-like yet strong and wiry, her mind razor-sharp, he *had* imagined she would remain indestructible for a good while yet. This stroke had come as a complete shock, as had the doctors' pronouncements that it was in no way a minor one. Aunt Jean would be in hospital for some time, and once they found out she lived alone, he was told she would need a lot of convalescence and rehabilitation before being allowed to return home… *if* that were possible.

Oh, how Alex hated that '*if*'.

By late afternoon, the doctors had said there was nothing more he could do and to get some rest.

On his way out of the hospital, he phoned Jules at Riverside. Business had been quiet, other than the large number of pumpkins sold, which he always bought in specially for Halloween. After this week, Riverside would match Fox Farm with winter hours, closing an hour early and switching from one closing day a week to two. Alex would normally use that extra time to catch up, but with Aunt Jean so ill, goodness knew what would happen. As he drove back towards Winterbridge, the prospect of colder days and darker nights ahead matched his mood.

Before going home, his mind set on a large glass of whisky, Alex pulled up outside Fox Farm. It was just past five, and all the buildings' lights were out except for Daisy's studio.

She opened the door to his knock, dressed in sturdy walking boots and an open cagoule over a pumpkin jumper.

Alex smiled at the motif. *Aunt Jean's work, no doubt.*

'Hi. I came with an update,' he said. 'Are you going out?'

'I need some fresh air. Today's been hard.' Hastily, she added, 'A lot harder for you, obviously.'

Alex hesitated. 'Mind if I join you?'

'No problem. I'd like to hear about Jean.'

'I'll get my boots and jacket from the truck.'

Kitted out, Alex re-joined her. She'd pulled on a bright woollen hat with a Peruvian-type design. It was cute.

Crikey. That's *not a word I normally think of. Must be more tired than I thought.*

'It's getting dark, so we'll have to keep it short.' Daisy led him over the road to a public footpath that would take them down to the river, a route Alex knew well.

As they walked, he filled her in on his day.

'Do they think she'll recover fully?' Daisy asked.

'She's strong and determined, so that's in her favour.' Touched by the wobble that had been in Daisy's voice, Alex said, 'You're fond of her.'

Daisy smiled – a lovely, natural smile in what his Uncle William might have called a bonnie face.

'Yes,' she agreed. 'She's been good to me ever since I moved to the Dales, taking my work in the gallery and recommending other places. When she offered me the studio for this year, I jumped at it. Somewhere to display, work *and* live? It was a no-brainer.'

'How on earth could you paint in that caravan at old Jack's?' Alex asked, curious.

'He let me use one of his downstairs rooms for working.'

'Jack lives in that big old farmhouse all alone. Couldn't he have given you a bedroom, too?'

'Ha! He said it wouldn't be proper. Didn't want everyone thinking he had a young flibbertigibbet in the house, looking after his "needs".'

Alex choked out a laugh. 'Jack's eighty if he's a day! Why would he imagine people might think that?'

'It wasn't just the idea of local disapproval – I'd hope nobody *would* think that. But he's loyal to his late wife's memory, and it would've felt wrong to him.'

'So he put you up in a rusting tin can instead?'

'I couldn't pay much, and he didn't charge much. I think he liked knowing someone was around.' Daisy winced. 'I don't visit him as often as I should.'

Alex was grateful they were talking about something other than the hospital. He needed normality right now. They reached the river, but the path there was muddy and the light almost gone. They turned back.

'You've settled in well, according to Aunt Jean,' Alex commented. His aunt had told him just recently that it felt like Daisy was a part of the fabric of Fox Farm – high praise indeed, and not something she'd said about any of Daisy's predecessors, much as she enjoyed having a new face around each year.

'Yes. There's something about Fox Farm, isn't there? The camaraderie, the atmosphere, the beautiful old buildings. And Jean, of course. I liked her before, but since I moved on site… Well, it's hard not to be friends with her. I've felt like she's taken me under her wing.' Daisy laughed, the sound ringing out across silent, darkening fields. 'That sounds silly. I'm thirty-one years old!'

'Aunt Jean's friendly with most people,' Alex agreed as they worked their way back up the incline. 'But the fact that she's taken you under her wing means you're special to her. And offering you the studio means she thinks you've got real talent.'

'Thank you.'

'I like your work. It's quirky and interesting.' He glanced sideways at her. 'Our paths haven't crossed much before now, have they? Still, we can put that right. Looks like I'll be spending more time at Fox Farm for a while.'

'What will you have to do?'

Alex had no idea. His aunt had a good set-up, and the staff were reliable, but until he knew more about her recovery, all he could do was keep everything ticking along.

'I don't know yet. But I can't expect everyone to keep going without feeling like someone's at the helm.'

Daisy accepted his offer of a hand as she negotiated a stile over a stone wall, although Alex doubted she needed it – she'd managed the hill from the river without any change of pace.

'What about Riverside?' she asked as they neared the farm.

'We'll manage somehow.' When they reached his truck, he said, 'Thanks for the walk. It was just what I needed.'

'You'll eat something when you get home?' Daisy asked, sounding so much like Aunt Jean that it made him smile. 'Not just have a strong drink?'

How did you guess? 'I will. I promise.'

'And you'll keep in touch? Let us know when Jean can have visitors?'

'Of course.' He glanced over at her studio. 'Will you be alright here, on your own?'

Daisy hesitated. 'It'll be a bit weird, knowing Jean's not around, but I'll be okay. Thanks for thinking about me.'

'You're welcome.'

Suddenly awkward – two strangers thrown together by difficult and emotional circumstances – they went their separate ways.

By the time Alex reached his small terraced house in Winterbridge, he was exhausted, but he still had a busy evening ahead. Word about his aunt would get around the village through Fox Farm's staff, so there was no need to trouble himself with contacting her friends and acquaintances. Family, however, was a different matter.

Throwing together cheese on toast, he glanced around while he waited for it to bubble under the grill. The small kitchen was looking dingy. He'd meant to refit it soon after he moved in. That was five years ago. The same could be said for the rest of the house. Alex had got it cheap because it needed updating – all he could afford at the time – but he'd only managed to give the worst rooms a lick of paint. Riverside took most of his time and resources, and he'd figured he'd sort the house out when he could. It wasn't like he was hosting elegant dinners or throwing fancy parties. But as he looked around the jaded kitchen, he couldn't help but compare it with Aunt Jean's. Hers was a warm, welcoming space, neat and well kept. His was somewhere to chill beer and make cheese on toast.

Ah, well. It'll have to wait a darned sight longer, the way things are going.

Once he'd eaten, Alex had no further excuse. He picked up the phone.

Aunt Jean's brother-in-law, Eric – Uncle William's older brother – was a widower, recently fitted with a pacemaker. He expressed concern but said he wasn't fit to travel from his home in Devon to visit her. Alex promised to keep him posted.

Eric and William's much younger sister, Nicky, also living in Devon, was Alex's mother. He would need a whisky for *that* call.

Gulping it down, he dialled.

'Alex. What a lovely surprise! How are you?' His mother's overly cheerful voice was one she employed to ensure they kept in touch – something he wasn't very good at.

'Not good, Mum. It's about Aunt Jean.'

His mother listened carefully, upset that the sister-in-law who had helped take care of her boy in difficult times was so ill.

'I'd struggle to get time off work at the moment,' she told him. 'Someone else is off sick. And since it's such a long way to come, I'd like to get the timing right. Perhaps it would be better when Jean's more fit for company? Or even if…' Her voice hitched. 'If she takes a turn for the worse. You'll let me know?'

'Of course.'

There was a long silence. 'Alex, I know this is hard on you; how fond you are of her. Take care of yourself, won't you?'

'I will. Bye, Mum.'

Alex sat brooding for a long time after that, nursing a second whisky.

It was a testament to his mother's generosity that she never held his fondness for Aunt Jean and his late Uncle William against them. Releasing him to their care during school holidays, she must have known a strong bond would develop. Had she also known it would make such a dent in their own bond? A dent that was still there, after all these years? Since they weren't heart-to-heart people, that wasn't something they were ever likely to discuss.

Finishing the whisky, Alex steeled himself to inform the one member of the family remaining – Eric's son and Jean's other nephew, Sebastian.

Sebastian was not Alex's favourite person, and the feeling was mutual. They had never been close cousins, even as children, and that chalk-and-cheese relationship had only magnified as they grew older. Alex owned his small rural business, growing and selling plants; Sebastian was some bigshot city accountant for a company that was called in when large businesses were going under, to either rescue them or put them into administration. It was *way* out of Alex's league.

Uncle Eric hadn't offered to contact his son, saying Sebastian was embroiled in an intensive job. Alex knew – because Sebastian had importantly bragged about it at many a family gathering – that once Sebastian was on a job, he was unavailable until it was sorted.

A fat lot of use he'd be with regard to keeping Fox Farm ticking over, whether available or not. Perhaps an email would do.

*

Daisy didn't feel like eating much. As she reheated some of Angie's pumpkin soup in her microwave, she worried about Jean and found herself thinking about Alex.

He'd looked tired and haunted with worry. As Jean's nearest relative, she supposed he suddenly had a great deal of responsibility on his shoulders. Visiting his aunt and liaising with medical staff would be hard enough, but there was Fox Farm to consider, on top of running his own business. Jean's stroke wasn't a minor health blip. This whole situation would be hard for him, both emotionally and in practical terms.

Still, Daisy was confident he would rise to the challenge. Angie and the others spoke fondly of Alex, and she knew they were appreciative of the way he looked out for Jean and helped around the place.

She took her soup over to her one chair and gazed out onto the silent farmyard. It felt eerily quiet, knowing the cottage was empty. Daisy couldn't believe it had been only twenty-four hours since they had all enjoyed Jean's hospitality in her cheery kitchen.

Her mobile's ringtone made her jump. Catching her bowl before she poured golden soup all down herself, she set it aside to answer.

'Hey, you. How's it going?' Grace's cheerful voice instantly relaxed Daisy's tense shoulders, and she smiled at her friend's equally cheerful face surrounded by enviable glossy black spiral curls.

'Hey. How're things with you?'

'Uh-uh.' Grace wagged a finger. 'Don't try that on me. If you were fine, you'd have answered my question first. I know you too well, Daisy Claybourne. Deflection is your middle name.'

She was right on both counts. Deflection *was* one of Daisy's better-honed skills. And Grace *did* know her too well.

Daisy had never been one for close friendships. They hadn't fit well with her childhood – it was painful making friends, only to leave them behind and move on. Her art course in Leeds had been different. Finding herself among like-minded people, she'd made an eclectic group of friends who had promised to stay in touch when their four years were up. That had proved surprisingly difficult, with some moving to London and some venturing abroad. Daisy didn't have the funds to travel and visit. But Grace had stuck like glue, and for that, Daisy was grateful.

She told Grace about her day. 'I can't bear the idea of Jean in hospital, so helpless,' she finished.

'That must be hard. I know you're fond of her.' Grace hesitated. 'Do you see her as a kind of surrogate mother, do you think?'

'I hadn't thought of it that way, but... maybe.'

'Well. That wouldn't be surprising, given your history.' Grace hesitated again before asking, 'Are you worried about your situation there?'

As usual, Grace had hit the nail on the head. Daisy wouldn't have admitted such selfish thoughts to herself, but Grace could wheedle them out of her without even trying.

'I suppose so. I'm sure the place can keep going under its own steam for a while. But Jean's the owner; the driving force. It's not clear what'll happen.'

'This nephew of hers will take over, though, by the sound of it?'

'I guess he'll keep an eye on things for now. But if Jean doesn't recover – heaven forbid – or even if she does but isn't well enough to keep the place going, what'll happen then?'

Grace frowned. 'But in theory – and I'm talking in practical, not emotional, terms – that's not your problem, is it? You're not an employee who could lose her job. Your year as guest artist finishes in the spring anyway.'

'I know. But even after that, if Fox Farm were to close, I'd lose one of the galleries that takes my work and therefore lose some income. It'll be bad enough going back to relying on commission again – we both know *that's* not much of a living. I'm hardly in the bright lights of London here. We're talking small galleries and gift shops in country villages and little towns.'

'Hmmm. There's more going on in that brain of yours. Tell Auntie Grace.'

Daisy gave in. 'I really like it here, Grace. You know me – I'm used to having to move around. I didn't expect to become so attached to a place or the people. They're kind and fun. And Jean's become a good friend. She's taken me under her wing.'

'Were you hoping she might keep you on at the studio?'

'Maybe.' Daisy sighed. 'I've tried not to think about it, because she's never done that before – Jean likes to give everyone a chance. The trouble is, I don't know how I'd manage without the studio now. It's so light for working in, and I'm getting something like an income for the first time in my life.' Daisy shrugged. 'That's partly because Jean let me have the place rent-free, of course, but I've agreed to give her a percentage of my takings, which is manageable, and it all feels... promising. I know the living space is tiny, but it's better than that grotty caravan at Jack's. The idea of leaving in the spring? Ah, I shouldn't hope.'

'Hope comes free, my lovely, but all you can do for now is hope that Jean recovers, keep your chin up and maybe support this Alex guy. He must be having a hell of a time.' Grace gave her a speculative look. 'What's he like? I don't remember you mentioning him before.'

'That's because I haven't come across him much, and I don't know much about him, other than how fond he is of Jean. He owns a small plant nursery, half a mile outside of Winterbridge.'

Grace's dark-brown eyes lit up. 'Oooh! An outdoor type. With muscles?'

'Since a Yorkshire October doesn't lend itself to bare-chested endeavours, I can't confirm that for you.' Daisy decided not to mention noticing Alex's T-shirt-clad torso in the summer. 'Haven't you got anyone of your own to ogle?'

'Not really.'

Daisy doubted that. Grace's striking good looks, flawless skin and incredible hair, added to her flamboyant artistic nature, meant that men – and women – were attracted to her like butterflies to nectar.

'How did the exhibition go?' Daisy asked her.

'They've agreed to another in the summer, but I wish I could paint full-time like you. Standing around selling other people's work in the gallery day in, day out is boring *and* galling.'

'That's what comes of living in London, my friend. If you were willing to brave the wilds of the north and live in a caravan and dine off baked beans, you *could* do it full-time.'

Grace laughed. 'No, thanks. Besides, I don't think my kind of work could be produced in a caravan, do you?'

Grace worked on very large canvases that required very large gallery walls to display them, and very rich people with very large loft apartments or office spaces to buy them. They were brilliant, but they had a limited market.

Grace's doorbell sounded. 'I need to go. Dinner with a middle-aged bloke with receding hair and a taste for slimline Italian suits that are too tight for his middle.'

'Does he own a gallery, by any chance?'

'You got it. Or manages one, anyway.'

'Okay, well, go get 'em. And thanks for phoning.'

'Anytime. Chin up, my lovely.'

Smiling, Daisy took her soup back to the microwave. Grace had cheered her up *and* spoken sense. She'd helped her to recognise what her secret hopes and fears were. And she'd reminded Daisy that it was too early to worry about what might happen; that she needed to trust Alex to step in and do whatever he needed to do.

Bless Grace. Although if she thinks I'll be sizing up Alex for muscle dimensions, she can think again!

Chapter Four

Alex arrived at Fox Farm early the following morning to thank the staff for holding the fort the previous day... and for the fact that they would be doing so for some time to come.

Daisy had already updated them on Aunt Jean's condition, saving him some explanation, and they assured him they would manage. Their concern for his aunt was plain, as was the fact that they didn't view her as any ordinary employer.

Angie patted his cheek. 'Jean won't let this keep her down, Alex. Come over to the café for something to eat later. You need nourishment. You have shadows under your eyes.'

That's hardly surprising, Alex thought as he climbed into his truck to head to Riverside. He'd been awake half the night wondering about the length of his aunt's hospitalisation, how good her recovery might be, even the possibility that she might need to go into residential care... and where that would leave Fox Farm.

Jules was reassuring with regard to his business, at least. 'The forced bulbs for Christmas are at the right stage. We'll have plenty of poinsettias in time. I spoke to the farm about the Christmas trees. I could do with selling the rest of these bloomin' pumpkins by the weekend. But swapping to two days' closing next week makes the staff rota easier if you'll be away a lot.' Seeing his long face, she said, 'It's as good a time as any for things to go wrong, Alex. It could've been spring, when you're up to your eyes in bedding plants and plug plants and hanging baskets.'

Alex rewarded her with a smile for trying. He would be forever grateful that he'd employed this petite, capable woman when he started Riverside ten years ago.

'You know you're a star and I appreciate you to the moon and back and I'd pay you more if I could?'

Jules laughed, her blonde bob bouncing. 'Yeah, yeah. Don't add guilt to everything else you've got to deal with. None of us wants to see you look any more down in the mouth than you already do.'

'Okay. I'll try to be here most mornings, and I'll spend afternoons and evenings between the hospital and Fox Farm.'

'How much will you have to do there?'

'I don't know. At the very least, there'll be paperwork to deal with; bills and salaries to pay.'

'Jean Fox is a capable woman, and that place has been going for years,' Jules reassured him. 'You won't hit any problems.'

'I'm sure you're right. Thanks, Jules.'

Alex worked through the more urgent tasks at Riverside, anxious not to let his staff down, before driving to the hospital for afternoon visiting.

Aunt Jean still looked pale and vulnerable. Her eyes were open, she knew Alex was there and she knew who he was, but that was about all.

'The confusion takes a while to clear sometimes,' the nurse told him. 'Don't worry. We'll take good care of her.'

Alex wanted to be reassured, but that would take a magic wand. Still, he was a practical bloke. Worrying could take over your life if you let it. He preferred looking at problems head-on, then finding solutions... although he had no idea, yet, what problems there might be. It would settle his mind to know.

Back at Fox Farm, Alex called in at the café first. The outdoor tables – usually heaving in the summer – were empty in the cold dusk, and there were only a few stragglers left inside. He loved the cosy space – it was like sitting in someone's large lounge, which of course it once had been, a very long time ago. The walls were a buttery cream colour, hung with labelled artwork to tempt people into the gallery rooms next door and upstairs; the pine tables and chairs gave it a farmhouse feel, with Jean's pottery jugs of dried flowers to add cheer; the tiled fireplace added to the homey atmosphere. Popping in there cost him twenty minutes of Angie and Sue asking questions, but it also gained him a toasted cheese and tomato sandwich and a large slab of lemon drizzle cake.

Fortified, he went next door to Aunt Jean's cottage, so quiet and cold without her. Alex turned on the heating – no point in lighting the range – and peeped into the downstairs room opposite the kitchen, long ago given over to her pottery. Shelves stacked with supplies and unfinished pieces, the floor splattered with clay and glaze, the kiln standing in the corner… All looked forlorn. Would his aunt ever get back to doing the thing she loved most?

Alex closed the door on the depressing emptiness and went upstairs to the second bedroom that served as an office. Should he ask his aunt's permission to do this? Alex only had to remember her pale face, her confusion, to know that wasn't an option. Besides, he'd had tacit permission for a long time. Aunt Jean had made sure he knew how Fox Farm ran.

'One day, Alex, something will go wrong and I'll need you to step in. No point in you being in the dark when that day comes.'

Well, that day had come, and it was time for him to step up to the mark.

*

Daisy had had a productive Friday. Now, with the café and gallery closed and dark, the lights at Jean's cottage stood out. Alex must still be there. She'd noticed lights the previous evening, too, and had been grateful for them – it weirded her out, knowing she was alone every night at Fox Farm.

Angie had given Daisy firm instructions before she'd left. 'Alex is over there again. Take him this flask of soup in a little while, will you?'

Daisy wasn't sure about that. If Alex was busy and hadn't come up for air – let alone food – then presumably he didn't want to be disturbed. But Angie never took 'No' for an answer.

Alex opened the door with his shirt hanging out of his jeans, his hair ruffled. It was a good look, actually. Daisy couldn't be doing with tidy men.

'From Angie. I'm under instruction.' She held up the soup flask.

Alex took it from her. 'Thanks. Do you want to come in for a cuppa?'

'No, I'm sure you're busy.' Daisy stared at the table covered in papers, a laptop, ring binders and box files. 'Crikey! What are you doing with that lot?'

'If I'm expected to hold the fort, I need to know where everything's at. Trouble is, I'm going cross-eyed.'

Daisy gave him a doubtful look. 'Does Jean know you're doing this?'

At that, Alex looked offended – which she supposed *she* would have, if the roles were reversed.

'Who'll pay the invoices, the salaries, if I don't? I know how Fox Farm works, Daisy. Aunt Jean discusses it with me. I just need to get myself back up to speed – it's a while since we last went through it all.' He neatly changed the subject. 'So, what have you been up to today?'

To make up for her earlier tone, Daisy told him, 'I made a few sales, finished a painting, decided which of my winter pieces to take to the other galleries. That's not so hard – they only take a few prints each. My studio's another matter, though – I need more variety to fill the walls, and I don't always get a clear run at painting new pieces with people wandering in and out.'

'Do you *have* to show seasonal stuff?'

'I have pieces that suit any season, obviously. But there's no point in displaying summer scenes at this time of year. People like to get in the mood. They want to see snowy fields and huddling sheep and windblown trees; white-topped farmhouses and winter wonderland villages. My main sellers will be Christmas cards. People who aren't willing to cough up for a print, let alone a framed picture or canvas, still need cards.'

'Sounds like you're busy.'

'Yes. And I can see that you are, too, so I'll leave you to it. Good luck with… whatever you're doing.'

Glancing at the mess on the table as she closed the door, Daisy frowned. When Alex had talked about taking the helm, she'd imagined he meant moral support, a bit of troubleshooting. But it looked as if he was going through every file and piece of paper that Jean possessed. Just to sort out a few invoices and deal with the monthly salaries?

*

Like Fox Farm, Riverside was open all weekend, so Alex spent his mornings there, pottering around his domain. It may not have been the busiest season, but it was a time people thought about planting hedges, trees, shrubs, climbers, bulbs… anything frost-hardy, so they would be ready to thrive when spring decided to arrive. And it wouldn't be long before they started thinking about Christmas. Alex couldn't believe it was that time of year already.

He spent time with Jim, divvying out tasks and deciding which could be given to Kieran, their apprentice. It was good to see Jim, in his mid-fifties, getting on so well with the young lad. Jim had introduced Kieran to Ian Dury and Blondie, and Kieran had got Jim into some of the latest podcasts. They enjoyed plenty of laughs while they worked together.

Alex's afternoons were spent with Aunt Jean – thankfully less pale and more lucid, but still not up to much conversation, her speech very slurred. Alex chattered at her anyway, hoping to divert her.

On Saturday night, his best mate Gary dragged him to the Masons Inn for a pint – well, several pints. Gary was concerned for Aunt Jean, but being the good friend he was, he knew Alex needed to forget all about it. They talked about football, the last movie Gary's wife Chelle dragged him to see at the cinema, and his eldest kid's eccentric primary school teacher. It was exactly what Alex needed.

But by Sunday evening, Alex knew he had to confront what he'd been trying to block out of his mind for the past two days – his discovery while looking through Aunt Jean's personal and business accounts.

When he'd first started on her papers, on Thursday evening, he'd only intended to make sure he knew when and how to pay the butcher or baker; deal with salaries; pay commission to artists – ongoing, everyday things.

But that had got him thinking. If Aunt Jean did come home but couldn't run the place, could they afford some kind of manager to take on her role?

And so, on the Friday night – the night Daisy had brought him soup and seemed suspicious about his activities – Alex had decided to look into that possibility.

He wished he hadn't.

It seemed that Fox Farm had been doing well until a couple of years ago. Then profits had taken a downturn – partly, he suspected, through his aunt not bothering to increase prices, even though everyday running costs had increased.

This past year was the worst. Despite declining profits, Aunt Jean had offered Daisy the studio rent-free for the year. *And* she'd kept Jamie on at the gallery full-time after his summer stint was over. Alex knew both those decisions were down to his aunt taking a special shine to someone, but they weren't appropriate for Fox Farm's state of affairs.

Then came the shocker. His aunt had not only stopped taking an income for herself – she had no profits to take it from – but she had also used some of her personal savings to cover the shortfall.

That made Alex sick to the stomach. As a still-young man, he could imagine using his own money to prop up Riverside in difficult times if he knew he could turn the situation around. But at Aunt Jean's age, it wasn't wise. And he couldn't help but be hurt that she hadn't confided in him. Through pride? Stubbornness? Because she'd decided it was none of his business?

In an attempt to take his mind off it all, he switched on the TV, a news channel, but he couldn't say he gave much of a damn about what was happening in the outside world. His world was problematical enough, thank you very much.

Speculative, Alex took a long pull at his beer before texting the Fox Farm staff and Daisy, apologising for the short notice and the fact that he was contacting them after work but asking if they could come in half an hour early the following morning. He hoped the unusual situation they all found themselves in would allow them to forgive him for his timing, but the fact was, he was going to have to take charge more than he'd expected to, and the sooner he eased everyone into that idea, the better.

Alex sighed. His initial idea that Fox Farm might employ a manager to take over his aunt's role was laughable. Instead, Fox Farm was in survival mode, and Aunt Jean couldn't continue to prop it up with her own money. In fact, Alex felt an obligation to see that that Fox Farm paid her back the savings she'd already used. She might well need those for care costs.

He supposed *obligation* was the wrong word, but Alex reckoned he owed his aunt for all those years she'd had him to stay at Fox Farm in school holidays, giving him a much-needed break from the toxic atmosphere at home. A time to feel free and run around in the fresh air; to eat good home cooking without fear that tempers would explode before he'd managed to bolt it down; to sit or lie in his room without listening to shouting and tears. A chance to learn at Uncle William's side in his cottage garden and vegetable plot, developing a love for growing that eventually gave him his vocation.

Alex felt a weight settling on his shoulders, knowing that everyone would be looking to him. The Fox Farm staff were brilliant, but they couldn't be expected to take on more responsibilities at their level of pay. Uncle Eric was too old and far away to help. His mother was also too far away.

Even cousin Sebastian, usually happy to meddle and lord it over everyone, had merely replied to Alex's email with platitudes like 'Sorry to hear that' and 'Don't worry, Jean's a tough old bird' and – setting Alex's teeth on edge – 'No doubt you'll be able to do more at Fox Farm, now it's heading for winter and your own little business will be quiet.'

Hmmph. Little *business? That cousin of mine is a total and utter...*

*

The October half-term holiday had passed in a blur. Angie and Sue had been inundated at the café – small children excited by ghosts and ghoulies worked up quite an appetite, and their fraught parents required sustenance, too.

The staff stayed after closing on Sunday afternoon to take down the Halloween Trail, so Daisy lent a hand packing away the things that could be used for next year and chucking or recycling those that couldn't.

Everyone had long gone home when she received a text from Alex asking them all to come in early on Monday morning. Daisy frowned. She presumed it would be an update on Jean, then remembered with unease the mounds of papers that Alex had spread across Jean's kitchen table. Would he have something to say about the running of Fox Farm?

Her curiosity was still eating at her when she saw Alex arrive at eight the following morning, well before the scheduled meeting. She walked over to his truck to greet him, noticing the shadows under his eyes in the early-morning light.

Alex gazed around, puzzled. 'The yard looks empty.'

'We packed up the Halloween Trail after closing yesterday,' she told him, wondering if he'd lost track of the days with everything that was going on.

Alex looked agitated. 'You didn't throw the pumpkins away, did you?'

'No. They're on the compost heap.'

Alex smiled with relief, and it lightened his whole face – a handsome face, if you didn't mind stubble or someone never getting round to a haircut.

'Uncle William made me promise to keep that compost heap going,' he explained. 'He'd haunt me if I allowed a zillion rotting pumpkins to go to waste!'

'No hauntings this year, then.'

Alex frowned. 'Do you get paid overtime for that kind of thing?'

'I don't think the others do – it's only once a year. You'd have to ask them. I don't get paid at all, remember.'

'Ah. No. Sorry. Well, it was good of you to help out. I guess I should have, too.'

'You have enough to do. I have a cafetière of coffee going, if you need to shore yourself up before the meeting?'

'Please.'

His heartfelt tone made her chuckle. Daisy led him over to her studio and poured him a cup.

He took it gratefully, glancing at the door to her living space. 'You *live* in that crappy old room?'

'Not so crappy any more. I jazzed it up. Throws, cushions. A chair. A bed.'

Daisy threw open the door for him to peep inside at the cramped but homey space, wondering too late if she'd left knickers on the floor or something equally embarrassing. 'Warmer and less rusty than Jack's caravan.' She closed the door again. 'How's Jean?'

'They moved her out of intensive care over the weekend, onto a stroke ward. She's properly conscious now. But her speech is slurred and she can't move one arm at all. She'll need a lot of therapy – speech and physio.'

'What about visitors? I'd like to go. So would the others.'

'I know, but she tires quickly. I've had to go in the afternoons rather than the evenings because she's sleepier later on. Could we leave it until she settles?'

'Of course. Whatever's best. So, what's the meeting about?'

'I… just wanted to touch base with everyone for now. There may be further meetings as we go along.'

Daisy wasn't sure she liked the sound of that. But since he clearly had no intention of saying anything further, she would have to wait and see, the same as everyone else.

*

With the coffee still spiking through his system, Alex began the meeting with an update on his aunt. *Best not mention there's a possibility she might not come home; that she might need residential care. That wouldn't do much for morale, would it?* Then he asked if anyone had any questions.

'What about the run-up to Christmas?' Lisa's tone was rather confrontational.

Mustering a soothing tone, he said, 'I'm sure you all know better than me how the café and gallery should run at this time of year. Just keep on doing what you've been doing. I'll let you know if anything changes.' *And it will have to. But changes are best served up in small doses, I reckon.* When nobody seemed impressed by this platitude, with trepidation he asked, 'Why? What do you think *I* need to know about Christmas?'

'The gallery starts to get really busy from mid-November onwards,' Lisa said. 'Jean likes to make sure all budgets are catered for. And we'll have to switch over to more seasonal pieces.'

That's what Daisy was saying last week about her work, wasn't it?

'You and Jamie will take care of that, surely?'

'This is Jamie's first Christmas at the gallery,' Lisa reminded him. 'And neither of us deal with taking on new work. Jean does that.'

Alex felt the beginning of panic. 'Don't you have stock left over from last year?'

'Some, at the cheaper end of the range, if we bought it outright. But most pieces are taken on a commission arrangement, so any seasonal items are handed back to the artists at the end of that season. We can't be responsible for storing delicate work for months. Jean usually contacts the artists around this time of year, or they contact her. Do you know how far she got with that?'

Alex's panic grew. He *wanted* to say he had his own business to run. That it was one thing lending moral support and keeping an eye on things, and quite another to be expected to have this level of knowledge and involvement.

'I've glanced at her emails,' he admitted. 'But only at those that meant anything to me or looked urgent. I don't suppose either of you…?'

Lisa shook her head. 'Sorry, Alex. I've got two young kids. I can't take on extra responsibilities, not in the run-up to Christmas.'

Jamie shrugged in an amiable way. 'I'm not an artist. I wouldn't know how to judge people's work or discuss it with them.'

Alex frowned. 'Judge? Discuss? I don't understand.'

'Jean doesn't accept people's work willy-nilly,' Lisa explained. 'They can't just wander in off the street and hand us things. Imagine what rubbish we'd have on display! Jean knows the artists, judges the quality, decides whether their work fits in and whether it suits the season. It takes an artist's eye, and sometimes a firm line is needed.'

'I can understand Aunt Jean vetting *new* artists,' Alex said. 'But don't the regular ones just hand their new stuff over to you?'

'If they're only topping up with a piece or two, yes. But Jean doesn't want that to turn into an open invitation, so she holds appointments with the artists a couple of times a year – summer and winter. It's a kind of quality control, using the seasons as an excuse.'

'Café-wise,' Angie butted in impatiently, 'we'll be switching to Christmas-themed food. And we're usually heaving from the end of

November, especially once all the Christmas decorations go up around the place.'

Alex ran a hand over his face. 'You're talking about the tree in the yard, lights and decorations on all the buildings, the whole rigmarole?'

Angie nodded. 'Don't forget Santa's cabin every weekend in December till Christmas.'

'Oh no!' Alex shook his head, adamant. 'I'm sorry, but I have to draw the line somewhere. That log cabin is a pain to put together, then there's Santa and an elf to find…'

'Santa is Lisa's dad. I'm sure Mike'll do it again this year.' Angie looked over at Lisa, who gave a noncommittal shrug. 'Jean usually collars some poor, unsuspecting sixth-former to be an elf. They need the money, so they're daft enough to do it.' When Alex said nothing, she went on, 'It's an added attraction, Alex. Parents or grandparents bring the kiddies to see Santa, then pop into the café for hot drinks and cakes or lunch, then take a look in the gallery – hopefully keeping those kiddies under control. It pulls the punters in.'

And that's what I can't ignore. More punters. Much-needed income for Fox Farm. Alex sighed. *Looks like I'm rebuilding that wretched log cabin this year, after all.*

Chapter Five

The following day was a closing day and the weather was glorious, so Daisy put aside her tasks and went out on a ramble.

Frosty fields that looked as though they had been dusted with icing sugar; the grey drystone walls that criss-crossed them, built with ancient skill and standing for hundreds of years with no mortar, defying the elements; sheep huddling in their thick fleeces – all made for iconic Yorkshire Dales scenery. The smattering of birch and oak trees were already losing their leaves, the autumn colours gone. It wouldn't be long before they gave way to winter bareness.

Daisy followed her secret path, narrow and less well known, down towards the river. Alongside, a stream bubbled through the trees, the chatter of it keeping her company. As the trees dropped back, she stopped to sit on her favourite rock, spreading a mat from her backpack over the moss that covered it. Ferns poked between the rocks, and a small waterfall tumbled into a still pool. It was idyllic.

In the spring and summer, the open field on the other side of the stream would be filled with wildflowers, deliberately left that way by the farmer, but for now the grass was an autumn yellow-brown. In the distance, on the hill over the other side of the river that ran through Winterbridge, above the pasture line, the bracken had turned bronze.

Daisy drank it all in as a sense of peace washed over her. After an upbringing filled with noise in what Daisy had always viewed as other people's homes despite the kindness of her foster families, followed by the hustle and bustle of her art course in Leeds, nowadays she wanted for nothing more than the trickle of a stream, the swish of leaves in a breeze, the baa-ing of sheep and the twitter of birds... Although spring was a better season for that – right now, all she could hear were blackbirds scolding each other.

Taking out her project book, she sketched a few ideas, taking an occasional absent-minded bite of her sandwich and wishing she'd brought a flask of soup to ward off the chill.

She was lost in her thoughts, pencil poised, when footsteps sounded in front of her, and she looked up to see Alex.

'Hi, Daisy. I didn't expect to see you here. Not many people know this spot.'

'That's why I come here.'

'Ah. Sorry to interrupt, then. Mind if I sit?'

Well, I do, but I can't say so.

'Help yourself. I thought you'd be catching up at Riverside.'

'Everything's under control, and I needed some fresh air. Are you thinking up some ideas?'

'I like to see what strikes me as I walk. This morning, I saw a sheep with the funniest face. She *has* to be in my next painting. And I need to do more wintry pieces before people start Christmas shopping. The more I sell, the more baked beans I get for tea!'

Alex frowned. 'You do alright, though, don't you?'

'Not in the past, when I was relying purely on commission from places. Hence the caravan at Jack's. But I've managed this year, with the studio. Browsers enjoy watching me work – it makes them more inclined to buy.' She made a face. 'Although one woman last week spent *ages* asking me question after question, then didn't buy a thing.'

'You don't overcharge.'

'No. The originals are dear, obviously, but the prints are reasonable.' She shrugged. 'People don't understand how much time goes into each piece. Never mind the paints, tools, my printer's costs, mounts, frames, canvases.'

Alex hesitated. 'Daisy, what Lisa was saying yesterday about taking on seasonal art needing an artist's judgement, I was wondering—'

'Oh no.' Guessing where he was heading, Daisy held up a hand. 'I've never done that kind of thing.'

'Neither have I.'

His miserable expression was almost comical, but Daisy couldn't afford to feel sympathy if she didn't want the task allocated to her.

'Daisy, *please*. I'm begging you.' Alex actually dropped off his rock and onto his knees on the muddy ground, his hands held in front of him. When her lips twitched, he added, 'Jean's begging you, too.'

Daisy narrowed her eyes. 'I thought you said her speech is affected. Besides, I wouldn't have thought you'd bother her about Fox Farm.'

He got back up, brushing dirt from his trousers. 'I'm bothering her as little as possible, but after what Lisa said, I did ask her if this was underway. She said no. I told her that neither Lisa nor Jamie felt capable of dealing with it. Her speech is slurred, and she can't get what's in her head to come out of her mouth properly, but she did suggest you.'

Ah, rats. How can I turn Jean down? Besides, my studio sales depend on footfall at Fox Farm. There won't be many customers if the gallery has bare walls or too much summer stock.

'*If* I were daft enough to agree, I wouldn't know how to go about it,' she complained.

'Me neither. But we could work it out together. Why don't you come to the cottage on Thursday evening? I'll cook dinner.' When she looked startled, Alex said, 'We both have to eat, don't we?'

Daisy hesitated. *It's only food and a chat, isn't it? Hardly a date.*

'I… Okay.'

'You'll do it?'

She sighed in resignation. 'Yes.'

Alex looked as surprised as Daisy felt. As he waved and walked away, Daisy wondered what she had let herself in for. She thought about those pleading hazel eyes, the twitch of mischief at his mouth when Alex had realised he'd got his way. She was having dinner with him?

It's just a business thing, Daisy. No need to panic. Yet.

*

Alex had needed a stroll in the fresh air for a reason – he was steeling himself before visiting Aunt Jean.

So far, his visits had been about reassuring her, instilling her with confidence about her recovery, explaining to her what the doctors were saying. Financial discussions hadn't felt appropriate. But she was out of her daze now and understood everything he was saying, so he'd decided that today was the day. He couldn't let things stay the way they were for weeks on end.

After leaving Daisy, he drove into Winterbridge to pick up a local magazine that his aunt had asked for – a positive sign for her recovery.

'Afternoon, Alex,' Harold greeted him at the village shop that served as grocery, newsagent and post office. 'How's our Jean?'

A five-minute update ensued, until Alex politely cut it short with, 'Well, I should get off to the hospital.'

'Give her our best.' Alex had reached the door when Harold called after him, 'I don't suppose you fancy moving into Jean's for a while and letting out your house, do you? There's a bloke looking for somewhere to rent between now and Christmas – an author chap from London. He phoned the other day asking me to place a notice. Phoned the other village shops around here, too.' Harold pointed to the corkboard on the wall. 'Wants to hide himself away. Panicking about his deadline, so he said.' Harold rolled his eyes, suggesting he didn't have much patience for an angsty writer.

To be polite, Alex walked over to read the notice. 'It says he wants a typical Dales cottage – somewhere atmospheric to feed his muse. I doubt my terraced house would fit *that* bill. Hasn't been decorated since I moved in.'

'Ah, well. Let me know if you think of anywhere.'

Alex left and climbed into his truck, dismissing the conversation, and turned on some music. Ten minutes later, he switched it off and pulled into a layby. His mind wasn't on the road.

Hmmm. A writer needed a traditional, cosy little cottage to rent for the few weeks coming up to Christmas. Somewhere with atmosphere. And he was willing to pay good money for the privilege.

Aunt Jean had a traditional, cosy little cottage that would likely be standing empty for those few weeks. Fox Farm certainly had atmosphere. And that money would help Aunt Jean with expenses when she came out of hospital.

Alex allowed his mind to race and then settle before restarting the engine. He should check with the doctors about how long they anticipated Aunt Jean staying in hospital or in recuperation before coming home… if she came home. And then he should speak to his aunt.

*

Daisy felt refreshed after her couple of days' closing, having enjoyed her walk, and pleased with her trips to the galleries and gift shops that took her work and to her printer with the pieces she wanted to reproduce on Christmas cards. Deciding she'd earned a treat, at lunchtime on Thursday she put up a *Back in Five Minutes* notice and popped over to Fox Farm's café for some of Angie's carrot and coriander soup. Angie always gave her an unofficial fifty per cent staff discount, and although Daisy's budget didn't stretch to indulgences like cake, there was no resisting delicious homemade soup. It would keep her going until her meal with Alex that evening, a 'date' she still felt odd about.

Angie potted up one tub, then another. 'Looks like Alex is over at Jean's again. Take this to him, will you? That lad'll turn to skin and bone with so much on his mind.'

Daisy doubted that Alex's broad chest and shoulders would wither away anytime soon, nor was she sure why a man in his mid-thirties wasn't capable of feeding himself without prompting, whether preoccupied or not, but she dutifully dropped her soup off at the studio and crossed the cobbles to Jean's cottage.

A gruff 'Come in' answered her knock.

'Hi.' Daisy frowned at the box in Alex's arms, which was full of photographs and ornaments. 'Having a clear-out?'

'Not quite.'

Hmmm. Not very talkative today, are you? 'I brought you some soup.'

'Oh, for goodness' sake. I'm awash with it! And I can fetch my own, you know.'

Not used to that kind of tone from him, Daisy retorted, 'Hey, don't shoot the messenger. Angie says you won't stop to eat if she doesn't make you.'

'Hmmph. She still thinks I'm twelve.'

'She remembers you when you were twelve?' Visions of a young Alex running around the farm, his hair flopping over his eyes, made her smile. She placed the soup on the table. 'Can I give you a hand with that?'

'No, thanks.'

Daisy frowned as she finally registered the contents of the box. 'Why are you packing Jean's things away?' Awful thoughts flitted across her mind. 'Is she alright? Isn't she coming home? Is she…?'

Alex dropped the box on the table so he could put a reassuring hand on her arm. 'She's fine. Well, as fine as she can be. Come and sit down for a minute.' He led her to the small, squishy sofa at the far end of the kitchen. 'I'm tidying away her personal effects and clothes because I'm renting out her cottage for a few weeks.'

Daisy was stunned. It was the last thing she'd expected him to say. 'You're *what*? Why would you *do* that? It's not as though she'll be gone forever!'

'Daisy. Please.' Alex hesitated. 'Look, I'm going to tell you something, but I need you to keep it to yourself, okay? Remember I told you that Aunt Jean always kept me in the loop over Fox Farm?' When she nodded, he went on. 'Well, we hadn't been through it together for a while, and… The fact is, it hasn't been doing as well as appearances would have you believe.'

Daisy did her best to hide her surprise at his revelation. She could see the worry in his eyes, the shadows beneath them – a combination of his concern for his aunt and now this, she supposed.

'Harold knows of a writer looking to rent a cottage temporarily,' he continued. 'It'll bring in a few weeks' money for Aunt Jean.'

'But what about her coming home?' Daisy insisted.

'The writer has to leave by Christmas. The doctors have said Aunt Jean's unlikely to be back before the new year.' Alex sighed. 'Would you *please* stop looking at me like that?'

Daisy shook her head. 'You honestly believe a few hundred quid will make any difference?'

'It's more than a few hundred. And it's needed. That's all I'm willing to say. I know you're fond of Aunt Jean, but I'm not prepared to discuss her finances with you in any detail. I shouldn't have said as much as I have, but you caught me on the hop.'

'How does Jean feel about this?' Daisy asked suspiciously.

'I hadn't wanted to bother her about finances, but I've had to. She knows there's a problem. I told her this had landed in our laps, and she's okay about it. I'm not heartless, Daisy. I'm doing what's best. You have to trust me.'

I don't have to trust you at all, Daisy thought, wondering whether Jean needed someone to stand up for her; wondering whether she *could* trust him – although, reading his expression, she knew she wanted to.

But it seemed that her lack of reply and attitude of potential mistrust were too much for Alex after the strain of recent days. He blew a gasket, standing and waving his arms about in anger and frustration.

'You don't believe me? You think I'd rent out a hospitalised woman's cottage for fun? You think I'd give myself all this extra work for the hell of it? We might not know each other very well, Daisy, but I'd hoped you might think better of me than that.' He huffed out a breath. 'Now, if you don't mind, I have things to do, and you have your *own* business to take care of.'

Well, that's being told, isn't it?

Not daring to try and soothe his ruffled feathers, Daisy made for the door, where she turned back.

'What about the staff? You'll have to tell them some stranger's coming to live in Jean's cottage.'

'Obviously. And I'm hoping they won't hold it against me too much.' He gave her an accusatory look. 'But as they're employees and I need to keep up morale, I'll be playing down the financial issues. With that in mind, I'd be grateful if you didn't say anything about what I've told you.'

'Fine. You've made it quite clear that it's none of my business.'

'I only told you what I did because you caught me off guard,' Alex snapped. 'I suppose I hoped you'd be on my side; that you might defend me with the rest of them when I can't admit what's really going on without worrying them. I shouldn't have expected that from you. I'm sorry.'

Daisy didn't know what to say to that. Instead, she waved at the soup. 'Don't forget that, or Angie'll have my hide. I'll get back to my own, although I imagine it'll be clap cold by now.'

She slammed the door, then stood for a moment to regain her equilibrium, eyes closed. Was this what it was going to be like around Fox Farm with Alex temporarily in charge? When Jean first fell ill, Daisy had felt relieved that he was available and willing and capable. But the side she'd just seen of him…? Perhaps he was just worried about Fox Farm's affairs – and worried he'd told her more than he wanted to. But what if he began to really take over? Did Jean honestly know what he was up to?

As Daisy headed back across the farmyard, it occurred to her there was something she could do about *that*, at least. But her step faltered as she remembered that she and Alex were supposed to have dinner that evening. *Great.* Would she still go? That all depended on what she found out... and on his attitude.

At her studio, she took down the *Back in Five Minutes* sign with a grimace. It had been nearer ten minutes – and not the pleasantest ten minutes she'd ever spent.

Angie could make her own soup delivery next time, lunch crowd or no!

Chapter Six

Daisy was locking up at four o'clock – new winter opening hours – when Alex walked across the farmyard to eat humble pie.

He'd been *way* too sharp with her at lunchtime. But that look she'd given him, the accusation in her voice… She had no right to judge. And if Daisy did that, what would it be like when Angie and Lisa joined in on the act?

But they were meant to be having dinner together, and since he was asking for her help, his outburst couldn't have been more ill-timed.

'Daisy.'

She turned. 'Alex.'

Oooh. Frosty. Can't expect much else, though, can I?

'I came to apologise,' he said. 'Things have been difficult, and I took it out on you. I shouldn't have.'

'No. You shouldn't.'

He opened his mouth, unsure how to say what he wanted to without sounding selfish.

But Daisy had him pegged. 'You're here to check if I'm still daft enough to come tonight, I take it?'

His shoulders sagged. 'Yes.'

'Is that why you're apologising?'

'Partly. After all, I already bought the lamb.' Alex tried a smile, but it fell on stony ground. 'But mainly because I know I spoke out of turn. The apology's genuine – it just happens to *look* self-serving. Listen, we can do dinner another time if you prefer. Or we can do the meeting without dinner, if that makes it more businesslike for you. Or you can tell me to shove the whole thing.'

'Hmmm. Lamb, you say? I don't get lamb on my budget.' Daisy sighed. 'Alright. Might as well get it over with. What time?'

'Seven?'

'Okay, but I may be a little late. I have to go somewhere first, and I don't know how traffic will be. I could text to let you know?'

'That's fine. See you then.' Alex stepped out of her way so she could head for her battered little car. He didn't like the look of that old banger – he sincerely hoped she wasn't going too far in it.

Crossing the yard to the cottage, Alex worried that he hadn't visited Aunt Jean today, but that couldn't be helped. N.J. Giles, the crime writer, wanted to move in on Saturday – just two days away – so he'd had too much to do. When he'd phoned Aunt Jean to let her know he couldn't come and to say sorry, she'd told him in her struggling way that she knew he was busy and not to be so daft.

At least he'd managed to make her laugh – first, by telling her that the reason N.J. Giles used his initials on his books was because his real name was a less-than-glamourous Nigel; and second, when he'd told her that the chap was thrilled about staying in a farm setting because he was writing about a grisly series of murders set in one.

Alex got started on the lamb casserole. He and Daisy could both do with a decent meal, and cooking relaxed him. Once it was in the range, he loaded boxes of his aunt's paperwork into his truck to take to his house before locking up her study, now filled with her clothes, ornaments and personal effects.

When Daisy texted to say she'd be there soon after seven, he checked his casserole. He was adept with the range – Aunt Jean had made sure of that.

'*There's nothing like good old-fashioned country cooking, Alex. Your future wife will appreciate it and thank me for it,*' she'd told him on many an occasion when he was too young to understand or care.

Now he was old enough to understand, but he still didn't care. Alex didn't see a wife in his future. Dalliances, yes. Short-lived relationships, maybe. But a wife? No, thanks. His parents hadn't exactly set a fine example for him. He'd seen at first hand how toxic a marriage could be, and he had no intention of trying it for himself.

That didn't mean he couldn't cook a tasty casserole for a woman who was helping him out, though.

He hoped he was forgiven. Of all the people to have had a go at! He liked Daisy. She was open and seemed comfortable in her own skin. Comfortable in saying what she thought, too, as proven today. And she wasn't obsessed with her appearance. Daisy was fresh-faced and natural, and that suited her personality.

The knock on the door made him jump.

'Hi.' Daisy stood awkwardly in the doorway, a bottle of wine in one hand.

'Red. Perfect,' he assured her as he took it.

'Dinner smells good.'

'Thanks.' He stood aside to let her in, noticing her hair was down for a change. 'Suits you,' he said, pointing.

'What? Oh. Thanks.' Daisy shrugged. 'I usually tie it up, otherwise it gets in the way or covered in paint.'

'Makes sense.' Alex dealt with the wine and handed her a glass, indicating that she should sit on the small sofa. 'Dinner won't be long.'

'Thanks. I'm starving. Sorry I'm a bit late. I went to see Jean.'

Alex struggled to contain his annoyance that she had gone to the hospital without telling him. And then he realised why. 'You didn't trust me.'

'I wouldn't say that,' Daisy said steadily. 'I know you have her best interests at heart. But I wanted to check for myself that she's as *compos mentis* as you say.' She held up a hand. 'And before you tell me that's high-handed and interfering, perhaps it is, but it'll stand you in good stead.' When he gave her a puzzled look, she explained, 'The minute you tell the others, they'll ask themselves the same thing. This way, I can tell them that I visited her and she's okay about it.' Daisy's chin wobbled. 'Although it's a struggle to understand her.'

Alex gave her a sympathetic smile. 'It's a shock, isn't it? Aunt Jean always seemed so indestructible before.'

'Yes. But she was pleased to see me. I chatted about Fox Farm and Halloween week. I had hoped she might advise me about the artists, but she was getting so frustrated, trying to say things she couldn't. In the end, I just sat and held her hand until she drifted to sleep.'

Alex nodded, and an awkward silence fell between them.

'So, have we forgiven each other for anything that needs to be forgiven?' he finally asked. 'I'm not serving food until I know we're friends. That's just a recipe for indigestion.'

'Then I'll have to say yes, because I'm really hungry.'

Alex grinned. 'Time to eat, then.'

When he put the casserole on the table, Daisy sniffed appreciatively. 'Where did you learn to cook like this, using a range?'

'Need you ask?' Alex served her a generous helping.

Daisy smiled. 'I hear you're a dab hand at everything else, too – Jean sings your praises a lot. I gather you spent almost all your school holidays here?'

'Yes, from about the age of eleven.'

Except for Christmas. I was always expected at home for Christmas. And 'festive' was the last word I'd apply to that *experience.*

Daisy took a bite. 'Delicious. The lamb's so tender.'

'Slow-cooked on a low heat, as per Aunt Jean.'

'It must have been odd for you, splitting your time between home and Fox Farm like that,' Daisy said.

Alex wasn't sure how much he wanted to say, or how much Daisy might have gleaned from her chats with Aunt Jean, although he knew his aunt wouldn't have gone into family troubles in detail. But she didn't comment – she simply left the space for him to fill it if he chose.

'Let's just say I had an unhappy childhood and leave it at that,' he finally said.

Daisy nodded, unoffended, and didn't pry further.

That's something to like about her.

Then Alex remembered what his aunt had told him when she offered Daisy the studio. He'd expressed amazement that Daisy was willing to live in that tiny end room, and Aunt Jean had mentioned the caravan at Jack's, saying that Daisy was used to temporary accommodation; that she'd spent her childhood moving around.

He winced. 'Sorry. I gather your childhood wasn't too bright, either. Aunt Jean told me you spent it with several different foster families.'

'Some of it was fine. Some of it wasn't.' Daisy shrugged. 'That was nobody's fault – it was just that I never felt I fit in anywhere. Not until I started my art course. Then I was as happy as a pig in clover.'

Alex wanted to ask what had happened to her family; *why* she'd spent her childhood in foster homes. But they weren't close enough for that. Instead, he asked, 'What got you into art? Beside natural talent, of course.'

'Flatterer!' Her laugh was a light, tinkling sound that shimmered over his tired bones. 'I was a solitary child – I always felt like I shouldn't be a bother to anyone. I didn't feel like I had the right to be an equal part of a family or to play with the others. Looking back, that was usually *my* perception, not the actual situation, but anyway, I kept myself to myself. Assuming I was just withdrawn and shy, my foster parents would buy me crayons and pencils and paints and stickers to keep me occupied. My love of doing something creative, something visual, grew from that.'

'Where did you do your art course?'

'Leeds.'

'But then you moved to the Dales?'

'Yeah. I enjoyed the city while I was at college because I had a lot of friends for the first time in my life. But after we graduated, everyone went off to do their own thing. A few, including my best friend, Grace, went to London – more opportunity there – but that was too expensive for me, without financial support. I stuck it out in Leeds for three more years, doing a minimum-wage job full-time and fitting my art into any spare hours, but I was too tired to create. I knew if I wanted to pursue it seriously, I had to devote more time to it. Besides, I couldn't find inspiration in the city – my style was more suited to the countryside. I moved to Grassington six years ago and worked part-time in a pub, but that wasn't ideal either – more inspiration and time to paint, but less money for rent.'

'That's the downside of living in a National Park on a small income,' Alex said with feeling.

'Yes. And my landlady didn't like me painting in my room. It was all too constrictive. I'd managed to get my work into places across the Dales, slowly but surely, so a couple of years ago, I decided to put the art above the job. Someone at the pub knew of a farmer a few miles away who might be willing to rent out an old caravan on his land, dirt cheap. The rest you know.'

'I imagine Jack misses you.'

'Yeah, but I think he expects to see me back there when my year runs out here.'

Alex could sense Daisy's disappointment at that idea. 'You're not tempted by his grotty caravan?' he quipped.

'Ha! No. Fox Farm has shown me that life at Jack's was *too* lonely, even for me. I like it here. It's nice having people around without having to interact unless I want to. And Jean's been so welcoming.' Daisy sat back in her chair. 'I ate too much. That was delicious. Thank you.'

'Glad you enjoyed it.' Alex could almost hear Jean's voice saying, *Told you our cooking lessons would come in useful someday, didn't I?* 'I'll make tea.'

Alex put the kettle on, then reached for the teapot and a jar of loose-leaf tea. No teabags allowed in Aunt Jean's house! When it was nicely brick-coloured – no wishy-washy stuff allowed here, either – he took it to the table and opened his aunt's laptop.

'So, we need to draft an email?'

'Yes. I reckon we should stick to the regular artists who already display in the gallery,' Daisy suggested. 'That'll limit how much time I have to spend on it all.'

'Can't we dispense with this altogether, under the circumstances?'

'Jean would be disappointed. And if you're worried about Fox Farm making money over Christmas…' Daisy stopped, obviously wary of bringing up Fox Farm's finances after their row at lunchtime.

'Go ahead,' he prompted.

'The gallery won't have the right atmosphere with a load of summer stuff up, and regular visitors expect to see something new. Besides, the artists who've worked on new pieces will want to swap them over.'

'You can't possibly meet with every single artist, Daisy. Surely Lisa can deal with top-ups? She already admitted she does that.'

'I know. We need a happy medium.' Daisy frowned in concentration, little lines appearing between her eyes. 'Be brief and firm. Tell them Jean's incapacitated, give my email address and say they should contact me if they want to hand over more than a couple of pieces or they've changed the nature of their work.'

'Will Lisa be okay with that?'

'She'll have to like it or lump it,' Daisy grumbled. 'More to the point, will Jean settle for that?'

Alex grinned. 'She'll have to like it or lump it.'

Sitting side by side so they could both see the screen as he typed, Alex became acutely aware of Daisy's leg pressed against his, and of her scent – not perfume but a fresh, fruity shower gel.

The wine must have gone to my head.

'I hope this won't take too much of your time.' He reread what he'd written. 'How about asking them to send photos first? If you're familiar with their work, you could accept it without meeting them and let Lisa know. Just meet those you're not sure about?'

'That *would* be less time-consuming.'

'Then that's what we'll do.'

When it was worded to their satisfaction, they found Jean's email list for the artists and pressed *Send* together, laughing, both with their index fingers on the mouse, like co-conspirators.

'I should go,' Daisy said, yawning. 'It's late.'

Alex walked her to the door. 'Thank you. I appreciate it. Especially after earlier. Again, I'm sorry.'

'That's okay. You have a lot on your mind.'

As he saw her out into the dimly lit farmyard and watched her cross to her studio, Alex was glad he'd begged her to help him. There were aspects of Fox Farm that weren't on his radar, and he was no artist.

Teamwork.

*

Daisy had enjoyed the previous night's dinner with Alex more than she'd expected. Of course, since she'd expected it to be horribly stilted after their lunchtime exchange, that wasn't saying much. She'd only gone because she'd agreed to help with the artists.

But Alex had made an effort with the food, and he'd taken a genuine interest in what she had to say about herself. He'd played his own cards close to his chest, though. Jean often spoke fondly about Alex's holidays at Fox Farm, but always stopped short of saying what was behind it, only indicating that he'd needed a break from his 'home atmosphere'. Alex hadn't wanted to elaborate last night, so Daisy hadn't pushed. She knew as well as anyone that people preferred to open up of their own accord.

Her contentment with her day took a downturn when Lisa stormed over mid-afternoon, looking most unhappy.

'There's an artist at the gallery saying you agreed he could drop off some glassware. That's the first *I've* heard of it. I thought you were meeting them all first?'

'Not necessarily.' Grateful she had no customers in, Daisy explained the arrangement that she and Alex had come up with.

'That's not how Jean does it,' Lisa complained. 'And it would've been nice if someone had bothered to tell me before I made a fool of myself! I've had to send him to the café for a free coffee while I find out what's going on.'

Daisy made an effort to contain the anger that wanted to bubble up. 'We're doing things differently because I don't have time to deal with everyone. I don't even work for Fox Farm, Lisa. I'm doing this as a favour.' *I'm doing your job for you.* 'I'm sorry you haven't been told the details yet, but Alex and I didn't finish till late last night, and I've been busy since, running *my* business. I'd planned to speak to you at the meeting Alex called after work today. I didn't realise anyone would come so soon. Is the glassware from Alan?'

'Yes.'

'Is it similar to his other pieces? Up to standard?'

'Yes.'

'Then feel free to take it. You can take anything where it's only a top-up or if I forward an email to you when I've accepted on photos alone. As long as they bring what they said, it's up to their usual standard and they take away unseasonal pieces, that's fine.'

'What about the others?'

'I'll be using my free time to meet with them.' *Unlike you.* 'Apologise to Alan for me, will you?'

Lisa turned on her heel and left, and Daisy sighed. She'd always got on well with everyone at Fox Farm, so she hoped that helping Alex and Jean didn't cause more of that sort of thing.

At four, she crossed the farmyard to the café. Alex had asked everyone to stay behind for ten minutes – presumably to tell them about Jean's cottage. Since it wouldn't do for the others to realise that Daisy already knew, she should be there as Alex imparted the news.

It went down like a lead balloon.

'You can't do that!' Angie puffed out her ample bosom.

'I can, Angie, and I am. Aunt Jean has agreed to it. We've been told she's unlikely to be home before New Year, and she might need the money for care when she comes back.'

Seeing the confrontational stances of everyone except Jamie, Daisy felt sorry for Alex. That was a good tactic, though, suggesting that Jean might need extra funds for her care, knowing they would have some sympathy with that. She could understand him not wanting them to know that Fox Farm was in trouble – he wouldn't want them panicking about their jobs. When he caught her eye, Daisy nodded to show she understood.

'When does this writer bloke move in, then?' Lisa asked.

'Tomorrow. He wanted it ASAP, and he's willing to pay for the privilege.'

'Sounds like we've not much say in the matter.' Angie picked up her coat. 'May as well go home.'

'Angie, I need a meeting with you about the café,' Alex said before she could leave. 'Monday morning?'

Angie frowned. '*Another* meeting?'

'This was just a polite update.' Daisy detected the slight warning tone in Alex's voice. 'I need a proper meeting with you in your capacity as café manager.'

'Fine,' Angie grumbled, and stalked off.

'How badly did that go?' Alex asked Daisy as they watched everyone leave.

'Could've been worse.'

Alex threw back his head and laughed, a deep rumble that rolled over Daisy like pebbles tumbling in the slip of a stream. 'Is that a regular motto of yours?'

'It's come in handy over the years.'

He studied her for a long moment, his hazel eyes kind, almost hypnotic. 'That's kind of a shame. Well, I'll be here tomorrow to meet the guy and show him around.'

'I'll let you know what the others think, once they've settled down.'

'Keep it upbeat, will you?' Alex made a face. 'I'm not sure how many more knocks I can take.'

'I'll do my best. Dare I ask what your meeting with Angie's about?'

'I need to talk to her about price increases.' Alex looked as though he was already dreading it.

'Ah. Well, good luck with that. I'd better get on. Emails are coming in thick and fast.' Daisy almost mentioned her altercation with Lisa, but Alex looked so woebegone, she refrained.

Back in her studio, she made tea and, with a rueful glance at a half-finished piece on her easel, reached for her laptop.

A dozen new emails sat in her inbox. Some, she could judge by the photos sent. Thank goodness Alex had come up with that idea! She replied to those first, giving the go-ahead and forwarding each to Lisa so she couldn't be told off again. But there were some artists she would have to meet with.

A plateful of sweet and sour noodles later, Daisy sent replies offering a limited time slot each on Tuesday or Wednesday – apologies, but she was a working artist herself. She ended by reminding them that she was acting on Jean's behalf and although she hoped to take their work, approval wasn't guaranteed.

Daisy didn't like having to say that. She knew what it was like to have your art judged – and rejected – and hoped she wouldn't face too many issues.

That idea plagued her for the rest of that evening and into the next morning. Her studio was quiet for a Saturday, the weather dreary and drizzly, but she got a few sales between making a to-do list: Retrieve Christmas cards and prints from the printer; Dig out last year's leftover Christmas cards; Deal with more emails from artists…

An estate car backing carefully into the farmyard was a welcome distraction. Curious, Daisy peeked through the window at the balding, middle-aged man who got out. Alex's truck drew up at the roadside and he came over to greet the driver, then the two of them unloaded a couple of suitcases and heaved them into Jean's cottage.

Hmmm. Not what I expected a writer to look like. Kind of boring.

Daisy had mixed feelings about N.J. Giles' arrival. It was good to know that someone else would be on the premises at night. But it also meant that Alex could no longer use the cottage as a base, so he might not be around as much. Daisy quickly dismissed her disappointment over that as ridiculous.

By closing time, N.J. Giles had popped into the café for a coffee and had a quick look around the gallery and studio, so Daisy had some sort of reaction from everybody. As promised, she texted Alex.

Angie's disappointed that he's not more handsome. She seems less cross with you about the cottage. Sue says she's too old to care one way or the other – I presume she meant about how fanciable the poor bloke is, not the cottage. Lisa thinks he's too quiet. She expected someone who peddles words for a living to be more gobby. Jamie's disappointed – he imagined someone in a velvet jacket and fedora.

I thought Mr Giles was nice enough, if a bit preoccupied. He said he's writing about a series of murders set on a farm. Not sure I like the sound of that! Daisy x

Oops! She'd put that kiss as a texting reflex. *Hope he doesn't take it the wrong way.*

Ten minutes later, her phone pinged with a reply.

Thanks. Quiet's better than a pain, I reckon. Don't work too late. Alex x

Hmmm. A kiss back. To be polite? Or because they were the kind of friends who put kisses after their texts now?

Chapter Seven

Alex's Monday morning meeting with Angie went better than he'd hoped it would. She agreed that prices hadn't gone up for far too long or kept up with supply costs. When he told her he'd spoken to his aunt and she was happy for them to implement something, Angie took his word for it.

The only sticky point came when she asked, 'Why are you suddenly so concerned about Fox Farm's profits, Alex?'

What profits? 'Like I said on Friday, Aunt Jean may need to pay for carers once she's home,' he said smoothly. Worried that might not be convincing enough, he added, 'Or she may need to employ an extra member of staff to take on some of the things she does around here.' *As if Fox Farm could stretch to that!*

But Angie nodded, satisfied. 'You're the boss.' She winked. 'For now.'

Breathing a sigh of relief, Alex drove to Riverside.

'How's it going?' Jules asked him. 'You look tired.'

'So do you.' Alex put a hand on her slim shoulder. 'Have you been doing unpaid overtime again?'

'I had some orders to catch up with, that's all.'

'Are you struggling because I'm not here as much, Jules?'

She shrugged. 'At this time of year, you and Jim tend to leave me to it while you play with your repairs anyway. But it might be a problem nearer Christmas. I wanted to get ahead with ordering things like the wreath frames and bases, so I won't have to worry when we're busier.'

Alex thought about the way Jules would stand to one side of the counter making festive masterpieces, surrounded by greenery that he and Jim brought her, only breaking off to ring up purchases. 'Won't you struggle with the wreaths if you're understaffed?'

'I'll manage. Kieran might have to cope with Christmas tree sales on his own, though – I'll need Jim to be the floater. Anyway, plenty of time before we have to worry about that.'

'You'll tell me if it's getting too much?'

'You'll *know*, because I'll start snapping at people, and that's never pretty. How're things with Jean and Fox Farm?'

'Too many "ifs", Jules. The doctors are impressed with her determination, but they can't say what'll happen yet.'

Alex had those 'ifs' in the back of his mind all morning as he worked… and it turned out he wasn't the only one worrying about them.

'Need to ask you about Fox Farm,' Aunt Jean said at the hospital that afternoon after he'd greeted her with a kiss and settled in a plastic chair. 'What'll happen?'

She was sitting up, and that made her look so much better, but Alex had to concentrate hard on her slurred speech whilst pretending he wasn't. He didn't want to discourage her.

'Everything's ticking along, Aunt Jean. Don't worry about it.'

She shook her head. 'What'll *happen*?'

Ah. She means in the future. I didn't want to have a conversation about that so soon.

'You should be thinking about *your* future, not Fox Farm's,' he hedged.

'Same thing.'

'Not necessarily.'

His aunt's face took on that stubborn, mutinous look he'd come to know so well as a lad whenever Uncle William suggested something to do with her precious Fox Farm. Alex was beginning to have a lot of belated sympathy for his late uncle. From inheriting a nice bit of land and buildings, to supporting his wife in developing her pottery hobby into a proper sideline, then opening the café, then the gallery, then the studio… How much had Uncle William worried about whether it was growing out of control? In the end, it had earned them a good living, but it must have caused his uncle many a panic attack along the way.

Aunt Jean was waiting. It wouldn't be kind to keep her hopes up *too* high.

'What about when you come home?' *If you come home.* 'Fox Farm can't carry on losing money. And we don't know how well you'll be.'

'Getting better.'

'Yes, you are.' The doctors had told Alex to be upbeat and optimistic. Aunt Jean had to *believe* she could get better, otherwise she might not try. 'You're tough, alright. But you're seventy-two, and Fox Farm was already a big ask, even without this setback. You might need helpers. You might not manage in your cottage like before. You might even have to move.'

He decided not to mention the possibility of a residential home. The idea depressed him to his core, and it would depress his aunt a darned sight more. But her questioning look gave him no choice but to voice the obvious option.

You have to put the idea in her head, Alex. Give her time to come to terms with the possibility.

'I think you should consider selling up, Aunt Jean.'

The result was predictable. His aunt's face turned ashen, and she pulled her hand away from his, withdrawing into herself.

So much for following the doc's instructions to not upset her.

Alex understood her reaction. It made him sick to the stomach, the idea of losing the place they loved so much. He sat patiently, allowing her to absorb the blow.

Finally, he could stand the silence no longer. 'Even before the stroke, you must have thought about what you'd do with Fox Farm as you got older.'

'Didn't plan to get old.'

Alex grinned. 'It looks like the universe has decided otherwise, you stubborn woman!'

That raised a small, crooked smile. 'But?'

'But running Fox Farm on your own will be too much for you. I think you know, deep down, it was already heading that way.'

Aunt Jean nodded, looking beaten, and Alex hated that he'd had to be so frank.

'I'm tired.' Her eyelids drooped.

'I'm sorry. I'll go now.'

'No.' She took his hand. 'Wait till I sleep.'

Alex sat, holding his beloved aunt's frail hand in his and feeling like a total bastard for suggesting she sell the place she loved.

*

Early on Tuesday morning, Daisy let herself into the closed gallery. Lisa – no doubt grateful that she didn't have to help – had lent her a key.

Daisy needed to look more closely at the work of the artists she had appointments with. Art was subjective. What Jean liked, Lisa might turn her nose up at, Daisy might love, Jamie might hate… But Jean was running a business, not a charity, and she'd been doing it for years. She knew what would sell, and she didn't want her walls and shelves filled with pieces that would sit gathering dust.

Lisa had given Daisy a list of instructions, ending with, 'Don't let them try it on. If you're unsure of yourself, they'll take advantage.'

Resentful, Daisy had asked pointedly, 'You're sure you don't want to be there?'

'I can't. Besides, I'm only paid five days a week.'

Daisy had sighed. 'Then I guess I'll do my best.'

The first couple of appointments went well. The artists were polite, decided what to take away from their space and suggested what they'd like to add. Daisy was happy with what they brought, followed Lisa's instructions on agreeing the price the pieces should be sold for, and even managed to keep them within their time slot.

Heaven forbid it should *all* be smooth sailing.

'I've been working on a new technique,' Lily said, showing Daisy a canvas. 'What do you think?'

Daisy wasn't sure what to think. 'What is it?'

'A cat, of course.'

Daisy studied the deformed feline as politely as she could. Lily usually employed bold strokes of acrylic paint to create her animals. For some reason known only to herself, she'd decided to incorporate other materials into her work, interspersing the paint strokes with strings and threads jabbed across the canvas from one end of the 'cat' to the other.

'Do you have more?' Daisy asked, hoping Lily had shown her a dud.

'Yes. They're all the same technique now. Look.'

Daisy looked. There was nothing she could take. She glanced at Lily's wall space with her colourful interpretations of *recognisable* animals. The addition of extra media simply didn't work, and Daisy knew from friends experimenting with mixed media at art college that these pieces would not be hardy. But how could she say that? It was different for Jean. She owned the place.

And I'm Jean's representative.

'Lily, I think your technique needs honing,' Daisy said carefully. 'The strings and twines… You've stretched them right across the canvas.'

'That was to give a continuous feel, to suggest fur or whatever.'

'Yes, but they'll give over time – with heat or dust, maybe, or storage if people like to swap pieces around.' Daisy gently placed a finger underneath a thread to show how it gapped away from the canvas. 'They're not robust enough.'

Lily's face fell. 'You won't take them?'

'Your others are bold and fun. They pop right out from the wall. The new pieces don't work the same way. I'm sorry.'

'Not half as sorry as I am!' Angry tears appeared in Lily's eyes.

'I understand.'

'I would have *thought* you should, being an artist yourself. I don't know who made *you* judge and jury at Fox Farm!'

Daisy felt sick. 'Lily, I can assure you that Jean wouldn't take these, either, but you're welcome to try again, when she's back. In the meantime, there's space on your wall, so if you have more of your old style…?'

'I already took them to a place in Skipton,' Lily said sulkily.

'Did you show them your new pieces?' Daisy asked, hoping to get validation for her refusal.

'Not yet. But I will.'

'Then I wish you luck.'

Daisy got through her last appointment without further incident. On the whole, she felt it was a morning's work well done. But the episode with Lily did not sit well with her. She could only hope the following day held nothing similarly unpleasant.

*

'How's the writer?' Aunt Jean asked Alex on his daily visit.

Alex was getting better at interpreting her speech, and she was becoming a little more confident with what she attempted, but it often depended on how tired she was.

Grateful that she was bringing up anything other than his traitorous suggestion to sell Fox Farm, he said, 'I told him to call if he needed anything. He hasn't, so I presume he's happy.'

'And Daisy?'

'She texted me to let me know how the others reacted to Nigel Giles.'

'You text each other?' His aunt gave him a speculative look. 'How's she getting on with the artists?'

Ah. Alex hadn't asked Daisy how that was going. When Aunt Jean glared at him, he said, 'I know, I should have followed it up. I will.'

'Alex, I've been thinking.'

Uh-oh. She looks serious.

'I always thought, when I die, you and Seb...' The name Sebastian was too difficult for her. Alex nodded to show he understood she meant his cousin. 'You'd sell up. But...' Her eyes filled with tears, tearing Alex's heart into a hundred pieces. 'The stroke made me think. I want to leave something behind.'

Alex frowned. 'You mean, like a legacy?'

'Yes. Fox Farm is my whole life. It'd be nice, for me and William... I want it to keep going after I die.'

Alex's heart sank right down to the hospital floor. After his suggestion to sell yesterday, he'd expected her to be awkward and terribly sad about the prospect, but Aunt Jean was nothing if not practical. *This* wasn't what he'd expected at all – not only wanting to keep Fox Farm going now, but even after her death? That was the tallest order he'd ever heard!

He tried to bring her gently back down to earth. 'Let's not worry about something so far away, eh? You should be thinking about what matters *now*.'

'I am,' she insisted, her eyes fierce. 'Keep Fox Farm going *now*, Alex, so that when I die, it can *still* keep going. My leg–'

'Legacy.'

'Yes. For all the folk who like to come. For the artists whose work we sell. The new ones we give a chance to. They rely on us.'

Alex studied her earnest face. He loved Fox Farm almost as much as she did, but he'd always assumed that once his aunt was no longer in this world – a thought he could barely stand and something he hoped was a very long way off – Fox Farm would be sold.

His brain scrambled. 'I'm not sure how that's even possible.'

'I'm asking too much.'

Yes! Yes, you are! But Alex remained silent.

'I'm sorry.' A tear ran down her cheek.

'Don't be sorry. It's just that I'm not sure it's practical.'

'But you'll think about it?'

I can give her that much, can't I? 'Yes. I'll think about it.'

Alex did just that on the long drive back, his mind turning it over. Once home, he ran a hot bath and lay with a warm flannel over his face so he didn't have to look at the shabby tiles.

One of these days, I'll get this house up to scratch.

Aunt Jean's request today was too huge to get his head around. She was emotional – that was understandable – but he couldn't make promises he couldn't keep. He had no idea where his life would be so many years ahead, where Riverside would be at, whether Fox Farm would be viable, how he could run two businesses at once. Besides, Fox Farm was left to both him *and* Sebastian.

Still, Alex was a practical man. If something felt too big to tackle, you broke it down into chunks. As he lay soaking, that was what he tried to do.

First, he needed to establish whether his aunt *would* need to go into residential care. If so, there was no question – Fox Farm must be sold.

If she came home but refused to sell – obvious from the steely glint in her eyes – then he would have to manoeuvre Fox Farm into a better position financially.

If he achieved that, and *if* it could eventually afford another member of staff to take over some or all of Aunt Jean's role, then maybe he could promise to *consider* keeping it going when she left it behind… *if* he could convince Sebastian that it was worth more as a source of income than selling.

And if they couldn't make Fox Farm profitable again in the short term? Aunt Jean would accept that they'd tried, if she knew he'd done his utmost.

The question is, how do I go about that?

A good Christmas season wouldn't be enough, even with the price increases. And Fox Farm couldn't manage with fewer staff. The only answer was to bring in more spending customers.

While the bath cooled, Alex's mind explored possibilities. He'd learned from building his business that you had to speculate to accumulate, and he couldn't see any other way with Fox Farm, even though it seemed contradictory to everything he'd said to his aunt.

By the time he was shrivelled like a prune, Alex had formulated a potential plan, but he had no idea if it would work or what it would cost.

His phone rang as he was towelling dry. *Gary.*

'Alex. Fancy a pint tonight?'

'Are you psychic, mate? I was just thinking about you.'

'Uh-oh.' Gary sighed. 'Why do I get the feeling that means offering my services for free?'

Sometimes it came in handy having a best friend who was a builder. 'How about offering some advice and an estimate in exchange for a Christmas tree for the kids?'

'Deal. See you at the Masons Inn at eight?'

Chapter Eight

Daisy spent the evening catching up on *her* work for a change. She was so absorbed, she didn't notice the creeping fog that curled around her cattle byre. When she heard a light rap at her window, she jumped a mile. And when her head jerked up to see nothing but engulfing mist and a face pressed against the glass, her heart hammered against her ribcage. The few seconds it took her eyes to adjust from working at close range to seeing into middle distance felt like the longest of her life, until she recognised the balding pate of N.J. Giles.

Pressing a hand to her heart to still it, she walked to the door.

I hope he only writes about murders and doesn't perform them.

'Evening,' he said. 'Sorry, did I startle you?'

Oh no, not at all. I'm used to people looming out of the fog and rapping at my window when there's nobody around.

'A little,' she said politely. 'Can I help?'

'I was hoping you might do me a favour.' His voice was quiet and considered. 'Could you come over to the cottage?'

At night, alone, in the fog, with someone who writes about murder? 'Do you have a problem with the range or something?'

'Oh no, nothing like that. I need a willing body, and with you being right here…'

'What?'

Realising what he'd said, N.J. Giles turned bright pink. 'I'm so sorry. That didn't come out right at all. I meant for my book. There are some logistics I need to work out, and cushions don't do the same job.'

'Uh-huh.' Daisy wasn't sure that him viewing her as a willing body in *any* context was good, but she couldn't see how to refuse. 'Well… Okay.'

She followed him across the farmyard, now like a scene from an old black-and-white horror film. She could barely see three feet in front of her.

'It's the perfect night for it, you see.' N.J. Giles' disembodied voice reached back to her through the gloom. 'Perfect conditions.'

Perfect for what?

When they arrived at the cottage, he ushered her in. Cushions from the sofa were huddled on the flagstone floor, forming the approximate length of a human being.

Gulp.

'Right.' He clapped his hands together, rather gleefully for Daisy's liking. 'First, I need to know how much you can see through the window.'

'Only the fog and dark,' Daisy said uncertainly.

'Good, good.' He shot out of the door, leaving it open, and once more his pale face loomed against the window. 'And now?' he called.

'Your face. Sudden. Scary.'

'Even better.' He came back in, beaming.

Are all writers this deranged?

'We'll do that again, with the door closed, and this time I need to know if you have enough time to reach it and lock it.' He held up a finger. 'But remember, you wouldn't react right away, because you'd be frightened out of your wits at first.'

That's not hard to imagine.

Allowing a couple of seconds for terror, Daisy enabled him to prove that he could indeed enter before she could lock the door.

'We need the knife block nearer the door,' he said, moving it to his satisfaction.

I don't like this game.

'And you'd be backing away at this stage.'

Damn right I would. Daisy followed her instincts and did as she was asked.

'And now I lunge.' She was backed against the far wall when he came at her – action only, no props, thank goodness.

'And you crumple.'

Tell me I'm dreaming. Daisy crumpled.

N.J. Giles stood over her, stroking his chin with dissatisfaction. 'No, no, that's no good at all.' When she stared up at him, he explained, 'You're blocking the door to the stairs, you see. The killer can't get up to his other victims. You'll have to fall elsewhere.'

Daisy stood and looked around. 'I could fall onto the sofa?'

'No, the floor's better. More dramatic for the reader to visualise.'

'But there's no other space to back into,' Daisy pointed out. 'Why would she back towards the range?'

'You're right. Unless…' He glanced overhead at the pan hooks. 'Hmmm. A heavy cast-iron skillet. If this were *on* the range, she might back up to it in the hope she could hit him over the head. Or it could have hot fat in it – she might plan to throw that in his face. Let's try that, shall we?'

Five minutes later they had established to Mr Giles' satisfaction that despite the victim's quick thinking, her nerves would prevent her from executing her plan of defence. That way, she could expire nearer the range, well away from the door, allowing her murderer access to the next floor and his next victim.

'Fantastic. Cup of tea?' he offered.

Triple vodka, more like. 'Er, no, thanks. I should get back to work.'

'Well, thank you so much for your time. I hope it hasn't unnerved you too much.'

You have no idea. 'I'll live. Unlike your poor stabbing victim. Goodnight, Mr Giles.'

Crossing the farmyard, Daisy felt distinctly spooked, the hoot of an owl causing her to jump out of her skin. Back in her studio, she pulled the blinds she rarely bothered with. And when she went to bed, she was still cursing N.J. Giles for his macabre weirdness… and cursing Alex for moving him into the cottage.

She was cursing Alex even more the next day after she'd finished a few more artist appointments. The two that went well took time she could have spent on her own work. The other two made Daisy miserable.

One was a potter who had changed her usually plain designs to look suspiciously like Jean's.

'They're too much like Jean Fox's,' Daisy had explained as she studied the mugs, glazed in a green-blue with a sheep design.

The woman had merely shrugged. 'Jean sticks mainly to mugs and jugs. I do plates and dishes, too. You have plenty of room for both of us.'

You copied her design, Daisy had wanted to say. *It would be bad enough if you took them elsewhere, but to bring them here…?*

'You won't take them?' the woman had realised. 'You're a *painter*. Who put *you* in charge?'

'Jean Fox put me in charge. You honestly can't expect me to take work so similar to the owner of this gallery.'

They did *not* part on the best of terms.

The other awkward encounter of the morning had been with an oil painter. He'd brought two winter scenes but had expected the rest of his work – trees in full summer leaf or spring wildflower meadows – to remain. Daisy had had to ask him to take those away.

'Why the hell do you want a gallery full of dreary pictures of winter?' he'd ranted.

'Many pieces here are unrelated to the seasons – animals, abstracts, nature. Ceramics, wood,' Daisy had said steadily. 'But with landscapes, Jean prefers to reflect the season. Your summer scenes are unlikely to sell at this time of year, but these two you brought in are perfect. Could you do more?'

'How much time do you think I have on my hands? Some of us have a full-time job. Some of us have mouths to feed. We can't all be Jean Fox's pet, swanning around in her cutesy little play-studio!'

Oh, I don't like this. Please let me go back to my cutesy little play-studio and lock the door.

'I'm only following Jean's instructions.' When he made no move to back down, she'd said, 'How about a compromise? You take the wildflowers and summer trees but leave the river scenes?'

'Whatever.' He'd started taking down the offending work. 'You'll take these back in the spring?'

'Yes. Hope to see you then.' *Like I hope to break an ankle.*

Crossing to her studio, Daisy glanced over at the barn. Alex was standing in the doorway with another man, both of them in scruffy jeans, Alex's soil-stained, the other man's covered in plaster or cement. Alex's companion was gesturing as he spoke, and as they parted ways, they slapped each other on the back. Alex was smiling when he came over to her.

'Hi. What're you up to in there?' she asked.

'Just checking on something.' He quickly changed the subject. 'I promised Aunt Jean I'd ask how you're getting on with the artists. Sorry – I should've done it sooner.'

'I'll live.'

'That good, huh?'

'I'm glad we decided to accept most by email or I'd never have had time, but I've still had to meet some. There've been… altercations. I'm not keen on conflict.'

'I'm sorry. And thank you. I owe you.'

'You owe me for more than that, mister. I was stabbed last night. Twice.'

'You were *what*?'

As Daisy related her tale of fog and murder, Alex's face turned from astonishment to laughter.

'I'm glad you find it amusing.' Daisy glared at him. 'I couldn't sleep last night.'

At that, Alex sobered. 'You don't *really* feel uncomfortable with him here, do you? I thought it would be good for you to have someone on site. I didn't like the idea of you being out here all alone. He seemed respectable.'

'He's a little odd, that's all.' She looked up as a florist's van pulled over at the roadside and the delivery driver took a bouquet from the back.

'I'm looking for Daisy Claybourne,' she said as she approached.

'Right here.' Alex pointed at Daisy.

'Thank you.' Daisy stared, bewildered, at the flowers in her arms as the lady nodded and left.

'Secret admirer?' Alex asked.

'I doubt it.' *Admirers are few and far between when you usually look a mess and have neither the time nor inclination to go out.* Daisy plucked the card from the bouquet and read out loud, '"Thank you for last night. Nigel Giles."'

Alex burst out laughing. '*That* could be taken the wrong way!'

'For a man who makes his living from words, he's not always clever with them, is he?' Daisy rolled her eyes. 'But this was sweet.'

'So, you're okay about him?' Alex asked. 'I don't want you to feel insecure.'

Daisy was touched by the concern on his face. 'I'll be fine, as long as there's no more fog.' She hesitated. Alex was looking careworn – unsurprising, since he did nothing other than work at Riverside, visit Jean and worry about Fox Farm. He could do with a change, and she had an idea. 'Will you be visiting Jean tomorrow evening?'

'No, I'll go in the afternoon. We have things to discuss, and I'd rather do it when she's less tired. Why?'

'I owe you supper after last week – not that you'll get anything as fancy as lamb casserole – and I have an idea to distract you from your troubles.'

Alex raised a cheeky eyebrow. 'Sounds promising.'

'Six thirty?'

'See you then.'

Daisy watched him go, then glanced back at the barn. Why had he been there with someone who looked like a builder? Was it about to collapse? They could do without that!

*

'Did you think about it?' Aunt Jean asked Alex when he visited on Thursday afternoon.

He knew she was referring to her legacy idea. *She's like a dog with a bone.*

Alex hadn't visited her the day before. Angie and Sue had asked to go, so he'd jumped at it. He'd had plenty to do.

First, he'd spoken to her doctor on the telephone. The consultant had told him she didn't see the need for residential care unless it was what his aunt wanted, then chuckled and said she knew *that* was highly unlikely, knowing Mrs Fox. She did, however, envisage her needing some level of home care, at least for a while.

With residential care – and therefore selling Fox Farm – no longer on the cards, Alex had had plans and calculations to make, Gary to consult…

Aunt Jean was waiting for an answer.

'Yes, I thought about it.' Alex chose his words carefully. 'But we can't consider that until we've sorted out the here and now.'

'Why?' Whether the simple question was down to Aunt Jean's usual blunt Yorkshire way or her current necessity for using fewer words, it was hard to say.

'Because there won't *be* any legacy unless we can make Fox Farm work. That requires changes. In the meantime, there's the question of *me*, Aunt Jean. Riverside is manageable at the moment, but come the spring, I won't be able to devote so much time to Fox Farm.'

'I'll run it,' his aunt said stubbornly. 'Same as always.'

He took her hand. 'To some extent, I hope, but not the way you did before. You'd end up right back in here again.' *Gotta be cruel to be kind.* 'And there's something else. At the moment, I can ask you for permission to do things, where to find stuff, what your online passwords are.' Alex had dropped his voice, not keen for the nursing staff to hear. 'But that's not ideal, is it?'

'You mean if I have another stroke?'

Straight to the point, as ever.

'I doubt you'll allow that to happen!' he said cheerily, desperate to buoy the spirits he was so busy dampening. 'But it's dodgy, and it doesn't sit well with me.'

'So, what can we do?'

This was a big step for both of them, one Alex had spent the previous evening researching in detail. 'You *could* consider giving me power of attorney so I can act on your behalf with organisations like the bank. Someone who knows you well has to sign to say you're not being coerced, and you need witnesses for signatures. Then it takes a few weeks to become official, so in the meantime, we'd have to carry on the way we are.' He winked. 'It'd be best if you didn't have another stroke before it comes through.'

'Do it.' His aunt's condition hadn't affected her capacity for swift decision-making.

'I want you to think about it first. Later on, you might not like that I can meddle in your affairs… although you could always cancel it.'

'I trust you, Alex. Maybe we should've done it before now. I'm getting old.'

Alex hated that his aunt was beginning to see herself that way. She had the mindset of someone twenty or thirty years younger. But he supposed seventy-two did take her out of spring chicken territory.

'You should consider naming more than one attorney, as a back-up,' he advised.

'No. Just you. Eric and your mum are too far away. Seb…' Frustrated at her inability to say the name still, her shoulders sagged. 'He's always busy. And you love Fox Farm.'

'Okay. I'll print off the forms. But I want you to *read* them. I'll ask Angie to sign to say you're sane.'

His aunt cackled. 'Sane as I'll ever be. Now, what about these changes you said are needed at Fox Farm?'

'That's enough for today.'

'Tell me.'

Alex sighed. His aunt was nothing if not determined. 'Only if you drink your tea.' He took the lidded beaker she was offered from a passing trolley and handed it to her.

'Feel like a baby,' she grumbled, glaring at it.

'Better than tipping it into your lap. Quit complaining.'

Aunt Jean sipped. 'Tell me.'

Alex took a deep breath. If his aunt agreed to this, he was letting himself in for an awful lot of work. 'First, the café.'

'What's wrong with it?'

'Nothing. It serves great food and it's popular. In good weather, people are happy to sit outside, especially walkers who don't want to push their way in with all their clobber. But in bad weather, people peer in, see there isn't a table and walk away. You can't afford to lose customers. And if they can't visit the café, they might not bother with the gallery.'

'You want to make it bigger?'

'The café could take over the entire ground floor.'

'But the gallery…' Her struggle with the word *gallery* made her cross. 'It'll have less space if it's just upstairs.'

'The upstairs has been limited for years, Aunt Jean. Access by a narrow staircase…? We get away with it because it's an old, historic building, but it costs you customers. Then there's the higgledy-piggledy nature of it – one room downstairs, three rooms upstairs. Even with the open doorways, Jamie and Lisa can't keep an eye on everything. We could provide access to all and make it more spacious by moving it altogether.'

'Where?'

'The barn.'

'The *barn*!'

'It's structurally sound. Uncle William had it repaired a couple of years before he died, remember – roof fixed, floors and walls sealed – when he planned to convert it into holiday accommodation. It's wasted, just sitting there, used for storage. I had a pint with Gary to discuss it, and he's looked it over. It needs a good clean-up, but it could be really atmospheric with the flagstone floors, wooden rafters, stone walls. We'd have to make some adjustments – screens for wall art, shelving, display tables, better lighting and spotlights, a basic heating system. That would mean expense, but I can keep it to a minimum. You'd have to see it as an investment – putting your money in and hoping it pays itself back.'

'Use my savings, you mean?'

They both chuckled at that – Alex had been adamant about her not using her savings, and now he was suggesting she do just that.

'Investing in improvements to increase revenue isn't the same as propping up a declining business,' he pointed out. 'If I thought you'd agree to sell, I wouldn't even suggest it. But if you're determined to keep Fox Farm going…'

'I am. When would we do it?'

I should have known that the minute I gave her an option other than selling, she'd go for it.

'It has to be now, to make Christmas the best we can. There's no point in leaving it till afterwards, when we head into a quiet season.

Besides, the longer we wait, the more money Fox Farm loses by the day. But you have to understand it could go wrong, and then you'll have lost more of your savings.' He sighed. 'I need a swift decision, though, and I'm not sure you're in the right state to make it.'

'I'm poorly, Alex, not stupid.'

'Even so, I want you to think carefully. I'll bring estimates tomorrow, and the power of attorney forms.' He picked up his coat.

'I'm glad you went out with Gary,' Jean said. 'You should get out more.'

In which spare minute of the day? Feeling that he was leaving her after far too heavy a discussion, Alex hovered another few minutes to tell her about Daisy's foggy encounter with N.J. Giles, and was rewarded by hearing her still laughing as he walked down the length of the ward. It was a wonderful sound.

Chapter Nine

Daisy panicked about what to cook for Alex. His lamb casserole had been impressive, but her options were limited with only a hob and microwave. In the end, she opted for hearty minestrone packed with vegetables and pasta, and it was bubbling nicely when he arrived.

'How was Jean?' she asked.

'She had a bit of sparkle back, especially when I told her about your murder role-play.'

'Ha! Glad to be of service.'

'The doctor's happy with her progress. I'm not sure how much Aunt Jean likes working with the physios and speech therapists, but she's putting up with it.'

Daisy smiled. 'That's good. Beer or wine?'

He accepted a beer and she led him to her work table at the far end of the studio, where he frowned at the array of materials she'd laid out.

'Do you paint?' she asked.

'Er. No.'

'It can be very therapeutic.'

'It can also look like a toddler's finger-painting. I would fit into that category.' Alex's eyes widened. 'You want me to paint? *That's* your idea of a distraction?'

'Why, what did you think I had in mind?'

'I hadn't given it any thought, luckily.'

'I decided the table would be easier for you – an easel takes some getting used to. Let the beer numb you a bit, I'll feed you, then we'll see how we go.' When he still looked askance, she said, 'It's a chance to put your mind to something different. Like I said, you might find it therapeutic.'

'I'd find more beer therapeutic. A hot bath. A massage.'

'Beer's limited – you're driving. There's no bath here. As for a massage? You and I do *not* know each other well enough!'

Alex grinned. 'I was talking in general terms.'

'Hmmm.' Daisy went through to her kitchenette to fetch supper, placing it on the sales counter.

Alex sniffed appreciatively, then tasted the soup. 'This is great.'

'Thanks. I'm limited in there.'

'I can imagine. Seen any more of our author friend?'

'I knocked to thank him for the flowers – in broad daylight, for my own peace of mind. He's always sitting at the kitchen table with his laptop. I've barely seen him outdoors.'

'Maybe he needs to ignore that the farm's full of people so he can imagine it all quiet and deserted for his murders.'

Daisy shivered. 'Delightful.'

'I'm glad he's only here for a few weeks,' Alex admitted. 'It doesn't feel right, him being in Aunt Jean's cottage.'

'She'll be back soon enough.'

'Yeah.' Alex stared out at the dark farmyard. 'You know, the best days of my life were at Fox Farm. Long days with no school. The freedom of the place – as long as I stayed away from the gallery and Aunt Jean's pottery room! Off on lone walks with the old collie dog they had back then. Fantastic home cooking from Aunt Jean and Angie. And Uncle

William…' He sounded wistful. 'He took a child brought up in a suburban house with a small lawn only fit for kicking a ball around, and let him loose in his glorious garden here. I had no idea what I was doing – or why I should even be interested – but he persevered, and he instilled that love of feeling my hands in the soil, of growing something from seed, of planting and nurturing.' He smiled. 'You should have seen the garden back then, Daisy. I try to keep up to it for Aunt Jean, but it's nothing like how it was when Uncle William was around.'

Happy to encourage Alex's reflective mood, Daisy asked, 'Is that why you started Riverside? Because he taught you gardening?'

'Yes. When I finished school, I had no desire to go to college or university. My father didn't push. Nobody in his family had been before, and he didn't see why they would start now. I think, in my naivety, I hoped I might be invited to live and work at Fox Farm, but Aunt Jean and Uncle William knew I needed to find my own feet. I got a job at a garden centre far enough from home to give me an excuse to leave. It paid bugger-all, so I couldn't afford much rent. I stayed in some fairly dire places. You know all about that! But I learned, watched everything that went on, saw how they planned ahead for each season. I had a knackered old car, so I spent my days off here at Fox Farm. Uncle William let me grow what I wanted and gave me my own greenhouse and patch of land. He looked after them for me when I wasn't here. I started selling at farmers' markets, but I had no idea how to move forward. There were no opportunities for promotion at the place where I worked.'

'Your uncle helped you?' Daisy guessed.

'Yes. I remember that evening so well. We sat drinking whisky after Aunt Jean had gone to bed, and I told him I felt in a rut but didn't know what to do about it. He looked at me for a long time, then said, "Are you going to carry on like this, lad, earning barely anything doing what you love for somebody else? Or do you want to earn barely anything doing what you love for *you*?"'

Daisy chuckled. 'So how did Riverside come about?'

'There was already a small nursery on that site by the river. It had been closed down a long while – the owner had gone into a home, and the place was a dilapidated eyesore, so everyone was keen to see it restored to something respectable. Uncle Willian loaned me the money, which I've repaid, slowly but surely. I pretty much had to rebuild the place from the ground up – ensuring I didn't tread on any regulations' toes, of course. At first it was me and Jules. Then Jim, and now Kieran, our apprentice. I wanted to give something back; provide someone with the same chances I had. I think Uncle William would be proud.'

'I'm sure he would.' Daisy gave him an encouraging smile. 'You know, I've never even been to Riverside. Never had cause to.'

'Drop in sometime.'

'I will.' She stood. 'Right. Come on over to the table.' Her lips twitched at the way Alex traipsed after her like a condemned man. 'Here's your canvas. Go for it.'

'You're not even going to give me pointers?'

'Okay, well, if you think you can't paint, try something that doesn't have to be accurate. Buildings can be hard to get right. So can people. Scenes – fields, sky, beach, sea – are sometimes easier for beginners. Picture something imprecise that you want to give a *sense* of. The colours, the textures. These are acrylics, so you can vary the thickness, and I have tools here for you to stipple or make waves – whatever you feel like. It doesn't matter if you make a mess of it. I'll put some music on. Try to relax.'

The background easy listening that Daisy favoured for her opening hours suited her purpose well. Alex was tense at first, but slowly he relaxed. At her easel, she played around with a painting of her own whilst watching his shoulders drop away from his ears as he concentrated. They didn't chat. She just let him be. She wasn't sure what he was aiming for – there were grey lines, some multicoloured dots, quite a lot of green – but it didn't matter. All she wanted was for him to forget his troubles for a while.

Eventually, she could stand it no longer and walked around the table to peer over his shoulder. As she studied his efforts, she became aware of Alex's woodsy scent – nothing artificial, no aftershave, just soap.

'Jean's cottage garden,' she stated.

'You recognise it?'

She pointed at his canvas. 'The grey stone of the corner of the cottage. Summer flowers growing up against the garden wall. Leaves, petals, stems. Bamboo canes. It's lovely.'

'Thanks.' He gave her a bashful smile. 'Not exactly Monet, though.'

'Did you enjoy doing it?'

'Very much.'

'Then that's all that matters. You can leave it here to dry.'

He glanced at his watch. 'I had no idea it was so late.'

'That's because your mind was occupied with something else. That's good.'

He stood and stretched. 'Thanks. I had fun tonight.'

Daisy laughed. 'You don't have to sound so surprised!'

*

Alex felt lighter as he went about his tasks at Riverside the following morning.

'You're in a good mood,' Jules commented as she handed him a list of repair jobs and a couple of large orders for him to give the go-ahead to.

'I had a night off.'

'Good for you. Who with? Gary?'

'No. Daisy. She owed me supper after last week – which was a *working* supper, by the way – and then she made me try my hand at painting a canvas.'

'You're kidding!'

'No, but I enjoyed myself, so I can't complain.'

'Good. It's about time you had fun. No *fun*, though?'

'No, Jules. Just a little R and R, which was what I needed. I have a lot to deal with at Aunt Jean's this afternoon.'

With that lead-in, Alex told Jules about his plans for Fox Farm. After all, she was the one who would bear the brunt of him spending even more time away from Riverside.

Jules stared at him. 'I'm not sure what to say!'

'You can tell me I'm mad, if you like.'

'I don't know about mad. Over-ambitious in terms of timescale, certainly, but you're right – if you're going to do it, you need to get on with it, to capitalise on Christmas.' She frowned. 'You're taking on an awful lot, Alex. And it could be risky, financially.'

'I am, and yes, it could. The idea that it might go wrong makes my stomach churn.' Alex rubbed circles on his temples, trying to ward off the headache that threatened. 'But Aunt Jean won't sell.'

'I can understand that. Fox Farm is everything to her.' Jules smiled. 'Well. Good luck.'

When he'd finished at Riverside, Alex drove to the hospital, the route now imprinted on his brain so well, he could have done it on autopilot.

'My legs are tired,' Aunt Jean complained. 'They've been making me do ex... Making me work.' She wrinkled her nose. 'My arm's still not good.'

Alex saw sadness in her eyes and knew she was wondering if it would ever be the same. How would that affect her doing the things she loved? Cooking and baking? Her pottery?

To distract her, he pulled out the sheaf of papers he'd printed off. 'This is the power of attorney. We'll read it together, section by section, so I know you understand it.'

Jean made a face but dutifully listened. When he'd finished, she simply crooked a finger and said, 'Pen.'

'You're sure?'

'Yes.' Luckily, it wasn't his aunt's writing arm that had been affected by the stroke. 'We need a witness.'

A nurse came over. 'I'd be happy to help.'

'Thank you.' After she'd gone, Alex told his aunt, 'Angie's coming tomorrow. She wants to make sure you're in your right mind before she signs her section.'

Aunt Jean cackled. 'How would we know? Now, what about those figures you promised me?'

This is going to be a long afternoon. Alex took out his notes and went through them with her in detail.

'Not too bad' was her verdict.

'I've kept it as low as I can,' he told her. 'I'll act as labourer for Gary, and he's heard of a café in Settle that's closing and selling off old tables and chairs. They won't match, but it keeps costs down.'

'A bigger café needs more staff. You haven't put that in here.' She prodded at his notes.

'It's counter service, not table service, so I reckon a part-timer would do, to cover lunchtimes. Maybe more in the summer. We have no money, but we do have Jamie for now.'

'He's with Lisa.'

'Yes, but he's not properly used, is he? I know you kept him on after the summer because he's a great lad, Aunt Jean, but that gallery does *not* need two full-timers. It certainly won't once it's in the barn, all in one space. He could do some hours in the café. I doubt he'll mind. In fact, I think he'll enjoy the hustle and bustle. I suspect he gets bored in the gallery.'

'Lisa won't like it.'

Alex *could* have said that Lisa hadn't exactly covered herself in glory lately, letting Daisy do all the hard work with the artists, but he decided his aunt didn't need to hear it.

'She'll have to put up with it. We can't really afford Jamie. This is the ideal way to put that right. It's bad enough that you don't charge Daisy rent. You always charged for the studio before. You shouldn't have made an exception, not when you were propping up Fox Farm with your own money.'

'Jack's farm was no good for her,' Aunt Jean snapped. 'I wanted to give her a better place to work, to live, but I knew she couldn't afford rent.'

'Oh, Aunt Jean.'

'Don't you "Oh, Aunt Jean" me,' she said crossly. 'That girl had a hard start in life. The least I could do was help her on her way.'

Alex sighed. 'You're too soft. You don't have to take every waif and stray under your wing.'

Her eyes gleamed fire. 'Took *you* in, didn't I?'

Chastened, Alex nodded. 'You did. But—'

'No "buts". I wanted to help her, and I can't change it now. But I agree about Jamie. Do what you have to do. All of this.' She waved the figures at him.

'If it doesn't work out, it's a chunk of your savings gone.'

'You can't take it with you when you die, Alex.' She patted his cheek with the hand she could lift high enough. 'And I'm not going on a world cruise anytime soon. I can spend it how I like. I want to do this.'

'Alright. But don't say anything to Angie tomorrow. I need to tell the staff in my own way, at the right time. And…'

'What, love?'

'They can't know how much trouble Fox Farm is in. It's not good for morale. The official line is that we want to improve profits to help you with carers and whatnot when you get home.'

'You're making out that I'm a frail old lady?'

'It serves our purpose for now.' He winked.

'Go ahead.'

And with that simple statement, Alex was looking at hard toil and sleepless nights for some time to come.

*

Daisy popped over to the café last thing on Saturday. Angie was going to visit Jean, and Daisy had bought a packet of Jean's favourite shortbread from the village shop.

'Could you take these to Jean, Angie? I haven't had a chance to visit this week.'

'Yes, will do. She likes those.' Angie was standing at the counter, cloth in hand, staring into space. She sounded distracted.

'Is something wrong?' Daisy asked, concerned.

'Hmmm? Oh. I was just thinking… I suppose with Jean out of it, Fox Farm is down to Alex, isn't it?'

Daisy frowned. 'Is this about Mr Giles taking over Jean's cottage?'

'No. I can see why Alex did that now. Money for old rope. You know he asked me to increase the café prices?'

Daisy nodded. 'Are you upset about it?'

'No. It's been hard work planning, and I'll have to stay after closing tomorrow to program the till ready for Monday morning, but I can see where he's coming from.' Angie bit her lip. 'But... Can you keep this in confidence?'

'If it'll help to talk, go ahead.'

'Jean's giving Alex power of attorney.'

Daisy thought about Alex having to go into Jean's emails and root through her paperwork. 'I can see why he'd want that. He must be doing all kinds of slightly dubious things. It must make him uncomfortable.'

'That's what he said. He asked if I'll sign to say that Jean's not being coerced.'

'Do you have a problem with that?'

'No.'

'Then what *is* the problem?' Daisy asked, frustrated with the conversation.

'I can't help wondering about the impact on us, Daisy. On Fox Farm. We expected Alex to take charge temporarily, but... He's called yet another staff meeting for tomorrow morning. What else will he come up with?'

'I doubt he has anything drastic in mind, Angie. He has so much on his plate already. Besides, he can't do anything Jean doesn't want.'

'You're right. I'm worrying over nothing.' Angie sighed. 'I've a couple of decades over you, and you'd be surprised – change doesn't always appeal as you get older. Anyway, thanks for listening.'

'Anytime.'

As she crossed the cobbles to her studio, Daisy noticed a light on in the barn. Changing direction, she peered around the door.

Alex stood in the middle of the huge open space, gazing around him, hands on hips.

'Hi.'

Alex jumped. 'Oh! Hi.'

'What are you up to?'

'Just taking a look around.'

'Oh?' Suspicion crept in. 'You were taking a look around the other day, too. With another bloke.'

'My mate, Gary. He's a builder.'

Daisy groaned. 'Don't say this place needs a ton of repairs?'

'No, that's not it. Can I speak to you in confidence?'

Crikey! This is turning out to be quite a day for confidences. 'Of course. What's up?'

'I'm going to be making some changes,' Alex told her.

And only a few minutes ago, Angie said she was worried about just that.

'I was hoping you'd help me out with the others if they're… resistant,' he went on.

A feeling of unease crept through Daisy's body. 'Why would they be resistant? What kind of changes?'

'Okay, hear me out.' His tone suggested he was expecting objections before he'd even started.

The unease spread, but Daisy did as he asked, listening carefully to his plans for expanding the café across the ground floor.

'I understand your line of thinking.' Daisy remembered what Angie had said about not liking the idea of change. 'But Angie's in her early fifties. Sue's in her early sixties. Expanding will put a strain on them.'

'I'll redistribute Jamie so he's part-time in the gallery and part-time in the café.'

'Because the gallery will be smaller?'

'No. I'm moving the gallery altogether.'

'You're *what*?' It came out aggressively, but Daisy couldn't help that. She hadn't imagined he'd meant such sweeping changes – not with Jean incapacitated. Angie's talk of legal paperwork floated in the back of her mind as she asked, 'Move it *where*? And why?'

'To here. The barn.'

Daisy goggled at him before glancing around. 'You can't hang people's artwork against stone walls, Alex. They're cold. Maybe damp. Uneven.'

'No, but you can hang huge white boards on wires in front of them. Gary did a similar thing for a place on the outskirts of Settle.' He ran a hand over his face. 'I asked you to hear me out, didn't I?'

Daisy bit back a dozen responses and allowed him to explain his vision for the barn. By the time he'd finished, Daisy couldn't deny it held appeal. 'When do you expect to do all this?'

'The alterations, this coming week. Then move the gallery across the week after, on the two closing days.'

'*What?*' Daisy squeaked. 'Why so soon? Why not January, when Fox Farm's quieter and Jean's back?'

'We'd lose out on the extra Christmas trade. As for Aunt Jean? It's better if she's not here during all the upheaval. She'd only want to get involved.'

At that, Daisy's eyes narrowed. 'Have you discussed this with her?'

'Of course I have! What do you take me for?'

'And she agrees?'

'She insists on keeping Fox Farm going, and she trusts me to do what I think's best.'

Daisy wasn't sure whether that sounded like *full* agreement. It sounded more like acquiescence from a frail, sick woman. And then there was this power of attorney business, which she couldn't say anything about without breaking Angie's confidence. Her mind raced. Why was Alex so determined to make such sudden, big changes?

Another thought occurred to her. 'If you move the gallery, what'll happen to the upstairs of the main house?'

'I don't know. Maybe I can convert it into self-catering accommodation – a holiday let.'

'Don't tell me you can get *that* done next week, too?' Daisy couldn't hide the sarcasm in her tone.

'Obviously not,' he snapped. 'I have the small task of making Fox Farm profitable first, let alone predicting what'll happen with Aunt Jean's health and planning for every other bloody eventuality!'

Daisy knew she should feel sympathy for that, but she couldn't ignore the coincidence of him persuading Jean to give him power of attorney and then doing all this.

'Do you have any idea what this sounds like, Alex?'

'No, but I can see that you're itching to tell me.'

'Damn right. I know you're appreciated for lending a hand around here.' Daisy knew she was about to overstep the mark, but she couldn't stop herself. 'But this is going *way* beyond that. Jean falls ill and suddenly you're reconfiguring the whole place? Besides, Fox Farm needing to make more money doesn't tally with *spending* it on converting this and moving that and expanding the other, does it? I don't understand you.'

Alex's tired expression hardened. 'You don't have to understand me. I'd hoped you would, but you only have to understand the situation.'

'But even as Jean's nephew, do you have the right…?'

'Daisy, I'm doing this for my aunt, whether you believe it or not, and whether you like it or not. You haven't been privy to the conversations I've had with her – which, by the way, have been emotionally gruelling for both of us – so please don't presume to understand her thought processes or mine. I have *every* right. I have a moral responsibility to look after Aunt Jean's affairs, and I'm doing that with her full knowledge and blessing. For your information, she's also granting me power of attorney to enable me to do what I need to.' He was livid now. 'I've been Jean's nephew for thirty-five years. You've only recently become her friend. If we're talking about rights, what right do *you* have to question me on this? I'll remind you that you're trading and living rent-free on Fox Farm premises with no official contract, so *you* have no rights whatsoever!'

Chapter Ten

Alex thought about apologising to Daisy but couldn't find the stomach for it. Yes, he'd been cruel, but she'd overstepped the mark. He'd hoped she would approve of his plans – as an artist, he'd expected her to appreciate the idea of using the barn as the gallery – but all he'd got was suspicion and recrimination.

That was disappointing. He didn't like the idea that she thought he was taking advantage of his aunt… although why anyone should think it was an advantage to him to run two businesses at once, he had no idea. Did she honestly believe he'd become some kind of property-grasping megalomaniac, intent on taking over?

His staff meeting at Fox Farm brought much the same reaction – surprise, suspicion, resentment. He *could* have told them Fox Farm was struggling financially; that their jobs might be at stake. Instead, he merely insisted that changes were needed to keep on making a profit – *Huh! Start making a profit, more like!* – reiterating that Aunt Jean might need extra income for her care.

Angie seemed resigned, as though she'd been expecting something along those lines. She was fine about having Jamie as her 'extra'. And Jamie was happy with the idea of dual roles.

Lisa, on the other hand, was incandescent. 'You expect me to move premises and then run it all on my own?'

'Hardly, Lisa. Jamie will still be with you part-time, so he can cover you for days off and breaks. You managed on your own before Jamie came along.'

'Jean covered for me then.'

'And Jamie will now.'

Daisy did not attend the meeting. On the surface, that made sense – she wasn't a member of staff. In reality, he knew she was avoiding him. That was fine by him.

By the time he got to Riverside, he was grateful to be back on his home patch. More than anything else, Alex wanted – *needed* – to spend time at *his* dream. *His* business. Aunt Jean's was beginning to overwhelm him.

'What do you need me to do?' he asked Jules.

'Isn't that rather odd, the manager telling the owner what to do?'

'Everything's odd lately,' Alex grumbled. 'I don't see why Riverside should be any different. Besides, you're far more in tune with this place than I am at the moment.'

'Poor Alex. You need to get your hands in the soil, don't you?'

'Yes. *Please.*'

'How about replanting the welcome bed out front? Jim hasn't had time. I was thinking winter pansies, but we have some winter-flowering heather that might look nicer if you can find something with silver foliage to go with it. You know best.'

'I'm on it.'

They called it the welcome bed because it stood between the small car park and the entrance to the main building, and it was overdue for a revamp. Fetching a trolley, Alex wheeled it around his domain, picking out what he wanted. Jules was right – the winter-flowering heather would look good, so maybe he'd stick with low ground cover in silvery shades for a frosty, winter tapestry look. Once he'd chosen, he dug out the old bed, enjoying the pale winter sun on his back.

Passing by, Jim called, 'I'd offer to help, but I can see you're as happy as a pig in muck' and left him to it.

Alex had begun planting, his movements well-practised, when he heard a familiar – and unwelcome – voice.

'Alexander. I thought I might find you kneeling in the dirt somewhere.'

Sebastian. Great.

Alex stood. Sebastian didn't hold out a hand, presumably because he didn't fancy getting soil on his manicured paws. It suited them both.

'Sebby! What the hell are you doing here?' Alex enjoyed seeing his cousin's displeased expression at the shortening of his name. It served him right. If Sebastian insisted on calling Alex 'Alexander' – which he had never gone by – then Alex could play that game, too. He also hated the way Sebastian lengthened the vowel – 'Alex*aaa*nder'. A true Yorkshireman would leave it as the short 'a' it should be, in Alex's opinion. But then Sebastian had been happy to shake off his northern roots and adopt a posh accent as soon as he could, hadn't he?

'That's a fine greeting, I must say,' Sebastian grumbled. 'I thought I'd better come up to make sure you haven't got yourself into too much of a mess, with Jean out of action.'

Alex's hackles rose. 'There's no mess, Sebastian. Everything's under control.' *Kind of.* 'I can't imagine why you'd think otherwise.'

'Dad phoned Jean a couple of times. He couldn't make head nor tail of what she was saying.'

'The poor woman's had a stroke. What does Uncle Eric expect?' Alex snapped. 'She's struggling with her speech. You have to get attuned to it. He could have phoned me.'

'He was trying to be considerate. Your mum said you're busy.'

Alex hoped his phone calls with his mother hadn't been relayed verbatim to Eric and thereby to Sebastian. But he knew, even as he thought it, that wouldn't be the case. He and his mother might not be close, but she knew when he was speaking in confidence.

'You should have let me know you were coming.' *I could have steeled myself. Had a large whisky.* 'How long will you be here for?' *Not long, I hope.*

'However long it takes to make sure everything's alright.' Sebastian's tone was arrogant.

'As I said, everything's under control,' Alex said through gritted teeth. 'But I can talk you through it, if you like.' *No choice, now you're here, have I?* 'Where are you staying?'

Sebastian frowned. 'What do you mean? At Jean's, obviously.'

Sebastian always stayed with Aunt Jean when he was obliged to venture north. Being pampered with home cooking went down well with him.

Alex suppressed a smug smile. 'Sorry, Seb. The cottage is let out till Christmas.'

'It's *what*? Why didn't you tell me?'

'I didn't know you were coming, did I?'

'I'll have to stay with you, then.'

You must be joking! 'The – er – the spare bedroom's damp,' Alex lied – although it wouldn't surprise him, the way he'd been neglecting the place. 'But you're welcome to the sofa.' That was a safe offer. Sebastian wouldn't lower himself that far.

'This flower place of yours can't be doing too well, if that's the state you're living in.'

And *that* was why Alex hated having his cousin around. At a distance, exchanging the occasional polite email about family news, Alex could just about handle his condescending attitude. But in person…

'You could try the B & B in the village. Or there's the Masons Inn,' Alex suggested.

'That'll cost a pretty penny, if I'm here for a while,' Sebastian complained.

At that, Alex felt true alarm. This didn't sound like a flying visit. Sebastian intended to stick his nose in where it wasn't wanted and throw his weight around. Well, maybe having to cough up for his stay might encourage him to keep it as short as possible.

'Why don't you find somewhere and let me know which establishment you decide to grace with your city presence?' he said. 'Then we can catch up over a pub meal.' *Anything to avoid you coming to the house and sneering at my humble abode.*

'They'd better have something more tempting than pie and peas or bangers and mash.' Sebastian sniffed.

Alex's patience was stretching thin. 'The pubs around here do good food and get great reviews – something you'd know from your occasional visits if you bothered to take Aunt Jean out for a change, instead of expecting her to cook for you.'

'Jean likes to cook for me,' Sebastian defended himself. 'It gives her pleasure.'

It gives you more. 'Well, she can't now, can she? You'll have to settle for the Masons Inn.'

To prevent any further discussion, Alex turned back to what he was doing. He'd rather kneel in the cold dirt than chat with that slimy cousin of his.

*

Daisy drove to the hospital after closing the studio, grateful that the ward was flexible with visiting hours. She didn't like driving too late in her rubbish car.

She'd been busy all day, using the time between customers to change the pieces on her walls to suit the oncoming winter, but she still felt the need to visit Jean, even though she was conscious that it was bound to annoy Alex further when he realised she was checking up on him again.

His words still smarted, as she suspected hers did with him, but she wasn't ready to apologise yet, and she guessed he wasn't, either.

'Hello, Jean. How are you?' Daisy kissed her friend's cheek, pleased to see her looking so much better than the last time she'd visited, and handed over the grapes she'd brought – a traditional offering but welcome, judging by the way Jean's eyes lit up.

'We don't get enough fruit in here,' Jean grumbled. 'The food's nowt to shout home about, I can tell you.'

Daisy sympathised. She didn't imagine hospital food could begin to compete with Jean's home cooking.

'How are you?' Jean asked.

Daisy filled Jean in on what she'd been up to in her studio and her progress with the artists, playing down the problems.

But Jean was too astute. 'I bet some were awkward. It must've been hard for you.'

If Daisy had been worried that Jean was confused or not herself, it seemed she was wrong... so she'd probably been wrong to speak to Alex the way she had. Still, she was here now. She may as well make sure.

'Alex told us about your plans for Fox Farm,' she said as casually as she could. 'Are you excited about them?'

Jean gave her a knowing look. 'You're asking if I know what I'm doing or if my mind is addled.'

'I just want to be sure you're not being pushed into anything.'

Jean took her hand. 'It's *me* pushing *Alex*. I'm asking too much of him, but I hope to make it up to him one day.'

Daisy was amazed at the improvement in Jean's speech – although she noticed she chose short, uncomplicated words and thought about them first. They chatted about her treatment and therapy, until Jean glanced at the clock on the wall.

'It's a long drive back, Daisy. You've done your duty and checked that Alex isn't taking adv…' She sighed. 'You know what I mean. Go and enjoy what's left of your evening. And don't annoy that writer, or he'll put you in his book. Alex told me about him.'

It was almost seven by the time Daisy got back to Fox Farm, yet the barn light was on again. Curious but wary, she peeped round the door. She had no intention of interacting with Alex after their last encounter, and yet it tugged at her heart to see him sitting on the stone floor, back to the wall, head in his hands. She hadn't forgiven him for what he'd said or the way he'd said it, but she couldn't ignore this.

'Alex,' she said softly. 'Are you okay?'

He jolted and looked up. 'I… Yes.' He heaved himself to his feet. 'I'm fine.'

'You don't look fine. Why are you in here?'

'Working out what needs doing and how long it'll take me.'

'I thought your builder friend…?'

'He'll do the technical stuff, but he's only got a narrow window, so I'll be his labourer.'

'You should take a break tonight.'

'Tonight, I have my hideous cousin to deal with.'

Oh dear. No love lost there, by the sound of it. Forgetting her resolve to not get embroiled, Daisy said, 'You look like you need a large mug of tea. Why don't you come over for five minutes?' It was against her better judgement, but she couldn't leave him alone in the cold barn, looking so desolate.

'I couldn't put you out. You and I...'

'You and I have our differences, but we can still drink tea together. C'mon.'

He followed her meekly. *As though he's lost his fighting spirit.*

While she made the tea in her kitchenette, he stood in the doorway to her room. Eventually, he said, 'I suppose you expect me to apologise.'

'I don't expect it. It's your choice.'

There was a long hesitation. 'Okay. I'm sorry for what I said about you having no rights or status here. It was unnecessary.'

'Thank you. But it's true enough – apart from one thing. I may not pay rent, Alex, nor do I have a contract, but I do give Jean a percentage of my takings.'

Alex frowned. 'I didn't know. I didn't see that in the accounts.'

'Jean said to do it at the end of the year, before I left. I've been putting money aside.' She shrugged. 'It's still not the same as previous artists here, though.'

'No, but Aunt Jean offered you the deal and I respect that. I shouldn't have said what I said.'

'You were stressed, and I pushed you into it. I apologise, too. I overstepped the mark, questioning you like that. I... I visited Jean this evening. I had to satisfy myself that she understood what you're planning.' She bit her lip. 'Does that annoy you?'

Alex sighed. 'I don't have a big ego, Daisy. It's good that she has others looking out for her welfare. Angie did the same over the power of attorney.'

Daisy handed him his mug of tea, glad they had cleared the air, although things still felt on the fragile side. 'So. Tell me about this cousin of yours.'

She waited patiently as Alex studied one of her pieces on the studio wall – a winter wonderland of snow-blanketed fields with a crooked, ramshackle farmhouse in the foreground and children sledging down the hillside behind it.

'I like this,' he said.

'Thank you. Stop evading the question. What don't you like about your cousin?'

'Sebastian is an arrogant, condescending arse.'

Daisy burst out laughing. 'Well, that's an honest start. Why?'

'Oh, he always has been, but he's got worse as he's got older. His parents had more money than mine and he went to a posh school, so between that and him being older than me, he always thought he knew best. It all started to go pear-shaped when I turned eighteen and he found out I had no intention of going to university to "better myself".' Alex made quotation marks in the air. 'He couldn't get it into his head that it doesn't suit everyone. It highlighted how little he understood me or even tried to. I wasn't driven in the same way as him. He washed his hands of me once he realised I didn't mind earning minimum wage working at the garden centre and helping Uncle William out for free. He thought I was wasting my life.'

'But you proved him wrong.' Daisy was surprised at how quickly the floodgates had opened, sweeping away any awkwardness between them. Sebastian had his uses, it seemed. 'You set up your own business. Riverside earns you a decent living.'

'Ha! Only just. But no, that doesn't impress him either. He's high-flying – a fancy accountant for a firm in London that gets called in when big companies are going under and decides if they can be salvaged or have to go bust, then deals with the aftermath. It's all very corporate. Riverside's a tinpot little business to Sebastian – nothing to be proud of.'

'But you're happy. Settled. There are more important things in life than money or what others perceive as success.'

'I couldn't agree more.' Alex glanced at the open door to Daisy's tiny living space. 'Maybe we're two of a kind, you and me.'

'Maybe we are.'

The sudden change in atmosphere took Daisy by surprise. For a brief moment, she imagined Alex might lean forward to kiss her. And for that moment, she hoped he would.

But that was all it was – her imagination. Alex shot her an awkward smile and placed his mug on the counter. 'Well. Time to go and explain myself to my big cousin.'

'Why do you have to explain yourself?'

'Aunt Jean only has two nephews, and she always did her best to treat me and Sebastian the same. That was difficult, because I spent so much more time here than he did, but she's always been scrupulously fair – the same amounts spent on us at birthdays and that sort of thing. Just because I'm the one dealing with everything here doesn't mean he won't expect to be kept up to speed. Besides, if he sticks around, he'll see for himself what's going on.'

Daisy walked him to the door. 'Don't let him bully you. You know what you're doing.'

'Thanks. This morning's staff meeting was bad enough. All I need is Sebastian on top.'

'Oh, hang on.' Daisy went to her store cupboard and brought Alex's canvas out. 'Don't forget this.'

'Thanks. Not sure what I'll do with it, though.' He opened the door. 'Daisy, are we okay now, you and me? I'd hate for us not to be.'

'Yes. I can't promise not to speak my mind or say the wrong thing again, and I'm sure you can't either. But we're friends, right? We should be able to handle it.'

As she watched Alex walk across the yard, the stoop in his shoulders, Daisy resolved that from then on, she would be as positive as she could about what he wanted to do at Fox Farm. She wouldn't always agree with him, and she would still speak her mind, but she would do it with good grace, knowing he was doing his best for the place and for Jean.

With that in mind, she went to her laptop to draft an email to the current artists, telling them about the upcoming changes to the gallery. They shouldn't have such a big change sprung on them, and Alex had enough to deal with, although he would have to approve what she'd written, of course.

The state of her inbox dismayed her – more artists to deal with, some she'd never even heard of. It seemed that word had got around that Jean was incapacitated, and people were hoping this was their chance to get in at Fox Farm. And so she had another email to draft – a firm reiteration that Jean was unavailable and Daisy was not in a position to accept new people's work. It sounded brusque, but once they thought they could get past her, it would be endless. She would have to run that by Alex, too.

As if he didn't have enough to worry about!

*

'How are you finding the Copper Kettle?' Alex asked Sebastian, a smirk on his lips.

The village teashop with rooms above had been run by Dot Deacon for decades, and 'quaint' was the kindest word to describe it. Faded floral chintz and lace predominated – Dot didn't believe in minimalism or reinvestment – and Sebastian fit in there as much as Alex would in a five-star hotel in London.

'It'll do.' Sebastian glared at his red wine as though he expected it to taste like vinegar, then looked around the room. 'This place hasn't changed much. You'd think they'd have done it out.'

Alex loved the Masons Inn with its cracked but cleanly painted walls, original beams, scuffed wooden tables, a bizarre collection of old country cartoons on the wall and a carpet that was merely a nod to comfort – Rebecca was not one of those landladies who asked walkers to kick off their boots and wellies in the porch, so the carpet was murky with ground-in mud. 'I run a country pub for country people,' she would often declare. 'If you want posh, there are plenty of other places round here.'

'Personally, I'm glad they've resisted the temptation to deck it out in that *faux country* style that's taken over so many places,' Alex said. 'We *could* have gone somewhere that doesn't offend your aesthetic sensibilities, but this avoids driving, and the food's good.'

Alex had recommended the fish pie. He hoped Sebastian liked it, or that would be another black mark against Winterbridge.

'Have you been to see Aunt Jean yet?' he asked.

'When did I have time for that? I had to find a room, then I had calls to make. I'm a busy man.'

Alex bit his tongue. If *he'd* been away when Aunt Jean had had a stroke, he would have been back a lot sooner and visiting her would have been top of his agenda.

'I realise you're a busy man, Sebastian, which is why you needn't worry about us. Aunt Jean will appreciate you visiting her, but she's getting good care, and I'm looking after everything for her in the meantime.'

'Are you, though?'

'What's that supposed to mean?'

'Oh, come on, Alex. You keep that little plant place of yours ticking over, but taking on Fox Farm's a bit much for you, don't you think?'

Alex bristled. 'No. I'm quite capable of dealing with it. I've been helping Aunt Jean for years – which you would well know if you spent any time around here.'

'Weeding and mending gate hinges is hardly the same as taking over the business.'

'It's as important a part as any other, but for your information, Aunt Jean has always kept me up to speed with how Fox Farm runs, in case we ever found ourselves in a situation like this.'

'Well, now I'm here, I can assist you with my expertise; make sure you *do* know what you're doing.'

The sneering doubt in Sebastian's voice made Alex's blood boil. 'I know a darned sight better than you, Seb. You're hardly ever here! I know where Aunt Jean keeps everything, how she runs everything, how she keeps her accounts.' At that, he inwardly winced. Aunt Jean had begun to fail on that score, hadn't she? But he forged on. 'Why you imagine your city wheeling and dealing qualifies you more than one experienced rural Yorkshire business owner looking after another rural Yorkshire business, I have no idea.'

'Now then, boys.' Rebecca interrupted to put plates of steaming fish pie with fresh vegetables in front of them. 'You'll get indigestion if you quarrel like that while you're eating.' She shook her head. 'Always the same, you two, ever since you were lads.'

Sebastian glowered after her, then turned back to Alex. 'You have a point. What you do *is* a different kettle of fish to what I do.' His tone made it plain that the one was very much beneath the other. 'That doesn't mean I don't have a duty of care to Jean.'

Alex almost choked on a floret of broccoli. Since when had Sebastian ever shown much duty of care to Aunt Jean? Flying visits, occasional lavish and unnecessary gifts... Nothing practical.

'As her nephew, I appreciate you might feel some responsibility,' Alex said carefully, reining in his temper. 'On that basis, I'm happy to fill you in on what's happening.' *If I must.*

Sebastian tried a forkful of fish pie, murmuring approval. 'You can start by telling me why you've rented Jean's cottage out. That seems like a drastic move.'

Only because you were expecting free run of the place. 'It's temporary – just until Christmas. A writer wanted somewhere to finish his novel, somewhere with atmosphere.' Alex ignored Sebastian's shake of the head that suggested bewilderment as to why anyone would come and freeze in the wilds of Yorkshire through choice. 'It seemed sensible to use the time it stood empty to bring in some income.'

'But why bother?' Sebastian asked, wolfing down his pie now he'd decided it wouldn't damage his refined tastebuds.

Alex couldn't lie, much as he wanted to. Sebastian was on an equal footing, family-wise, and he wouldn't leave the subject alone.

'Aunt Jean could do with the money,' Alex said quietly, glancing around to make sure nobody was too close.

'Why does she need money?' Sebastian asked suspiciously and far too loudly.

'Could you keep it down, Seb? We don't want all of Winterbridge to know our business.'

'Fine.' Sebastian huffed and lowered his voice. 'Is Fox Farm going bankrupt or something?' He said it as though it wasn't of much consequence to him – which it probably wasn't.

'Jump to the worst conclusion, why don't you? No, it is not going bankrupt. Fox Farm has been ticking along nicely. But over the past couple of years, there've been a few blips, and apparently Aunt Jean decided to cover those by using some of her savings.'

'*What?*'

'We're not talking millions, Sebastian, just a few thousand,' Alex hastened to defend his aunt. 'It's no big deal.'

'It *is* a big deal. She shouldn't be using her savings to prop up that business of hers. Jean loses all sense of proportion when it comes to that place.'

Alex concentrated on chewing his food. He would be gulping down indigestion tablets all night at this rate.

'That's because Fox Farm is her life,' he said as calmly as he could. 'She built it up from nothing, and now, with Uncle William gone, it's what keeps her going.'

'It's given her a stroke, more like.'

'I doubt Fox Farm was responsible,' Alex snapped, although he couldn't deny it had crossed his mind. 'But I agree she shouldn't have dipped into her savings. Since there's a likelihood that she'll need some care when she's discharged, I wanted to get that money back for her, and renting her cottage was a good way to start.'

'I suppose it can't do any harm,' Sebastian agreed. 'Even if it does mean I have to stay at that pathetic Copper Kettle.' He cleared his plate. 'But in my mind, it should be Fox Farm – the business – paying her back. And it shouldn't be allowed to happen again.'

'I agree, which is why I'm implementing some changes.'

'What for? Surely she'll sell now?'

'No. She refuses to consider it.'

'Stubborn old woman.' Sebastian eyed Alex. 'What kind of changes?'

Alex knew he needed to sound as practical, as knowledgeable and in charge as he possibly could, to pre-empt Sebastian's objections. His cousin deciding to meddle would make everyone's lives a misery. Over whisky – which he hoped Sebastian was paying for, since he was the one who'd ordered it – Alex explained his plans and reasoning.

'We've never bothered about disabled access before,' Sebastian grumbled when he'd done.

Alex ignored that 'we'. *As if Sebastian has ever taken the slightest interest.* 'Then it's time we should,' he said.

'The staff are amenable?'

'Yes.' Alex tried not to think about that morning's mixed reactions.

'And Jean agreed to all this, you say?' Sebastian sounded cynical.

'Yes. She understands every last detail. It's what she wants.'

Sebastian swirled the golden liquid in his glass. 'Changes cost money.'

'I'll be doing a lot of it myself, with help from people who are willing.' Alex paused, giving Sebastian the opportunity to volunteer to don jeans and help out but, unsurprisingly, the void remained unfilled.

'It's throwing good money after bad,' Sebastian declared.

'No. It's investing with a view to recouping.'

'You must have plenty of time on your hands. Isn't that River-wotsit of yours doing so well?'

'River*side*,' Alex ground out, 'is doing perfectly well, thank you, but luckily it's not the busiest time of year, and I'm fortunate to have excellent, loyal staff who are doing their best to cover me while I drop *every part* of my own life to keep everything that matters to Aunt Jean going until she comes home.' He swallowed the last of his whisky, stood, and leaned down into Sebastian's face. 'Feel free to drop everything in *your* life to help out. And by that, I don't mean by interfering in things you know nothing about. I mean by taking that fancy overcoat of yours off and doing something useful – scrubbing floors, lugging furniture around, whatever. Goodnight, Sebastian.'

Outside the pub, Alex took in a deep breath of sharp, cold air. As he walked home, his gut told him that snow was imminent. The landscape would look like one of Daisy's paintings. That thought, at least, made him smile.

Chapter Eleven

Daisy woke on Tuesday morning to a fresh covering of pristine white snow, thick and substantial and satisfying – yesterday's frosting coming to fruition. She opened the door of her studio to gaze out at the farmyard, as yet untouched by human footprints. It was tempting to throw on wellies and be the first to make some, but she didn't have the heart to spoil the smooth whiteness yet. Lines of snow lay along the branches of the trees, and the roofs of the buildings wore a layer like white marzipan.

A winter wonderland.

Daisy had seen plenty of snow in her years living in the Yorkshire Dales, but she'd never been staying at Fox Farm before, and she couldn't believe how perfect it looked – like something on a calendar or a TV programme.

I'm so lucky to be here, even if it is just for this year. And my studio's a darned sight warmer than that old caravan at Jack's!

Closing the door on the cold, Daisy nursed a large mug of tea as she thought about her day ahead. She had a small number of meetings with artists booked in this week, but they were evening appointments to accommodate their day jobs. That meant she could paint during the daytime, when the light was better. Now that she'd seen the snow, though, there was no doubt she should get outdoors at some point.

Sipping her tea, she worked a little, still in her pyjamas, and wondered how Alex had got on with his cousin on Sunday night. He'd spent the previous day working hard in the barn with his builder mate, and she hadn't wanted to interrupt.

Sebastian sounded thoroughly dislikeable, and Daisy imagined Alex would struggle to find the patience to deal with him when he was so stretched already. She considered Sebastian's attitude to Alex's life choices a disgrace. Alex was a calm, rounded character, happy with his path in life, content with his achievements without feeling the need to seek status or become obsessed with money. She and Alex had much in common in terms of valuing contentedness over material concerns, Daisy reckoned, and they shared a desire to create, albeit in different ways.

When Alex poked his head around her studio door, she jumped, almost dolloping paint over her work. It was still really early.

'What are you doing this morning?' he asked.

'Working.'

'Haven't you heard that old saying, "All work and no play makes Jill a dull girl"?'

'You're one to talk. If you're not working at Riverside, you're working here.'

'I go to the hospital for light relief,' Alex reminded her with a wry smile. 'Sebastian's supposed to be doing that while he's here, though. Whether that's a blessing is another matter.'

'How did it go with him?'

'To cut a long story short, he doesn't like me renting out Aunt Jean's cottage, he doesn't agree with the changes I'm making, he thinks we're throwing good money after bad... You get the picture.'

'Ignore him.'

'I'm trying to. Which is why I'm here. I've decided we both need a little playtime.'

'Oh?' Daisy's pulse skipped as stray thoughts flitted across her brain as to what Alex might think constituted play. And for a creative woman whose imagination was pre-set to conjure up visuals... 'What kind of playtime?'

'You'll see.' He grinned, and Daisy could have sworn he'd guessed where her mind had wandered off to. 'Do you have waterproof over-trousers?'

So now those sensual images are dissipating a little...

'Dress up warm,' he warned. 'Meet me outside in five minutes.'

'Just like that?'

'Just like that.'

He was gone, leaving Daisy to belatedly remember she was still in her scratty pyjamas. *Great.* Should she abandon what she was doing on Alex's say-so? *Hmmm.* If she didn't, she wouldn't find out what he meant by 'playtime', would she?

Unable to resist, five minutes later she was warmly bundled up, but there was no sign of Alex in the farmyard. She could, however, hear his curses, along with the odd crash and bang. Following the noise, she went around the back of the cattle byre.

Alex was inside the doorway of an old outbuilding, battling with something.

'Can I help?'

'No, I've got it... Ow! Yep, here it comes.'

As whatever he was after came loose from whatever it had been tangled with, he staggered back through the doorway, and Daisy only just sidestepped in time. Alex was clutching a beautiful old wooden sledge with metal runners.

'Wow! That must be an antique.'

'It is.' Alex inspected his prize. 'It was Uncle William's when he was a boy.'

'Looks in good condition. Well-varnished. How come the metal hasn't rusted?'

'I dragged it out last winter. Aunt Jean wanted me to lend it to Lisa's boys – their plastic one broke and the shops had sold out. But it was in a state, so I ended up renovating it. Are you ready?'

Realisation dawned. 'You want me to go *sledging*?'

'Yep. Problem?'

'Sledging's for kids, Alex.'

'Why should they have all the fun? When did you last go sledging? Or have you ever?'

'Once.' It wasn't one of Daisy's fonder memories. 'The other kids were older and bigger and expected me to keep up. I got a lot of ice in my face that day. And my sledge was cracked.'

'That's plastic for you. Won't happen with this. Come on.'

'Do I have a choice?'

'Nope.'

Taken aback by this newly forceful Alex, Daisy followed him over to his truck, where he hefted the sledge into the back.

'Looks heavy,' she commented.

'It is. They don't make them like this any more.'

'Won't it be slow?'

'You'll see.'

Daisy frowned. 'Aren't you supposed to be working in the barn today?'

'Gary can't make it till mid-morning. He has another job to finish first.'

Alex sounded so gleeful about the prospect, Daisy couldn't help but smile.

'When did *you* last go sledging?' she asked as she climbed in.

'As a teenager, with Gary. There are some great slopes around here.'

'Where are we going?'

'You painted it. The hill behind old Jack's.'

Jack never complained about sledgers using his land – he loved to sit in his back room, watching the kids laughing and shouting and enjoying themselves. It was a form of company, Daisy supposed, feeling a stab of guilt that she hadn't visited him for a while.

'What's the rush?' she asked. 'Why so early?'

'You lived there, Daisy. You must remember how busy that slope gets after a good snowfall. The older kids are at school, but the little ones will be brought along soon enough. I want to get out there on virgin snow.'

'You're taking this seriously.'

'When I decide to play, I decide to play,' he said, his smile mischievous enough to make her pulse stutter.

He parked in a lay-by, Daisy helped him lift the sledge out, and Alex helped her climb over the fence.

He set the sledge down, eyeing the slope with apparent expertise. 'Not here.' He moved it along a few feet. 'That's better.'

Daisy shook her head. *Boys and their toys.*

'On your own or with me?' he asked.

Daisy weighed it up – a scary ride on her own, something she hadn't tried since childhood… or with Alex, in close proximity.

'You go on *your* own first. I'll watch. Then I'll decide.'

Alex laughed. 'Coward.' Without a moment's hesitation, he sat astride the sledge and pushed off, whooping and yelling like a four-year-old as it gathered speed. At the bottom, he ground to a halt, jumped up and waved his arms in triumph... and Daisy's heart took her by surprise as it swelled in happiness for him.

Looks like I'm joining in and having a good time, whether I want to or not. For Alex's sake.

Alex dragged the sledge back up the slope, positioned it for her and handed over the reins. 'Your turn. You steer with these.'

'I do?'

She sat, and Alex pushed. The sledge was slow at first but gathered momentum at an alarming speed. Daisy had no idea how to steer. She just closed her eyes and hoped to survive the experience. And she did. And it wasn't so bad.

Alex cheered as she came to a halt, then hopped impatiently from foot to foot while she brought the sledge back up. 'Now together.'

'Why?'

'You'll see. Hop on.'

Against her better judgement, Daisy got on behind him – there was plenty of room on the long, wooden seat – and clutched her arms around his waist. *Mmmm. Cosy.*

'Ready?'

Alex kicked off, and they were on their way. If Daisy had been startled at the speed of the sledge on her lone run, she couldn't believe the speed of it with two of them on it. The fields and walls were a blur of white and grey as they whizzed down the slope, but Daisy trusted Alex and tried not to panic... until they approached the bottom, where a grey stone wall loomed alarmingly.

'Stop!' she shrieked, even though Alex was already pulling on the rope and digging his heels in. When it became obvious the sledge wouldn't stop in time, Alex did the only thing he could do – he tipped them over.

Daisy, planted face-first in the powdery snow, gasped at the cold on her skin. She would have rolled over, but Alex landed half on top of her. Spluttering, she pushed ineffectually at him.

'Gerroff!' she managed through a mouthful of snow.

'Sorry.' He clambered off and sat in the snow, laughing.

'Not funny.'

'Yes, it is.'

As she glared into those smiling, hazel eyes, slowly overcoming the shock of being tipped face first into the cold snow, Daisy decided that maybe it had been fun after all.

'Again!' Alex pulled her to her feet and dragged both her and the sledge back up the hill.

'Why does it go so fast when there's two?' She puffed as they climbed. 'Shouldn't it be heavier?'

'It is. So, if the snow's the right consistency, the runners bite in and glide faster.' He shrugged. 'I'm no physicist.'

No. But you're a very hunky gardener with kind eyes and a great smile.

They got in several more runs before the little kids began to arrive with their parents and their red or blue plastic sleds, then Alex declared it unsafe for them to carry on.

'If we plough into them on this thing, we'll do them some damage. Time to call it quits.'

They were hefting the sledge back into Alex's truck when they heard a shout.

Jack hung out of a bedroom window of his farmhouse, beckoning. 'Hot tea!' he shouted, barely audible across the space between them, the shouts of excited toddlers hindering transmission.

Alex looked at Daisy. 'Do you have time?'

'If you do. I owe him a visit, and a hot drink wouldn't go amiss.'

They trudged back down the slope to Jack's farmhouse, peeling off layers as he greeted them at the door, clearly pleased to have company.

'I'm so sorry I haven't been for a while, Jack,' Daisy told him.

'Eee, that's alright, lass. I know tha's allus busy.'

'It has been rather manic.'

'Tha works too 'ard, too, lad,' Jack said to Alex, then beamed at them both. 'Good to see you two taking a bit o' time out. You fair steamed down that hill. Quite the courting couple!'

'Oh no, Jack, we're not…' Daisy protested.

But he was already shuffling down the hall. 'Tea's in t'kitchen.'

Alex began to laugh, and Daisy jabbed him in the ribs with an elbow before following Jack through to where steaming hot, strong tea waited.

An hour later, they were back in Alex's truck for the ride home. As they passed Riverside, Daisy said, 'I still haven't seen your life's work properly.'

'Do you have time now?'

'I can make time.'

Pleased, Alex swerved in and parked in front of the quiet buildings. 'One personalised tour of Riverside coming up.'

He unlocked the main building, a long structure with wooden beams overhead and many glass windows. There were long tables of house plants; a whole aisle devoted to hardware – spades, hoes, secateurs, hoses and the like; a row of shelving with plant food, pest control and so on; and then the counter near the entrance with an office behind. Fairy lights had been strung above the counter, and several stands to one side held artificial Christmas decorations.

When Daisy raised an eyebrow at those, Alex gave her a sheepish shrug. 'No choice at this time of year. People expect it. And we do sell the trees for them to go on. I only stock a limited number of artificial trees, though. It's the real ones that people come here for. We get those in from a tree farm, obviously. Nearer Christmas, Jules'll have us putting up all the usual festive decorations, I suppose.'

Smiling at his natural reluctance – he certainly had plenty to do at the moment without worrying about that sort of thing – Daisy gazed around the airy space, neat but rustic, the plants arranged in logical groups. She was no expert, but as she wandered up and down the rows, she could tell they were all in good condition.

They left through the far end, and he showed her his various public greenhouses; the staff greenhouse for growing, propagating and potting; the covered, gravelled area where he sold terracotta or glazed pots and troughs. Everything was on a small scale compared with many garden centres, but Daisy liked it all the more for that.

As though he could read her mind, Alex said, 'I'd like to expand a bit more, but I prefer quality over quantity. Besides, I doubt the planners would let me do much more building, square-footage-wise. It's more a question of offering variety, increasing footfall, making the most use of any outside space, improving the buildings, maybe making it more cohesive and aesthetically pleasing.'

'That's a lot to think about.' *No wonder Fox Farm feels like an extra burden to him.*

As they passed large piles of compost bags and gravel, Daisy reckoned that must be how he earned his muscles. 'They must weigh a ton!'

'They do. Jim got a hernia a couple of years back through hefting those.' Back at the entrance, Alex asked, 'Like what you see?'

Daisy smiled at this kind, modest man with hazel eyes, in need of a haircut and maybe a shave, the man who had taken her sledging for the first time in twenty-five years, and almost said something unwise.

'I love it,' she managed instead. 'I can see why you're proud of it and want to make it even better.'

He beamed. 'Thanks. Well, let's get you home. You have your work to do.'

'I do. But could you approve a couple of things first?' On the ride back, Daisy explained about the email she'd drafted to the regular artists.

At her studio, Alex read it, then said, 'Thanks for doing this. I'd like to hang fire, though, in case something goes wrong. We could send it the day we swap the gallery over. That way, it's a done deal and they can come and see for themselves.'

'Okay. Thanks. And I had to do another.' Daisy sighed. 'They're all crawling out of the woodwork.'

'What? Who?' he asked, alarmed.

'Artists who don't display here. Completely new ones, and ones who tried in the past but Jean turned away through lack of room... or lack of talent. They think they can get a foot in the door with someone new and naïve in charge.'

Alex shook his head. 'We tried to limit who you'd be dealing with, but it's opened the floodgates?'

'Yeah. The wording sounds harsh,' Daisy said as he read it. 'I know what it's like to be an artist trying to make a go of it. I hate being mean.'

'You're not being mean. We're in a specific situation here and we need to be practical. You have to put your foot down.' He placed a hand on her shoulder. 'You're already putting too much time into this, and I feel guilty as hell. Send this to anybody you need to, and don't worry about it.'

'Okay. Thank you.'

'No. Thank *you*. For this – and for a great morning.'

As she watched him leave, Daisy smiled. It *had* been a great morning – unexpected and fun, the very definition of 'playtime'. If Alex had any more spontaneous ideas like that, she wouldn't turn him down.

*

'Alex. I'd like a word.'

Sebastian.

Alex wished he hadn't answered without checking caller display first. He'd had a wonderful time sledging with Daisy yesterday and catching up with Jack, who had been determined to believe they were an item despite their protests. Daisy had been kind enough to draft those emails to the artists, something that hadn't occurred to him but should have. It had reminded him why he needed her on his side. And he and Gary were making good progress on the barn. He didn't need his cousin bursting his bubble.

'Sebastian, I'm up a ladder with a heavy chain in my hand. Now's not a good time.'

'Nor is it for me. I've just finished visiting Jean.'

'Did you go yesterday, too?' Alex didn't like the idea of Aunt Jean not having any visitors on a given day.

'No. I went on Monday, and she told me some woman called Sue was going yesterday. Suited me because I had work to do. The world doesn't stop just because Jean's in hospital and I'm up here in the northern wastelands, you know.'

It's stopped for me. But you don't care about that, do you? 'You didn't have to come up here, Seb.'

'It's a good job I did, though. You and I have things to discuss. In person.'

Uh-oh. 'I already gave you the rundown the other night.' Alex blew out a long breath, causing Gary to look across in concern. 'I'm up to my eyes working on the barn all week, but if you're determined, I could meet you at the pub tonight. I suppose I need to eat.' *If I'm not too tired to put food in my mouth and chew it.*

'Fine. See you at seven.' Sebastian clicked off before Alex could reply.

'Everything alright, mate?' Gary asked.

'Nothing's ever alright where that cousin of mine's concerned.'

'He always was a pompous arse,' Gary agreed. 'Whenever he came to stay, we could never get him to play outdoors or do anything physical, remember? All he'd play were board games that involved greed and cunning. He loved thrashing us at those.' He shook his head. 'I can't believe the pair of you are related.'

'I'll take that as a compliment.'

'It was intended as one. Don't let him push you around, Alex. What you're doing here will work – I can feel it in my bones. And it's what Jean wants. What Sebastian thinks is neither here nor there.'

'Do *you* want to tell him that?'

'I'd probably punch him.'

If Alex had known how his dinner with Sebastian would go later, he might have felt much the same way.

It started out better than the last time – Sebastian had higher expectations that his meal might be gastronomically acceptable, venturing to try the game pie and commenting on its edibility. But it didn't take long for the evening to go downhill.

'How was Jean?' Alex asked.

'She seems very frail.'

'She's seventy-two and had a stroke, Sebastian, so that's hardly surprising. But the doctors are pleased with her progress.'

'That's good news, of course,' Sebastian said. 'Dad's been asking after her. He's very concerned.'

Alex refrained from comment. Uncle Eric had shown precious little interest in his sister-in-law, even given his own health problems, and hadn't bothered phoning Alex for updates. Perhaps he got them from Alex's mum, since she phoned Alex or Jean every few days. She was hoping to come up to visit sometime soon, too. *Something else to worry about.*

'We're *all* concerned, Sebastian.'

'I suspect my concerns are different to yours, though,' Sebastian said cryptically.

Alex's fork, loaded with beef hotpot, paused halfway to his mouth. 'What do you mean?'

'You're busy making all these expensive changes, but I've yet to assess them for you.'

Alex ground his teeth together. '*I've* assessed. Aunt Jean's assessed.'

'And that's where my concerns come in – Jean, and how much of this she understands.'

'Oh, come on. Aunt Jean's perfectly "with it". She wasn't at the beginning, I grant you, but she is now. She's run Fox Farm for donkey's years, Sebastian, and she still has vision for it, but she can see that it needs to move on, and she's embracing that.'

'With a great deal of coercion from you.'

'*What?* Alex put his fork down on his plate before he could stab his cousin in the eye with it. 'You make it sound like I have nothing better to do with my time than invent new problems for myself! I'm doing this for Aunt Jean because she doesn't want to give the place up – something I originally suggested she should do, bear in mind. I have my own life. My own business. I wouldn't involve myself in hers unless I had to. And I *have* had to.' His eyes narrowed dangerously. 'Coercion is a strong word. You should be careful how you use it.'

'Oh, I am.' Sebastian allowed a dramatic pause, taking a bite of his pie and chewing slowly. 'Jean told me about the power of attorney you asked her for.'

Ah. I wish she hadn't. But Alex supposed the family were bound to find out sooner or later. Besides, Aunt Jean *not* telling Sebastian might have made it look like they were trying to keep it from him.

Alex kept his voice steady. 'I didn't *ask* her for it. I suggested it might be helpful to us both while she's incapacitated, now or in the future. She was happy to go ahead. There was no coercion. Angie signed to say so.'

'Angie's hardly impartial, is she?'

'It had to be someone who knows Aunt Jean well. Angie's known her for over twenty years.'

Sebastian jabbed his fork in Alex's direction. 'Why only you as an attorney?'

'Your dad's older than Aunt Jean, he's ill and he lives too far away. Mum's too far south, too.'

'What about me?'

Alex suppressed his impatience. 'How could that work? You live in London, spend your whole time reminding everyone what a busy man you are, and your work makes you uncontactable for days or weeks at a time. You know nothing about how Fox Farm runs or Aunt Jean's personal affairs. I do.'

'There should be someone to hold you to account,' Sebastian insisted.

'*I'm* holding me to account. And for your information, while Aunt Jean still has mental capacity, I can only act with her permission. Even if she loses it, I'd be legally obliged to act in her best interests, not my own.' *Something I wouldn't trust you to do, you self-serving…*

'What if I want to contest it?'

'*What?* It's already been sent off!'

'It won't become official for a while yet, though, will it? I have time to object.'

Alex couldn't believe what he was hearing. Panicked, he mentally flitted through the reams of guidance he'd read online.

'You're not named on it,' he said as calmly as he could. 'As an outsider, you can object before it's registered, but there'd be a sizeable fee and it has to go through a court of some sort. You'd have to prove coercion or whatever your nasty, suspicious little mind has dreamed up. That's up to you, if you can find time in your busy schedule for something so idiotic.' Alex stood, leaving his hotpot half-eaten – his stomach was churning so much, another bite might make it rebel altogether. 'You and I have never been friends, Sebastian, but we are family, and I'd have liked to think you could trust me.' He shook his head. 'I suggest you speak to Aunt Jean again before you take this any further, because I genuinely believe you'd be laughed out of court. And I doubt you think that egg on your face is a good look for you.'

Chapter Twelve

'How's the book going, Mr Giles?' Daisy asked their resident writer as she saw him crossing the farmyard, carrying groceries. The air had warmed, turning much of the snow to slush.

'Not bad, thank you. Two more victims dispatched. One more to go. The snow helped, much like the fog the other week – that feeling of being trapped, you know?'

Daisy tried not to look disconcerted. *She'd* thought of the snow as a gorgeous winter wonderland; a white comfort blanket. It hadn't occurred to her to see it as a threat. Besides, Alex had made it so much fun on Tuesday, it was hard to equate it with murder.

'The killer still has to be caught, of course,' he went on.

'Of course. Will you be finished on time?'

'Oh, yes. Peace and quiet was what I needed. And Fox Farm has given me inspiration – as long as I pretend there's no café or gallery or people here.'

'It inspires me, too, only not in the same way as you.'

'I should hope not! Your artwork would have rather a sinister air to it if that were the case. I should pop into your studio again sometime, and the gallery. It'd be good to get an unusual Christmas present for my wife, to make up for being away so long. She's long-suffering, the poor woman. Although perhaps my being away is actually a nice break for her.'

Daisy chuckled. 'Well, I'm glad your book's going well.'

Back in her studio, she made a cuppa, grateful that she had no more appointments with artists to worry about. The few this week had all been brief and gone well. Feeling relaxed, she reached for her laptop and settled down for a chat with Grace. Their messages between face-to-face calls never quite did the trick.

'So, how're things?' Grace asked.

'There's so much going on,' Daisy gushed, surprised at how enthused she felt about the general chaos in her life at Fox Farm recently.

Grace's eyes lit up. 'Oooh! Tell all.'

Daisy did tell all – an update on Jean; her agreements and disagreements with Alex; her dealings with the artists, making Grace roll her eyes over those that had not gone so well. And Daisy made her hoot with laughter over Mr Giles and the foggy night of mock-murder.

'He sent you *flowers?*'

'To be fair, he did frighten me to death, lock me in a dark kitchen and stab me twice,' Daisy pointed out.

'True enough. So, this Alex sounds harassed, poor bloke.'

'His cousin isn't helping on that score.' Daisy went on to tell Grace the little she knew about Sebastian.

Grace wrinkled her nose. 'I don't like the sound of him. Alex sounds like a *much* better prospect.' She allowed a dramatic pause. 'You're talking a lot about him. And seeing a lot of him.'

'I've barely seen him this week, he's been so busy in the barn. Apart from when we went sledging.'

'*Sledging?*'

'He called by early one morning and made me go.'

'*Made* you go? Hmmm. Did you have fun?'

Daisy didn't have to think about it for long. 'Yes. More fun than I've had in a long time.'

'Good. You should have more fun. You're not very good at it.'

'I wasn't good at sledging, that's for sure. It was an old, heavy sledge that went *way* too fast with two on it, so we ended up in a heap in the snow…'

A neatly shaped brow rose on the screen in front of her. 'You rode together? Pillion-style, you clutching your arms around his waist? And you ended up in a heap?'

'Don't read anything into it, Grace. I was clutching him because my life depended on it. And the heap we landed in was neither elegant nor sexy.'

'Did you *want* it to be sexy?'

I'm not sure I can answer that honestly without letting myself in for further interrogation. 'Oh, stop it.'

'I can't. It's so good to see you with a twinkle in your eye, Daisy Claybourne. Where's it going, this thing between you and Alex?'

'Nowhere. We're good friends, that's all.' Daisy thought about that brief moment a few nights ago when she'd imagined he might kiss her; when she'd even wanted him to. 'I'm trying to be supportive over Fox Farm because some of the staff are a bit sceptical. That's all there is to it. Anyway, enough about me. What about you? Did the middle-aged gallery manager take you on for an exhibition?'

'No. It was a ruse to take me to dinner and put a hand on my knee. He got short shrift. And scalding hot coffee in his lap.'

'Good for you.'

Grace made Daisy laugh with her blow-by-blow account of the evening.

Oh, I miss this. I miss her.

'I do have some good news, though,' Grace said. 'I got a commission from a big law firm who want original art for their new offices.'

'That's fantastic! How many?'

'A dozen. Two large ones for the lobby, a medium for the conference room and nine smaller canvases – one for each office. They said they love my style and the bold colours will cheer up the walls. They think that abstract designs are less likely to distract colleagues and clients than "proper" pictures.' Grace made quote marks in the air. 'Luckily for me, they're too upmarket – as are their clients – to look at a bunch of factory-produced canvases from a homeware store.'

'I'm so thrilled for you!'

'My stomach's thrilled too,' Grace said. 'It might get the occasional square meal. I was even thinking of spending some of my advance on a train fare.'

'Oooh. Where to?'

'I hear Yorkshire's nice at this time of year.'

Daisy whooped. 'You're coming to see me?'

'I'm hoping to, if there's room?'

'No room at all. I only have a single bed, but I'll get a put-me-up from somewhere – we can use the studio at night. There are blinds we can close. We'll manage. When?'

'How about for Christmas?'

'*Christmas?*' Daisy's eyes misted over. 'That would be perfect. Won't you be at your parents'?'

'I fancy somewhere different this year. Your little part of the world sounds like just the ticket. And someone needs to rescue you from being on your own again.'

'I had Christmas dinner with old Jack last year,' Daisy said defensively.

'Full of excitement, I'm sure. By the way, do you remember Andreas from our course?'

'Didn't he specialise in wildlife?'

'Yup. You ought to look him up. He's narrowed down to cats and dogs, and he's doing really well online selling prints, mugs, cushions, tote bags… I thought that now you have the studio, you could try stuff like that. They'd make great Christmas presents.'

'Yeah, they would. But it's too late this year, I reckon. I haven't got enough capital to buy the goods. If I were here longer, I might have, but I leave in the spring, remember?'

'Look him up anyway.'

'I will.' Daisy beamed. 'I can't wait to see you, Grace.'

*

Saturday evening saw Alex back at the hospital. He hated that he'd been too busy all week to visit – and he didn't like leaving Aunt Jean to Sebastian, especially after the things he'd said.

'A young lad like you should be out with his mates on a weekend,' Aunt Jean told him, smiling as he kissed her cheek.

'My mates have given up on me. As for Gary, I worked him to the bone this week. Chelle will be furious if he doesn't take the weekend off, and that includes having a pint with me.'

'You should be out with a girl, then.'

Alex laughed. 'You *must* be feeling better if you're nattering me about that! And it's women, not girls, Aunt Jean – I'm thirty-five years old. Besides, you know me and women.'

'I know you're an idiot, keeping yourself from them.'

'I don't.'

'I didn't mean physically,' Jean said, struggling with the word. 'I'm not *that* old. I meant emot…' That word did defeat her.

'Leave me alone,' Alex warned. 'I'm happy enough.'

'What about Daisy?'

'What about her?'

'She's smart, pretty, talented, and plenty of other things my brain wants to say but my mouth won't let me. Stupid stroke.'

'Yes, well, maybe that stroke comes in handy occasionally. It might help you to mind your own business.'

Mischief twinkled in his aunt's eyes. 'Why? *Is* there something going on?'

'No. Daisy's a good friend. She's been very supportive, and she's easy to talk to.' *I loved the feel of her arms around my waist when we went sledging. The sound of her squealing at the speed, and her laughter when she realised it was fun. The understanding in her eyes when we chat. And I keep wanting to kiss her whenever we're alone together.* Alex's eyes widened as these thoughts flitted through his brain. Where had they come from?

His aunt gave him a speculative look. 'If you say so. How's the barn?'

'Looking good. Gary's done his bit. I need to tidy up and scrub the floors. Tuesday, I'll move the gallery across. Wednesday, I'll put the café to rights. Then it's all go from Thursday.'

'I wish I could see it.'

'We'll take photos and do a video tour for you.'

'You've worked so hard.' She patted his hand.

'Yes.' There was no denying it. 'But it'll be worth it.' *I hope.*

'Sebastian thinks we're wasting money.'

'Yes, well, it's not his money, is it?'

'That's what I told him,' Aunt Jean said crossly.

'Good for you.'

Alex wasn't happy, though. Aunt Jean's determination to recover, return home and see Fox Farm do better than before was what made her try so hard. He didn't want Sebastian putting doubts in her mind, giving her any reason to give up on herself.

Aunt Jean put a hand on his cheek. 'Don't worry,' she soothed. 'It's nice to see him, and he is family, after all. He's kept me company, telling me all about London and his job and how well he's doing.'

I bet he has.

'But he is unhappy about that power thing.'

'The power of attorney?' Alex had tried to convince himself that was just Sebastian throwing his weight around after feeling that he'd been left out.

'Yes. He wanted to be sure I knew what I was doing. I said I'm not senile and you're not that kind of man. Told him off, good and proper.'

Alex smiled. 'Did it do the trick?'

'He said I trust you too much. That I should be careful. But I think he'll stop making a fuss.'

'Well done, Aunt Jean.'

'Go home and put your feet up,' she said. 'I'm worried about you driving when you're so tired.'

Alex felt as if he could put his feet up on his aunt's bed and fall asleep in the hard plastic chair he was in.

He kissed her goodnight. 'See you soon.'

By the time he got home, he wasn't even fit for a beer. Instead, he made a large mug of tea and nursed it, thinking about the gruelling week to come.

Once this week's over, Alex, you can relax a bit.

But even as he thought it, he remembered that the end of the next week was also the end of November.

So, only the tree to put up in Fox Farm's yard, decorations and lights outside every building and inside the café and gallery, Santa's log cabin to build, and an elf to find if Santa a.k.a. Lisa's dad hasn't found one yet… Then there's the tree-selling to set up at Riverside, helping with decorations and lights there…

Ho bloomin' ho!

*

Daisy brushed a hand across her face. Her back and shoulders were aching. When she'd offered to lend Alex a hand to scrub the barn's stone floor on Sunday after closing, she hadn't taken into account how big a surface area it was.

'You're tired.'

His voice startled her. She hadn't even heard him come up behind her.

'Not used to all this manual work. My neck and shoulders already struggle with tension from painting.' She rubbed ineffectually at them.

Alex propped his brush against the wall and dug his thumbs into the sore spots.

'Ow!'

'Quit complaining.'

'I'll complain if I want to.'

'Yeah, I guess you will.' But he continued kneading, and Daisy didn't stop him. Something had to be done, or she'd be too stiff to work tomorrow… which was what she should be doing now, instead of sloshing soapy water around.

'Not sure it looks any better,' she grumbled.

'It will. I'll go over it with clean water, and we'll see what happens when it dries off.' He looked worried. 'Or did you mean the whole barn?'

'No, just the floor. The barn's amazing. I can't believe what you and Gary achieved in a week.'

'Gary's a good mate. He had to juggle his other jobs to fit it in, but he knew how urgent it was.' His hands still at her shoulders, he bent to speak at her ear. 'Thank you for helping. It means a lot.'

'Having a mug to skivvy for you?'

He turned her to face him, his eyes earnest. 'Knowing you're supporting me. Lisa doesn't. And neither she nor Angie like me taking charge to this extent.'

'Maybe you should be honest with them, Alex. Tell them it *has* to be done for financial reasons. That it's not a whim.'

'They could work that out for themselves if they tried. It's not my place to give away Aunt Jean's business affairs.' His phone rang, and he dug it out of his pocket. 'Hi, Mum.'

Daisy busied herself with the floor until he clicked off. 'I gather your mother's planning to visit?' she ventured, since she couldn't help catching the gist of the call.

'Yes. She's finally managed to get time off at the gift shop where she works.'

'It'll be nice for you, her visiting, won't it?' Daisy faltered. She knew Alex had had an unhappy childhood, but she still didn't know why.

'Yes. But it's a long way for her to come, all the way from Devon. And I hadn't expected such short notice.'

'When's she arriving?'

'Tomorrow.'

Daisy winced. 'Can I do anything to help?'

'Can you redecorate an entire house and refit a kitchen and bath-room in twenty-four hours?'

Daisy frowned. 'She's stayed with you before, hasn't she?'

'On and off. She doesn't come up often. But every time she does, the house looks another year worse.'

'Alex.' Daisy laid a hand on his arm. 'She's your mother. She won't care, as long as it's dry and warm. All she cares about is seeing you and Jean.'

'You're right.' He sighed. 'Still, plenty to do.'

'C'mon, then. Let's get this finished.'

'You go. I'll finish.'

'No. We're in this together, remember?'

Daisy wondered why she'd made it sound so 'us against the world'. She was beginning to care more and more about Alex. But she was only helping him at a difficult time, right? For Jean's sake. *And* her own. After all, between now and when her year was up, extra success for Fox Farm meant extra success for her.

Taking up her brush, she plunged it into her bucket of soapy water. Unfortunately, Alex had dropped to all fours to scrub at a stain he'd spotted. Distracted by the sight of his very fine backside in denim, Daisy's aim was off, her brush hit the side of the bucket, and it tipped, pouring its contents across the floor in Alex's direction.

'Alex!'

Her warning came too late. The water swam beneath him before he could leap out of the way.

'Oh, for…'

'Sorry.' Daisy gave him her best apologetic look as he stared down at his dripping legs. But it was late and she was tired. She started to laugh.

'Oh, you think that's funny? I can find things funny too, you know.' Alex scooped his hands into his own bucket and flung them in her direction, showering her with water.

'Hey! That's grubby.'

'So are you.' Alex pointed at her filthy dungarees.

'Charmer.'

When he merely stood there grinning, she came after him with her wet brush. Clearly unsure what she intended to do with it, Alex hurriedly backed up until he hit a wall. Daisy jabbed the sopping bristly brush-head in his chest, pinning him in place with a firm grip on the handle.

'There. See how you like that!'

'How do I like being pinned against a wall by an attractive woman in sexy dungarees? Can't say I'm complaining.'

Taken aback by the sudden change in Alex's tone from playful to sultry, the smoulder in his eyes, the smirk on those full lips, Daisy struggled for a comeback. He'd called her attractive. Sexy. She didn't know he thought of her that way, despite that one time she'd wondered if he might kiss her. But he hadn't, had he? She'd been imagining things.

A comeback was required. 'You're not being pinned by *me*. You're being pinned by a scrubbing brush.'

'A man can dream.' He cocked his head to one side. 'He can act, too.'

In one swift move, he pushed the brush away from his chest and caught her by the arms. He could have pulled her close. Her body wished he would. But he held her with a foot of space between them, staring at her mouth for what felt like an age, as her heart thudded against her ribcage.

And then she yawned.

Really sexy, Daisy.

Alex smiled. 'Go to bed,' he said gruffly. He lifted his hand to her cheek and kissed her forehead. 'Go to bed before I kiss you properly.'

What if I want you to kiss me properly? It was on the tip of her tongue. But she was too tired to know if it was a good idea, so she simply nodded and left.

She'd almost reached her studio when he called after her. 'Daisy! You left your phone. And you have my brush.'

Oh. And that had been such a neat getaway.

Daisy turned back and met him halfway across the yard where he handed over her phone, his own long-handled brush still in his other hand. She handed him hers.

'Well, what have we here? Looks like the chimney sweep scene from *Mary Poppins*!'

The voice came through the dark, its owner looming into the light cast across the cobbles by the outside lamps of the buildings. Wearing a wool overcoat that Daisy suspected had cost a good few hundred quid, the man had slicked-back hair and a face she wouldn't trust in this lifetime.

'Sebastian.'

Daisy detected the distaste in Alex's tone, and her heart sank. *Oh, joy. I'm meeting Alex's stuck-up cousin looking like I climbed out of a dustbin.*

'Evening, Alexander. And who is this?'

'Daisy Claybourne, meet my cousin Sebastian.'

Sebastian nodded rather than offer his hand to shake – unsurprising, since she must look filthy. 'Pleased to meet you, Daisy.'

No, you're not. And the feeling's mutual. But Daisy managed a brittle smile.

'What are you two up to, so late?' he asked.

'Daisy's been helping me in the barn.'

'That's very community-spirited, Daisy. And when you're not scrubbing floors, you work here as…?'

'I don't. I'm this year's artist-in-residence. And I should get back to my studio. If you'll excuse me…?'

Without waiting to see if she was excused or not, Daisy scarpered to the safety of her own space, where she messaged Grace to tell her she suspected that Alex's cousin was the spawn of the devil.

Chapter Thirteen

'Hello, Alex.'

'Mum.'

They hugged with genuine affection but also the reserve that had somehow crept into their lives and never left. It saddened them both, but neither knew how to fix it.

'You changed your hair,' he stated.

'You noticed! Yes. Blonde didn't look quite right any more. My stylist suggested mixed highlights so I can fade gradually to grey as befits my sixty years.' She made a face at the number. 'But the layers make it perkier, don't you think?' She laughed. 'As if you're interested! Now, how's Jean? I mean, how is she *really*? You know I can tell if you lie to me face to face.'

Alex smiled at that. 'She's holding her own. It'll take more than a major stroke to keep her down.'

'I'm glad. I know how much she means to you.'

Alex knew there was no unspoken recrimination that he might be fonder of his aunt than he was of his mother. Besides, that simply wasn't true. He was closer to Aunt Jean, that was all.

'Let me take your things up to your room,' he said. 'You must be tired.'

'Thanks. I'll put the kettle on. I'm parched.'

When they were settled with a cuppa, his mother looked around the house. 'This hasn't changed since the last time I was here.'

'I haven't had time, what with Riverside, and now Fox Farm and Aunt Jean…'

'Sorry, love. I wasn't criticising,' his mother said quickly. 'But a home should be more than a place to throw off your boots and crawl into bed, you know. It should be somewhere with warmth at its heart – a place you feel truly yourself.' She sighed. 'You never had that as a child. When you bought this little house, I hoped you'd find it here.'

'I suppose I will, eventually. But for now, you're right – I treat it more like a motel.'

She studied him. 'I *would* say you're looking well, but you look tired. You've been overdoing things.'

'Yes. But it's not like I've had any choice.'

'Bring me up to speed.'

Alex didn't hold anything back. Aunt Jean was Nicky's sister-in-law, and she had a right to an update. Besides, his mother had no axe to grind with him or the situation. As for Sebastian…

'That wretched cousin of yours!' she said when he told her about Sebastian's latest shenanigans.

'Last night, he came to Fox Farm to tell me he's decided *not* to object to the power of attorney, after all, as though he's doing us all a huge favour,' Alex concluded his tale of woe. 'He's still dubious that Aunt Jean's in her right mind, and he doesn't like the fact that I'm taking *advantage*, but he doesn't want to upset her any more.'

'More like he knows he'd have no chance of proving his case. What right has he got to come up here, poking his nose in? Jean's fonder of that boy than she should be. He's always been a nasty piece of work, if you ask me. He bullied you when you were little.' When Alex raised an eyebrow, his mother said, 'Don't think I didn't notice. And don't think I didn't know you didn't tell me because you knew I had enough to worry about with your father.'

'I can't say he treats me any better now. But I'm older and wiser. And I have more muscles than I used to.' Alex grinned, but then his expression became serious again. 'Aunt Jean wants to be fair, Mum – to treat us both the same.'

'Being fair could be her undoing, if she listens to Sebastian about Fox Farm. Although I have to say, I can see his point. That place *is* too much for her. Selling seems a sensible option when you stand back and look at it objectively. The trouble is, Sebastian doesn't take people's *feelings* into account. I suppose he couldn't do the job he does if he was sentimental.'

'I *am* sentimental about Fox Farm,' Alex admitted, 'but I'm trying to be objective, too. Aunt Jean wouldn't sell, and this was the only way forward that I could see.'

'You've a good head on your shoulders, Alex, and the difference between you and Sebastian is that you have Jean's best interests at heart. The only interests Sebastian has at heart are his own.'

'He told me he's going back to London this week, so we'll all get a bit of relief.'

'At least *I* won't have to have anything to do with him, then,' his mother said with feeling. 'And it'll give me a chance to undo some of his poisonous ideas with Jean.'

Alex leaned over to kiss her cheek. 'Thanks, Mum.'

Over a meal at the Masons Inn, they talked about what his mother had been up to in Devon – her job in the gift store, the reading club she'd set up for her friends and neighbours, the watercolour classes she was taking. All these years after his father's death, his mother was finally thriving, and Alex couldn't be more pleased for her. Boldly, he told her so.

'Thank you. That means a lot, love. How about you? Any "outside interests"?'

'Are you trying to find out if I have a girlfriend? You're as bad as Aunt Jean.'

His mother laughed, her cheeks a little rosy from the wine, the way they used to get after she'd had a glass at Sunday lunch. Alex pushed away the childhood memory. It was best to only look forward.

'You never mention women much,' she complained. 'I'm beginning to wonder if you became a monk and neglected to tell me.'

'I date, now and again.'

'Nothing more serious?'

'No.'

'Oh, Alex. Don't let my marriage to your father define how you live your life.'

'I'm not.' But they both knew that was a lie. 'I haven't met the right person up until now, that's all.'

His mother's eyes lit up. '"Up until now"? Does that mean there *is* someone?'

'No. Poor choice of words. Don't turn them into something they're not.' *Although why* did *I use that specific phrase?*

'You keep mentioning this Daisy person. She's helping out an awful lot.'

'She's become a good friend since Aunt Jean fell ill,' Alex admitted. 'Frankly, I couldn't have managed without her.' The memory of her pinning him against the wall in the barn with a scrubbing brush slid into his mind, and his pulse stuttered as he remembered how much he'd wanted to pull her to him and kiss her senseless. *Get a grip, Alex.* 'Please don't read any more into it.'

'Okay.' She sighed sadly. 'But I'm your mother, Alex. All I ever wanted was for you to be happy. I couldn't give you a happy childhood, but I would like you to be a happy grown-up.'

'I *am* happy, Mum. I'm doing what I love with Riverside. I'm where I want to be, here in the Dales. I belong here.'

'Well. That's wonderful.' His mother teared up a little. 'Still, you should share that *with* someone, if the right person comes along. Don't lock yourself away. Your dad's caused enough damage already.'

Alex couldn't get his mother's words out of his head that night as he tried to sleep. It was the nearest they had got to a heart-to-heart in years. He'd thought it would feel uncomfortable, but it hadn't. As for avoiding sharing his life with anyone? She was right about that, but it hadn't been a difficult choice so far. If he thought back to the women he'd spent time with over the years, he couldn't imagine being married to any of them now. He didn't feel as if he'd missed out on a soulmate.

But Daisy... Was he in denial? His heart lifted when he saw her. *You're having a crap time, Alex. It isn't surprising that a friendly face would cheer you up.* His blood pumped faster when he was with her. *You're only human. She's an attractive woman with a great smile.* He kept wanting to kiss her. *Don't have an answer to that one, mate. Sorry.* Was he flirting with her just for fun? Or to cover up a yearning for something more?

Quit the analysis, Alex, and go to sleep.

*

Jamie didn't mind doing overtime on one of his days off to help move the gallery. Lisa was more grudging about it.

'As long as I finish in time to pick the kids up from school,' she grumbled. 'I don't have childcare on a Tuesday.'

'You can go when you need to, Lisa,' Alex said. 'And your help is appreciated. It's your gallery, after all – we don't want to do anything you're not happy with.'

Daisy admired Alex's tact. She suspected he wanted to shout, *It's for your benefit, if you want Fox Farm to keep going so you can keep your job!'*

Less reluctant was Alex's mother, Nicky, who turned up with him, wearing practical jeans and a sweater, and declaring herself willing to muck in. Since Angie wanted to visit Jean that afternoon, Nicky would go in the evening, leaving her free to help all day.

Daisy studied Alex's mother with interest. Alex had her eyes, she decided, but he must have got his broad shoulders and height from his father.

If Daisy had a curious eye on Nicky, she could have sworn that Nicky cast an eye over her, too. Had Alex spoken to his mother about her? What would he have said?

But there wasn't time to think about that during a back-breaking day that entailed Jamie and Nicky carefully packing up goods at the old gallery; Alex carrying the boxes over to the barn; Lisa and Daisy deciding where everything should go.

Nor was there time to think about Alex, which was a blessing when Daisy's overly creative mind kept wandering back to their sultry mock-tussle on Sunday.

At three, Lisa looked pointedly at her watch. 'I have to go.'

'Of course. We'll make sure it's up and running for you by Thursday morning,' Alex promised.

'Thanks.' Perhaps realising she could be more enthusiastic, she added, 'It's looking good. I imagine it'll grow on me.'

'High praise indeed,' Alex grumbled when she'd left.

Daisy laughed. 'She didn't say she hated it. We Yorkshire folk aren't known for our effusiveness, are we?'

'True.' He looked around. 'Plenty left to arrange, though. I hope she won't mind us deciding for her.'

'Then perhaps she should have tried to stay longer,' Nicky said curtly.

Alex smiled. 'I can see you're champing at the bit, Mum. Go for it.'

For the next two hours, Nicky ordered them all around, and Daisy had to admit she had good ideas about how to group things; where they would be lost and where they would stand out. They even moved a few of Lisa's placements, hoping she wouldn't notice.

At five, Nicky brushed her hands on her jeans. 'I should get changed and grab something to eat if I'm going to see Jean.'

'Thanks for today, Mum. Drive safely.' Alex looked at Jamie. 'Can you do another hour or two? There's still the counter to bring over.'

'No problem,' Jamie said affably. 'I'll make a start. See you over there.'

When he'd gone, Alex turned to Daisy. 'What do you think?'

Daisy gazed around the space at the chain-hung white display 'walls' contrasting against the grey stone walls of the barn, the art on them popping. Chunky wooden shelves in the spaces between held an array of pottery, wood-turned crafts and glassware. The glass cabinet from the old gallery displayed handmade jewellery. And an eclectic mix of old wooden coffee and dining tables that Alex and Gary had hunted down on local websites and at charity shops, laden with cheaper, unbreakable goods, was an inspired idea, breaking up the large area of stone-flagged floor.

'It looks great. Less cosy but definitely more stylish. I can't believe you did it in such a short time.'

'Thanks. But I couldn't have managed without all this teamwork today. I appreciate you giving up your day off, Daisy. And, let's face it, Lisa would never have offered to spend an evening scrubbing the floors.'

'She has two small children to take care of.'

'And you have your own work to do.'

'Talking of which, I'd like to put in a couple of hours at the studio before I crash.' At the door, Daisy turned back, curiosity niggling. 'What did your cousin want the other night? He looked very determined.'

'The good news is, he's gone back to London this week. The bad news is, he still doesn't approve of any of this.'

'It's not up to him to approve or otherwise, though, is it?'

'No, but as family, he is entitled to an opinion.'

'I can't see him putting in the work or worry you're putting in,' Daisy said hotly, resentful at the way Sebastian treated Alex.

'It's not just the alterations and investment. He went mad about the power of attorney, too.'

'Why? It's a sensible idea, for both you and Jean.'

'He doesn't like that it's only me who can act on Aunt Jean's behalf. This is the first time she's not treated us the same. She leaves Fox Farm to us equally in her will, and I suppose he believes this should be likewise.'

The idea that Sebastian might inherit half of the place Alex worked so hard on and loved so much horrified Daisy. But that was none of her business, so she stuck to the power of attorney.

'But you're the one dealing with everyone and everything. He's hardly ever here.'

'I told him that. So did Aunt Jean. But he's always on at her.'

Daisy bristled. 'That's not right.'

Alex gave her an amused look. '*You've* been to check she was on board with things a couple of times, remember? I have no quibble with you – or him – checking with her. But I don't like him haranguing her or trying to influence her. Sebastian's not in tune with Aunt Jean, with her wants or needs. He…' Alex stopped, frustrated.

'He doesn't love her the way you do,' Daisy said softly.

'You understand.'

The expression on Alex's face made Daisy melt – his profound relief that there was someone he could talk to like this.

He came to her and placed a hand on her cheek. 'Thank you.'

After a second's hesitation, he popped a kiss on her other cheek, but she'd smiled, so the kiss hit the corner of her mouth instead.

Without realising what she was doing, Daisy moved a fraction so her lips were under his. He kissed her again, quick and gentle. Pulling back to see if he'd done the wrong thing, he looked into her eyes, an unspoken question there.

Daisy didn't want questions. She covered his lips with hers, a slow kiss that gently simmered. Already feeling bold that she'd been the one to initiate it, she didn't dare push it further. Her head wasn't sure how she felt about this, although her pulse was pretty certain.

When they broke it off, he still had his hand on her cheek. He stroked it with his thumb. 'Daisy.'

She bit her lip, not sure where they stood now. The tussle in the barn had been jokey, sultry. This kiss had been tender, with feeling. Goodness knew what would happen if they allowed the two different moods to come together!

'I should go,' she said quietly.

'I hope you won't regret that kiss in the morning. I might want to do it again sometime.' Alex's smile was mischievous, lightening the atmosphere between them.

Daisy's pulse thrummed. 'Likewise.'

Chapter Fourteen

By the time Alex left the barn, his body ached. He was used to hard labour, but every task used a different set of muscles, and the past couple of weeks had tested every single set he owned.

Once Daisy had left and he'd pulled himself together – not an easy task, when his lips tingled and his blood hummed in his veins – he and Jamie had begun the job of transferring the heavy counter from the old gallery. Alex hadn't taken into account how slight Jamie was. He was a keen runner, but that didn't help when it came to a broad back or strong arm muscles. They'd had to semi-dismantle the wooden counter and carry it across the farmyard piecemeal, Alex taking as much weight as he could.

After that, he'd sent Jamie home with a heartfelt thank you for all his hard work and was rewarded with a broad smile from the lad, who had clearly enjoyed his day – and no doubt appreciated the idea of extra funds.

Glancing at the transformed barn as he left, Alex felt vindicated. The old gallery was quirky because of the way it had developed over time, but it no longer served its purpose. The barn was an *excellent* new space.

Out in the farmyard, his breath misted in the cold air, and he shivered. Lights were still on in Daisy's studio, and he felt a stab of desire before a stronger stab of guilt overtook it. She had devoted a whole day of her free time – again – for no monetary reward. Every time she did this, it set her back with her work, her livelihood.

Crossing the yard, he peered in at the window. She sat at her easel, her hair piled randomly on top of her head, frown lines between her eyes as she concentrated. It was late. Had she eaten yet? He could see a mug at her side, but no plate or bowl.

Making a decision, he crossed to his truck, climbed in and drove into Winterbridge, to the welcoming lights of the Jolly Fisherman takeaway. Ten minutes later, he was rapping at the studio door, steaming hot fish and chips in his arms.

Daisy looked up, startled, then came over to let him in. 'What's up?'

He held out the packages. 'These are up.'

She stood aside to let him in, inhaling deeply. 'Mmmm. How did you know I haven't eaten?'

'I peeked in at the window and couldn't see any evidence.'

'That sounds rather stalkerish.'

He winced. 'It does, doesn't it?'

'But I forgive you.' She relieved him of the parcels so he could remove his coat, then made space on her serving counter. 'Thank you.'

'You earned them,' he said as they unwrapped their treat and tucked in.

'These are so good,' she murmured. 'I haven't had fish and chips in ages.'

'You don't treat yourself often?'

'No. I like to cook homemade, mainly.'

Alex kicked himself as he realised there was probably another reason. 'And lack of funds?'

'Yeah, that too. I'm not down to my last fiver, but I try not to splurge on anything unnecessary. I have no choice but to keep that old banger of a car going – I need it for running my work to galleries, shopping and so on – but…' She waggled her paint-stained hands at him. 'Luckily, my vocation doesn't lend itself to indulgences like manicures, and as for facials or whatever, I've long since stopped worrying about what I look like.' She chose another chip.

'Why on earth would you worry about it?'

'Er… Duh!' Her hand wafted at her jeans and jumper, her untidy hair, her unmade-up face.

Alex frowned. 'You think you have to be all dressed up and coated in make-up to look good?'

'I suspect it doesn't go amiss,' she said wryly.

Alex shook his head. 'I like the way you dress. It suits your personality.'

'Messy?'

'Creative. And you don't need make-up. You have the loveliest eyes.' *Soft brown. Gentle. Kind.*

'Well… Thank you.'

An awkward silence followed, until Alex filled it with a clumsy, 'Besides, I'm hardly one to talk.' He pointed at his sweater and jeans.

'Well, I like the way *you* look and dress, too.' Daisy smiled. 'A sartorial kindred spirit.'

'I can't remember the last time I wore a suit.' Alex shrugged. 'Uncle William's funeral, probably.'

'You still miss him?'

'Yes. He was a big influence on my life.'

'He helped to make you who you are.'

Alex saw her wistful look. 'You didn't have that luxury.'

'No. I try not to think of it that way, though. I just figure I was who I was in the past, I am who I am now, and I'll be who I'll be in the future.' Daisy rolled her eyes. 'You can tell I didn't do a degree in philosophy.'

Alex wondered if he dared ask more, then thought, *What the heck? Nothing ventured, nothing gained.*

'What happened to your parents?' he asked, steadily eating his fish and chips to deflect from the fact that he was getting personal.

Daisy hesitated, then said, 'I never knew my father. My mother was a serious drug addict. In and out of hospital, in and out of rehab, in and out of prison. So, from a young age, *I* was in and out of foster homes. The social workers kept on hoping they could turn her around, so full-on adoption was never on the cards. But as time wore on, that became less and less likely. My mother died of an overdose when I was fourteen. My foster family at the time offered to adopt me, but I didn't like the idea that they were doing it out of pity, although I'm sure they weren't.' She shrugged. 'I was old enough to have a say, and I decided that since my life had been temporary all along, it may as well stay that way until I became an adult. I didn't want to cause anyone any trouble.'

Alex had stopped eating. He knew there must have been tragedy in her childhood, but this? 'Daisy, I'm so sorry. I don't know what to say.'

'It was what it was, Alex. I don't remember my mum very well from when I was little. As I got older and she got worse, any time I spent with her was supervised, and even then, it often didn't happen for months at a time, depending on whether she was... elsewhere.'

Alex covered her hand with his. 'You missed out on so much.'

'I suppose I did. But most of the families I was with did their best. It could have been worse.'

He smiled. 'And there you go with that phrase again.'

'Like I said, it comes in handy when I start to feel too sorry for myself.'

Alex thought back to his own unhappy childhood – nothing like Daisy's, but he knew how easy it was to indulge in self-pity. He'd tried to just get on with his life, living it the way he wanted to. But Daisy's story reminded him that he at least had his mother, and they did love each other. Perhaps he ought to appreciate that more.

They had fallen into another awkward silence.

Alex changed the subject. 'Listen, Daisy, I've been thinking.'

'You're going to demolish Jean's cottage and garden to make way for a retail mall? You're making space in the farmyard for a helipad?'

'Ha! No. It's to do with you, actually.'

'Oh?'

He could have laughed at the suspicion in her voice. After that kiss in the barn, she was probably worried he was about to suggest something untoward.

'I'm developing a guilty conscience,' he told her. 'I think Fox Farm should pay you for all the time you've put in.'

'I did it to help you and Jean.'

'I know, but could you tot up what time you think you've spent on the artists and helping me? It'll only be minimum wage…'

'I gave my time as favours, Alex. Besides, it'd cause you no end of headaches to set me up as a casual employee, surely?'

'Ye-es, but it's worth it.'

'Look, it's kind of you, and I appreciate you understanding how much this has cut into my time, but the fact is, you were right.'

'I was? When?'

His deliberately shocked expression made her laugh. Daisy's whole face lit up when she laughed.

'When you reminded me that I'm living and working here rent-free with no official contract.'

'Ah. Sorry about that. I honestly didn't know about the percentage arrangement at the time.'

'You still had a point. I'm here on the cheap. Consider my helping out in Fox Farm's hour of need as a contribution.'

Alex saw the stubborn set of her mouth. She had pride, and one hell of a work ethic. He didn't want to dent either.

'Then thank you. I'm too tired to argue.'

She gave him a sympathetic look. 'Another crazy day tomorrow?'

'Yup. I'll be in trouble with Angie if I get that café wrong.'

'I wouldn't like to get on Angie's wrong side, I must admit. But it'll look fine. You know what you're doing, considering you'd rather be digging your hands into pots of soil. Does Jamie know what he'll be doing?'

'Angie and Lisa can fight it out amongst themselves.' He made a face. 'There may be fireworks.'

Daisy placed her hand over his. 'Try not to worry.'

Alex's skin hummed where her fingers touched. He wanted to take up her hand and press her palm to his lips.

Instead, he gathered the fish-and-chip wrappers and stood. 'I should go. Mum'll be back from the hospital by now. She'll wonder where I've got to.'

Daisy gave him a knowing smile. 'What will you tell her?'

'I could tell her I was working late. Or I could tell her I brought supper to a talented, beautiful artist and kissed her goodnight.'

The lyrical way he'd said that surprised and embarrassed him. But the delight on Daisy's face made it worthwhile.

'You haven't kissed me goodnight, though,' she pointed out as she stood, too.

'No, but I'm going to.'

He moved around the counter and put an arm around her waist. This was no peck on the cheek turning into something else by accident. This time, Alex kissed her properly. Daisy responded properly, too, her mouth softening under his, her body loosely pliant against him, making his blood drum loudly in his ears.

Alex broke it off, resting his forehead against hers. 'This could become a habit.'

'Do you have a problem with that?'

'No. I don't think I do.'

As he drove home, Alex thought about that. His mother had told him to stop holding back from emotional entanglement. She'd also asked if there was something about Daisy.

Mothers know too much. There is something about Daisy. I can't deny that, not after today. Still, kissing is just kissing. Emotional entanglement would be another matter.

*

When Daisy saw Alex arrive early the next morning, she went out to greet him. She told herself it was simply to offer to lend a hand – not to see him again or stare at the mouth she was becoming familiar with.

'Hi. Can I help today?'

Alex shivered in the chill wind. 'Absolutely not. You lost a day yesterday.'

When he shivered again, Daisy frowned. 'You're cold.'

'Didn't grab a hot drink before I set out, that's all. I didn't want to wake Mum. She probably overdid it yesterday, helping us all day and then going to the hospital in the evening. And I wanted to make an early start on the café.'

'You're not doing anything till you have a hot drink inside you,' Daisy decided, taking his arm and dragging him over to the studio, where she put the kettle on.

He didn't resist.

'I like your mother,' she commented as they waited for the water to boil. 'I meant to say yesterday.' *But I was blindsided by the unexpected fish-and-chip treat and the kiss.*

'I like her too.'

Daisy laughed. 'I should hope so! It's nice that she came such a long way to see Jean. And that she's staying with you, so you get a chance to catch up.'

'Yeah. It's been good this time.'

This time? What did he mean by that? Daisy was curious about his childhood but, so far, he hadn't offered to share and she hadn't felt she could pry. But she'd told him about her mother, hadn't she?

Handing him a large mug of tea, strong with a dash of milk, just as he liked it – *How do I know that? Have I absorbed that about him without noticing?* – she said, 'Tell me about you and your mother.'

'Not much to tell. We don't see much of each other nowadays, partly because we live so far apart and partly because…' Alex stopped, seeming to decide whether to go on. 'Look, she's my mother, and I love her, but things between us were – I don't know – damaged, a long time ago.'

Daisy hesitated, then plunged in. 'Why *did* you spend your school holidays here at Fox Farm instead of at home with your parents?'

'My father…' Alex shrugged. 'He had a temper. Oh, he worked hard and provided for us. But he had precious little patience, and he didn't seem interested in spending much time with me when I was a child. Maybe he was tired from work. Maybe he believed that child-rearing was a woman's job. He and I... We had no real bond. He was a builder, and I showed no aptitude for that kind of thing when I was little, despite the wooden blocks and stuff he expected me to enjoy playing with.' When Daisy raised an eyebrow at that, he said, 'I may be a practical soul now, but I wasn't back then. I was a bit of a dreamer, if truth be told. I struggled to concentrate, especially at school. My reports always disappointed him – comments like "Alex is a bright child but needs to concentrate better". The more frustrated my dad got, the less I was able to give him what he wanted, so the more frustrated he got... It was a vicious circle for both of us.'

Alex stopped, and Daisy could imagine his young world – a boy wanting to please his father and yet always getting it wrong.

'And his temper?' she prompted.

'Ah, yes. His temper.' Alex blew on his tea and took a sip. 'He shouted at us. A *lot*. When he had a go at me, Mum would step in to defend me and then she took the brunt. We both learned as the years went by that it was easier not to rile him in the first place. We spent our whole lives creeping around, trying not to say or do the wrong thing.'

'That must have been hard. Young boys should be free-spirited.'

'And wives shouldn't have to tiptoe around their husbands every minute of every day,' Alex said bitterly.

'Did he hit either of you?' Daisy asked, horrified at the idea.

'When I was younger, just the occasional smack when angry words hadn't been enough to make me behave. I don't *think* he ever hit my mother. But when I was eleven or twelve, around the time I switched from primary to secondary school, things began to change. I was taller, broader. Maybe he found that a threat. Even though Mum and I tried not to wind him up, his behaviour became worse. I was too old for him to slap any more, so the house was always filled with arguments and shouting and him proving he was in charge. Mum could see it coming – the day I'd turn round and thump him. She wanted to avoid that at all costs. Term-time wasn't as bad – I was at school, he was at work, so we only had evenings and weekends to contend with. School holidays were more dangerous, because I got bored quickly – more potential for disaster. So, Mum and Uncle William cooked up the idea of me spending school holidays at Fox Farm with him and Aunt Jean. They told Dad it was to give me something to do. Dad was happy to have me out from under his feet. As for Mum…' His voice hitched. 'I know she missed me. And I know she gave up a lot, losing me to others when we should have spent that time together. I didn't understand that back then, but I do now. She did what she thought was best to keep the peace. The trouble was, we grew apart. Fox Farm was the place I came to love, away from all that drama and ill feeling. Aunt Jean and Uncle William were firm but kind. Aunt Jean taught me to cook and help around the house. Uncle William taught me to grow things and gave me my vocation. They gave me the space to *be*.'

'It wasn't your mother's fault that she couldn't provide that, Alex.'

'I know.'

'She never considered leaving your father?'

'She told me she thought about it so many times. But she still loved the man he once was, when she married him. And she was scared that, if we left, we might not make ends meet. That he would make our lives a misery, even from a distance. My mother was all about keeping the status quo. I understand and respect that.'

'Where's your father now?'

'He was killed in an accident on a building site when I was twenty-two. There was compensation. After the shock, I think my mother found a kind of relief in it. She sold the house and moved down to Devon, well away from Leeds and the memories.'

'She didn't consider the Dales, to be near you?'

'I wasn't settled at that point. I could have ended up anywhere. And…' He paused, as though searching for the right words. 'The damage was done. We do our best under the circumstances, but we lost something along the way. Seeing each other too often reminds us both of a deeply unhappy time, a time we'd prefer to put behind us.'

'That's so sad.' Daisy couldn't help the tears that sprang to her eyes.

Alex shook his head. 'I must sound like the most selfish person in the world, complaining about that, when you have no bond at all with your parents.'

'Unlike you, I can't mourn what I never had. There were times I wished for a family of my own so hard, it was like a physical pain. But I got to experience several versions of family life, so I try to be grateful for that. And I'm still in touch with one of my foster parents. I do get jealous of what others have, now and again. And sometimes I wonder what it might be like to… Oh, I don't know, to go Christmas shopping with a mother, for example.' She gave him a weak smile. 'That would be nice.'

'You can borrow mine, if you like,' he quipped.

'I'd take you up on that if I had any money for Christmas shopping,' she said with a sigh.

'Ah. Sorry.' Alex hesitated. 'But Mum loves it, and I refused to let her help me today. Jamie's going to the hospital this afternoon – he hasn't seen Aunt Jean yet, and he's anxious to go, bless him – so Mum's on an evening visit again. She was talking about a day trip to Settle. Why don't you go with her? Take her to a couple of your favourite galleries. Have coffee or lunch. She'd enjoy your company.'

Daisy warred with temptation. She should paint today. Then again…
A day away from here. A drive along country roads on a cold but sunny day. With Alex's mother.

'I do need to drop Christmas cards off at a few places,' she mused.

'Go for it, Daisy. My mum's a good woman.'

'Of course she is. She had you, didn't she?'

It was a joshing comment, but Alex put down his tea and folded his arms around her. 'Thank you.'

'What for?' she asked, muffled against his chest.

'For listening and not judging me for how I feel. Others might think I was… cold.'

'I would never think that.' *Quite the opposite.* 'And it's not my place to judge.'

When she pulled away, he asked, 'Shall I phone Mum to promise her a fun day out with you?'

'Okay. But afternoon only, if that's okay – I need to finish this painting and then sort out what I'm taking with me.'

And so, after lunch, Daisy found herself standing in Alex's small lounge while Nicky fetched her coat. She looked around with interest. The room had the potential to be cosy, but it felt sad, neglected. A quick peep at the adjacent galley kitchen didn't dispel the impression.

'He knows, Daisy,' Nicky said as she came back down the stairs.

'Sorry?'

Nicky gave her a knowing look. 'You were thinking the house isn't at its best.'

'Oh, no, I…' Daisy shrugged. 'He's a busy man.'

'Yes. And he puts all his time and money into Riverside; never into his own comfort. I told him a home isn't just a place to eat and sleep. But I'm not sure this house is *him*. If it were, he'd have found the time to get it how he wants it. He bought it to get on the property ladder, and it was all he could afford at the time. But I'm not sure it suits him.'

Interesting. Alex believes that he and his mother have grown apart, but if that were true, why does she have this kind of insight into how he ticks?

'I think a proper little cottage would suit him better, out of the village, with its own garden,' Nicky went on. 'But I know for a fact he doesn't have *that* kind of money. They cost a bomb around here. Well. Shall we go?'

'Talking about things not being at their best…' Daisy said as they approached her car. 'This was all *I* could afford.'

'As long as it gets from A to B,' Nicky reassured her. 'I've never been one for fancy props.'

Like mother, like son.

As they drove along the country lanes, what Daisy appreciated most about Alex's mother was that she didn't immediately try to wheedle Daisy's personal life out of her. Instead, Nicky enjoyed the drive, admiring the view and pointing things out as they took her eye. That gave Daisy the opportunity to talk about her work, how and where she found inspiration, and Nicky took a genuine interest, expressing a desire to have a good look in Daisy's studio before she went back home, and telling her about the watercolour classes she had started taking.

They parked on the outskirts of Settle and walked in.

As they were about to enter the first gallery, Nicky grabbed Daisy's arm, saying, 'Don't let me buy anything in here if I can get something similar at Fox Farm. Jean would have my guts for garters!'

Nicky browsed while Daisy dealt with the gallery owner, handing over packets of cards. Nicky spotted them, and the moment they were out of the shop, she put in her own order.

'They're perfect for my book club and the other staff at the gift shop.' At the gallery, she'd bought a hand-blown glass ornament for her next-door neighbour. 'A thank you for taking care of Scar while I'm up here.'

'Scar?'

Nicky laughed at Daisy's expression. 'My cat. He got in a nasty scrap before I took him in, and his nose took the brunt, but he's a softie, really. How about a cuppa before we move on?'

Settled in the tea room down the street, Nicky asked, 'How are you managing, Daisy? Alex told me how much you've been doing for Jean and him.'

'I'm happy to help. I've enjoyed it. But my own work...? It's lucky I had winter and Christmas pieces in storage from last year, and I'd already anticipated and made a start on a few new ones in the summer. It's not easy, coming up with snowy hills in the middle of July.'

'You can't just get more prints of your existing work?'

'I can and do. But people get bored seeing the same old thing. I need to keep adding fresh pieces. And *I'd* get bored if I didn't.'

'Well, I know that both Jean and Alex appreciate your help.' Nicky hesitated. 'What do you think of my son?'

Daisy spluttered on her tea. 'I... Er. He's a nice man. I wouldn't be doing all this otherwise, would I?'

Nicky's eyes, the same colour as Alex's, twinkled. 'No other reason?'

Daisy thought about all the time she and Alex had been spending together; the hard toil and the furtive glances at his chest and arm muscles as he worked; the joshing and laughing and sharing – something she suspected he didn't do with many others. And then there were those kisses. They were pretty darned impressive. Her pulse spiked just thinking about it, and she knew she was blushing.

Nicky smiled. 'Sorry. Not my business, love, and not fair when we don't know each other. I can never get much information out of Alex. We're not as close as I'd like. Has he... Has he spoken to you about that?'

'A little,' Daisy said cautiously.

'Well. That's good. He doesn't talk about it much. Anyway, I only want to say – and I have a feeling I'm preaching to the converted – that Alex is a good man. And if you're not materialistic – because I doubt Riverside will ever run to owning fancy cars and posh houses – I'd say he's quite a catch. But then, I would say that, wouldn't I? I am his mother, after all.' Nicky picked up her handbag. 'Right. Where to next?'

Chapter Fifteen

Alex was almost finished in the café when Jules arrived.

'Hey. What are you doing here?' he asked.

'I came to see if losing Riverside's owner to Fox Farm for all those many hours was worth it.' Jules gazed around the café.

'Hope so. Nearly done here.'

It had been a long day. First, Alex fixed a chain across the staircase to the old gallery, then he stacked the existing tables and chairs so he could thoroughly clean the floor and walls. Jim had given up part of his day off so they could drive their trucks to Settle to fetch the second-hand tables and chairs Alex had bought. After Jim had helped him unload and left, Alex had placed the furniture, interspersing the just-purchased dark wood with the existing pine, hoping the mix and match approach would look quirkily rustic. Finally, he'd put the artwork back on the walls.

'Looks good,' Jules said. 'The archway between the two rooms means each space looks cosy if it's quiet, but also part of a whole. Now you just have to fill it with customers.'

'That won't be a problem in the run-up to Christmas. Nor in the summer – although people'll sit outside then, too. The point is, we won't be turning people away. Want to see the gallery?' He led her over to the barn.

Jules gaped. 'Alex, it's fabulous! The old one had its charms, but this is something else.'

Alex kissed her cheek. 'Thanks. I needed to hear that.'

'Who did all the arranging? Lisa?'

'Some, but she's been lacklustre about the whole thing. Young Jamie's been more helpful than her – he's the one who's done all the touting of it on social media. And a lot of yesterday was down to Daisy and my mother.'

'Well, now. There's a pairing!'

'Yeah. They went to Settle this afternoon, too. I have a feeling they could become a formidable twosome.'

Jules gave him a piercing look. 'Why should that matter? Daisy's just a friend, isn't she?'

'She is.' Alex nodded like one of those bobbing toy dogs in the back of a car. 'She is.'

'Hmmm. Not sure I believe you. I haven't even met her yet. I may have to come and inspect her.'

'You'll have to wait until my mother's finished with her. Anyway, you'll only find a nice, ordinary woman.'

'But that's what you like about her, right?'

In trying to put Jules off from further speculation, Alex knew he'd done Daisy a disservice with such a pedestrian description. 'That, and her talent and brains and kindness. And her endless capacity for hard work and doing favours, of course.' He smiled. 'A quality you also have in abundance. I'm sorry for what I'm putting you through.'

'You're at Riverside as much as you can be, and you do what you can when you're there. I need to talk to you about the next few weeks, though. Orders. Quantities. Christmas trees. I can judge the wreaths as I go along, but some of the other things we buy in – the wicker snowmen and reindeer and whatnot? We don't have storage space if we get it wrong. Jim's already stringing lights up, but he could do with a hand. I know you'll need to borrow Jim and Kieran to put the tree up at Fox Farm, but I was wondering if they might be willing to help you on one of their days off, because I can't spare them in opening hours. As for building the Santa cabin, I doubt they can help you this year…'

'Jules. Slow down.' Alarmed at her rapid chattering – so unlike her – Alex took her by both arms. 'Take a breath.' When she had, he asked, 'Is this becoming too much for you?'

'It's not like I haven't done it before.' Her slim shoulders sagged. 'But this year, it feels like things are running away from me. If we could sit down together, go through it all, set dates for who's doing what when? I'd feel better about it.'

'Then that's what we'll do,' Alex promised. 'You'll have my undivided attention at Riverside for the rest of this week.'

'But it's the first day of the new café and gallery tomorrow. Don't you want to be here?'

'No. I've put everything in place. Now other people need to do their jobs. It might be good to work on my own business for once!'

*

Daisy was up early on Thursday, with painting as her main priority. She had no intention of trooping to any more galleries between now and Christmas.

And after Christmas, it will only be three months before I have to leave Fox Farm.

Her heart sank at the thought. Fox Farm was a part of her now, and she felt like a part of it. How had previous artists-in-residence felt after their year was up? Had they become as attached to this place?

She was sure they must have missed the studio space, but they had lived elsewhere and had lives of their own. Daisy didn't – not really. The one thing this year had taught her was that she had been merely existing up until now – temporary accommodation, temporary jobs. Nowhere she could call home.

Fox Farm felt like home. But come April, a different artist would be here, and she would be... wherever. Back at Jack's? Some other cheap accommodation? The idea depressed her. Was it time to give up trying to make a living from her art? Having this studio was the first time she had made enough money to live off, mainly because Jean had taken pity on her and only asked for a small percentage of her takings rather than rent. To go back to living off commission from Fox Farm and the other galleries, trying to afford somewhere cheap to live but where she could also paint... She would have to take a part-time job of some kind. It felt like going backwards, and it certainly didn't seem like much of a prospect for a thirty-one-year-old.

Noise from the yard gradually filtered through as Fox Farm's day began. It was looking busy out there – word had got around about the new gallery.

Time to stop moping, Daisy.

The curiosity that brought business to the gallery and café was good for Daisy, too. She sold plenty of Christmas cards, far more in one day in the studio than she would sell across all the galleries and gift shops who took them from her – *Must contact the printer with another order* – as well as several prints and one original. If it was this busy today, she imagined it would be even busier at the weekend.

At the end of the afternoon, she looked up as Nicky entered. 'Hi.'

'Hi, Daisy. I promised to take a look, didn't I?'

'You did. Can I make you a cup of tea?'

'I'd kill for one, but I don't want your other customers to think I'm getting preferential treatment.'

'I'll put it in a reusable takeaway cup so they'll think you got it from the café.'

'Deal. I couldn't've got near the café anyway. It's heaving in there.'

'That's good to hear.'

Nicky smiled her thanks as Daisy handed her the tea. 'It vindicates all Alex's hard work and Jean's faith in him. She's so proud.'

'You saw her this afternoon?'

'Yes. Alex is concentrating on Riverside for a few days, but he promised her a video tour, so I did that this morning and went to the hospital after lunch to show her.'

Daisy dismissed her disappointment that Alex might not be around for a while. He was entitled to spend time at Riverside for a change.

'I've only visited her a couple of times,' Daisy admitted. 'I should try harder.'

'Jean knows how much time you've spent helping, and she appreciates it. The hospital's a long round trip, and you have this place to keep up with. Talking of which…' Nicky walked over to the walls to study the work there. 'I love your style. So much to see in each piece. A hint of comedy. Fun details.' She took a few paces back. 'Each one is different, yet the style defines it as *you*.'

Daisy thanked her. 'You have a good eye, Nicky. I liked your ideas in the gallery the other day.'

Nicky smiled. 'You know, when Alex was little, I had a part-time job in a bakery to fit in with his school hours, and then I became the manager as he got older. I can't say that sausage rolls and sliced loaves excited me, but it brought in extra money. When I moved to Devon after Keith died, I wanted to work somewhere I *enjoyed*. There's always something new coming in at the gift shop, and the owner gives me a free hand in how it's arranged.' She studied a painting that depicted a typical Dales scene in winter – snow and stone walls and sheep; a bridge over a frozen river. 'I must say, it's beautiful up here in the Dales. I never came out this way much, other than to bring Alex over for his stays. I was always stuck in the suburbs.'

Daisy wondered whether she dare be bold with this woman she barely knew. 'Nicky, why didn't you come to Fox Farm with Alex for the school holidays? Wouldn't it have been nicer for you to be together?'

Nicky smiled sadly. 'Oh, yes. I would have been with my son; watched him thrive here. I could have spent more time with my brother. Nobody expected to lose William in his sixties. I still miss him – he was the one I felt closest to. Eric was the eldest, then William, and me the youngest. There was a twelve-year gap between me and William! I was a late-life accident, I'm told.' She chuckled. 'But in answer to your question... Because of the bakery, I couldn't get that amount of holiday time. We needed the money. And Keith wouldn't have countenanced it, having to look after himself for weeks on end. I did what I thought was best for all of us at the time, but especially for Alex.' Her voice hitched. 'I'm not sure he knows that.'

Moved, Daisy took her hand. 'He *does* know that. He told me only the other day.'

'That's good.' Nicky dabbed at a tear. 'Well, I should leave you to it.' She handed over the cup. 'Thank you for the tea. And the chat.'

As she turned to leave, N.J. Giles entered.

'Hello.' He frowned. 'It's busy round here.'

'The new gallery opened today,' Daisy said. 'Didn't you realise?'

'No.' He jerked a thumb at Jean's cottage. 'I've been caught up.'

'Nicky, I'd like you to meet Mr Giles, our resident writer, the one who's taken Jean's cottage. Mr Giles, this is Alex Hirst's mother, Nicky.'

'Nice to meet…' N.J. Giles stopped, his mouth agape, as he looked at Nicky properly for the first time. 'I… You!'

'Me?' Nicky looked puzzled. 'I'm sorry, do we know each other?'

'No, not at all. Not in the sense *you* mean.' He moved back a few paces, drinking Nicky in, eyeing her from top to toe. 'Oh dear, oh dear, oh dear.'

'Mr Giles, you're unnerving us. Not that *that's* anything new.' Daisy turned to Nicky. 'He stabbed me in his kitchen once. It's the way he works.' She laughed at Nicky's expression. 'Ask Alex to fill you in sometime. Now then, Mr Giles, what's all this about?'

'Oh dear,' he repeated. 'You, madam, have cost me a great deal of work,' he said to Nicky.

'I'd say sorry if I knew why,' Nicky replied, perturbed.

'I don't suppose you're in the police?'

'No. I work in a gift shop.'

'Oh. Ah.' He gave a disappointed sigh. 'My DCI, you see – that's Detective Chief Inspector – well, she's a female DCI, and I've got her tall and masculine. Kind of beaky. She's all wrong. Stereotyped. I couldn't picture her properly. But she *could* be you. You could be her. A striking woman, with presence. Attractive for her age.'

Nicky raised an eyebrow. 'Thank you. I think.'

'Do you mind if I take photos?'

Amused now, Nicky said, 'Be my guest' and posed patiently while N.J. Giles snapped her from all angles.

'Thank you.' He shook her hand. 'You've saved the book. Although I'm very cross with you. So much work to do, altering everything. So much.' And off he scuttled.

Daisy and Nicky waited until he was halfway across the yard before bursting into delighted laughter.

'Well!' Nicky puffed out her cheeks. 'It's never dull around here, is it?'

*

On Friday afternoon, Alex's mother insisted on visiting Riverside before setting off home. He'd surprised them both by asking her if she could stay the weekend, but Saturdays were too busy at the shop where she worked.

Nicky admired all the changes and expansions he'd made since the last time she'd visited. 'It's doing well?'

'We do alright. It could always be bigger and better.'

'Bigger and better isn't necessarily best, Alex. There'll always be somewhere else that does the all-singing, all-dancing thing. Let them get on with it. You haven't got the capital. What you're offering is a different experience. If people don't want to drive miles, if they want to go somewhere local that they can trust for reliable advice and quality, then they'll come to you. That's what matters.' She gazed around. 'This place has a cosy, old-fashioned, rustic feel about it. Your staff are friendly and knowledgeable. People appreciate that.'

Alex stared at his mother. She was turning into quite a revelation, what with her expert eye in the gallery and now understanding exactly what he was trying to achieve at Riverside.

'Thanks, Mum.'

'I'm proud of you, Alex. And what you're doing for Jean is incredible. But I'm worried about you. I know Fox Farm means a lot to you. But don't allow it to *consume* you, love. Fox Farm is Jean's dream, and she's entitled to hang on to it for as long as possible. But you're still young and Riverside is *your* dream. You're entitled to see it flourish.'

They walked to her car, pulling their coats around them against the biting wind.

'Now, before I go, I want to talk to you about Daisy.'

Alex suppressed a groan. 'In what respect?'

'You're different with her.'

'Don't be daft.'

She fixed him with a steely glare. 'I'm your mother, and I've never seen you like this. When Daisy's around, your eyes light up, you smile more. You're softer.'

'A thirty-five-year-old outdoorsman does *not* want to be told he's soft, Mum.'

She laughed, the sound reminding him of happier days when they baked together or went to the park; days when his father was at work or down the pub. The memory gave him a physical pang. *Oh, I miss that.*

'She's good for you,' his mother said simply.

I can't deny that. 'Yes, she is.'

'Then why don't you do something about it? Stop hanging back.'

'I'm busy enough, without adding complications.'

'Alex Hirst, you've been avoiding complications like this all your life. Don't let her slip through your fingers.'

'You and Aunt Jean have been talking, haven't you?'

'What difference does it make?'

Alex ran a hand through his hair and wondered when he'd get time for something as simple as a haircut, let alone a relationship.

'Let's say this scenario that you and Aunt Jean have cooked up has some smidgen of truth, and I like Daisy more than I admit. What makes you and that temporarily bedridden matchmaker think *she's* interested in *me*?'

'I'm a woman, aren't I? I have eyes. Daisy looks at you the way you look at her. I'm not talking full-on, gooey, lovey-dovey – yet – but with interest and fondness. There's a chemistry between you. It would be a shame to let that fizzle out. Christmas is a magical time of year. Let a little magic into your life, son.'

She placed a hand on his cheek, the way she used to so long ago, and Alex wanted her to keep it there forever.

'We'll see,' he murmured.

'I'll take that. Better than a "Bugger off and mind your own business"! It's Friday night. Why don't you ask her out?'

'Because tonight I have to do Fox Farm's accounts. It's the end of the month. Suppliers like getting paid for what they've delivered. Staff expect to see their salary appear in the bank. It's tradition, you know.'

'Ha. Well, don't work too hard.'

They hugged, and he watched her climb into her car and drive away. He would miss her. They had been closer this visit than any other. There had been more camaraderie between them, more affection, more understanding. He longed for that to continue, for their relationship to grow into something it should have been all along.

As for what she'd said about him and Daisy... It seemed they weren't pulling the wool over his mother's or Aunt Jean's eyes, even if they were trying to pull it over their own. Did his eyes light up when he was with her? Did he smile more? If so, that was a miracle, because he couldn't see that he'd had much to smile about lately.

He felt comfortable with Daisy. He could talk to her. What he'd told her about his parents and childhood... With previous girlfriends, he would have brushed the question off, but with Daisy, he hadn't just told her the facts – his father's temper, the unhappy home – but so much more. He'd never confessed to anyone about his damaged bond with his mother. Saying it out loud would have felt disloyal to his mother who tried so hard, and in anyone else's eyes, he imagined he would sound almost callous towards her. But with Daisy, the tenderness in her tone had made him want to curl up in her arms and pour it all out. He'd never felt that way with *any* woman he'd dated. And she hadn't judged him.

Because she likes you for who you are. She doesn't look for anyone else within you.

That was worth a lot, in Alex's eyes.

Chapter Sixteen

It was almost the end of November, and Angie, Sue and Jamie had begun adding festive touches to the café, using decorations that looked like they harked back to the 1970s and 80s… although that vintage look suited the old building. They had also swapped to festive music in the background, favouring well-loved Christmas hits to match the decorations.

'The old 'uns are the good 'uns,' Sue declared, jiggling along, when Daisy popped over for her lunchtime soup. 'Although they'll start driving me mad after a couple of weeks!'

'Jean would kill us if she knew we were getting Christmassy already,' Angie confided. 'She doesn't believe in it before December. But we needed to get a head start – we're already busy, and it'll only get worse.'

'Well, what she can't see won't hurt her,' Daisy said. 'When do you switch to the Christmas menu?'

'Monday.' Angie handed her a scribbled list.

The drinks included cinnamon latte, mulled wine, hot spiced apple and elderflower… and the food made Daisy's mouth water. How could anyone resist spicy roasted parsnip soup or warm turkey and bacon salad, let alone jam-filled star-shaped shortbread, gingerbread snowmen or spiced clementine brownies?

'Looks like I might have to treat myself,' Daisy said.

'There's always the odd item that comes out imperfect.' Angie winked. 'I'll make sure something heads your way, shall I?'

Jamie had helped Lisa decorate the barn, too, but they were keeping that muted. Too much glitz would detract from the goods on display, so they stuck to strings of fairy lights around the counter and along the shelves, and artificial but realistic swags of greenery. Jamie had braved the tall stepladder to hang bunches of holly from the beams, which he'd cut himself from Jean's garden. Daisy was impressed with his gumption and efforts. It was a shame he would leave next year.

Lisa was less enthusiastic about the new space and Christmas. 'Easier access is all very well,' she complained. 'I suppose I can cope with wheelchairs and old dears using walking frames – they know not to touch. But pushchairs and small kiddies? At least in the old building, they were limited to downstairs, where we could keep the less breakable items. And we were always busy in the run-up to Christmas, but it's even busier now.'

Daisy *could* have pointed out that better access meant more customers and therefore more sales and therefore more chance that Fox Farm wouldn't slowly decline to the point where Lisa lost her job. Ditto about being busy in the coming weeks. She could also have pointed out that the new gallery had been carefully arranged to ensure that anything breakable was out of reach of small fingers. But it would have fallen on deaf ears, and besides, it wasn't her place to interfere.

On Sunday evening, she set off for the hospital.

'Daisy! Lovely to see you.' Jean smiled, sitting upright in her bed and looking well. 'You shouldn't have come. You're too busy.'

Daisy was pleased to hear her friend's improved speech. 'Never too busy for you, Jean. Sorry I haven't been for a while.'

'Don't be silly. I know how much you've been doing. The gallery and café look incr… They look grand. Nicky showed me on her phone. I can't wait to see them.'

'You'll love them, I promise.'

'Angie phoned to say they're coping with the bigger café and Jamie's great, so all's well there. Now then, tell me about the artists – about who else you saw.'

Daisy did, but knowing Jean felt guilty, added, 'Anyway, I'm finished now. It's too near to Christmas for anyone else to bother.'

'Lisa should've helped.' Jean fixed Daisy with a gimlet eye. 'What's going on with her?'

That's a conversation you can have with your nephew. 'She's probably just stressed about all the changes at such a busy time of year.' *Although everyone else has managed to step up to the mark.* To deflect the conversation away from Lisa, Daisy told Jean about Nicky's ideas and her eye for presentation at the gallery.

Jean looked thoughtful. 'I never knew she had that in her. I don't suppose she had much chance to find out, stuck with Keith. She seems happy enough now, although there was something about her this time. A melanc… Oh, I wish the words would come.'

'Melancholy?'

'Yes. She told me that she and Alex got on really well this time. They talked a lot, and he didn't hold back. I think she wishes she lived nearer.' Jean sighed. 'I wish she'd move back up north. I'd love for those two to be how they *should* be. I feel so guilty.'

'Guilty? Why?'

'I stole Alex's affection from Nicky. I didn't mean to.'

'It couldn't be helped, Jean. You all did your best for him, and it just worked out that way.'

Jean gave her a speculative look. 'Nicky *said* Alex had told you about it. You and Alex must be getting close.'

'Oh, I don't know about that.'

'Tosh!'

'Anyway…' Daisy was anxious to veer away from *that* line of enquiry. 'There's still time for Alex and Nicky to fix things. This past week proves that.'

Jean nodded, but Daisy could see she was getting tired, so she took her leave.

By the time Daisy had driven home and eaten, she was ready to collapse into bed and allow sleep to take her.

The full eight hours she got was a blessing, allowing her to concentrate well the next day. Late in the afternoon, she looked up when a woman entered the studio, her arms full of greenery.

'Hi. I'm Jules from Riverside. You're Daisy?'

'Yes. Pleased to meet you.' Daisy came around the counter to help the woman with her load. 'What's this?'

'A bundle for your door.' Jules shrugged. 'Sorry, I can't call it anything better than that. I usually do wreaths for the studio, gallery, café and Jean's cottage, but I couldn't this year. I can barely keep up with customer demand at Riverside. Everyone wants the natural look, which fits nicely with Riverside's ethos, but I only have one pair of hands.' She waggled slender fingers. 'And they're currently like sieves, due to the holly pricking its way through my gloves.'

'Ouch! Well, it's good of you to do these.' Daisy lifted the bunch of greenery tied together at the stalks by a ribbon; a mixture of evergreen and holly and pinecones. 'It looks lovely – really natural. Thank you.'

Jules dug in her pocket. 'Here's a rubber hook with a sucker. It'll hold on the glass – don't worry about the weight.'

Daisy positioned the arrangement on her door and admired it. 'It looks great. Can I make you a cuppa?'

'I'd kill for one, thanks. Angie was looking harassed in the café. Besides, it's nice to chat to someone new.'

As Daisy boiled the kettle, she surreptitiously studied Jules from the corner of her eye while the other woman admired Daisy's art. Jules was slim, blonde, attractive, with enviable bone structure. Somewhere in her early forties maybe...

Not too old for Alex, Daisy thought with a surprising stab of jealousy. He spoke highly of her, they worked closely together and were obviously good friends. *Has he ever kissed her? Have they had an affair?*

Seemingly unaware of Daisy's scrutiny, Jules took the tea gratefully. 'Thanks. I love your work. Especially that piece.' She pointed to a large print on canvas, a winter scene of the bridge over the river, with snowy hills in the background and the stone buildings of the Masons Inn and the village store to one side. 'I have a summery beach canvas in the lounge, but it looks daft in the winter. It'd be good to swap them over for the seasons. If Alex paid me more, bless him, I'd treat myself.'

'I'm glad you like it. Maybe you'll get a Christmas bonus?'

'Alex'll forget his head at this rate, let alone the wine or chocolates he usually buys us.'

'I haven't seen Alex since midweek,' Daisy said, hoping that nonchalance rather than disappointment came through in her voice.

'That's my fault. I was feeling overwhelmed, so I commandeered him. He has all the Christmas stuff to do here at Fox Farm this coming week, so I wanted to make sure Riverside got his attention first. And I'll need him at weekends from now on for tree sales.' Jules laughed. 'That won't be hard, though – Alex loves that netting machine. He's like a kid when they get that out of storage.'

Daisy smiled at that. 'How much does he have to do at Fox Farm?'

'Lights. Outdoor decorations. The tree. That'll take Alex, Jim *and* Kieran, because it's so big. He's hoping to do that tomorrow.'

'Aren't Jim and Kieran off work tomorrow?'

'Yes, but they're soft as putty, the pair of them, when it comes to Alex. He's on his own with Santa's cabin, though – that would be a favour too far.'

'Building a cabin sounds like a lot of work for just three weekends of Santa.'

'Yeah, but it brings in revenue and creates a captive audience for hot chocolate and cake from the café or Christmas shopping at the gallery. Your studio, too.'

'Sounds good to me. You're not tempted to have a Santa's grotto at Riverside?'

'Jean's had hers for years, long before Riverside got off the ground, and we're not far enough away to sustain two. Alex decided it wasn't fair to compete – he's soft as putty, too. Well, thanks for the tea. It was good to chat with you.'

'You too. Thanks for the greenery.'

'You're welcome. See you sometime.' Jules cast one last wistful glance at the canvas she'd been admiring before leaving.

Daisy watched her walk away, her jeans and slimline jacket emphasising a neat figure, and looked down at her own baggy, faded jeans and splodged jumper.

Ah, well. Some have it, some don't.

After closing, shamed by Jules' door decoration into finally doing something about the lack of festive decoration in her studio, Daisy dredged through her storage cupboard and her creative brain to come up with something she could do cheaply that wouldn't detract from her work. Something classy and understated. Her studio floor scattered with possibilities, she set to.

By midnight, Daisy had neat, elongated triangles of stiff craft paper laid out all over the studio to dry, each sporting a painted holly leaf or fir tree or mistletoe sprig, and each edged with gold paint. Once they were dry, she would string them along the walls above her pictures and along her counter, like bunting. She might even sneak out in the morning and cut holly from Jean's garden.

Rubbing her aching shoulders, she admired her evening's work. It would look so festive when Grace came to stay. *Can't wait for that!*

As a final task before going to bed, she compiled a music playlist. The café had their vintage hits, the gallery had opted for classical and acoustic, but for Daisy, it was a no-brainer – it could only be Bing Crosby, Frank Sinatra, Doris Day, Dean Martin and friends. Surely Christmas wasn't Christmas without them?

*

Alex was looking forward to seeing his aunt again. While his mother was around, he hadn't needed to, although he'd phoned every day. But Aunt Jean had been moved to a rehabilitation ward, to reteach her the skills she needed before she could come home, and he wanted to check up on that.

'Aunt Jean, you're looking so well.'

She had more colour in her face and sat upright in her bedside chair without slumping.

'Thank you.' She beamed. 'I can go up and down the ward with the walking frame now. Do you want to see?'

'Of course!' He made a move to help her out of her chair, but she batted him away. 'I have to do it myself.' Using more strength from one arm than the other, she pulled herself up to grip the walking frame and shuffled slowly down the length of the ward and back.

Alex applauded, cursing the tears in his eyes that he knew his aunt would think were soft.

She was tired when she sat back down, but triumphant. 'They're talking about stairs next. They have a little set to try – just two or three. I have to do it,' she said, determined, 'or they won't let me go home – I'd have to do stairs morning and night there.'

'Thank goodness you have a downstairs loo, eh?'

'*And* they took the lid off my beaker.' She indicated her tea on the bedside table. 'I feel less like a child now.'

Her speech was clearer and less monosyllabic. Alex hadn't noticed that on the phone. Face-to-face was so much better.

'Nicky showed me Fox Farm on her mobile,' Jean said. 'You've done a fant... A great job. Thank you.'

'You're welcome. I'm really pleased with it, and it's busy – both the café and the gallery. Takings will be higher than last year.'

'Good. They say I'll need carers for a while, for showers or baths. A cleaner, too. So, you were right about money.' She paused. 'Seb came this afternoon.'

Alex smirked at the idea that Aunt Jean still called his cousin by the shortened form he hated – but the news that Sebastian was back startled him.

'I didn't know he was up here.' *What does he want now? He's made it clear he doesn't approve of anything we're doing. He's also made it clear he has no intention of pitching in.*

'He asked what we were up to. I told him to see for himself. Told him it's grand.'

'Good for you.' *Although I could do without him inspecting it and telling us how we could have done it better if he'd been in charge.*

'He asked about the main house. About the upstairs. The holiday flat.'

Ah. 'You told him?'

'No choice, if it's going to happen.'

Alex bit down irritation that his aunt assumed that *could* go ahead. It had been a suggestion, made in haste. He hadn't costed it out yet, but it would need a kitchenette, and the old bathroom, unused for decades, would need replacing – a complete overhaul, in other words. Carpets, curtains, furniture… Then someone would have to list it, deal with bookings or an agency – that someone being him, no doubt. He'd shoved the whole idea to the back of his mind, treating it as a second phase he might never have to deal with, depending on how the first phase went.

His mother's words echoed in his head – '*Don't allow it to consume you. Fox Farm is Jean's dream.*'

'One step at a time, Aunt Jean,' he said patiently. 'We have to be sure that what we've already done was worth the investment first.'

'I know.' Aunt Jean changed tack. 'Your mum had a good time up here with you.'

'She did. *We* did.'

'Maybe she'll come more often.' She gave him a speculative look. 'She likes Devon and her job. But she said she loves the Dales.'

'It's a darned sight colder than Devon. And the sea's not exactly on our doorstep.'

'I know. But it has family.'

'Mum needed distance from memories of Dad and her marriage, Aunt Jean. She likes it where she is. Don't meddle.'

'Not meddling. Just saying.'

Time to change the subject. 'I'm putting Fox Farm's tree up tomorrow. And I'll build Santa's cabin on Wednesday, ready to open at the weekend.'

'Send me pictures. Is Mike being Santa again?'

'Yes.' Alex thought back to his phone call with Lisa's dad. He was a lot more enthusiastic than his daughter, *and* he was doing it for free because he loved it.

'Who's the elf this year?' Aunt Jean asked.

'Mike's neighbour's daughter. A sixth-former again.'

'And what about the presents?'

'Jamie dealt with ordering those, and he's spent his evenings wrapping them. He won't take any money for the extra work. Says he's happy doing it while he watches telly. He's been brilliant, Aunt Jean. Full of energy. Willing to go the extra mile.' *Unlike Lisa.* 'Well. I should go. I haven't eaten yet.'

At that, his aunt frowned. 'You have to eat, Alex.'

I barely have time to breathe, let alone eat. 'I will.'

'Are you going to the barn dance this year?'

'The *barn* dance?'

Aunt Jean never missed the annual Winterbridge barn dance, and Alex always accompanied her. It made him sad that she wouldn't be there this year.

'I doubt it.' He winked. 'I can't take my usual beautiful partner, can I?'

'Ask someone else. Ask Daisy.'

'I…' Alex was about to argue, but a little voice said, *Why not? You both need a break. A bit of fun.* 'I'll think about it. See you soon.'

*

'That's a big tree,' Daisy stated the obvious as she watched Jim, Kieran and Alex haul it into position on Tuesday afternoon.

'Yep, and Aunt Jean wants pictures to prove it,' Alex grumbled.

'She appreciates everything you're doing.' Daisy put a reassuring hand on his arm, then quickly withdrew it when Jim and Kieran exchanged a meaningful glance. 'What can I do to help?'

'You can go and do your own work. We'll get the lights on this monster. Jim and Kieran can go after that – this is an annual freebie from them, eh, lads?' He smiled, reminding her how much she'd missed seeing him around. 'You could help me decorate after that, but there's no point in freezing your ar… backside off until you have to.'

'Okay.' Daisy hurried back indoors to the warmth of her studio and perched at her easel, but the piece she'd been working on stared back at her, uninspiring. What with using her closing days and evenings to see the artists or help Alex or catch up, she hadn't been getting out much for walks or drives, where things might catch her eye and spark ideas. She also liked to inject a little humour into her work – and humour had been rather lacking lately.

In the spring and summer, she'd always tried to take a short walk before opening the studio, but in the winter, it was too cold and dark that early. Now the Fox Farm alterations were done, and she'd finished with the artists, she should use her free days more constructively, if the weather allowed. In fact, she should have gone somewhere today, but she'd had some mounts and frames to do… and she'd known Alex was coming with the tree.

Gazing unseeingly through the studio window, her eyes gradually refocused on the scene out there. Three burly men in a cobbled farmyard, hoisting a giant Christmas tree upright, against a backdrop of old, grey-stone farm buildings…? *Hmmm.*

Daisy got to work. She became so absorbed that she didn't hear the door opening.

'Do you want to decorate? Or are you too involved?' Alex came over to see what she'd been up to. A tree was taking shape, and a red jumper similar to his. 'You find me inspiring?'

'I found the *scene* inspiring. Goodness knows, there's been little enough inspiration recently.'

'Well, I need some out there. Aunt Jean usually orders me about with the tree.' Alex gazed around the studio. 'I like the handmade bunting, by the way. Very tasteful.'

'Thank you.'

'Did you nick the holly from the cottage garden?'

'Ah. Er. Yes. I hope you don't mind. Jamie did it for the gallery.'

'No, I don't mind. Get wrapped up. It's brass monkeys out there.'

When Daisy had pulled on a jacket and hat, Alex took her hand and dragged her outside. Three large plastic crates held ornaments suitable for outdoors.

'That's a lot of ornaments.'

'It's a lot of tree.' Alex fetched a stepladder and began to climb. 'Pass me something and point to where.'

They worked like that for ten minutes – ten minutes in which Daisy's artistic judgement regarding ornament placement was somewhat impaired by her tendency to spend the time admiring Alex's backside in faded jeans as he climbed up and down the stepladder.

'It'd go quicker if we had two ladders,' she said, in a desperate attempt to remove herself from temptation.

'Not if you broke your neck.'

'You think I can't handle a stepladder?'

'Be my guest. But we'll stick with one ladder, and I'll stand by to catch you if you fall.'

That could be a lyric to a romantic song, Daisy thought as she gathered up several ornaments and made her way gingerly up the ladder, using her other hand for support. It was wobblier than she'd expected on the uneven cobbles, and she was grateful that Alex was there to steady it. She placed her ornaments where she wanted, directed Alex to pass her more, got more confident, made her way higher up the ladder each time, reached higher each time... until the inevitable happened.

'Daisy!' Alex warned, but it was too late.

His steadying the ladder wasn't much use when she lost her footing at the very top, with nowhere for her hands to grip but the tree – and she had no intention of grabbing *that* and bringing the whole thing crashing down.

With a panicked wobble worthy of Stan Laurel, Daisy came off the ladder completely and fell backwards. If this had been one of those romantic Christmas movies that old Jack watched on the telly when he thought she wasn't looking, she would have fallen right into Alex's strong, capable arms and they would have gazed into each other's eyes, smiling with relief.

Instead, there was much squealing from Daisy, shouting from Alex and a flailing of arms and legs from both of them as she hit him square in the chest, the impact sending them flying to the cobbles. Alex and his thankfully well-padded jacket bore the brunt, Daisy landed on top of him, and both let out an undignified 'Oooff!'

'Well, isn't this cosy?' Sebastian drawled as he strode over to where they lay, out of breath. 'Can I help? Or would you prefer to lie on top of one another a while longer?'

Daisy didn't like his tone. If Grace had turned up and said the same thing, she would have laughed – but when Sebastian said it, it sounded full of nasty insinuation. Judging by the look in Alex's eyes, he felt the same way.

'Sorry,' Daisy mumbled.

'Are you hurt?'

'Only my pride.'

Alex grinned. 'Same here.'

They struggled to their feet and brushed themselves down, then Alex righted the stepladder, shooting Sebastian a filthy look for not lending a hand.

'What can I do for you, Sebby? Here to help?'

'Hardly,' Sebastian sneered. 'Some of us have work to do. We can't all play around with Christmas trees.'

'I have plenty of work to do, too, but Aunt Jean wants me to do this.'

'I've already done my duty with Jean today. I went to the hospital this afternoon.' Sebastian looked Daisy up and down as though he remained unimpressed with her. 'Besides, you have your own little helper.'

'Yes, well, this *little helper* also has work to do,' Daisy said pointedly. 'If you two will excuse me?'

Her cheeks still red from the fall and Sebastian's snide remarks, Daisy made a hurried retreat to her safe space, where she wouldn't be tempted to slap that hateful man's face. Talk about how to ruin an afternoon!

Chapter Seventeen

'I want to speak to you, Alex.' Sebastian's tone was strident.

'I assumed so, otherwise why would you take time out from your busy schedule?' Alex shot back, still winded by his fall with Daisy and disappointed it hadn't turned into a fun tussle and a steamy kiss. *That* would have made the hassle of putting up the tree so much more worthwhile, in his opinion. 'What about?'

Sebastian hugged his arms to his chest. 'Can't we go somewhere warm?'

Alex sighed. 'I'll open up the café.' Grabbing his keys from his truck, he let them in and offered Sebastian tea.

'No macchiato?' Sebastian whined.

'I am *not* firing up an industrial coffee machine for you to have a barista coffee. It's tea or nothing. Now, what's up?'

'I'm concerned about what's going on around here, Alex.'

'I don't see why.' Alex slammed Sebastian's mug down in front of him, sloshing tea over the top. It would have been an added bonus if some had landed on Sebastian's cashmere sweater, but no such luck. 'It's not as though you're involved in any practical sense. In fact, I'm not sure why you're back here. Everything's going to plan. You've seen for yourself that Aunt Jean's recovering well. What else is there?'

Sebastian inspected the café. 'Hmmm. I don't deny there's more space – which is all well and good, *if* you can fill it with customers.'

'We have been doing.'

'Only because it's a busy time of year. What about when it's quiet?'

'We can't have our cake and eat it, Sebastian.' *Although I bet you try.* 'The capacity's here, if needed. It wasn't before.'

'What about that barn you've been pratting about in?'

Alex took a deep breath. 'Ignoring your offensive turn of phrase… Have you seen it since it was finished?'

'The last I knew of it, you and that arty-farty woman had been knee-deep in suds and brushes in there,' Sebastian commented. 'You're spending a lot of time together, aren't you?'

I'm not rising to that *bait.* Alex stood. 'Come with me.'

'I haven't drunk my tea!'

Alex led the way across the yard to the barn, Sebastian trailing reluctantly behind him, unlocked the door and stood aside for Sebastian to enter, then waited – not for Sebastian's approval, because he knew he would never get that, but for an acknowledgement, at least.

Sebastian took his time assessing the new space that Alex was so proud of. How could his cousin have any quibble with this?

'It's smart,' Sebastian grudgingly agreed.

Alex was annoyed to feel relief. He didn't need Sebastian's blessing. Aunt Jean and the staff were the only ones who mattered.

'But we still need to talk,' his cousin insisted. 'Let's go back to the café so I can finish my tea.'

The tea you didn't want? Sure.

Back at their table, Sebastian said, 'The café looks fine. The gallery looks good. Better than the old one, although that wouldn't be hard.'

'The old gallery was the way it was because it grew over time. But we needed to rethink it to suit modern needs.'

'And *that*,' Sebastian said, wagging a finger at Alex in that condescending way of his, 'is where you've gone wrong. When I first came up here, I *said* you were throwing good money after bad. You've done the café. The gallery. And now, I gather you're planning to turn upstairs into a holiday let? You're pouring money into this place like there's no tomorrow. It's a ridiculous strategy.'

'Just because you're in the business of giving up on an enterprise when it's down on its luck, winding it up without a second thought…'

'No.' Sebastian wagged a finger again. 'It's a question of recognising when a business has no chance of recovering – or in Fox Farm's case, when there's no point in trying – and making the best of it for all concerned.'

'No *point?*' Alex's blood pressure was rising by the second.

'Alex, you're so fond of Aunt Jean, you're not looking at this objectively.'

'But you're going to put me straight, are you?' *Best get on with it, before I punch you. Actually, I may punch you anyway.*

'I can spell it out for you, if you like.' Sebastian didn't wait to see if Alex *did* like. 'The way I see it, it could go three ways with Jean. One: She could be alright for a while, but since the stress of Fox Farm is obviously too much for her, why expand and invest? She should cut her losses and sell. Two: Jean's already been told she needs care, and she may well need more in the future. Whether that's in her cottage or a residential home, she'd soon run out of savings, and Fox Farm wouldn't cover it. She'd have to sell.'

Alex's mouth set in a thin line. 'Any more delightful options?'

'Third: Jean could die. She will eventually, of course, but after a major stroke, it could be sooner rather than later. Then we'd sell. In other words, two of those three scenarios involve *having* to sell, and the other has a strong case for selling… Hence, no point in taking this nonsensical investment any further.'

Alex's blood had run cold at the clinical way Sebastian talked about their aunt's death. 'You're trying to protect your inheritance, aren't you?'

'It's not about inheritance.' Sebastian's tone was indignant but unconvincing. 'It's about financial sense, and it applies whether Fox Farm is sold before or after Jean dies – the chances of it selling as a business are slim, more likely as just property and land, therefore all your "improvements" wouldn't have any effect on the price we could get for it.'

Alex noted the 'we', as though this was his and Sebastian's decision, not their aunt's. 'Is that all Fox Farm means to you? A bottom line?'

'Perhaps you should try to see it the same way.'

'I *can't* see it the same way, because Aunt Jean doesn't. She's put her *entire life* into starting it from nothing and building it up into a successful place that people love.'

'Not so successful, though, is it?'

'She made a few poor decisions, that's all. I wish she'd come to me.'

'Well, you're involved now, and look what's happening. You're worn out, pandering to an old woman's pet project, with no vision as to how it'll pan out.'

That was the last straw. 'I'm worn out, alright – by you and your negative attitude. And I wish you'd stop referring to Aunt Jean as an old woman, saying it won't be long before she'll die. She's only seventy-two. That's nothing these days. And she has the will of a woman half her age.' He stood. 'Please go, Sebastian.'

'You'd see I'm right if you could stop being so sentimental.' His cousin stood, too. 'One more thing. I want to see the accounts.'

'You *what?*'

'You've had access to them. I'm as entitled as you are.'

'No, you're not. Your name isn't on the power of attorney, remember?'

'Be careful,' Sebastian warned. 'That power of attorney hasn't gone through yet, so neither are you, officially. You looked at Jean's accounts, made all those decisions, without any proper standing.'

'I didn't need it. Aunt Jean has mental capacity. I'm simply carrying out her wishes.'

'I have equal standing as her other nephew.'

'That's the whole point, Sebastian – you don't any more.'

'So, you won't let me see them? Sounds like you have something to hide.'

'No,' Alex said through gritted teeth. 'Despite my better judgement, I've kept you in the loop ever since you showed your unpleasant face here, but that's as far as I'm willing to go.'

'I could ask Jean's permission.'

'You could, if you *want* to harangue a poor woman recovering from a stroke for no good reason. Let me know if that works out for you, and I'll comply. Now, please leave before I do something I regret.'

Sebastian headed for the door, then turned back. 'Oh, and I'm not happy about that Daisy woman.'

'What the hell do you mean by that?'

'If you ask me, she's getting far too involved for someone with no status. Jean's fond of her, I gather, and Daisy's using that to get what she wants. Wheedling her way in with you, too; using the fact that, for some obscure reason, you fancy her.'

For some obscure reason? 'Oh, and what's she hoping to achieve with these Machiavellian ploys?' Alex's tone was dangerous.

Sebastian either didn't notice or didn't care. 'You really can't see it? She's making herself indispensable to Fox Farm, right?'

'She *has* been indispensable,' Alex agreed. 'She's been up to her eyes with the artists on Aunt Jean's behalf. She wasn't paid a penny and lost precious time on her own work. The same applies to the times she helped me. If you took a proper interest in what goes on around here instead of concentrating on the pound signs ringing up behind your eyeballs every time you think about selling off Aunt Jean's life's work, you'd know that.'

Sebastian let that slide. 'Oh, come on, Alex. The woman even scrubbed floors for you. Why aren't the others helping?'

'The others have done what they can, but they're employees, and beyond a certain point they expect to be paid overtime – which we can't afford. That's why I've done as much of it myself as I could. Daisy's not an employee and hasn't expected to be paid. She's doing it out of the goodness of her heart – something you would know very little about.'

'You're a naïve fool.' Sebastian shook his head in contempt. 'She's either after you—'

At that, Alex snorted. 'According to you, I'm not worth having and never have been!'

'Or she's after something to do with Fox Farm. It's my guess that she wants to carry on taking advantage of Jean and live here rent-free *ad infinitum*. Why else would she do all that?'

'Because she's a good person.'

'Hmmph. Like I said. Naïve.'

When Alex's fists clenched at his sides, Sebastian smirked. 'On the feisty side nowadays, young Alexander, aren't you? I thought growing flowers was supposed to soothe the soul. Perhaps you take after your old man, after all.'

And with that – the worst thing he could have thrown at Alex; the secret fear that Alex spent his life forcing deep down into his subconscious – Sebastian took his leave… which was a very good thing. Alex was a placid man. He'd seen enough sparks of temper from his father to know he never wanted to be that person. But Sebastian brought out the worst in him, and Alex hated him for that.

*

Daisy was determined to go for a walk on Wednesday. It was a beautiful day, although she wrapped up against the cold.

The banging and the muffled curses she heard as she came out of her studio drew her across the yard and around the back of the barn, where Alex was dragging large wooden pieces from an outbuilding.

'What on earth…?' she asked him.

'Sodding Santa's sodding cabin,' he muttered.

Daisy laughed. 'That's not a very festive response.'

'Best you'll get from me.'

'Let me help.'

'You can't lift them.'

Ignoring him, Daisy went inside and pushed the pieces out towards him, then helped him carry them to a space in the corner between the barn and her byre.

'Will it take long to build?' she asked.

'Nah. Been doing it for years.' He frowned. 'Are you going somewhere, or do you always wrap yourself in ten protective layers to greet me?'

'Ha! No, I was going for a walk. Haven't had a decent one in ages.'

Alex gave her a wistful look. 'Well, enjoy.'

'Why don't you come?'

'I can't. I… Oh, why not? Let me grab an extra layer.'

Suitably bundled up, they set out. A pheasant scuttled in front of them as they turned onto a footpath that led through a small copse of beech trees until it opened out, looking down over the glittering ribbon of river spanned by the stone bridge at the village.

The Masons Inn, the village store, Dot's Copper Kettle café and B & B, the Jolly Fisherman takeaway huddled side by side, the village hall and ancient church behind, its steeple poking up above the houses.

Alex breathed deeply. 'You can never get tired of a view like that.'

'No.' Daisy smiled, pleased that she'd dragged him away from hard toil.

Alex turned her towards him. 'Maybe I didn't only mean the landscape.'

'That's a cheesy line, Alex Hirst.' She waved a hand at her many layers of ancient outerwear. 'This is not a view. *That's* a view.'

'It's all subjective.' He leaned in for a kiss, his lips lightly touching hers, warming them. 'We haven't done this for a while.'

'No. You've been busy. And your pesky cousin keeps on turning up.'

'He's not here now.'

'Wouldn't put it past him.'

'Nah. Sebastian's a city boy. He doesn't like the countryside. Stop thinking about him. Think about me.'

That's not hard.

Daisy leaned in for another kiss. This time, Alex's arms came around her waist, pulling her close. They wore too many layers for the contact to be sexy, but the kiss smouldered with more heat than should be possible on an extremely cold winter's day in Yorkshire.

'Mmmm.' Daisy's eyes flew open. 'Oops! Did I say that out loud?'

'You did.' Alex grinned, looking pleased with himself. 'Come on. It's too cold to stand around.'

He took her gloved hand and kept hold of it as they went down the gentle slope towards the river, past bare rosehip branches that still held red fruit and burdock whose burs Daisy knew she would find stuck to her clothing when she got back.

'How's Jean?' she asked.

Alex filled her in on Jean's new ward. Daisy was pleased to hear about her progress. She was less pleased to hear about Sebastian's constant interference, in particular his wanting to see the accounts.

'The cheek! What right has he got to throw his weight around like that?'

'No legal right,' Alex said wearily. '*Some* moral right as Jean's relative.'

'Rubbish! I hate the idea of Jean sitting in the hospital, having to listen to him. You and she discussed everything, and she's happy with it.'

'I know. But…'

Daisy turned to him. 'You're having doubts?'

'Ah, I don't know. I couldn't see any other option – Aunt Jean refused to sell, and Fox Farm was haemorrhaging money. I had to do what I did. But… I'm sure you already guessed we used some of her savings for the alterations. That's all well and good if we get it back. But what if I've made a colossal mistake, and we don't?' He bit his lip, looking more unsure of himself than Daisy had ever seen him.

'You did what Jean wants, in order to keep Fox Farm going.'

Alex ran a hand over his face. He looked so tired. 'Yes, but she's not being practical. I'm trying to bite this off in chunks, but she wants the whole pie. And it isn't sustainable, Daisy. She won't be able to run it properly when she gets back, but I can't carry on doing what I'm doing, and Fox Farm can't afford a manager. I can't see where this is all going, to be honest.'

Alarmed at his despondent tone, Daisy took his arm. 'You need to take time for your*self* and think about something else for a change. Are you going to the hospital today?'

'No. Angie's going this afternoon, and my delightful cousin's going this evening, no doubt to spread more poison.'

'Right. We are going to walk along the river to the village, get a takeaway coffee and head back to Fox Farm. You are going to build that "sodding Santa's sodding cabin", I am going to finish some work, then I'm going to feed you supper and force-feed you a Christmas movie.'

Alex looked taken aback by the way she was taking charge, but he acquiesced. 'Sounds good.' He frowned. 'Not sure about the Christmas movie, though.'

'No arguments.'

Chapter Eighteen

Alex had a great day. How did Daisy know exactly what he needed?

They enjoyed their walk, drinking their takeaway coffee from the Copper Kettle whilst leaning against the stone bridge, listening to the water tumble over rocks and watching a dipper catch its lunch. A robin came to perch on the wall a foot away from Daisy, hoping for crumbs, and they both apologised profusely to it for the lack thereof.

They walked through the village and out the other side, past the churchyard with its crumbling, lichen-covered gravestones, taking a different route back to Fox Farm, where Daisy made Alex a bacon butty to shore him up for his task ahead.

Refreshed from the walk and Daisy's company, Alex spent the afternoon contentedly enough, working on the cabin. When he was almost done, she came out to admire his handiwork.

'Impressive,' she said, hands on hips.

'Yeah. It was one of the first things Uncle William and I built together,' Alex said. 'He got the half-sawn logs from a forest estate a few miles away – he wanted flat walls on the inside and the logs on the outside. We made them into panels so it was easier to put together, but each panel couldn't be too heavy to lift. Then we added fixings to hold each panel to the next. Pitched roof. This little walkway out front for the elf to stand under the eaves – she'll probably still freeze but won't get wet if it rains. And voilà!'

Alex smiled at those memories of long summer days as a teenager, helping his uncle design and build the cabin because Aunt Jean had got it into her head that Fox Farm should have a Santa grotto ('*And I don't want a piddly little shed. I want it done proper!*').

'Now for the chair.'

Daisy helped him manoeuvre an old rocking chair from the outbuilding into the yard, and they placed it in one corner of the cabin.

'Cushions? A rug?' she asked.

'They might be in Aunt Jean's cottage.'

Daisy harrumphed. 'If you think I'm knocking to ask Mr Giles, you can think again. He'd probably drag me in so he could decide which method of strangling works best. Did your mum tell you she's now a detective chief inspector?'

'She did. It really cheered her up. I have a feeling she'll be using that anecdote for a long while.'

Daisy chuckled. 'We can use something of mine.' She popped inside and came back out with a cushion and small rag rug.

'You don't mind? They might get damp.'

'They're old. And it looks cosier.'

'Thanks. Next, the tree.'

'This is quite a job, isn't it? Now I know why you were so reticent when Angie first mentioned it.'

'That feels like a lifetime ago already.'

Daisy helped him set up and decorate a small, artificial tree in a corner of the cabin, then she strung lights along the eaves while he extended electrics from the barn to the cabin. When he switched the lights on against the dusk, Alex smiled with satisfaction. It really did look like Santa's log cabin, inside and out, and with a sack of gifts next to the little tree, it would be perfect. Perhaps it had been worth his while, after all.

'I'm frozen,' Daisy declared. 'Hot cider?'

'You don't need to ask me twice!'

The warm alcohol thawed him, even made him feel a little woozy on an empty stomach. Daisy's cheeks were rosy red from the cold and the cider.

Man, she's so pretty. Those brown eyes, like a gentle doe's, and that smile... Alex stared into his glass, as if the thoughts had jumped out at him from the golden liquid there.

'Time for something to eat,' Daisy declared, making Alex wonder if she was thinking the same thing – not about his eyes or smile, but about alcohol on an empty stomach. 'I didn't plan this, so it'll be pot luck.'

Alex let her get organised in peace while he wandered her studio, studying her pieces on the wall, her style familiar to him now.

When Daisy came back out, he was lingering over one of her winter scenes.

'Jules loves that one,' she told him. 'She wishes she could afford to treat herself.'

'Jules deserves a big, fat bonus this year,' Alex said with feeling. 'They all do, for the extra work they've put in these past few weeks. I'm not sure Riverside can stretch to much, but I do know chocolates and wine won't do the trick.'

Daisy mused a while, then clicked her fingers. 'Do Kieran and Jim like beer?'

'Does a plant need water?'

She laughed. 'I saw an advert online for a new craft brewery near Skipton. They have a Christmas offer on – twenty per cent off gift crates or something. Can't remember the name...' She pulled her phone from her pocket, tapped until she found what she wanted, and handed it to him.

He read the advert. 'Perfect. You're a star.'

'Doesn't solve the Jules problem, though,' Daisy said – over-brightly, Alex thought. She returned to her hob, stirring a pan before muttering, 'She's attractive, isn't she?'

'Jules? Yes, she is.' Was it his imagination, or did Daisy's shoulders droop? *Is she jealous? Only one way to find out.* Alex moved close behind her, ostensibly to peer into the pan. 'Does that bother you?'

'Bother me? Why should it?'

'I'm not sure. But you and I...'

'What about you and I?'

He gently removed the wooden spoon she had in a death grip and turned her to face him. 'We have a little something going on. Now you're talking about Jules.'

'Well, I wouldn't want this little something, as you put it, to tread on anyone's toes.'

'No toes to tread on. When I first hired her, she was married. Eventually she got divorced, but that made no difference to our dynamic. Jules and I get along like a house on fire, but there's nothing else between us and there never has been.' He placed a hand on her cheek. 'Unlike you and me.'

He brought his mouth down on hers, gently at first, then more firmly, deepening the kiss. Her response was... knee-melting, frankly.

Oh, these kisses are killing me. I want more.

That was enough to make him break away. This was becoming more than a flirting game. And whatever his mother thought about Daisy being good for him, he would have to think carefully before he risked hurting her. He cared too much about her to do that.

'What's for supper?' he asked lightly.

'Oh. Er. Fancy ravioli your mother treated me to from the deli in Settle, with pasta sauce. Not sure the salad leaves I have in are still edible, though.'

Daisy rummaged in her small fridge, while Alex regretted breaking the spell. But until he knew how far he wanted to take this, it was necessary.

*

They ate at her sales counter. The ravioli was rich and warming, and Daisy was pleased with the relaxed look on Alex's face as he sat back, one hand on his middle. She'd seen too much of his worn expression lately – unsurprising, given the circumstances – but she'd been even more worried on their walk today, when he'd admitted to all those doubts about Jean and Fox Farm. Daisy had struggled to find words of comfort. Much of what he'd said was true – it *was* a gamble, and he was bound to feel responsible for the consequences. Daisy was glad that he'd felt able to confide in her, though, and happy that she'd taken him in hand for the day. He seemed better for it.

And now for the promised movie. 'What do you fancy?' she asked him.

A wolfish grin spread across his face. 'That's quite a question.'

'I meant movies, you idiot. Any favourites?'

'Not really.'

'Jean didn't make you watch *her* favourites?'

'I didn't spend Christmases at Fox Farm. They were the one holiday I spent at home.'

'Ah.' Daisy could imagine what Christmases must have been like at the Hirst household – wary, volatile, dreary. *Poor Alex.* 'But I bet you've spent your adult Christmases here?'

'Naturally. Aunt Jean's Christmas cake with Wensleydale cheese; Angie's mince pies... A traditional Christmas Eve trip with Aunt Jean to Bolton Abbey, walking along the river, a hot drink at the café, feeding the ducks. And then Christmas Day, sometimes just the two of us, sometimes with one or two of her friends from the village, occasionally my mother. Always so much Christmas dinner we can hardly budge, then card games – no television allowed.' He sighed. 'There won't be any of that this year.'

'There might be. Let's keep our fingers crossed, shall we?' Daisy shot him an encouraging smile. 'So, as you were deprived of Christmas movies, it looks like it's up to me to choose. *Love Actually* or *Elf*?'

'I haven't seen either, but *Elf* sounds like fun. Especially after a day building a cabin for an elf to stand outside.'

Interesting. Instant avoidance of anything with 'Love' in the title...

'*Elf* it is, then.' Daisy led him through to her room and reached for her laptop.

Confused, Alex looked around. 'You don't have a TV?'

'Where would it go?'

'Ah. Point taken. Sorry. I should have asked you round to my house. There's a TV *and* you wouldn't have had to cook.'

'Do you have much in your fridge?'

'Mouldy cheese? Out-of-date ham?'

Daisy made a face. 'Tempting, but no.' She looked around. 'The studio's too uncomfortable to sit through a whole movie, but I hadn't thought about how small this room is with two people in it. Would you prefer your house?'

'You've seen that place, Daisy. It's like a mausoleum. I like it here. It's cosy.'

'Well, it's about to get a whole lot cosier, because the only way we can do this is to sit on the bed together with the laptop on our legs.'

Alex raised an eyebrow. 'I never imagined I'd get into your bed so soon, Daisy Claybourne!'

Am I blushing? I'm thirty-one, for goodness' sake! 'I didn't know you wanted to,' she managed a comeback.

'You have no idea,' he muttered under his breath, but Daisy heard it. 'I'll wash the dishes while you set it up.'

He clattered around at the small sink in the kitchenette area while Daisy fiddled with her laptop, wondering if this was a good idea after all. Her bed was a single, and Alex was a big bloke.

There's cosy and there's cosy...

For the next two hours, shoulder to shoulder with Alex, their backs against the headboard, their thighs pressed together, Daisy sensed Alex shudder when he laughed; felt his breath on her cheek when he commented; caught the light woodsy scent she was coming to know, a scent of the outdoors... It was a good job she knew the movie inside out, because she would have struggled to follow it otherwise.

When it was over, Alex stretched his arms over his head, bringing one down around her shoulders and resting his head on top of hers. 'Thank you. I didn't think I'd enjoy that, but it was perfect.' He gave her a quizzical look. 'I didn't have you down as a Christmas movie kind of girl.'

She shrugged. 'It's my friend Grace's fault. She's obsessed with them. She made me watch every single one in existence when we were at college.'

'Do you see her much?'

'No. We chat and message, but neither of us has the funds for to-ing and fro-ing.' Daisy beamed. 'But she got a commission, so she's coming up at Christmas!'

'That's great. Do you usually spend Christmas alone?'

'Mostly. But last year, I spent it with Jack.'

'I bet that was a barrel of laughs.'

'It's only one day a year, isn't it? But this year will be special, with Grace here.'

'I'm glad. Well, I should go. It's late.' He wriggled off the bed, walked through to the studio, glanced again at the snow scene and took his wallet from his back pocket. 'Will you wrap that for me? Jules should get a decent thank you this year.'

'She'll love it, I promise.' Daisy took the canvas down and wrapped it carefully. 'Ten per cent off.'

'No, Daisy, you can't…'

'I can and I am.'

'Well, thank you.' He pulled on his jacket, then hesitated before asking, 'Are you going to the barn dance in the village hall on Saturday night?'

The question took Daisy by surprise. She hadn't been to that event before, even though Jack had tried to get her to go last year.

'I hadn't thought about it. Anyway, I don't have a partner.' *Oops. Did that sound pointed?*

'You don't need one. Everyone just turns up. But you could come with me, if you like. Aunt Jean's insisting I make the effort.'

He sounded more awkward than a thirty-five-year-old man should. *Because he's asking me on a date? Or because he isn't, and he doesn't want it to sound like he is?*

'I'd love to. Thanks.'

He bent his head to kiss her lightly. 'G'night, Daisy.'

As she watched him walk across the yard, Daisy wondered if this was all getting too complicated. Becoming friends was one thing. But the kisses – no longer occasional, more of a habit – and now attending a public event together? Whether Alex saw it as a date or not, she suspected the rest of the village would. Did he realise that? Would it bother him? She knew nothing about his personal life.

And if Alex did intend it as a date, how did *she* feel about that? Daisy had worked hard at being self-sufficient, and she'd learned to be content in her self-protecting bubble. Why wreck it?

It's only a barn dance, Daisy. Like Alex said, the whole village goes. It's no big deal.

*

'Did you sell lots of trees today?' Aunt Jean asked Alex late on Saturday afternoon.

'Loads, but my arm aches from holding the trees at the top and trying to stand to one side so people can see them properly. You wouldn't believe how long they take to decide – too tall, too small, too broad, not evenly shaped, not bushy enough, have you got anything narrower? Let alone the decisions over varieties – Fraser Fir, Norway Spruce, Nordmann Fir, Scots Pine...'

His aunt's lips twitched. 'Did you hog the netting machine again?'

'How did you guess?' Alex loved that thing – feeding a bushy tree in at one end and watching it come out at the other, neatly pinioned by net. So simple, and yet like magic. It brought out the boy in him. He'd been sorry to hand over to Kieran so he could fit in a quick hospital visit before the barn dance tonight.

'So, you made money today *and* had fun. Couldn't ask for more. Talking of fun… What time are you picking Daisy up?'

'Seven fifteen.'

His aunt beamed. 'I'm so pleased you asked her. She's a lovely girl.'

'Yes, she is. You've got what you wanted, so you can stop meddling now. What about Sebastian? Will you let him see the accounts?'

'Cert… Abs…' Jean growled in frustration. 'No. We fell out.'

'Ah.' Alex wasn't sure if that was ideal. It was good that Aunt Jean was standing up for herself, but he didn't want Sebastian to feel driven to make life difficult for them all. 'In what way?'

'I told him I didn't see why he needs to see them. That I trust you. He said I should get a second opinion. In the end, I told him I was too tired to talk.' She huffed. 'I wasn't – I just wanted him to go away. Hoped he might cool down and forget about it.'

'But he didn't?'

'No. He was back again yesterday, harping on. I had to be firm. Eric and his mum should've been firmer with him when he was little, if you ask me. He said he had a right. I said that being my nephew doesn't give him that right. He said, "In that case, why have I spent all this time up here, staying at that awful B & B?" I told him that I *thought* it was so he could visit me, because he *cared* about me.' Her voice wobbled.

Alex cursed Sebastian. *What a self-serving, unfeeling…*

'He does care, in his own way, Aunt Jean.' Alex struggled to believe that, but he knew his aunt needed to. 'He's used to being in charge, that's all. Thinks he…' Alex was about to say that his cousin felt he had a stake in the farm, but stopped himself.

Jean fixed him with a knowing look. 'Because he's in my will.'

'Maybe. The will puts him on an equal footing with me, so I suppose he expects to have an equal footing in everything else. But once the power of attorney comes through, he'll have to accept that's not the case.'

'Anyway.' Aunt Jean waved a hand, dismissing the topic. 'Angie's pleased with Jamie in the café. Says he's like a breath of fresh air. Jamie phoned to tell me the new elf was in the year below him at school, bless him. Sue's promised to visit again soon.'

'You haven't heard from Lisa?'

'No, but she's got enough on with the gallery and her family. Has the Santa cabin been busy?'

'I don't know. I wasn't at Fox Farm today. I had to be at Riverside to sell Christmas trees, remember?' He immediately bit his lip. 'Sorry.'

To make up for being sharp with her, Alex came up with a few snippets of gossip from Riverside.

By the time he left, under instruction to dress smartly and shave before picking Daisy up, Alex was already tired. Finding Sebastian on his doorstep didn't improve matters.

'Where the hell have you been?'

'Hello to you, too.' Alex unlocked his door. 'How long have you been here? I wasn't under the impression we had an arrangement.'

'Fifteen minutes. And we didn't.' Sebastian pushed his way in, then looked around in undisguised dismay. 'Haven't done much with this place, have you?'

'No, but there's this thing called time, Sebastian, and I find I only have so much of it.'

'Why don't you get someone else in to do things? Oh, that's right. That would cost money, and you don't have much of that, either.'

Alex tried for patience. 'Are you here to insult me and my home, or can I help in some other way?'

'Not going to offer me a drink?'

'I was hoping you wouldn't be here long enough.'

'Then I'll get to the point.' Sebastian's expression was hard. 'Jean has denied me access to the accounts. Was that your doing?'

'No. You got to her before I could. But I'm hoping that'll be an end to the matter.'

'I haven't decided about that yet.'

Does that mean he intends to take some fancy, expensive legal advice?

'I'm going back to London for a while,' Sebastian said. 'I may speak to my solicitor.'

Nothing if not predictable.

'You're well within your rights, of course,' Alex said, knowing his voice sounded weary. *Don't send him away in a combative mood, Alex. It won't achieve anything.* 'But Aunt Jean is of sound mind, and you won't be able to prove otherwise. It's her choice who she confides in, who she asks to act on her behalf. You keep harping on about preserving her funds. Don't drag her into a situation where she has to pay a solicitor to fight you. That will only eat away at what she has.' Alex closed his eyes. The idea of prancing around at a barn dance felt quite beyond him. Opening them again, he said, 'Now, if you'll excuse me, I need to have a bath and a nap – probably at the same time – before I go out.'

'With Daisy?' Sebastian couldn't have sounded more scornful if he tried.

'We're going to the barn dance – along with the rest of the village.' Suddenly keen to build any bridge that might stop Sebastian making their lives difficult, Alex said, 'You're welcome to join us.'

Sebastian snorted. 'A barn dance? You must be joking! What am I, a country cowboy? I have work to do. I'm leaving in the morning… although I'll be back soon.'

No doubt you will. 'Have a good journey.' *And don't hurry back.*

Chapter Nineteen

The festive atmosphere had gathered pace at Fox Farm. Since Daisy's day with Alex midweek, he had strung lights along the eaves of all the buildings, and a family of fairy-lit wicker reindeer had taken up residence outside the café. With all the lights twinkling, the huge Christmas tree in the centre of the courtyard and Jules' greenery on all the doors, Fox Farm looked like the perfect country Christmas. It was magical.

Daisy's studio looked good with the homemade bunting – she received several compliments – and she noticed customers happily humming along to her Christmas playlist. As Sue had said, *'the old 'uns are the good 'uns'*, and relaxed customers often led to a sale.

Saturday was opening day for Santa's cabin, and the queues were impressive. Daisy spotted Jamie running over from time to time with another sack of presents – presumably Santa had a mobile phone to call for extra supplies. She felt sorry for Lauren, the teenage elf, looking cold in her elf dress and tights. *Rather her than me.* Daisy took her and Santa – a.k.a. Lisa's dad, Mike – mugs of tea when she could spare the time, and she saw Sue come over with hot drinks, too.

Mid-afternoon, they were treated to a glorious hour of carol-singing by the church choir who spent their December Saturdays moving from venue to venue around the village, their voices soaring into the cold air, making everyone feel a little goodwill to all men.

Finally, all was quiet, and Daisy had time to talk to Grace before getting ready for the barn dance – an invitation that Grace took much delight in.

'Very "country".' Grace made quote marks in the air. 'What are you wearing?'

'Jeans and a shirt. It's a barn dance, not cocktails in Mayfair.'

'Has that poor boy seen you in anything other than denim?'

'Only pyjamas.'

'Oooh!'

'Hardly. That was one morning when he called early. I looked a mess.'

'You look cute when you look a mess.'

'If you say so.'

Grace's dark-brown eyes were piercing. 'There is a great deal you're not telling me, Daisy Claybourne. I want to hear it *all*. Now spill.'

Cornered, Daisy spilled. Too much had been happening to keep it all in, and Grace was the only person she could speak to. The odd cup of tea with Jack, occasional drinks in Grassington with a couple of women she'd worked with at the pub… They were just social relationships, and the way things had been, she hadn't even been doing those lately. She got on well with Angie, Sue and Jamie, but not in the *confidante* sort of way. She was closest to Jean, but she could hardly talk to *her* about this!

Half an hour later, Grace goggled. 'Let me get this straight. You've been flirting with and kissing this hunky guy on a regular basis without telling me. You watched TV *in bed* together. You met his *mother*. And yet you don't know if he's had a love of his life that escaped, or even a recent girlfriend?'

'Correct.'

'Well, *that* needs fixing. And tonight's as good a night as any.'

'We'll be busy.'

'Getting sweaty together? Yeah. But you'll have to take a break from that sometime.'

'I'll see. How about you?'

Grace looked at her watch. 'You need to get ready now, so I'll move onto the main news.' Her face fell. 'Daisy, I'm so sorry, but I won't be able to come and see you, after all.'

A lump formed in Daisy's throat. 'Why?'

'My family have booked us all plane tickets to Nigeria. My grandparents aren't well, and they haven't seen us for five years. My parents want to go, and they asked me and my sister to go, too. I couldn't say no.'

Daisy put on a bright voice and a false smile. 'Of course you couldn't. Family is important.'

Grace looked miserable. 'I've let you down.'

'Don't be silly. It wasn't set in stone, and even if it was, this would totally override it. I hope you have a fab time and your grandparents enjoy the visit.'

'Thank you for being so sweet. I love you. Now, go and put on a *decent* shirt and a *clean* pair of jeans. And there's this amazing stuff called mascara and lipstick. It comes in tubes...'

'Okay, okay. I'll doll up for you.'

'Not for me, my lovely. For your man.'

'He's not my man,' Daisy said crossly, still terribly disappointed at their plans falling through.

'Sure sounds like it to me.'

*

An hour previously, Alex couldn't imagine being ready for the barn dance. But by the time he'd soaked Sebastian out of his system, followed Jean's instructions to shave and dress smartly (a newer shirt, newer jeans and unscuffed boots), he couldn't wait to see Daisy again. After their Christmas movie evening, he'd wanted to back up a little; make sure he wasn't making a mistake with her. And yet here he was, like a teenager going on a first date.

When he arrived at her studio, there was no sign of her, but the door was unlocked, so he let himself in.

'Hello there!'

Alex jumped a mile, spinning around to see Daisy's laptop on the counter, from which a very attractive woman appraised him.

'You must be the infamous Alex,' she declared.

'Er. Yes. Hi?' he managed.

'I'm Grace. Pleased to meet you.'

'Daisy's friend from art college? Pleased to meet you, too.'

'I've been hearing a lot about you,' Grace said, her smile mischievous, and Alex could immediately see why this woman was Daisy's best friend. Openness and humour shone from her eyes.

Alex gave a nervous chuckle. 'Why are you here on your own?'

'Daisy dashed off to get changed and forgot to disconnect. I was going to, but then I thought, why not hang on? See if Alex turns up?' She grinned. 'You're worth the wait.'

'Er. Thanks?'

Her expression turned serious. 'I'm glad I caught you. I want to talk to you about Christmas. Did you know I was meant to be coming up for a few days?'

'Yes. Daisy's looking forward to it.' His face fell. 'You said "was"?'

'Yes. My family are flying us all out to Nigeria to see my grandparents. I didn't want to let Daisy down, but...'

'I'm sure she understands.'

'She does, because she's a sweet-hearted sap. But Christmas is a difficult time of year for her. I don't want her to be alone too much. Will you keep an eye on her for me?'

'Of course.' *Daisy shouldn't be alone at Christmas.* 'I don't know about my aunt yet, but if she's home by then, I'll make sure Daisy's invited.'

'And if your aunt isn't home?'

'Then Daisy and I can be depressed together.'

Grace's eyes twinkled. 'I'm sure there are better things you two could do together, but I'll refrain from making suggestions.'

'Ha. Hmmm.'

'Aww, and he even blushes.'

Alex was grateful for Daisy's appearance. She looked startled when she saw him chatting with Grace.

'Oh! Sorry, Grace, did I leave you turned on?'

'And again, I'll refrain from comment.' Grace cast Alex a smouldering look. 'Nice to meet you.'

'You too.' *Gosh, these arty London women are forward, aren't they?*

Daisy shut down her laptop, laughing at his expression. 'Are you okay?'

'I'm not sure. Grace is very…'

'Yes, she is. *Very.* Come on.'

Daisy was quiet on the short drive to the village, presumably still upset at Grace's news, so he let her be. He couldn't say anything without admitting that Grace had made him promise to keep Daisy occupied at Christmas, and he didn't want her to think he might include her out of pity.

As they parked along the roadside and walked towards the village hall, Daisy said, 'This makes no sense at all. You've just driven out of the village to fetch me all the way back into it. And you won't be able to have much to drink.'

'I don't need much to drink.' *You're enough of an intoxication.* 'I don't trust that old banger of yours in the dark. I wanted to be gallant.'

'Well, thank you, kind sir.' Daisy linked her arm in his.

When they walked into the old building next to the church, Daisy's face lit up, a smile spreading across her face as she took in the Yorkshire Rose bunting, brightly lit bulbs strung along the rafters, and the Christmas tree taking up so much of the stage that Alex wondered where the band would go.

'This is wonderful,' she breathed.

Alex could feel her enthusiasm rubbing off on him. 'Harold and Maureen are on the committee. They do a grand job. Let's grab a seat while we can, shall we?' He led her to a small table in a corner. Bigger groups had taken long trestle tables lining all four sides of the hall. 'Look, there's Jack.'

'I should go and talk to him,' Daisy said. 'Can I grab you a beer?'

'I can allow myself the one. Thanks.'

Alex settled back in his seat, taking in the noise and babble. There was a real community feel to it – people waving and calling across the room to each other, or standing at each other's tables chattering. This was Winterbridge at its best – although if you liked to keep yourself to yourself, it didn't always suit. His eyes drifted to Daisy, who had stopped by Jack's table on the way to the temporary bar and was chatting with him, her face animated, her hands moving as she spoke. Her jeans fit her perfectly – no paint tonight – and her checked shirt was open enough to allow a glimpse of pale skin at her throat. He couldn't drag his eyes away.

Are you falling for her, Alex?

Don't be daft. I haven't fallen for anyone so far. I'm not about to start now.

He was mercifully distracted by Harold's wife, Maureen, but his relief didn't last long.

'I saw you arrive with Daisy,' she said pointedly.

'I gave her a lift, Maureen, that's all.'

'If you say so, love.'

Best to distract her from that *line of enquiry, or we'll be the talk of the village.* 'I went to see Aunt Jean today…'

It was fifteen minutes before Daisy came to his rescue, bringing a couple of beers with her.

'Sorry. I owed Jack a chat.'

'No worries. Maureen kept me company. Sit down and don't you dare leave me again.'

Daisy laughed. 'Aren't we supposed to mingle?'

'I don't want to mingle. I want to be with you.' *Take it easy, Alex.* 'Besides, there'll be plenty of opportunity once the music gets going.'

'Jack's convinced we're an item,' Daisy told him.

'Does that bother you?'

'I don't know. Does it bother you?'

'I don't know. Are we? An item?'

'I don't know. Are we?'

Alex rolled his eyes. 'What I do know is that we're the worst conversationalists ever.' He hesitated. 'So, have you… been involved with anyone recently?' *Subtle, Alex.*

But Daisy took the question in her stride. 'No. My relationship history's rather limited and boring, I'm afraid. To pick out the highlights? Four months with a lad in the sixth form. Turned out he was two-timing me with twins in a neighbouring school. Or is that three-timing? Then two years at art college with Eoin, an Irish lad with a soft, southern accent that melted my bones.'

A stab of jealousy took Alex by surprise. His Yorkshire accent couldn't compete with that, could it? 'What happened?'

'We graduated. He wanted to try Dublin. I couldn't see the point of swapping one city for another. If I had to be a city girl for my art's sake, it may as well be the devil I knew.' She shrugged. 'We were drifting apart anyway.'

'And since?'

'Not much to report. A few dates in Leeds that didn't work out – friends of friends. When I moved to Grassington, a few locals asked me out. I agreed now and again, but nobody appealed for more than a date or two.' She sighed. 'I'm an insular kind of person. Dating doesn't come easily.'

'Does that apply to me?'

Daisy hesitated. 'Well, first off, we just concluded that we don't know if dating is what we're doing. But whatever it is has grown out of getting to know each other, becoming friends, and that's been nice. Less forced.' She turned the tables on him. 'How about you? Do you date much?'

Alex was saved by the screech of a microphone, Maureen shouting 'Testing, testing', and then the small band began to play.

Keen to avoid answering – they were here to dance, weren't they? – Alex dragged Daisy out onto the floor.

She thew herself into it with good humour, not blinking an eye as partners swapped with alarming regularity, directed by the caller, and she was spun around the floor. Alex was always happy when Daisy landed back with him for a brief time before being spun elsewhere.

By the time the caller announced a break, everyone was out of breath but smiling and laughing.

At the bar, waiting for orange juice, Gary nudged Alex's arm. 'I see you brought a date, mate. Ha. That rhymes.'

Alex rolled his eyes. 'Daisy. And not a date. We're… accompanying each other.'

'If you say so. She's got a great figure. Nice eyes.'

'Hey!' Gary's wife dug him in the ribs. 'You noticed her *eyes*?'

'I partnered her a couple of times. What am I supposed to do, Chelle? Better to stare at her eyes than her cleavage.'

'You dare…'

'Married bliss, eh?' Gary chuckled. 'Where are you sitting? We could come over.'

But Chelle jabbed him in the ribs again. 'We're sitting somewhere else,' she said firmly. 'And their table's too small.'

'But I…'

'Don't be so *dim*, Gary. Come with me.'

Smiling after them, Alex got the juice and walked back to Daisy, but it seemed he wasn't off the hook.

'So, you were going to tell me about your past relationships?' Daisy said.

Alex had always made it clear to the women he dated that he didn't want anything long term. Most accepted it. Some thought they could change his mind, forcing him to end it sooner than he might have. He just wasn't sure how to explain all that to Daisy without sounding uncaring. He had always cared about the women he'd chosen to see – just not enough.

'I… haven't wanted to get too involved up until now.' *There it is again: 'Up until now'. You used that phrase with Mum, too.* 'When I was younger, I was working, learning my trade; helping Aunt Jean and Uncle William. Once I started Riverside, I didn't feel there was room for me to commit to anything serious.'

Daisy gave him a studied look. 'Your parents' situation can't have helped. It must have tainted your view of relationships. Of marriage.'

'It didn't help. But I'm not stupid – I know other people can be happy. Look at Aunt Jean and Uncle William. Still, I always felt the odds were too hit-and-miss for my liking. Didn't fancy my chances.'

'Alex, you don't subscribe to that old "acorn not falling far from the tree" saying, do you? Turning out like your father? Because you couldn't possibly! I know I never met him, but you're nothing like that.'

This is getting a little too close to home. 'I used to worry about that when I was younger,' Alex admitted. He'd never told anyone that, although his mother and Aunt Jean both guessed. 'Now I'm older, more mature, I'd like to think you're right. Apart from when I'm with Sebastian. He brings out the worst in me.'

'I should imagine he brings out the worst in most people.' Daisy smiled. 'I reckon that if you don't want a long-term relationship because it doesn't fit with your lifestyle, your needs, your dreams, that's fine. But you shouldn't avoid them because of your childhood. That would be too sad.'

*

Daisy had had a wonderful evening. Why on earth didn't she go last year, with Jack? Had her insular nature really made her so unsociable?

Jack had been chuffed to see her there tonight, though, and Daisy had loved watching him gad about the dance floor – well, shuffle, but he'd had a good time, and everyone went easy on him. The same could be said for many of the older residents – they all joined in, and nobody had an arm pulled out of its socket by overzealous young 'uns.

'You've got yourself a fine young man in Alex,' Jack had said. 'Could do a lot worse.'

'I'm sure I could, but…'

'Runs his own business. Hard-workin'. Handsome. But he's a slippery one, yon Alex is. Nobody's managed to tie 'im down yet. You might be t'exception to t'rule, lass.'

Daisy wasn't sure about that. Alex had been candid with her about his past relationships and the fact that he avoided anything serious.

Does that matter? Aren't you two just flirting and kissing? Do you want more than that?

All these thoughts flitted through her head as she and Alex pulled on their jackets, left the hall and carefully drove the narrow lanes back to Fox Farm.

As she climbed out of the truck, Daisy pointed to Jean's cottage. 'I never thought to ask Mr Giles if he wanted to join us.'

'That would've put a dampener on the evening! Material for a new book – *Slaughter at the Village Hall* or something equally cheery.' Alex shuddered. 'Anyway, he must've seen the posters all over the place.' He draped an arm around her shoulder. 'Your trouble is, you're too soft.' He glanced over at Santa's cabin. 'Did it look busy today?'

'*Really* busy. Does it make much money?'

'Aunt Jean sees it more as a community service than money-making.' Alex gave an indulgent shake of his head. 'But there is a profit margin, mainly because my labour's free and Mike plays Santa for the love of it. Jamie ordered and wrapped the gifts out of the good of his heart this year, too. So, the only cost is the gifts and paper, and minimum wage for whichever sixth-former we rope into being an elf.'

'I took her a couple of hot drinks,' Daisy said. 'She looked frozen in that ridiculous outfit.'

'I bet you'd look good in it.'

Daisy gave him a look that would have felled an ox. 'You'd never catch *me* in tights and pointy boots, let alone a short dress that barely covers my knickers!'

Alex grinned. 'That's a sight to think about.'

'You can think all you like, but it'll never happen.'

'Shame.'

At her door, she invited him in, but he shook his head.

'I'm too tired. And I wouldn't trust myself – not now I've got visions of you dressed as an elf in my head.'

'Pervert.'

He laughed. 'Wouldn't say no to a kiss, though.'

Daisy wouldn't say no, either. She leaned in for him to wrap his arms around her, his padded jacket soft between them as he brought his mouth down to hers. His lips were cold from the drive home, but she did her best to warm them up, delighted to hear him moan as she succeeded.

'For a woman who says she doesn't have much of a relationship history, you sure as hell know how to kiss,' he said.

Daisy smiled against his mouth. 'Right back at you.'

Another kiss, and Daisy could no longer feel her feet. 'It's too cold to stand out here. Are you sure you don't want to come in?'

'No, I need to sleep. And like I said, I don't feel particularly trustworthy right now. G'night, Daisy.'

She watched him leave, then scuttled inside, straight into her small living space where she'd left the heat on low. As she got ready for bed, Daisy grinned. No man had ever told her they couldn't trust themselves around her, suggesting she drove them wild or some such nonsense.

'He's deluded and going mad with overwork.'

But when she looked at her reflection in the bathroom mirror, a glowing face stared back at her, her eyes bright, her lips still swollen from Alex's kiss.

'Perhaps I'm going mad, too.'

Chapter Twenty

Alex spent the next few days at Riverside. He told himself he'd done enough at Fox Farm last week, putting up all the Christmas stuff, but the fact was, he was avoiding Daisy.

She had got under his skin. Seeing her, spending time with her… She'd looked radiant and happy at the barn dance. She'd even put on lipstick and mascara. For him? Or for the general populace of Winterbridge?

Their goodbye kiss had been heated despite the late-night cold, and when he'd told her he had to go because he was tired, that was true enough. It was also true that he wouldn't have trusted himself to go inside with her, because at that point in the evening he'd wanted a great deal more than he'd felt was wise.

Why wouldn't it be wise?

Because until I know that I won't hurt her, the handbrake stays on.

Christmas-tree sales were busy all week. Jim shook his head, smiling, as Alex put the gazillionth tree through the netting machine. 'You're like a kid in a sweet shop with that thing.'

'I know. Can't help it. Why, do you want a go with it?'

'Don't worry, Kieran and I see plenty of it when you're not here.' Jim hesitated. 'I'm worried you're overdoing it, Alex. Riverside, Fox

Farm, the hospital, putting up with that hoity-toity cousin of yours…
I don't know how you manage not to clock him one.'

'Years of practice, Jim. Anyway, the overwork's temporary, I hope.
I could have done without all the extras at Fox Farm last week, but it's
as though it was designed for Christmas. I couldn't not do it.'

Alex may have groused and grumbled to himself all last week, but
once Fox Farm looked as good as it did every year, he was pleased that
he hadn't stinted. Having missed out on Christmases there as a child,
as an adult he revelled in them.

'Daisy's been helping you a lot, I hear,' Jim said in an apparently casual
tone. 'And I saw you together at the barn dance. Is it more than business?'

Alex's lips twitched. 'Isn't that rather a forward question from an
employee to his boss?'

Jim shuffled on the spot. 'Jules told me to be subtle, but subtle
isn't my strong suit.'

'Why doesn't Jules ask me herself?'

'She said that hinting's got her nowhere. She thought *mano a mano*
might work better.'

Hmmm. Alex would have to lie. Until he knew for himself what
this was, he wasn't going to declare it to anyone else.

'Well, you can report that you got nowhere because there's nowhere
to get. Besides, when would I have time to indulge in anything more
than friendship right now?'

'That's true. Jack said that Daisy's a grand lass, though.'

'She is a grand lass.'

*And that's why I shouldn't let this get out of hand. Daisy deserves
someone who wants a relationship, not just a flirt and a kiss when the
mood takes him.*

*

Daisy hadn't seen Alex since the barn dance, but she knew he was just busy, as was she. Christmas shopping was in full swing now, and the studio was doing well. In between helping customers, she worked on a new painting of Fox Farm that could be at any time of year, the sky blue, the buildings in her usual quirky style.

By the time Friday night rolled around, she was exhausted, despite her two days closing midweek – one of which she had used to visit Jean, who was full of questions about Fox Farm, how the Santa cabin had done on its first weekend, and the barn dance. Daisy's head was spinning by the time the visit was over, but at least she had managed not to fess up about her and Alex's kissing habit or the fact that she fancied him more than any man she could remember fancying, including her youthful love, Eoin.

When she heard the rap on her studio door at six on Friday evening and saw Alex huddled against the biting wind that had whipped up outside, she was happy to let him in.

'Hello, stranger.'

'Hi. Sorry I haven't been around all week.'

'I understand. Tea? Beer?'

'No, thanks. I popped by to ask a favour.'

The charming smile he plastered on his face made Daisy immediately suspicious. 'What kind of favour?'

'Lauren has a sickness bug. It started this afternoon at school, and she can't stop throwing up. That means we're short of an elf for tomorrow, and I was wondering…'

Realisation dawned. 'Oh no! There is no way in this lifetime—'

'Daisy, pleeaase!' Alex held out his hands in a begging gesture. 'I've asked everyone I know.'

'I told you last weekend that you wouldn't catch me in striped tights and a short skirt, and nothing's changed.'

'But it *has* changed. Lauren's throwing up and Fox Farm has no elf. I'm desperate!'

He looked so woebegone, Daisy couldn't help but feel sorry for him – but that didn't mean she would relent. Hell would freeze over first.

'What about Jamie?'

'The café and gallery can't manage without him, not on a December weekend.'

'But there must be somebody…'

'They're either indispensable or they've point-blank refused.'

Daisy glared at him. '*I* point-blank refused.'

'Yeah, but I reckon you'll soften up if I work on you.'

The charming smile was back, and Daisy's pulse stuttered as her mind wandered off on a tangent, imagining all the ways Alex could work on her that she *wouldn't* mind.

'What about my studio?' Daisy asked indignantly. 'I can't afford to close just to be an elf!'

'Of course not. Riverside will have to manage without me so *I* can run your studio for you.'

'And you'll paint while people watch, will you? Answer their technical questions?'

'No… But you'll only be a few yards away. I can come and ask if I need to.'

'Wouldn't it be easier if *you* played the elf?'

Alex guffawed. 'I doubt I'd suit tights and a short skirt. We're not trying to frighten the kids away!'

Daisy had to laugh – and that was when Alex moved in for the kill.

'It's only for one day. Do it for Aunt Jean. Please?'

Jean. The trump card he plays every time.

Daisy sighed. This was too tiring for a Friday night. He would wear her down in the end. Might as well save them both the trouble.

'Alright. But if my backside gets too cold in those stupid tights or Santa breathes whisky over me or' – she wagged a stern finger at him – 'if I lose *one single sale*, then I'll quit before the end of the day. And if Lauren isn't back on Sunday, that's *your* problem. Understood?'

'Understood.' Alex bent to kiss the top of her head. 'Thank you. You're a star.'

'Hmmph. You'll be seeing stars if I get any comments about that outfit. What if I don't fit into it?'

Alex eyed her from top to toe. 'It'll fit. And you'll look good. I promise.'

*

Saturday morning was a harried affair for Alex. First, he made sure that Jim and Kieran were ready for the rush on trees at Riverside. Last week was probably the busiest, but he expected plenty more sales this weekend. Then he checked in with Jules, who was tying twine around sprigs of mistletoe to hang near the counter as a point-of-sale temptation. The woman had more poinsettias on display than he imagined possible, but they always sold.

'They're going like hot cakes,' she told him. 'We're selling plenty of decorations, too.' At that, she huffed. 'I thought nurseries were supposed to sell *living* things, but needs must. At this time of year, everything else fades into the background.'

'People aren't worrying about their gardens right now,' Alex agreed. 'And for once, I'm grateful for that. I haven't time to grow any living things. Besides, it's the only time of year that we give in to the commercial crap.'

Spotting a Christmas cactus that was beginning to flower, Alex plucked it up.

'Pilfering the stock?' Jules asked.

He gave her a sheepish smile. 'I need to take *something* as a thank you for making Daisy dress up like an elf.'

'It's a good job you haven't chosen a spikier cactus. That would hurt when she shoved it up your—'

'Thanks, Jules. See you.'

When he arrived at Daisy's studio, her expression told him the plant was woefully inadequate as a way to make up for what he was putting her through. Since Santa's cabin opened an hour after the rest of Fox Farm, she had plenty of time to explain what she expected of him for the day.

Daisy became so animated when she spoke about her work, so involved, as though she lost track of everything else around her. Alex knew what that was like. He felt the same way about his business, his skills.

At half past nine, Santa – a.k.a. Mike – poked his head around the door. 'Cooee! I gather my elf is in here?'

Daisy groaned. 'Hi, Mike. She's a very unwilling elf.'

'They're not *all* brats, I promise. All you have to do is keep the queue orderly, build up the excitement, ask their names when it's their turn, introduce them to me like it's a privilege for them – which it is, of course – and cut it short if they linger too long. You'll soon get the hang of it.'

'Unlikely. But since I don't intend ever doing it again, I doubt it matters.'

Mike wagged a finger. 'Kids love their annual visit to Santa, Daisy. Don't sell them short. Don't you remember how excited you were for yours?'

Alex shot Daisy a sympathetic look, guessing she might not have had as many visits to Santa as some children.

Mike handed over a carrier bag. 'Lauren said to tell you her mum washed it. She didn't want you to catch any germs.'

Daisy took it from him. 'Thanks. I think.' She slouched off to her room to change.

Alex couldn't blame her for her reluctance. Dressing up as an elf wouldn't be top of his 'Fun Things to Do' list, either... although it *was* currently top of his 'Fun Things to See' list.

Fifteen minutes later, he wasn't disappointed. Daisy scuttled out in all her elf-like glory – green-and-red striped tights, pointy boots (too big for her), green woollen dress with red buttons and a red zig-zag collar, the dress cinched with a wide, black belt and trimmed with red fur at the short hem – *Man, she has good legs. Who would know, when she wears denim all the time?* – and that pointy hat with the bell on top.

'You can take that smirk off your face,' Daisy warned.

'I'm sorry, I can't.' Alex went up to her and tinkled her bell. So to speak.

'Get *off*!' She batted his hand away.

'You look great, Daisy.' He swapped to what he hoped was an encouraging smile. 'Really cute.'

'Huh. I've never looked cute in my life. I don't intend to start now.'

She thinks she never looks cute? Not with the dungarees and the oversized men's shirts and the paint in her hair? That was a damned shame. He would have to do something about that. But perhaps now wasn't the best moment, when she looked like she might kill him.

Mike poked his head around the door. 'Ready, Daisy? You look grand.'

'Thanks.' Daisy squared her shoulders. 'Right. Let's get this day over with.' She turned to Alex. 'One lost sale, and you're dead. And if I catch a cold, you're looking after me, snot and all. Understood?'

'Understood.' He nodded solemnly as she followed Mike out to the log cabin, her feet slipping in the oversized boots. *Bless you, Daisy. You're a real trouper.*

*

The day wasn't as bad as Daisy had imagined it would be, but she wouldn't say it was something she'd care to repeat. The kids waiting to see Santa were excitable and occasionally downright rude. Huddling in the porch of the cabin, it was sheltered enough for her not to freeze, but she became chilled despite the hot drinks sent over regularly from the café.

Luckily, Daisy was used to the cold – she often left her studio doors open so people felt free to wander in – but then she was dressed accordingly. Pulling on a warm fleece would hardly help the elf look. As for *that,* at least she and Lauren were a similar size, other than their feet, but she still felt like an idiot. Thirty-one years old, and this was what she was reduced to! She wasn't thrilled about having to pose in so many photos, either – many would end up on social media, she suspected, and whilst she was keen to get herself 'out there', she would have preferred to do so as an artist, not as a bloomin' elf.

The afternoon visit from the church carol-singers, gathered around the tree, cheered her up, especially when her queue sang along. And Mike was brilliant with the kids. He'd been doing this for years and knew how to get the best from them. They came out beaming, clutching their gift, then often headed with their parents or grandparents for the café or gallery. As Jules had said, Santa was good for business.

Her gaze often strayed to the studio, where Alex appeared to be holding his own. She'd instructed him to allow visitors to browse before approaching them, but it looked as if there weren't many women who minded being accosted by a broad-shouldered, handsome man with day-old stubble and a welcoming smile. Since she saw plenty leaving with packages, she couldn't complain. The means justified the end, as far as her income was concerned.

By the time she and Mike closed the cabin at three o'clock, her feet were like ice, and she wanted nothing more than a hot shower to warm her chilled bones.

'Thanks, Daisy,' Mike said, patting her shoulder before dragging off his red coat. 'You did really well.'

'You're welcome.' Daisy frowned as he unhooked his fluffy white beard. 'Are you alright, Mike? You look peaky.'

'Nothing a hot toddy won't fix. See you tomorrow.'

'With Lauren in tow, I hope.'

'She said it was bound to be just a twenty-four-hour bug.'

As Daisy crossed to her studio, she figured the hot shower would have to wait. There was still an hour till closing.

But Alex was having none of it. 'You look frozen.' He reached out to rub her arms, bringing the warmth back to them surprisingly quickly. 'Take a shower and get into something warm. I can carry on here.' When she looked dubious, he showed her the sales figures for the day so far.

'Wow! Maybe I should have you in here more often.'

'Maybe you should.' The ambiguous wording hung between them before he smiled and said, 'Go.'

Daisy was too cold to argue. Stripping off the elf costume with relief, she stepped into her shower where she stayed for as long as the old hot water tank allowed, then dried off and pulled on jeans and her warmest jumper, even fingerless gloves, before going back through.

'Better?'

'Yes. Thanks.' She pointed after a woman just leaving. 'Another sale?'

'The sheep huddling against the wall in the snow. Angie sent this over. She says you deserve a medal, but this will have to do.'

Daisy took the mulled wine he handed her with relish, breathing in the fruity scent and spices. 'Mmmm. Thanks for all you did today.'

'Thank *you* for being an elf.' When she made a face, he said, 'You looked the part. And I know you hated every minute, so it's doubly appreciated.'

'I didn't hate *every* minute,' Daisy admitted. 'Although I can't say I appreciated the kid who hugged me whilst holding a lolly and got it stuck in my hair. Or the girl who got so giddy she threatened to throw up over my boots.'

He chuckled. 'You're not a children person?'

'They're okay in small doses. Or if they belong to you.'

'Is that something you see in your future? A family of your own?' He gave an embarrassed shrug. 'Sorry. That's a personal question. I shouldn't have asked.'

But Daisy didn't mind answering. 'I haven't thought about it much – I haven't been in a relationship where the question arose. And I learned a long time ago to only ever look one step ahead at a time. It was the only way to cope with moving from family to family, college, temporary jobs, temporary accommodation.' She sighed. 'Turns out my whole life has been temporary.' Her voice hitched, surprising and embarrassing her. *This mulled wine must have quite a kick.*

Alex moved a step closer. 'You'd like something more permanent now?'

'I… I thought I was happy enough the way things were, as long as I could paint. But being at Fox Farm has changed things. I finally feel like I belong somewhere.' Daisy straightened her spine. 'And I'm well aware it can't last, so don't worry.'

'I'm not worried.' Alex took the mug from her hand and placed it on the counter. 'I'm sorry you had a difficult childhood, Daisy. A difficult adulthood, too.'

'My adulthood, at least, was my choice, and I'm doing what I love, in a place I love – for now. That's all that matters.'

His face was inches from hers, his eyes on hers, his mouth so close…

A kerfuffle outside had them jumping apart before a party of four entered the studio.

Daisy glanced at her watch. Quarter of an hour to closing. 'Thanks, Alex. You go now.'

'Okay. I'll check on the others.'

Daisy didn't have the magic touch that Alex had, it seemed. There were no purchases by the party of four – not even a Christmas card. *Ah, well.*

He slid back in as she was about to close up.

'Alex! I thought you'd gone. Is there something you want?'

'There certainly is.' And with no preamble whatsoever, he kicked the door shut, turned the 'Closed' sign, took her face in his hands and planted his lips on hers.

Daisy was taken completely by surprise. She hadn't expected him to come back and… Oh, his lips were turning softer, melting hers, and she greedily returned the kiss, sliding her hands up his chest to wind around his neck, needing him to be closer, needing *him*…

She broke it off. This was getting out of hand, wasn't it? These whims of kisses, with both of them hedging around the topic of what was going on between them. 'Alex, I...'

His hazel eyes twinkled. 'Did you have something to say?'

'I... No.'

'Good.'

His mouth closed over hers again, and Daisy told her conflicted mind to let it alone. It did – Alex was a great kisser.

This time, it was Alex who broke it off. 'Footsteps.'

Daisy moved away before there was a light tap on the door and Sue entered. 'I came for the mug,' she said, glancing from one to the other of them. 'Good day as an elf?'

'I'll live, thanks. As long as I never have to do it again.' When Sue had gone, Daisy turned back to Alex. 'Do you think she guessed?'

'Maybe. Does it matter?'

'I'm not sure.' She sighed. 'But I am sure I need to restock before tomorrow.'

'Need a hand?'

'No, thanks.' *You've done quite enough already!*

*

Alex struggled to sleep that night. It had been a long, strange day.

Despite his apparent nonchalance, he hadn't felt at all confident about manning Daisy's studio. And he'd felt guilty all day – it had been a low shot, begging Daisy to play an elf for Aunt Jean's sake.

She'd looked amazing in that outfit, though. Then again, Alex fancied her in jeans and baggy jumpers, too, didn't he? Their kisses had become an addictive habit. He *could* put that down to the stress of them being thrown together in difficult circumstances, alongside a dose of mutual attraction. But today…? He hadn't wanted to walk away when those customers had interrupted them. And at four o'clock, when he'd seen them leave, his feet had marched him right back over there, his lips had taken what they felt they were owed, and it seemed his brain had had little say in the matter.

Deep down, Alex knew that what was between them was no longer light-hearted fun. But he didn't do anything *other* than light-hearted, did he? He didn't *want* messy feelings and emotions that might lead to commitment. Even if he did, he had enough complications with Aunt Jean in hospital and Riverside and Fox Farm, let alone Sebastian sticking his oar in at every opportunity.

Kissing Daisy was a nice distraction, one that took his mind off other things – *totally* off them – for a few minutes. She was good company. They were in tune with each other. But anything more would go against the way he'd chosen to live his life so far.

And people were beginning to notice. Turning up together at the barn dance had raised a few eyebrows. Old Jack was convinced. Jules knew something was going on. Jim and Kieran made the occasional comment. Sue must have sensed the charged atmosphere when she'd called in for that empty mug. Creating gossip and speculation at Fox Farm probably wasn't a good idea right now.

And yet the idea of calling a halt to it, the thought of not kissing Daisy again, left a hollow space somewhere deep inside. Alex didn't like *that* feeling at all.

He also didn't like being woken at six on a Sunday morning when he'd had precious little sleep. He may be an early riser, but after such a bad night, he might have given himself some leeway.

'What? Who? Huh?' he managed, after a mad scramble to find the phone and make his fingers work.

'Alex. It's Mike.'

Uh-oh. 'What's up? Or don't I want to know?'

'You don't want to know, but I can't help that. I've been throwing up all night. I must have caught what Lauren has. Sorry, but there's no way I can be Santa today. I can't infect a load of kiddies in the run-up to Christmas. Besides, I feel like death warmed up. I'd scare the poor little mites to death – I look more like the Grim Reaper than Old Saint Nick.'

Alex ran a hand over his face. 'I'm sorry, Mike. You sound awful. I don't suppose you know of anyone…?'

'Alex, you know and I know that every available Santa already has a gig at weekend grottos across the Dales. Listen, I left the costume in the cabin. Any germs will have gone overnight in that cold. All you have to do is sit there and be jolly…'

Alex sat bolt upright in bed. 'Whoa! *Me?* You must be joking!'

'It's either that or shut the cabin for the day. You'd get a lot of disappointed kids turning up, and it wouldn't look good. Besides, Fox Farm's only open eleven till four on a Sunday, so the cabin's only open twelve till three. You can do it.'

'I… Huh. What about Lauren? She'll be back, won't she?'

'Doubt it. I rang her last night, when I first started chucking up, and she could barely move. Aching legs and a blinding headache. Guess I've got *that* to look forward to.'

Alex did his best to quell his panic and summon up suitable sympathy. 'I'm sorry, Mike. Kids are nothing but a bag of germs, if you ask me.'

'Spoken by a non-parent. Although many a parent would be inclined to agree with you.' He made a retching noise. 'Gotta go. Good luck.'

Alex stared at his phone. 'No, no, no.'

Stumbling out of bed, he went into the bathroom to splash cold water on his face, then sat on the side of the bath, trying to drum up the names of anyone willing to play Santa at short notice. He wondered about asking Gary but soon dismissed that idea. Chelle had already complained about all the extra time he'd put in at Fox Farm. Dragging him away on a Sunday would not go down well. Otherwise, Alex's mind was a blank.

Staggering downstairs, he switched on the kettle to make a strong brew. Was he really going to play Santa today? A man who generally avoided children if at all possible? As for Lauren… How on earth was he going to tell Daisy?

Chapter Twenty-One

Daisy began work early. After Alex had left yesterday, she'd struggled to focus on restocking – those kisses of his had a lot to answer for, concentration-wise – but she'd managed some, done more this morning, and now she could feel free to settle down and paint for a while, still in her pyjamas, a baggy jumper over them, relieved she would be back in her studio all day.

She was so engrossed, she didn't notice the rattle on the door at first. When it became a thump, she looked up to see Alex, his fist raised, phone in hand. Scraping hair from her eyes, she shuffled over to the door.

Alex swept in, shivering from the cold. 'I've been trying to phone you for the past hour!'

'Sorry. My phone's charging through there.' She pointed to her bedroom. 'What's up? Is Jean alright?'

'She's fine.' Daisy's relief was short-lived as Alex said, 'It's Lauren. She's still ill.'

'Poor Lauren.' The truth slowly dawned. 'Oh no, Alex. Not again!'

'I don't know what to say, apart from a big, fat "please". It's only for three hours today.' When she folded her arms across her chest in a confrontational stance, he added, 'If it makes you feel any better, Mike's ill, too.'

'Why on earth would that make me feel better?'

'Because I'll have to…'

Daisy choked out a laugh. '*You're* going to be Santa?'

'Who the hell else?' he snapped. 'Go ahead and laugh. But I can tell you, I don't find it funny. I have my own business to run, let alone this place, and now I have to play Father Christmas and be nice to a bunch of hyper kids? Yeah. Enjoy your fun.'

'Welcome to my world!' Daisy snapped back. 'You were happy to take me away from my business yesterday and dress me up as a stupid elf!'

'I took care of it for you, didn't I?'

'You did,' she conceded, only now realising what she must look like – her hair loose and unbrushed, her pyjamas old, the baggy jumper with its holes, the scruffy woollen socks. *Ah, what do I care what I look like for him?* 'But if you're playing Santa – hilarious though I might ordinarily find that – who would take care of my studio today?'

'I've asked Jamie to do it. He'll be great. Jules' daughter Hannah will do a one-off helping Lisa in the gallery – Lisa's not happy about it, but she never is, these days – and Kieran's brother wants a free go on the tree netting machine, so that's Riverside covered as best it can be.'

Daisy studied the worry lines at Alex's eyes; the pinch of his mouth. 'You've gone to an awful lot of trouble to see me in tights again,' she grumbled.

He grinned. 'Worth every effort I can make.' His face serious once more, he said, 'I don't want to close the cabin when kids have been promised by their parents, Daisy. I could try doing it on my own, but I don't want anyone to feel short-changed. I'd rather you were there by my side.'

Daisy hesitated. Alex *could* manage on his own, but it wouldn't be easy for him, coping with the queue outside as he gave his attention to each child inside. She'd come to understand from her stint the previous day that the elf added to the atmosphere and excitement for the children. She sighed. 'Okay.'

Alex's expression was one of pure relief. 'Thank you. I know I'm taking advantage of you, and I'm sorry.' He kissed her cheek. 'See you soon.'

Daisy watched him leave with a roll of her eyes. How on earth had he managed to get around her *again*?

*

By the time Alex had checked in with Jules at Riverside then driven back to Fox Farm and delivered Hannah into Lisa's sulking clutches, there was already a queue for the cabin. He cursed when he remembered the Santa suit was inside it. He could hardly go in there as Alex and transform into Santa, could he?

Daisy called to him from the door of her studio, her elf outfit hidden under a coat. 'Quick! In here.' When he was through the door, she pulled him into her room.

'Watch out, Alex,' Jamie warned from his place at the counter. 'She's feisty today.'

The Santa suit was laid out on Daisy's bed.

'Thanks for bringing it in.' Alex stared at it. 'How many clothes am I taking off?'

'What?' Daisy looked alarmed.

'I mean, how cold is the cabin? I don't want to freeze, but I don't want to stifle under all that.'

Daisy rolled her eyes. 'What am I, your mother? You're a big boy.' When he wavered, she huffed. 'I'd say, trousers off – these look warm. Thicker jumper off, leave your polo neck on under the red coat. Oh, what *am* I saying? Just get on with it.'

Alex did as she suggested, donned the beard, looked in the mirror in her bathroom, couldn't believe how ridiculous he felt, and called to her from the doorway. 'Is the beard alright?'

Daisy adjusted it for him. 'Perfect. Now all you need to do is look jolly all day. Can you manage that?'

'I very much doubt it.'

Laughing, Daisy shrugged off her coat and hooked her arm in his. 'Into the fray, my friend.' And she dragged him off to his doom.

Except it wasn't such a terrible day, Alex decided as their stint drew to a close. At over six feet, he'd felt cramped in the cabin, and he could have done with stretching his legs at some point, but Angie had sent over a toasted turkey and cranberry sandwich, and Daisy held the brats off while he ate it – 'Santa needs to keep his strength up as much as you girls and boys do,' he heard her declare brightly – and he'd been supplied with tea… although he reckoned Santa must be a whisky man, because that was what he hankered after.

Through the open doorway of the cabin, the sight of the waiting children's excited faces helped him feel that his sacrifice was worthwhile. Daisy was brilliant, keeping the kids – and their parents – occupied, telling them all about the North Pole. For a woman who hadn't had the happiest of childhoods, she did a great job at keeping the sense of wonder alive out there. Even though she'd told him that most of her foster families were happy ones, it had to be hard for her, watching these children standing with their parents when she had lost a mother she had barely known, and never known her father at all.

They ran well over time, the queue was so long. After Daisy had ushered the last child away, Alex was about to pull off his beard when she slapped at his hand.

'Don't you dare! What if someone looks back?'

'Shut the door, then.'

Daisy kicked it shut but still stood over him. Impulsively, Alex pulled her onto his lap.

'Stop it!' Pushing at his chest, she fought to get free. 'They may look through the window.'

'What does it matter?'

'Do you want a small child to be scarred for life by seeing Santa fooling around with an elf?'

'Who knows what they get up to at the North Pole?'

'Well, I doubt Mrs Claus would approve. Let me go, and come over to my place so we can get these outfits off.'

'That sounds more like it.'

Daisy gave him a withering look. 'You're incorrigible.'

'I've spent nearly four hours cooped up in an eight-foot-square room. I literally have cabin fever... and a lot of unexpended energy.'

'Then go for a walk.'

'It's almost dark.' He trailed after her, but inside the studio, he slapped his forehead. 'I almost forgot! Jules wants a photo or she's going on strike.' He handed Jamie his phone. 'Could you do the honours?'

'With pleasure.' As Jamie took photos of Alex on his own and with Daisy by his side, Alex smiled at the lad's alternately red-and-green painted nails to go with his Christmas-tree jumper, and the red streak in his hair.

'How did we do?' Daisy asked Jamie.

'Good. Plenty of cards and smaller prints. A couple of canvases.' Jamie showed her the figures. 'I enjoyed it. It was a nice change.'

'Well, thanks for today. Enjoy your evening.' As she locked the door after him, she turned to Alex. 'I'm not surprised he enjoyed a change from Lisa. How about you? Was today so bad?'

'No. Not so bad.'

'Good.' She opened the door to her room and waved him in. 'You first.'

'Thanks.' As he went through the doorway, Alex pulled Daisy in with him. His intention was merely to kiss her – her beckoning him into her bedroom was too much to ignore after a stressful day – but he caught her off balance, and the room was so small, he ended up tumbling onto the bed, Daisy landing on top of him with an 'Oooff!'

'Sorry.'

'No, you're not.' Daisy pushed ineffectually at him, but he kept his arms banded tightly around her waist.

'No,' he agreed. 'I'm not.'

Alex loosened his grip enough to allow her to pull away if she wanted to, but she stilled in his arms, so he lifted his lips to meet hers in a long kiss, his night-time worries that he was getting in over his head already forgotten.

When they came up for air, she said, 'I'm sure this isn't right.'

'I'm pretty sure it is.' He kissed her again to prove it.

'I meant, Santa and an elf together.'

'That's what's bothering you? Easily fixed. All we have to do is get out of these costumes.'

'You have an answer for everything, don't you?'

'Yup.' He silenced her with another kiss.

*

Daisy wasn't sure how it happened – that split second that took them from her ordering Alex into her room, to her lying on top of him in her bed, her heart beating faster than seemed good for her.

Alex's hair was tousled from the Santa hat, making him look incredibly sexy, and his eyes looked *hungry*. Daisy had never been looked at quite that way before.

She should pull away. But those kisses… She'd kept on wondering whether this habit was a good idea, but it was hard to remember why, with Alex *looking* at her like that.

'What are you thinking so hard about?' he murmured.

'I don't think—'

'No. Don't think. That's for the best.'

In one deft move, Alex flipped them so she was on her back, and his mouth took hers again. His kisses were addictive. *What would making love to him be like?* Broad shoulders, muscled chest… not that she could see them, with that stupid Santa jacket he was wearing. And it was so *hot* in here, out of the wind and cold.

As though Alex was thinking the same, he moved away long enough to pull off the jacket, revealing a tight polo neck clinging to those sculpted muscles she already knew from sneaking peeks at him when they'd worked together in the gallery. This time, it wasn't enough.

'More,' she murmured.

'What?' He nuzzled her neck, making her gasp.

'Take it off.'

His eyes widening in surprise, Alex did as he was told, pulling off his jumper to reveal the chest and shoulders she'd imagined.

Oh my. Daisy kissed his shoulder, running her hands over the muscles of his chest and then his back. There was a lot to be said for a man who did so much manual work.

Alex quivered under her touch. 'This is a little one-sided.'

'Hmmm?' Daisy's teeth were nibbling his shoulder now – of their own volition. What was *happening* to her?

'I'm half-naked. You're not,' he pointed out.

'You want me half-naked?' Daisy had no idea where her provocative tone had come from.

'I want you fully naked, but I'll settle for halfway to start with. That's only fair, isn't it?'

Daisy's belly flipped with excitement, her pulse racing. Alex was right. It was only fair.

He ran his hands over her tunic, finding the zip at the side. Daisy was acutely aware of his fingers against her skin as he pulled it down.

'Under or over?' he asked.

'Hmmm?' *What sort of a question is that?* Daisy's mind had become fogged.

'This dress. It's cute on. It's a pain to get off.'

'Oh. It'll have to go over my head.'

But as Alex tugged at the hem, an awful thought struck her. If he took the dress off, that would leave her only in her bra and the stripy red-and-green tights. *No* woman could look good in *that* combination!

'No!' she squeaked.

'No?' Alex groaned.

'No, I mean… Let *me* do it.'

Not wanting to explain and thereby dampen his enthusiasm, Daisy climbed off the bed and stood, demurely wriggling the tights down and off. *Now* he could take the dress off. But he wouldn't, would he? She'd already said, 'Let me'. There he lay on the bed, watching her. She would have to go ahead and take the dress off herself, as if she were stripping for him.

Her pulse racing, Daisy gathered up her courage and pulled the tunic over her head.

Alex let out a long, low whistle. 'How on earth have you been hiding a body like that? And why?'

Daisy felt suddenly exposed in bra and pants. At least they were matching – and that was only by chance. She shrugged. 'Cold studio. Practicalities.'

He tugged her back to the bed. 'I thought you only agreed to get *half*-naked?'

'I'm still wearing something.'

'Not much.' His grin was wolflike, making her blood thrum. 'And not for long, if I have my way.'

If you have your way, I'm going to have serious trouble breathing.

But Daisy didn't care. Alex's kiss was more tender this time, as though he could sense that she was nervous now that they were moving beyond the fun and frivolity of their previous encounters. He kissed her neck, her shoulders, ran his hands over her breasts, then pulled her on top of him.

Daisy squirmed. 'Take your trousers off. They're scratchy.'

'You haven't had to wear them all day!' But Alex complied in a lithe move and had her back in his arms in seconds, both of them with hands and lips running out of control.

'Can we get full-on naked yet?' he asked her, his need as apparent as hers. 'Please?'

'Yes.' Daisy could barely speak. 'Definitely yes.'

As Alex helped them both with that, the dim part of Daisy's brain that was trying to tell her this was a bad idea, or at least not thought through, was drowned out by her aching body.

Daisy had never felt like this with *anyone* before, and she wanted the whole experience, no holds barred.

*

Alex woke in the narrow bed with Daisy in his arms, her head on his shoulder, her breathing steady. He glanced at her bedside clock. It was late evening now, and he was hungry – he'd had nothing since the sandwich at lunchtime. But Daisy was exhausted from her weekend as an elf and showed no sign of stirring.

His mind played over their lovemaking in excruciating detail, and although it made his pulse beat faster just thinking about it, it made him uncomfortable, too.

Alex cared about Daisy, and even though he'd wanted to make love to her more than he'd wanted to make love to any woman in a long time, he didn't want her to get the wrong idea.

You don't do relationships, Alex, remember? Friendship, companionship, sex if both parties are willing to accept that that's all it is...

He'd come a cropper a couple of times with that philosophy, when women had begun to care more for him than he for them. Those occasions had been awkward, but he'd done his best to end things with consideration.

Would he have to do the same with Daisy, if she thought this meant more than it did?

Sex complicated things. As he looked down at Daisy's tousled hair, felt her breath on his chest, he knew he could never see theirs as a 'friends with benefits' situation. He shouldn't have allowed himself to get carried away. And yet even as he thought it, he knew he'd had little control over what had happened. Daisy hadn't seemed to, either, and Alex suspected that wanton sex was *not* her style. It was touching that she'd let go with him.

Would she regret it? He hoped not. It had been amazing. But whether it should happen again was another matter.

Daisy stirred, murmured, then jolted when she realised she was in his arms.

He smiled at her. 'Good evening.'

She looked up at him, her eyes large. He could imagine what was going through her head as she replayed their lovemaking.

'Oh!' Her embarrassed exclamation was endearing… and irresistible.

Alex lifted her chin to kiss her, his intention merely to reassure her that it had been great for him, too; that he was as surprised as she was. But as her lips melted beneath his, as she let out a shaky breath, that intention was forgotten. Any idea that there shouldn't be a repeat performance, even his stomach's growling hunger… Everything was overridden by his desperate desire for Daisy.

Chapter Twenty-Two

They made love a second time, as frenetic as the first. Daisy could sense Alex trying to slow it down, make it more tender, but the fire their bodies generated made it impossible.

Afterwards, as they lay squashed in her bed, Daisy's head spun.

What on earth just happened? And why did it happen twice?

From where she lay, she could see Alex's Santa outfit thrown over the footboard of the bed and her elf accessories strewn across the floor.

Did I actually strip *for him? I can't believe I did that, even if I did have a good reason.*

'What's going on in that head of yours?' Alex asked.

'I don't know. I think we destroyed most of my brain cells.'

Alex burst out laughing, his teeth white in the lamplight. 'No woman has ever said I had *that* effect on her before!' He stroked a finger along her cheek. 'Seriously. Are you okay?'

'I think so. Are you?' As soon as she'd said it, Daisy knew how stupid it must have sounded. Men weren't emotionally affected by first times with a new partner, she reckoned, not in the same way women were. And the impression she'd got from Alex was that he hadn't been particularly short of such occasions. 'Well. Of course you are,' she blustered.

She was saved by a loud growl of hunger from Alex's stomach.

He winced. 'Sorry.'

'Don't be silly. You must be starving. But I don't have much in.'

'That's okay. I should get home. I have some calls to make. I'm sure Aunt Jean will enjoy taking the mickey over my day as Santa.' He gave her a mischievous look. 'I'll leave out the finale, shall I?'

'I think that's best.' Self-conscious, Daisy sat up, reached for a nearby T-shirt and pulled it over her head.

With no such inhibitions, Alex extricated himself from the bed and stood in all his naked glory, stretching before hunting for his clothes. He really did have an impressive body.

What he does with it is pretty impressive, too.

Dressed, he stepped back to her. 'You're sure you don't mind me dashing off like this?'

'Of course not. You have things to catch up on, and I should do some work.'

The chances of me being able to concentrate on anything for the rest of this evening are nil.

'Okay. I'll speak to you soon.' The awkwardness between them was palpable as he bent to kiss her lightly on the lips.

Daisy managed a smile. 'Could you let yourself out? I can't find a bottom half.'

Alex wiggled his eyebrows. 'No problem.' And he was gone.

Daisy sat for a long time in the half-light, her knees drawn up to her chin, going over the turn of events. Whilst she couldn't regret the incredible sex they'd had, she *could* regret that they were suddenly so awkward together, in a way they had never been before.

With a sigh, she hauled herself off the bed and into the shower, forcing her mind to go blank as the water ran over her.

In her pyjamas, she rummaged in her kitchenette for something edible. Scrambled egg on toast? And maybe tomatoes, albeit on the mushy side. It was a good job Alex hadn't stayed to eat, after all. Then again, it was obvious he had no intention of staying. That didn't surprise her. He hadn't hidden the fact that he was casual about relationships; that he avoided involvement. Why should it be different with her?

Cracking eggs into a pan, Daisy stirred without paying much attention. As her neglected eggs became rubbery around her wooden spoon, she had one of those light-bulb moments that make you feel so stupid for not realising before.

When she and Eoin had split up at the end of college, even though it was mutual and nobody's fault, it had still been painful, leaving her wondering why she'd put so much energy, so much of herself, into two years of a relationship for no real reward. Over the decade since, had she genuinely not been interested in the people she'd dated? Had she honestly not been attracted to those she declined outright? Or had she too, in her own way, avoided involvement, persuading herself that her art came first?

A smell of burning brought her attention back to her eggs. They were only fit for the bin.

Giving up on food, Daisy wandered through to her studio. Oh, she loved this place. Her own space to display whatever she wanted, to work whenever she wanted, slap bang in the heart of the area that inspired her paintings and from where she could radiate outwards to the other galleries. More than that, these past few months had almost made her believe that her art was a 'proper' job. Up until now, she hadn't had that feeling. The years developing her style, touting her work, working at the pub, quitting to paint more but earn less; the lonely existence at Jack's…

Here at Fox Farm, for the first time, Daisy felt that she was properly running her own business. It could do better. She could expand. She needed to get herself organised to sell online. She would have to, because by spring she would be back out in the wilderness, looking for cheap accommodation, relying on mere commission from other galleries. Daisy didn't want to go back to that. She wanted to move forward.

You could ask Jean to keep you on.

No, Daisy wouldn't do that. Jean had enough on her plate without pressure from her. She didn't want to be seen to be influencing or manipulating her.

Over in her work area, her painting of Alex, Jim and Kieran erecting the Christmas tree caught her eye. She'd toyed with the idea of giving it to Alex as a Christmas present, once she'd taken it to her printer to capture and store the image, ready to make prints for next year, but then she'd wondered if such a present might seem too intimate.

At that, Daisy gave a strangled laugh. *What we just did was pretty intimate. A mere picture pales in comparison.*

Oh, Alex. What am I going to do about you? About us?

*

'The photos were fab,' Jules told Alex the next morning at Riverside.

'Photos?'

'Surely you can't have forgotten your stint as Santa already?'

I think I forgot my entire head yesterday. 'Oh. Well, I survived.' *My body and dignity, anyway. Not sure about my senses.*

'Daisy looked cute.' Jules' tone was pointed.

'S'pose.'

'Oh, c'mon, Alex. You can't deny it.'

'No. Guess not.' He picked up a crate of fir branches that Jules used for wreaths from behind the counter and moved it to another location three feet away. Then back again.

'If you're trying to look busy, I've got actual useful tasks for you that'll produce the same effect,' Jules said. 'Hey! Earth to Alex?'

'What? Oh. Sorry. What do you need me to do?'

'I need you to fetch me a cup of tea. One for yourself, too.'

Alex went into the office behind the counter and did as he was told. Taking hers from him, Jules gave him a direct look.

'We have fifteen minutes before we open. Jim and Kieran are out in the greenhouses. We're all alone. What's up?'

'Nothing. I'm just distracted,' Alex hedged, aware his voice was tinged with desperation. 'That's hardly surprising, with everything that's going on, is it?'

'True. But today you've taken it to a whole new level, and my gut's telling me it has something to do with a certain elf.' Her voice softened. 'Alex, we've known each other a long time. Tell me what's going on.'

'Nothing's going on.' *Too quick, Alex. Too defensive.*

'And there's my confirmation. You two are more than friends now? Enjoyed too much festive *bonhomie* this weekend?'

'I…' *Oh, this is hopeless.* 'Yes. If you tell one living soul, I will kill you. And Daisy would kill *me* for telling you.'

'Alex, you've had girlfriends before. Why are you so flustered about this one?' Jules' eyes widened. 'Oh, my giddy aunt. You've fallen for her!'

'What? No, of course not! I mean, I *like* her. A lot. Obviously. Otherwise I wouldn't have…'

'Uh-huh. And how does Daisy feel about it?'

'I don't know. We both had stuff to do… after.'

'Maybe you should ask her.'

'I asked her if she was okay about it.'

'Not the same thing, and you know it.'

'Jules, you know I don't go in for all that touchy-feely stuff. Besides, Daisy and I already had a conversation about our pasts. She knows I don't do "serious".'

'Does she know that might have changed for you?'

'What *are* you talking about?'

'I'm talking about the fact that you've fallen for her. I can see the signs, Alex. You haven't been this way with anyone in the whole time I've known you. She's good for you, I reckon.'

'Well, I didn't ask for your opinion or for you to dredge my weekend secrets out of me. Let's get some work done, shall we?'

Alex could see the hurt in Jules' eyes and regretted his tone, but he was fed up with all these women analysing him, telling him how he was around Daisy, thinking they knew best – Aunt Jean, his mother, Jules. And why would he ask Daisy how she felt until he knew how *he* felt?

His visit with Aunt Jean that evening was no better. Naturally, she wanted to hear all about how they had managed as Santa and his elf. To satisfy her curiosity, he regaled her with some of the funny things the kids had said and complimented Daisy's stoicism.

'She's a gem, that one,' Aunt Jean said.

'Yes. It was good of her to help us out.'

'I don't just mean that. I mean an all-round gem.'

'Yes.' He couldn't deny that.

'So why the long face?'

I don't want to think about Daisy – and yet I do, in what feels like every waking moment. I'm worried that what happened between us yesterday will affect our friendship. I should be thinking about that unexpected, incredible interlude with a smile, and instead I'm agonising about it. It's taking all the fun out of it!

Aunt Jean was waiting for an answer. Alex had to say something to deflect her.

'I'm worried I've asked too much of her. Where I haven't asked, she's given.'

Aunt Jean nodded. 'We should pay her.'

'I already offered. She wouldn't hear of it. She thinks it's a way of paying you back for the fact that she doesn't pay rent.'

'Silly girl. That was my choice. Besides, she gives me a percentage.'

'So I gather.' *I wish I'd known that before I accused her of all sorts that time we argued.*

'I'm glad you and she have become good friends,' she said.

There was a speculative look in his aunt's eyes that Alex could have done without. *There she goes, on the same track as Jules. Spare me!*

He changed the subject, asking Aunt Jean about how far she was getting with the physio exercises and letting her relay all the gossip she'd prised out of the staff on the ward, until he could safely take his leave.

But as he drove home, Alex's mind wasn't fully on the roads – so much so that he pulled over, his truck idling in a dark layby.

Do I need to speak to Daisy about this? Weren't we just two adults taking flirting and kissing to the next level after a stressful weekend? A bit of fun and release of tension? She knows I'm not looking for anything more, doesn't she?

Jules' words came back to him – her assertion that this time, it was different for him. *Had* he fallen for Daisy? He knew he felt differently about her than anyone he'd dated before. But their situation was different, wasn't it? Everything had been so intense. That might explain it.

Besides, he didn't know why everyone was on at *him*. Daisy came across as a fairly impenetrable fortress, too. She hadn't exactly rushed from one relationship to the other. In fact, she seemed to go out of her way to stay in her solitary little world. Maybe she didn't want this to get serious, either. Perhaps Jules and Aunt Jean should consider *that*.

*

Daisy was desperate for a day out by the time Tuesday came. A chance to clear her head.

First, she took her Fox Farm Christmas tree painting to her printer. He was amenable to storing the image for her until she wanted prints next year, and she pacified him by ordering prints of the other Fox Farm painting she'd been working on, the one with blue skies. As she handed them over, she thought about how great the Christmas one would look on mugs… But that would have to wait until next year, *if* she'd set herself up to sell online by then and *if* she had the money to pay for stocks and somewhere to store them – not a given. Afterwards, she drove to Grassington for a coffee and a visit to the bookshop.

Daisy only stayed in touch with one of her foster mothers, the one who had her the longest in her teen years, and she always bought her a small gift at Christmas. Sheila loved thrillers, although Daisy had no idea which she'd already read. When the name N.J. Giles jumped out at her from a shelf, she smiled broadly. He owed her a signature, surely? That would make it special, even if Sheila already had it.

With the book stowed safely in her car, Daisy put on her small backpack and set off to Linton Falls, a walk she'd enjoyed regularly when she lived in Grassington.

It was a glorious day, cold but with the sky so bright, she wished she'd brought her sunglasses. Trees stood out like black skeletons against the blue. Daisy loved winter trees, the shape of them firing her imagination. The landscape wasn't enough to stop her thinking about Alex, though, and eventually she texted Grace.

Are you free to chat sometime today?

Grace's reply soon came back.

I'm not in the gallery, but I am working on a canvas. I could call you in maybe half an hour. Do I need to prepare myself for a particular topic or crisis?

Daisy forwarded the photo of Alex and herself as Santa and his elf that Jamie had taken. Her phone pinged almost immediately.

Not sure what to make of that! Can't wait to hear about it, though.

Daisy reached the falls, crossed the footbridge and found a spot to sit and eat her lunch, enjoying the sound of the water. The falls weren't tall, but they could be full and gushing. In the summer, there were sometimes kayakers negotiating the rushing waters, something she couldn't imagine wanting to try herself. She'd finished her sandwich and moved on to her flask of tea when Grace rang.

'You have my full attention. What gives?'

Daisy described her weekend as an elf to a backdrop of Grace laughing uproariously… until she got to Sunday evening. 'And then we slept together!' she wailed.

Grace whistled. 'That isn't anything to get upset about, is it? It was inevitable, if you ask me. Dare I ask if it was as good as I imagine?'

'That and beyond,' Daisy admitted. 'We started out in costume.'

'Kinky!'

'It got us going, that's for sure. The chemistry… I've never known anything like it, Grace.' She dropped her voice as a pair of ramblers came over the bridge. 'After, we dozed off, then we did it all over again, and it was just as good.'

'Daisy, forgive me, but I'm not getting what the problem is here.'

'The problem,' Daisy said slowly, 'is that Alex avoids serious relationships. He told me so at the barn dance.'

'So you *did* ask?'

'You told me to, remember? But that's why I shouldn't have slept with him. I mean, it was fun, but it was so awkward when he left, and I don't want it to spoil the friendship.'

'Are you positive he doesn't want a relationship with you?'

'I didn't say *that*.' Daisy thought how best to put it. 'I think he'd be happy for us to be friends and lovers, but nothing more. I'll be at Fox Farm for another three months, and there's Jean to consider. I need to fix any awkwardness as soon as possible.'

'How do you propose to do that?'

'I should tell him that I appreciate it was only a one-night stand; that I know he prefers casual.'

'Or you could carry on being friends and lovers? Enjoy it for as long as it lasts?'

'That's just delaying the inevitable. Better to put it behind us now, right?' Daisy ignored the painful pang caused by the idea of not being close to Alex again.

'Or it gives you time to see where it leads. One or both of you might change your minds about what you want.'

'He already said what he wants at the barn dance. Sunday night was… We got carried away, that's all. I need to tell him I understand that.'

'Well, I don't advocate it, but I guess you'll have to speak to each other about it sometime. Good luck.'

'Thanks, Grace.'

Daisy sat for a long time after she'd ended the call. Was Grace right? Could she let things be and see how they panned out? The trouble was, Daisy didn't like uncertainty. She'd experienced plenty of it in the course of her life, and she preferred to know where she stood, so she could steel herself. Alex hadn't asked anything of her. He'd been honest with her. He didn't need anything messy to complicate his already-complicated life. She could give him that, at least.

The thoughts buzzed in her head like wasps as she retraced her steps to Grassington, not seeing the landscape as she had before. By the time she'd driven back to Winterbridge, called in at the village shop and was heading back to her car, she'd wound herself up over the whole Alex thing.

And there he was, walking towards her.

*

There were no groceries in the house again, forcing Alex to walk to the village shop. He really should get more organised – Harold and Maureen held limited stocks.

Coming in the other direction was Daisy.

'Hi, Daisy.'

'Hi, Alex.'

This isn't good. She can hardly look me in the eye. He tried a smile. 'I'm not sure why this is so awkward. We're both adults, right?'

Her return smile was strained. 'Yes. I guess Sunday took us both by surprise.'

'Nice surprise, though?'

'Of course.'

Thank goodness for that small morsel!

She shuffled on the spot. 'But…'

Alex didn't like the sound of that 'but', even though he had no idea what he wanted her to say. 'But…?'

Daisy took a deep breath. 'Alex, you and I have been playing around for a while now, and perhaps Sunday was inevitable. But I want to say that I understand it was a one-off. I know you don't want it to continue, and that's okay with me.'

Taken aback, Alex experienced an odd feeling of anger. Even though he wasn't sure what he wanted, he'd imagined they would have a conversation about what had happened between them. He hadn't expected it to be so cut and dried.

'That's a lot of assumption,' he said.

'I'm just trying to be helpful. You told me yourself that you don't like to get too involved. I'm simply saying that I respect that.'

Talk about being hoisted by your own petard. He *had* said that, and she wasn't to know that *maybe* he felt differently in her case, but she shouldn't just assume. The creeping anger got stronger.

'Oh, well, if we're going on *assumptions*… I'm not the only one side-stepping relationships, am I? You're pretty good at it yourself.'

Daisy frowned. 'What's that supposed to mean?'

'Other than that bloke in college, you've shown no real interest in anything permanent, either. Why should I be made out to be the bad guy, when you're the same?'

'Nobody's making you out to be the bad guy, Alex. I was merely stating facts. But if, as you say, I'm the same as you, then that suits both of us, doesn't it? Perhaps it's better that we had this little *conversation* before this all got out of hand!'

She marched past him without a backward glance.

That didn't go too well, did it?

Alex couldn't handle Harold or Maureen now. Instead, he trod gingerly across soggy grass to a wet bench by the river and sat, ignoring the damp and cold seeping through his jeans.

What the hell just happened? In past relationships, he'd always known when it was time for it to end. This time, he was being told before he'd decided. Had Daisy just been handing him a get-out before he asked for one, to save face? Or was she genuinely okay with ending this now?

Alex thought about Daisy's lifestyle so far, one that seemed to have filtered through to her relationships. Was it that she hadn't found someone she wanted to be with? Was it that she never felt secure enough to put down roots? Or was she merely content in her world? She came across as self-contained. Maybe she *was* happy with the status quo.

Alex would have said that of himself a few weeks ago. He wasn't stupid – he knew his parents had set a bad example, and he knew other people enjoyed good, non-toxic relationships. But he'd never felt the need to work hard towards finding that for himself.

His time with Daisy hadn't felt like hard work, though. They chatted easily, laughed easily. He'd shared memories and commentary on his life that he rarely shared with anyone. He felt at *home* with her. Was that what a good relationship was about? Why had he never felt it before? Because the others weren't right for him? Or because he wouldn't allow himself to explore the possibility?

Finally braving the shop and escaping Harold's clutches without too much conversation but with a measly haul of eggs, bacon and frozen peas to make an omelette, Alex walked back to his house in a bad mood. The eggs suffered for it – his omelette came out not so much light and fluffy as verging on murdered. N.J. Giles would be proud.

He'd only just finished eating when his phone rang.

'Hi, Mum.'

'You sound glum.'

'You can tell I'm glum from two words?'

'You're my son. What's up?'

'Just tired.'

'Liar.'

Alex closed his eyes. He *was* tired, but he wouldn't get away with that, would he?

'Is it about Daisy?' his mother asked.

His eyes flew open. What was she, psychic? This was the downside of them growing closer recently.

'Why would you think that?'

'I spoke to Jean today, and she's fine. Sebastian isn't up there, annoying you. You should have got over the trauma of playing Santa by now, although it must've been quite a trauma, because you sounded spaced out on Sunday night when I rang. Barely the energy to speak! That leaves only one variable – Daisy.'

Mothers. How do they do it? 'We had words, that's all.'

'What about?'

'It's personal,' Alex said quickly to head her off at the pass, then kicked himself. That would only fire her curiosity. Sure enough…

'Personal, eh? That sounds promising.'

'Don't get your hopes up.'

'You don't want to talk to your mother about it?'

'Er. No.'

'Right, well, I'll go out on a limb and guess that you and Daisy have been getting closer. Both of you are scared to death, so you've fallen out over it. How am I doing so far?'

'Can I put the phone down yet?'

'Not until I've given you a little parental advice. You and Daisy are loners, Alex – or you have been, up until now – but that doesn't have to be a lifelong choice. Two loners can find a mate, same as anyone else. In fact, they go well together because they understand each other's need for space. Don't let a little tiff stop you from exploring this further. If one or both of you decide it's not for you, then so be it, but it would be an awful shame not to give it a chance. That chance may not come along again.' She hesitated. 'Maybe one day *I'll* find someone else. If I do, I hope I'll have courage, because that's what any relationship takes – courage. A leap of faith. You're not getting down on one knee and proposing. You're just giving it a bit more time, to find out whether you're a good fit.'

His mother spoke perfect sense. Alex knew it. And he hated it.

When he remained silent, she chuckled. '*Now* you can put the phone down.'

Chapter Twenty-Three

'Daisy, could you visit me sometime today? I'd like a chat with you.'

Jean sounded serious. Daisy's mind ran over her plans for the day. *Walk. Work. Avoid Alex.*

'I know you're busy, love,' Jean cut into her thoughts. 'But it is important.'

'No problem, Jean. I'd love to see you.' *True enough.* 'I'd like to go for a quick walk this morning, while the weather's good – they're forecasting rain later – but I could come this afternoon, before it sets in.' *That still gives me this evening to work.*

'Good. I don't trust that car of yours in bad weather.'

'Alex won't be there, will he?'

'Why? Is that a problem?' Jean's voice was sharp; knowing.

'It… makes sense not to clash, that's all.'

'Hmmm. No, he said he might come tonight.'

'See you this afternoon, then.'

Packing up some lunch so she could drive straight to the hospital afterwards, Daisy drove to Burnsall and walked along the river to Appletreewick, the weather fine for now. It was good to go somewhere she hadn't been for a while. Walks like yesterday's and today were what she'd been missing lately, and the bright flit of a kingfisher made up for the muddy riverside path – so muddy, she decided to turn it into a circular walk, making her way back along country roads to eat her lunch on a cold bench by the river at Burnsall.

Daisy gave scant attention to her sandwich. Her encounter with Alex had not gone well, and Daisy couldn't understand why. He didn't want to get serious; she'd pre-empted making it awkward for him by explaining that she understood. What had she done wrong? He'd looked offended, angry – not what she'd expected at all. He'd accused her of making assumptions. How could it be an assumption, when it was something he'd actually told her? Never mind the assumptions he'd made about her!

With her sandwich finished and her Alex dilemma still unresolved, she drove to the hospital, where she found Jean looking immensely pleased with herself.

'I did it, Daisy. Twelve steps on a proper staircase. They took me out of the ward, and I did it!'

'Oh, Jean, that's wonderful.' Daisy kissed her friend's cheek. 'Well done.'

'Thanks, love. No chance of being allowed to shower or bath alone, though. Not for a few months. Maybe never.' Jean harrumphed. 'Bloomin' invasion of privacy.'

'I know. But it could've been so much worse,' Daisy said. 'And your speech has improved such a lot. You'll be as good as new in no time.'

'My arm's still not right, though. I'm not sure it ever will be.' A tear appeared. 'I think my pottery days are over.'

That tugged at Daisy's heartstrings. She loved Jean's cheerful mugs and jugs, glazed in muted country greens, blues or browns, her signature sheep on each. It was Jean's pottery that had started Fox Farm in the first place.

'It might come back,' Daisy tried to reassure her. 'And even if it doesn't, you could still paint and glaze, right? Hold it in your bad hand, use your good hand? Maybe there's a way of finding someone to make the pots for you. Some kind of teamwork.'

Jean patted Daisy's hand. 'You're a good girl, trying to find a solution. That's not a bad idea. I'd hate to give it up altogether.'

'Good.' Daisy hadn't mentioned the potter who had copied Jean's designs too closely. Jean *was* Fox Farm, and people liked to buy the wares that reminded them of a place they had enjoyed visiting. *Long may that continue.* 'So, why did you want to speak to me?'

'It's about the studio in the spring.'

Daisy's heart sank. She'd known this was coming, but she hadn't expected Jean to bring it up so soon.

'Don't worry, Jean. I know the score. I appreciate what you did for me, and it's made a massive difference – space to work, the opportunity to show more pieces to more people. I've seen what a proper income looks like. Thank you.' She smiled, trying not to let it wobble. 'Have you decided who's taking it on next?'

'Yes. You.'

Daisy frowned. 'I don't understand.'

'Alex keeps on telling me I won't be able to run Fox Farm the way I used to.' Jean made a face. 'So, I've been thinking – let's face it, there's bugger-all else to do in here – and I've decided that one of the things I don't need to do is change the studio artist. It's been good for Fox Farm to have a new face there each year, but that time is coming to a close. You're happy and doing well. I'd like you to stay. What do you say?'

Daisy's heart lifted. 'Oh, Jean, I'd love to stay. The studio is perfect.'

'The living space isn't.'

'It suits me for now. Maybe someday, I can aspire to greater heights.' Daisy beamed, but then her face fell as she thought about the implications. Alex would still be spending a lot of time at Fox Farm, yet things were so awkward between them. Could she cope with that? With seeing him and perhaps wishing things were different between them? And then there was the question of rent.

'Jean, it was so kind of you to let me have it rent-free this year, but I don't think Alex approves.'

'I know. We'd have to come to some sort of arran...' Jean sighed. 'Long words. Hate 'em. A deal.'

'I agree. I'd have to pay rent somewhere else if I moved, and this way, I get to be somewhere I love. I've done well at the studio. Enough to know I can afford rent, anyway.'

'Good. No more caravans for you. We'll sort out the details in the new year, but I wanted you to know now, so you can plan ahead.'

'Thank you, Jean. Thank you *so much*!'

They chatted about Fox Farm, and Jean took the opportunity to interrogate her about being elf to Alex's Santa, but Daisy managed to keep her cool until she could get away.

She struggled to concentrate on the drive home. Knowing she had a permanent place to work meant she could build her business in ways that hadn't been feasible before, increasing the products she sold and looking into selling online. Not only that, she had a *home*. Not her tiny living space – she would want to move on from that if she could increase her income – but somewhere she *belonged*. That sense of belonging was what she had lacked her entire life. The feeling of relief and contentment was incredible.

The rain began as she drove, and by the time she reached Winterbridge, it was torrential. Her windscreen wipers batted furiously to and fro, squeaking worryingly. A narrow miss with another car as she crossed the stone bridge had her peering over the steering wheel in a panic for the last mile.

If my income improves, a newer car wouldn't go amiss.

Parking at the back of the byre, Daisy pulled on her cagoule before dashing to the door, but by the time she'd got inside, she was drenched. Through the window, she could see the rain bouncing off the cobbles. The gallery and café were dark, but the cottage's lights were on, as usual. Perhaps Mr Giles found the weather atmospheric for his writing. She wondered if he ever wrote a thriller set in the brightness and warmth of summer, but she supposed it wouldn't fit.

Shaking off her wet clothes, Daisy put on warm jogging bottoms and an old hoodie, dried her hair carelessly and made herself a quick stir-fry before starting work. Jean's news had fired her up, and it was all she could do to stop herself from planning. That would have to wait till the new year. For now, she had to keep her walls filled. Digging around in her store cupboard, she got out more prints and frames, and the last few packs of Christmas cards, and restocked.

That done, she felt she could relax with a little painting... which was what this was all about, after all.

*

Alex spent a long day at Riverside on Wednesday, working his way through every task that Jules had left for him on a list. He was hoping to visit the hospital that evening. When the rain began, he reckoned it sounded worse than it was, the way rain always did on glass or corrugated metal roofs. He carried on working.

Despite the dark moving in alongside the rain, being alone didn't spook Alex. Riverside was *his* domain, his dream in his beloved Dales. Devoting an entire day to it felt like a luxury.

Still, the hard work wasn't enough to stop his mind from going over his encounter with Daisy yesterday – the awkwardness, his surprise over her pronouncement that they shouldn't continue the way they were, her assumption that he'd feel the same way… and his assumptions about her motivations.

For a bloke who preferred not to discuss emotions if at all possible, Alex couldn't help but feel that a decent conversation might be sensible.

Was he really missing out on something? His mother was right – he was a loner. That didn't mean he couldn't enjoy good company and good sex when the mood took him and the right woman came along. But his mother wanted him to find more than that, or at least have the courage not to turn away the opportunity.

Alex could be himself with Daisy. They could laugh at themselves and each other. He missed her when he hadn't been to Fox Farm for a while. His pulse raced when he saw her, when he anticipated kissing her… And their lovemaking had been special. Was that too strong a word? No, it wasn't.

He hated the sudden awkwardness between them.

The rain was so loud now, Alex began to worry about his property. Downing tools, he went to the doorway and peered out. The downpour was torrential, lashing the buildings and churning the ground into mud.

I'll need to spread more gravel on the paths before we open tomorrow.

Checking that everything was locked and secure got Alex drenched, despite his waterproofs. His truck took him the short way home, and then he was in the shower, rinsing off the rain and sweat, and feeling thoroughly depressed.

It's the weather, Alex. It's enough to depress the sheep in the fields.

After reheating a desultory offering of macaroni cheese from the freezer – Aunt Jean would be appalled – Alex thought about the hospital. But when he looked at his watch, he saw it was already seven. Too late to go, and even his trusty truck would struggle with the roads in these conditions. He texted his aunt to let her know he couldn't make it after all, then, not wanting to be alone in his dreary house in the dreary rain, he texted Gary.

Fancy a pint at the Masons Inn?

The reply soon came back.

Sorry, mate. It's our tenth wedding anniversary. Big night for us! The missus – I'm entitled to call her that now we're an old married couple – is cooking a fancy meal, the kids are going to bed early, and I'm hoping to get lucky.

And two minutes later…

Actually, I may be a bit drunk on prosecco, but the fact is, I don't need to get lucky. I already AM lucky to be married to this wonderful woman who was daft enough to say "I do" a decade ago today. Have a pint for me, mate. Cheers!

Alex stared at his phone, a lump in his throat.

See, Alex? There are people who take a chance and don't regret it. Not just old-timers like Aunt Jean and Uncle William, but people the same age as you. Will you still be happy on your own in fifteen years' time, when

Gary and Chelle celebrate their Silver Wedding Anniversary, or will you regret never taking a chance?

It only took him a moment to decide. Grabbing his phone, he pulled on a jacket and dashed out to his truck.

The mile to Fox Farm in such appalling conditions felt like a lifetime, and was certainly foolhardy, but Alex drove into the farmyard with a sense of purpose. Daisy was in the studio, and he almost battered the door down in his desire to get out of the rain. He saw her jump before coming over to let him in.

'Alex, what on earth…?'

He pushed his way inside, shaking himself like a wet dog and making her hop out of his way.

'Watch it!'

'Sorry.'

'Is everything alright?'

'I need to talk to you.'

Daisy eyed him warily. 'Tea?'

'Please.'

Alex took off his wet coat and draped it over the counter, then watched from her bedroom doorway while she made tea. Her scratty hoodie and saggy jogging bottoms made him smile. He knew what lay underneath now, didn't he? As for her hair… She must have been caught in the rain earlier because her brown mane, usually straight and mostly up in a ponytail, was loose around her face and shoulders, wavy and a little frizzy. It looked incredibly sexy.

Get a grip, Alex. You're not here to persuade her into bed. Although if that's the end result…

Daisy caught him studying her. 'What are you looking at?' She glanced down at her attire. 'I didn't expect any visitors tonight.'

'I like your hair like that. It's sexy.'

'It's a mess, that's what it is.' She handed him his tea and indicated that he should sit in the chair while she took the bed. 'What are you doing here?'

Alex's brain scrambled. He hadn't thought this through before he'd run to his truck, and the driving conditions had prevented him from rehearsing on the way. He would have to wing it. Maybe that wasn't a bad thing. At least whatever came out of his mouth would sound heartfelt.

'It's about us.'

'Us?' She looked alarmed. Uncomfortable.

'Yesterday, you said you knew I wouldn't want to continue after what happened on Sunday. I got a little mad because you caught me off guard. I thought Sunday night was amazing. I know it was spontaneous, but I didn't think it was a mistake – for either of us. And I know we haven't had a… formal arrangement up until now – dating or whatever. But I didn't expect you to put an end to it, just like that.'

Daisy hugged her mug in her hands, rising steam causing strands of hair around her face to turn damp.

'I was trying to make it easier for you,' she said. 'I spoke to Grace and…'

Uh-oh. Women chatting with their best friends never boded well for the bloke, in Alex's experience. He'd been branded a louse on more than one occasion via *that* route.

'She told you to dump me?'

Daisy glared at him. 'Quite the opposite. She said to see how it goes, maybe ask how *you* felt about it. But talking it through with her…' She shrugged. 'I thought that by asking you, I'd be putting you in an awkward position – that you'd feel obliged to say nice things so you didn't hurt my feelings. I know you don't want to get involved, so what's the point? It seemed best not to let it get out of hand.'

'Forget about me for a minute. Is that what *you* want?' Alex asked her.

'I… I don't know.'

There's hope, then. 'Okay, let me clear something up for you. Yes, I've avoided involvement in the past, for so many reasons – fear of failure, trauma from living through my parents' marriage, even plain old selfishness. But that might have changed.' He watched her carefully, seeing her expression alter from wariness to confusion. 'I like you, Daisy. More than like you. People who know me well can see that – my mother, Aunt Jean, Jules. They're all urging me to make an effort. To not let this whatever-it-is slip through my fingers. Things feel different with you. I can't ignore that any longer.'

He fell silent. There wasn't much more he could say – but what he had said was the truth, however badly expressed.

Daisy's mouth gaped in an 'O' shape before she closed it. She stared into her tea, then took a sip. 'Ow. Hot.' She placed it carefully on her bedside table. 'I… I wasn't expecting you to say that.'

'How do you feel about it?' he asked, exasperated. 'How do you feel about *me*?'

She chewed her lip. 'Much the same as you, I guess – I haven't felt this way about someone, even Eoin. I think there could be something worth exploring here. But we've become such good friends, Alex. I'd hate to lose that for the sake of a sexual relationship.'

Alex shook his head at the way she made it sound so clinical, when there had been nothing clinical about Sunday night at all.

'Does that mean I haven't been discarded, after all?'

Daisy considered him from those soft brown eyes. 'Maybe not.'

'So, can I come over there?'

'I suppose so.'

Placing his tea next to hers, Alex sat beside her on the bed. 'Let's take it as it comes, Daisy. No expectations. And no more assumptions.'

He thrust his fingers into her wild hair. And when she opened her mouth to reply, he silenced her with his.

Chapter Twenty-Four

Daisy wasn't sure what to think. One minute she was working in her studio, the rain pounding down outside, and the next, Alex was telling her he had feelings for her.

And then his lips were on hers, possessive and unstoppable.

She should feel ridiculously unsexy in her old, comfy clothes chosen only to get her warm after the rain, but Alex's kisses made her feel sexier than she ever had, and the clothes' warmth was no longer necessary.

As though he'd read her mind, Alex tugged at the zip of her hoodie. Their mouths being apart for even the time it took to get undressed was too long, and when his lips met hers again, as they lay in the narrow bed, skin to skin, Daisy felt a new kind of coming home in his arms.

If she had expected the playfulness and heat of their previous love-making, she was wrong. When he had her naked, all activity stopped for a moment as Alex surveyed her body. Once upon a time, that would have made her incredibly uncomfortable, but not with Alex.

'You're beautiful. Stop trying to hide it,' he murmured as he allowed his fingers to drift across her skin, making every last nerve end jump under his touch.

Daisy opened her mouth to make some self-deprecating remark, then closed it again. If he thought she was beautiful, why argue?

His hands stroked gently across her shoulders, her breasts, her hips. How he held himself in check she had no idea, because she could barely breathe now. It was as though he was making a deliberate effort not to rush this time, to show her how much he meant what he'd said about his feelings for her. That was touching… and excruciating. Unable to just lie there, her senses swamped, she began to stroke his back, his stomach, but he pushed her hands away.

'Don't. I won't be able to behave if you touch me. I want to concentrate on you for now.'

And he did… and oh, it was delicious. No man had ever concentrated their energies solely on her in bed. Any self-consciousness melted away under his touch, until he achieved his aim and she lay spent, her cheeks flushed and self-awareness returning.

'*Now* you can touch me,' Alex groaned. '*Please.*'

Daisy happily obeyed, until the small room was filled with heat and sighs.

As they lay together afterwards, breathless, all Daisy could think was, *Thank goodness he had the courage to come here tonight. To tell me how he felt. I wouldn't have been able to do the same.* She drifted to sleep with a smile on her face.

When she woke, she couldn't believe they'd slept till morning in that single bed – most of which Alex took up by himself through necessity. But he had her clutched tight in his arms and she hadn't fallen off, and they woke with a shy smile for each other.

'I have to get up. I'm stiff,' Daisy complained.

Inevitably, this led to Alex raising a comical eyebrow. 'Ditto.'

Daisy rolled her eyes. 'Don't get any ideas. We both have to work today.'

'True. But at the risk of yet another *double entendre*, we're both early risers. Make love to me, Daisy. It'll see me through the day.'

How can I refuse a plea like that?

By the time they were up, showered and dressed, it was a later start than either of them was used to.

At the door, Alex rubbed his back. 'I'm too old for a single bed.'

'I could come to yours?'

'You could, if you want to be depressed by the décor.'

'I won't be concentrating on the décor.'

'Glad to hear it.' He kissed her lightly on the lips. 'See ya.' And he was gone.

Grinning like an idiot, Daisy made herself tea and took it to her easel, where she spent five minutes staring unseeingly at her painting, like a moonstruck teenager. *Pull yourself together, Daisy!*

A light knock at her door had her looking up as Angie came in.

'Morning. I saw Alex's truck along the lane. Bit early for him to be at Fox Farm, isn't it? Everything alright?'

'Oh, er, not sure. He was… rummaging in one of the outbuildings. Maybe he was picking something up.'

'Maybe he was,' Angie commented wryly. 'How were your days off? The weather was awful yesterday.'

'I got a walk in before the rain started and I visited Jean in the afternoon. She's managed twelve steps!' *And she offered me a permanent place here at Fox Farm, which I'm thrilled about but probably not allowed to tell you yet.* 'How's Jamie doing at the café?'

'Brilliant. I like that lad. Shame he'll leave in September. And if Sue retires soon, I'll have new staff to find and train. Still, Alex was right about the café – it's less cramped, and it's doing well.'

'I'm sure he'd be pleased to hear that.'

'I'll tell him when I see him. He deserves a bit of slack. As for Lisa, I'm not convinced she'll be here much longer. She was losing interest in the gallery *before* the changes.'

'You'd think the new space would have fired up her enthusiasm.'

'I agree. But I think she feels that she and Jean had an understanding, and she doesn't like Alex interfering.'

'He only interfered where necessary, acting on Jean's wishes. Jean isn't up to dealing with Lisa leaving.'

'I reckon Jean's health is the only reason Lisa's stuck it out. You mark my words, she'll hand in her notice come the spring. I can feel it in my bones. Well, I'd better get going. Have a good day.'

'You too.'

Daisy sat musing after Angie had gone. It sounded like there could be more changes at Fox Farm in the near future – just as she was due to become a permanent part of it. And yet that was what life was about, wasn't it? Things evolved. Nothing stayed static. She, of all people, knew that.

Looking around her studio, Daisy felt deep contentment that this was now hers. Jean would draw up a contract, and that was fine. What Jean did for her this year was kind, but Daisy would rather be on an official footing now that she was staying.

She hadn't got around to telling Alex about it last night, she realised – although that wasn't surprising, once he'd started telling her how he felt about her. *Showing* her how he felt. General business chit-chat wouldn't exactly have been appropriate then.

Anyway, surely he knew? Jean wouldn't have made the offer without consulting him. Or would she? After all, Fox Farm was Jean's, not Alex's.

Daisy would check next time she saw him. It was hardly urgent, was it?

*

Alex felt so *good* as he drove to Riverside that morning. He probably had his mother to thank for that. She'd told him to find courage; take a leap of faith. He had, and it had paid off. He had no idea where he and Daisy were heading, but they were on a journey together, which was more than they had been a couple of days ago.

Heaven forbid that his elation should last. His day became a rollercoaster from the moment he arrived at Riverside.

'Alex, I need to speak to you.' Jim, a barrow full of gravel in hand, collared him the moment his truck drew up.

'Are you doing the paths?' Alex asked. 'Sorry, Jim. I meant to be here earlier, so we could do it together.'

'Least of our worries.'

Alex's heart sank. 'Why?'

'We lost some roof panes in the propagation greenhouse. Hail in the night.'

'Hail?' Alex hadn't heard hail. He'd slept like a log, with Daisy in his arms. 'How bad is it?'

'We need plastic over for now. Repairs ASAP. Not too many plants underneath at this time of year, thank goodness.'

'Okay, I'll get to it, if you and Kieran can deal with the paths.' He glanced around him. 'It'd be cheaper to put slabs down, in the long run.'

'They get slippery with rain and ice, though, Alex. Bit of a liability.'

'Yeah. I'll think about it, if I ever get time.'

Alex went to examine the greenhouse damage, then fetched supplies with a cursory wave at Jules along the way. Some panes got damaged every year, but he could have done without it right now.

As he got started, his phone rang.

'Aunt Jean, this is early for you. Is everything alright?'

'I'll say. Marvellous, actually, love. The doctor's been round. She says I can be home for Christmas!'

'*Really?*' Alex hadn't expected that. How long since he'd spoken to the doctor about Aunt Jean's progress? A few days? A week? He'd been so busy.

'Isn't that wonderful?' Jean insisted.

'Yes. Wonderful. What date do they have in mind?'

'They're hoping the beginning of next week.'

Alex's mind raced. Nigel Giles was due to leave this weekend, but Alex would have to clean the cottage, put all his aunt's belongings back, get supplies in, organise carers… He felt sick at how much there was to do. Let alone Christmas being just over a week away.

'The discharge team want a meeting about what I'll need,' Aunt Jean went on. 'Can you come tomorrow at eleven?'

No choice, have I? 'No problem.'

'Will the writer be out in time?'

'He's due to leave Saturday.'

'Good. Home for Christmas. Bliss!' She rang off.

Her voice had been so gleeful, and Alex felt guilty. He knew his heart should be full for her; he should be grateful she'd made such a good recovery and could be at home for Christmas. He *did* feel all of that, but the sense of overwhelm took much of it away. So much to do, so little time…

Leaving what he was doing, he went back to the main building to update Jules before they opened.

'Jules. I need a quick word.'

'Actually, Alex, so do I.'

'But…'

'Please, Alex. Me first. It's important, and it's no good when we have customers. There's never a good time to catch you nowadays.'

'Sounds serious.' He followed her into the office, ducking under the string of fairy lights draped over the doorway.

'Alex, when did you last look at the books? Riverside's, not Fox Farm's?'

'Not since Aunt Jean's stroke. Why?'

'I think you should. I wasn't going to bother you before Christmas, but you may need to do a little planning over the festive season.'

His heart hit his boots. 'What are you trying to tell me?'

Jules turned the PC monitor towards him. 'We're down on the same time last year. It's not horrendous, but it is worrying.'

Alex frowned, trying to take in the figures on the spreadsheet. 'We're doing the same things, selling the same things. Is it because I haven't been here as much? Have customers had to walk away without getting served?'

Jules looked mutinous at that. 'We've done our best to cover you. Sometimes customers got a little impatient waiting for assistance. Luckily, it's not the season for doling out too much advice. But spring will be a different matter. You know what it's like – everyone gets garden crazy. TV programmes get people all fired up to want this, that and the other, and they need the guidance to go with it. You're good at that, and it's *you* the regular customers want. We've got away with your absences so far, other than some income loss. But spring is the big money-making season for us, and if people can't chat to you – their local, trusted font-of-all-knowledge – they may consider going elsewhere. I know Fox Farm had to be a priority for you, but if you've got it on an even keel now, you need to start worrying about Riverside again, before too much damage is done.'

'But I have been here…'

'A few hours here, a couple there. In the flesh, doing little jobs. But not *here*, Alex.' She tapped the side of his head. 'We need you back in control, planning, knowing what's going on around here. I can't do it all myself.' She blew out a shaky breath. 'Sorry. That's a lot to throw at you.'

Alex put an arm around her shoulders and hugged her to him. 'I'm sorry, Jules.'

'I know you are.' She laid her head on his shoulder. 'You're only trying to do what's best for everybody. But you've been spreading yourself too thin. You have to choose where your priorities lie. Taking charge of Fox Farm is temporary. Riverside is permanent. It's *yours*.'

He heard the wobble in her voice; knew she took real pride in what they'd achieved together over the years.

Taking charge of Fox Farm is temporary, is it? Hmmph. Aunt Jean hadn't mentioned her notion of leaving a legacy for a while, but knowing her, she wouldn't let it lie forever.

'I'll look at the books over Christmas, I promise. We'll work something out.'

She managed a teary smile. 'Thanks. So, what did you need to tell me?'

With a sigh, Alex explained why he wouldn't be at Riverside much over the next few days.

'It's wonderful news, that Jean's coming home,' Jules said. 'But hard work for you.'

'Yes. And hard cheese on Riverside. Yet again.'

He left her, got his temporary covers up in the greenhouse and was fetching the spare panes they kept on hand when he heard his mobile tone.

N.J. Giles. Good. I can ask him what time he's leaving on Saturday.

'Nigel. How are you?'

'Fine, Alex, thanks, but I thought you should know about the cottage.'

For what felt like the tenth time already that day, Alex's heart plummeted south. 'What about the cottage?'

'There're a couple of broken roof tiles and a damaged gutter. I wouldn't have spotted them – I've no reason to go round the back – but I could hear the rain pouring off the gutter last night so I took a look, and part of it's broken off.'

You have got to be kidding me. 'I appreciate you letting me know. I'll be round when I can. Don't be alarmed if a ladder appears at the window – I know you're usually the scare-giver, not the scare-recipient.'

The writer chuckled. 'Indeed. Well, sorry to be the bearer of bad news.'

'Not your fault. Listen, could I ask what time you're planning to leave on Saturday?'

'First thing.'

'Your book's all finished?'

'Yes.' Alex could hear the relief in the man's voice. 'Thanks for the cottage, Alex. The solitude, the lack of distractions, made all the difference. And the atmosphere was perfect on closing days and evenings, without the hordes. Can't say the Christmas tree or Santa cabin fit in, but I suppose that's what I have an imagination for.' Nigel chuckled.

'Glad it worked out.'

Clicking off, Alex called Gary. 'Gary, mate. My best friend. How are you this fine morning?'

'Hmmph. What do you want?'

Alex explained. 'I wouldn't ask, but with Aunt Jean coming home soon…'

Gary gave a sigh of resignation. 'I'll meet you there at two-ish. But I'm not a roofer, Alex. I can only fix the gutter and maybe patch the roof for now.'

'Understood. I owe you.'

Relieved that he had that underway, Alex got on with his repairs. With everything that was going on, Daisy had been pushed to the back of his mind, and when she popped to the front, he pushed her right back again. He didn't want to think about her, the loveliness of her, alongside all this other crap going on. Instead, he tried to slot into place all the things he had to do over the next few days to get Aunt Jean home and sorted. Then there was Christmas itself. Aunt Jean usually cooked Christmas dinner for them both and whoever else she invited, but of course that wouldn't happen this year.

So now I have to go shopping at the height of the mad season? Turkey and all the trimmings? Plan it? Cook it? Give me strength!

He felt immediately guilty for complaining. Aunt Jean *deserved* a Christmas dinner, after all she'd been through. And after all the wonderful Christmases he'd spent with her since moving to Winterbridge, it was the least he could do to give her the same.

But as Alex fixed the new panes in, checked for any other damage, made sure Jules wasn't having a nervous breakdown, ensured he gave customers who stopped him the time and help they needed – mindful of what Jules had said – he realised that the short term wasn't what worried him. He could clean and sort the cottage; deal with whatever the hospital said Jean needed; cook Christmas dinner. In a couple of weeks, all that would be behind him.

No, what worried him was moving forward into the new year, and the ongoing level of his involvement with Fox Farm. After what Jules had told him that morning, he couldn't, *wouldn't* neglect Riverside in the run-up to spring. Somehow, he had to back away from Fox Farm.

And yet he couldn't see how to make that happen. Did Aunt Jean honestly expect him to run both businesses for the foreseeable future and beyond?

*

Daisy was having a fantastic day. The studio was busy from the moment she opened, with people looking for last-minute presents. Her Christmas cards were almost gone, but with only a week to go till Christmas, there was no point in ordering more.

That got her thinking about next year already. Grace was right – there was so much more she could sell that would make great presents, both at Christmas and all year round. Her prints would look good on mugs, tote bags, cushions. In the new year, she would draw up a plan, source the materials, talk to her printer… Between customers, she scribbled a rough to-do list. She couldn't help herself. Everything was finally falling into place with her business – and with Alex. She admired him for making the first move, for being willing to talk things through… not that they'd done much talking. Perhaps they should do more, but for now, Daisy was content knowing he wanted to be with her and she with him.

Early in the afternoon, N.J. Giles came into her studio. 'Christmas shopping,' he explained. 'I leave on Saturday.'

'Did you finish?'

'Yes. First draft, anyway. I can relax over Christmas.' He made a face. 'Until the edits come back in January.'

Daisy smiled. 'Oh! I have a favour to ask,' she remembered. 'I bought one of your books as a gift for someone. Would you sign it for me?'

'With pleasure. Just tell me what to write – within reason.' He winked.

Daisy fetched the book from her room, and he obliged.

'Thank you. So, are you looking for something in particular, or would you prefer to browse?'

'I'd love one of your paintings of the farm,' he said decisively. 'For my wife – to show her where she lost me to. Do you have a wintry one?'

When Daisy showed him the couple of prints she had up, he asked, 'Do you have the original of that one?' He pointed at the one he preferred.

Daisy tried to hide her surprise. She did display *some* original paintings, but she tried not to fill the wall with them – the prices tended to put people off. Prints were far more affordable. 'I do, but it would be a lot more expensive.'

'That's fine. My wife deserves it.'

'Then I'll fetch it.'

When Daisy brought it out from her store cupboard, he said instantly, 'Perfect. I'll take it.'

'I'll wrap it for you.'

As she handed him his package, he said, 'Now the gallery, to find something for my daughters, sister-in-law and an ancient aunt.' He headed for the door, then turned back. 'Thank you again, for letting me stab you that foggy night. It was much appreciated.' He smiled and left.

Embarrassed by the startled looks from her other browsers, Daisy declared, 'He's a writer. What can I say? They're an odd bunch.'

Daisy watched N.J. Giles walk across the yard with mixed feelings. Like the others, she'd resented him taking over Jean's cottage at first, but now, she would miss knowing he was there. She would feel isolated, on her own at Fox Farm again. Still, the way things were going between her and Alex, she didn't anticipate being alone *every* single night from now on.

Sebastian, walking through the door an hour later, was a far less welcome visitor – and a total surprise. Giving her a mere nod – she was dealing with a customer at the counter – he studied the art on her wall as though he had hoped for Renoir and found kindergarten.

When she was free, she went over to him. 'Sebastian. Can I help?'

He jerked a thumb at the wall. 'Making a decent living?'

Offended – and grateful there were currently no other customers – Daisy said cautiously, 'I'm getting by. The studio's been a bonus.'

'I can imagine. It must help that you're here on a freebie, eh?'

'That's not quite…'

'Jean tells me that's set to continue,' he cut her off. 'A favourable arrangement for you.'

'Jean has offered me the studio, but…'

'Lucky you.'

Daisy bristled. 'I wouldn't call it *luck*. Jean loves my work and likes having me here. That's her decision, surely?'

'If you choose to look at it that way.'

Daisy frowned. 'What other way is there to look at it?'

'Well, first of all, you're talking about a frail, sick woman. You *could* be seen to be taking advantage of her.'

'How *dare* you?'

Sebastian held up a hand. 'And then there's the question of how Alex will feel about it. He seems determined to take over here. He might not agree with the arrangement. I wouldn't get too settled, if I were you, or make a lot of plans. Jean's offer could be rescinded at any time.'

Daisy couldn't believe what she was hearing. But the truth was, she *didn't* know how Alex felt about Jean's offer. She hadn't had a chance to discuss it with him yet.

'But Alex…'

'Ah, yes.' Sebastian gave her a knowing look. 'You think you've got him twisted around your little finger, don't you, with that scruffy, ditzy artist look? Scrubbing floors and helping out and wheedling your way in. I imagine you've thrown in sex as an added incentive?' When Daisy gaped at him, he went on smoothly, 'If you imagine that'll work, you're sadly mistaken. Alex has had plenty of women, and not one of them has managed to get their claws into him. What makes you think you're any different? Don't fool yourself, Daisy. Alex is a lost cause, relationship-wise. Both he and Fox Farm will only ever be temporary for you. Even if you manage to spin out your stay here, the clock will always be ticking. Alex will tire of you, or this place will go downhill, or eventually, Jean will have to give it up.' He shrugged. 'Like I said, I wouldn't get too settled, if I were you.' And with that, he swept out, his expensive coat flapping.

'Well!' Daisy staggered to her counter stool and sat, shaking with shock and anger. Who on *earth* did that man think he was, speaking to her like that? Replaying the conversation in her head, she knew she should have stood up for herself more… But it had been hard enough absorbing his accusations and spiteful comments, and besides, he'd cut across her before she could think of a decent comeback. She hadn't stood a chance. Was this what it was like for Alex?

Alex.

Daisy knew she shouldn't let them, but the seeds of doubt that Sebastian had planted were already snaking their way into her brain, driving away the pleasure of the night's lovemaking; the joy of the things

Alex had said to her. Had he meant those things? Or did he only think they were true… for now? *Could* she expect him to change for her?

As for the studio? Daisy's gaze landed on her new year to-do list. All those hopes and plans to expand, explore new things with her art, her business… Was Sebastian right? Would her temporary status at Fox Farm always be just that?

Daisy didn't *want* a temporary life any more. She wanted a home. And she'd hoped her home was right here.

Chapter Twenty-Five

Alex lost track of time, so he'd missed lunch and was starving by the time he met Gary at Fox Farm.

'Got any food?' he asked.

'Bag of crisps in the truck. Doubt they're in date.'

'Beggars can't be choosers.' Alex ate them – tasteless and soggy – whilst holding the foot of the ladder for Gary, who rooted around up there, came back down and inspected the broken tiles on the ground.

'The gutter, we can fix,' he said. 'I brought a new piece with me. But *all* the guttering needs replacing, Alex. It's ancient. The tiles, I can patch for now. But that roof…'

The crisps turned to cement in Alex's stomach. 'What about it?'

'I reckon it's had it.' Gary picked up a piece of tile and showed Alex how easily it broke; that it was spongy. 'Round the back here, with those trees overgrown, you get moss, and what with age…' Seeing Alex's stricken expression, he put a hand on his shoulder. 'But I'm no roofer. You need a proper opinion and estimate. I know a good bloke.'

'Gary, I can't… Aunt Jean…'

'Hey. Take deep breaths, mate.' Gary looked alarmed. 'I might be wrong. But if not, you might be best moving Jean out for a while during the repairs.'

'She'll only just be back in!'

'It might not need doing straight away. Wait till the roofer gives his verdict. He probably won't have time to even look till the new year, anyway. Then you and Jean can decide what to do.'

'Roofs don't come cheap.'

'No, but Jean has savings, right? Repairs like this come up every now and again. It is what it is.' Gary looked at him, concerned. 'Are you alright?'

'Yeah. Just having a bad day.'

At the sound of footsteps, Gary poked his head around the corner of the cottage. 'Well, don't look now, but your day's about to get a whole lot worse. Sebastian's here.'

Alex's heart sank. Again. 'Great.'

'We need to talk,' Sebastian said as he approached.

Gary quietly packed up and scuttled off to his truck.

'I'm busy here, Sebastian,' Alex told him, his tone curt.

'Problems?'

'Jean's gutters and roof aren't sound.'

Sebastian merely nodded. No '*I told you so*' or sarcasm. That was quite a novelty. 'You look like you could do with a pot of tea,' he said instead.

Surprised at his cousin's demeanour, Alex indicated the café, but Sebastian shook his head.

'Privately,' he insisted. 'We have a lot to discuss. Your place?'

'I thought you hated my place.'

'I didn't say that. I only said you hadn't done much with it, and you rightly pointed out that you hadn't had much time.'

'Who is this new Sebastian? Where's the old one?'

'Look, Alex, you and I have never seen eye to eye, especially recently. But I've done a lot of thinking, and we need to put aside our differences for a while. C'mon.'

Meekly, Alex got in his truck and followed Sebastian's fancy car down to the village. In his chilly lounge, he turned the heating on and made a pot of tea while Sebastian settled in the armchair. His stomach growling, Alex grabbed a packet of biscuits and put them on the tray.

'Did Aunt Jean tell you she's coming home next week?' Alex asked as he poured the tea.

'She phoned this morning. Great news, of course. I'd already visited her last night, before she knew about that.'

'Oh?' Aunt Jean hadn't told Alex that Sebastian was back already. She must have been too excited about the doctor's news.

'We were chatting, and I'm worried,' his cousin said.

Here we go again. But Sebastian was using a different tone this time, and that in itself was intriguing enough for Alex not to lose his cool... yet.

'What about?'

'Alex, I want to make one more appeal to you to see sense.' Sebastian held up a hand. 'And before you jump down my throat or storm out – which I wouldn't advise, since you're in your own home – I'm begging you to hear me out.'

'Okay...'

'Jean says you're on track to recoup the investment in Fox Farm as well as the savings she already used?'

'It'll take at least the summer to do it, but yes, I think so.'

'And then what?'

'How do you mean?'

'It's a straightforward question. Jean's coming home. She needs some care, which is to be paid for. You have no idea how much more care she'll need in the future or how much that will cost. The cottage, for example. Could a stair lift be fitted in such an old, awkward building? How expensive would that be?'

'What are you driving at?'

'I'm suggesting the cottage might not be the best place for her. She lives alone. What if she falls? Perhaps she should consider moving. There are specially designed flats for older people. I've looked online. Admittedly the nearest are a few miles away, but she would have neighbours, a warden…' Sebastian leaned forward, his manicured fingers steepled together. 'Alex, you've done a great job these past few weeks. I know how much you love Fox Farm, and I'm sorry if I've been unsympathetic to that. I was frustrated because I couldn't make you see.'

'See what?' Alex was becoming alarmed at how calm and reasonable Sebastian sounded.

'That it simply isn't sustainable. I spoke to the staff nurse last night. She said Jean will be advised to avoid stress. Not for a while. *Forever*. How could she possibly run Fox Farm without stress? And before you tell me that you're around, how can *that* work? You have your own business. You'll end up having to choose.'

Jules had said the exact same thing, hadn't she? Not that Alex hadn't thought it a hundred times already.

'You want Aunt Jean to sell up and move to a poky flat? Why don't you just shove her in an old people's home and be done with it?' Alex's eyes narrowed. 'This is all about your inheritance again, isn't it?'

Sebastian held his hands out, palms up. 'If it were, how would shoving her in an old people's home be to my advantage? Those places cost a fortune. As you said, she's only seventy-two. She'd go through all her savings, Fox Farm would be sold and there'd hardly be anything left.'

Alex's mind raced. Everything Sebastian said made sense – and that scared him. He *hadn't* worked out how he could help run Fox Farm without watching Riverside decline… let alone his aunt's fanciful notion of keeping Fox Farm going after she left this earth. Sebastian didn't know about *that* yet, did he? Imagine the fun they would have after she'd gone, argy-bargying about it! Was Sebastian right? Moving Aunt Jean would be painful, but at least if she sold Fox Farm, she would no longer be tied to the stress of it.

'So, you're going to try to persuade her to sell?' Alex asked.

'She won't listen to me. She doesn't trust me. She trusts *you*. It would have to be you.'

'I've been her source of hope, and now you want me to be her executioner?'

'You need to be her voice of reason.'

Alex shook his head. 'I tried, and she wouldn't have it.'

'That was early on. Now she knows how much you've put into this. You have to tell her you can't keep it up.'

'What's in it for you?'

'Does something have to be in it for me?'

'Usually, yes.'

Sebastian shrugged. 'This is a big responsibility for us both, and I'd like to see it resolved; see Jean settled. See you free to do your own thing.'

Hmmm. There has got *to be another angle here, but I'm not seeing it.*

'But you'll have to move fast,' Sebastian went on. 'Disabuse her of all her notions. The longer you carry on like this, the more she'll expect it.'

'I was waiting for her to get settled before we had any discussions about it.' *Perhaps I was hoping she'd see for herself that it isn't sustainable.* 'We can talk in the new year.'

'Except she's already making long-term plans, isn't she?'

Alex frowned. 'Such as?'

'Such as offering the studio to Daisy on a permanent basis yesterday.' When Alex failed to hide his surprise, Sebastian enquired innocently, 'You didn't know?'

'I… No. Aunt Jean was too excited about coming home when she phoned me this morning.'

Daisy could have mentioned it last night, though. Why didn't she?

Because you were busy discussing other things, Alex. Doing *other things.*

'Anyway, I can see why,' Alex defended his aunt. 'Changing the artist over each year is a pain. Daisy's thriving there. She's done a lot for Fox Farm lately, and she's become good friends with Aunt Jean.'

'That doesn't worry you?'

Alex gave Sebastian a puzzled look. 'Why should it?'

'It doesn't bother you, the way Daisy's inveigled her way into Jean's heart so quickly? Into yours?' He gave Alex a knowing look that made him squirm. 'Made herself so indispensable? No wonder you didn't want to show me the books. You think I don't know how Fox Farm runs, but I do remember Jean telling me about letting Daisy have the studio rent-free. And now, Daisy's managed to turn that into a permanent arrangement. Odd that she hasn't told you yet. Smells fishy to me.'

Sebastian's insinuations lodged in Alex's brain – nasty little niggles of doubt.

'I'd have to speak to Aunt Jean about it,' Alex said carefully.

'Well.' Sebastian stood. 'Daisy isn't really the issue, is she? I was merely using her to illustrate that Jean's making promises and commitments she may not be able to keep, and the sooner you speak to her, the better, or you'll be stuck with running Fox Farm, your own business playing second fiddle, for the rest of Jean's lifetime. Think about it.'

Alex sat for a long time after Sebastian left, doing just that, his tea going cold, the biscuits untouched, his growling stomach ignored.

When his phone rang, he realised it was dark outside.

'Jean called me with the good news. I'm so excited for her!' his mother gushed. 'Will you be okay getting her cottage sorted? The carers? I know there's Christmas dinner to do, but don't worry – you'll only have to do the shopping. I'll send you a list. I spoke to my boss and she's giving me Christmas Eve off. If I set off really early, I could be there by mid-afternoon. That way I can help you prep and we can spend the evening together with Jean. Then you and I can cook Christmas dinner for her. How does that sound?'

Alex's head was spinning. Actually, he felt downright nauseous. Telling himself it was lack of food, he mumbled into the phone, 'Sounds fine, Mum. But I have to go now. Sorry.' He threw the phone down and gulped in deep breaths.

When he'd stabilised, he forced himself into the kitchen to make toast which felt like eating cardboard, microwaved his tea and took the mug with him to bed. It was only six o'clock.

*

Daisy was disappointed that Alex hadn't been in touch since she'd waved him off the previous morning. She hadn't expected them to suddenly be in each other's pockets, but she had hoped for a text or a call. She'd taken out her phone several times, then changed her mind. Sebastian's words had got to her, despite her best efforts to block them out, and she didn't want Alex to think she was clingy if he needed space.

Mid-morning, Angie came over to the studio with a mocha and a deformed gingerbread snowman for her. 'On the house,' she declared. 'I needed a break. Sue's ratty today – she's coming down with a cold, and that's panicking Lisa, who's worried Sue'll be off sick so that Jamie'll have to cover. Face like a wet weekend, Lisa has!'

'Well, you're welcome here. I'm not busy at the moment. Have a perch.'

Angie settled on the stool behind Daisy's counter. 'You've heard the news?'

'What news?'

'About Jean coming home. Beginning of next week.'

'No. I hadn't.' *Why didn't Jean call to tell me? Why didn't Alex?*

'Alex is at the hospital, for a meeting about what's required. He'll have a lot to do – Mr Giles doesn't leave till tomorrow, so he's got the whole cottage to sort out this weekend, poor lad.'

'That'll keep him busy.' *And it explains why he's not been in contact, with so much on his mind. Even so…*

'And that dreadful cousin of his is back,' Angie went on. 'I saw him yesterday, bothering Alex when he was over at Jean's with Gary, trying to deal with her broken gutters.'

Oh, I know Sebastian was here, alright. I hadn't realised Alex was around, though. Why didn't he pop by?

'Sebastian dragged him off,' Angie said, as though in explanation. 'No doubt he wanted to bother him about Jean again. The nerve of him! Never here, and yet interfering all the time.'

Daisy tried a smile. 'Well, it's brilliant news about Jean. Home before Christmas! And Mr Giles seems pleased with himself. He bought one of my originals.'

'Jamie said he spent a fortune in the gallery, too,' Angie said. 'Making up for his absence, he said, or some such. And he placed an order with me for a whole lemon drizzle cake and a batch of fresh mince pies to take with him tomorrow morning. He's been rather partial to my lemon cake while he's been here.' Angie puffed out her chest in pride.

'I'm not surprised. It's the nicest *I've* ever tasted.'

Pleased by the compliment, Angie stood. 'Well, I'd better get back to see if Sue's gone into a decline yet.'

'Thanks for the coffee.'

'Thank *you* for the chat, love. I'll miss that when you leave in the spring.'

Daisy smiled a secret smile as Angie left. *You won't have to, Angie, because I'm staying.* But her face soon fell. Sebastian's many scenarios as to why Jean's offer might not hold may have been spiteful, but they were all valid possibilities. She shouldn't count her chickens.

Surely Alex could at least have sent her a text to tell her about Jean coming home? At lunchtime, she decided to make the first move and texted him to say she'd heard the news about Jean and hoped the meeting at the hospital had gone well.

His curt reply – *Thanks* – fell far short of what she'd hoped for, but she told herself it wasn't surprising that all this would make him a bit short-tempered.

She wasn't wrong. Alex appeared not long after she'd closed up for the day, his rap on the glass door impatient.

'Hi. How are you?' she asked.

'I'll live. Can I come in?'

Daisy moved aside. 'Tea?' She went to her kettle with an element of dismay. Shouldn't they kiss when they greeted each other, now that they were… together? She hadn't even got a peck on the cheek.

Bringing his tea through to the studio, she perched on her stool and watched him pace. 'How did the meeting at the hospital go?'

'They'll send a team ahead of Aunt Jean to check out the cottage, then they'll make sure she can manage when she gets back – that she can get upstairs and what-have-you. I'm not sure how I'm expected to be at the cottage with them *and* fetch her home, both at the same time.'

'Can't Sebastian bring her?' *He might as well be useful for something other than making a hateful nuisance of himself.*

'Maybe. I'll ask him. Then they've organised carers to help her shower or bath every other day – she'll have to pay for that, of course. They were helpful and kind enough.'

Then why do you sound so unhappy? 'Jean must be over the moon.'

'Yes, she's very chipper.' At that, he finally smiled. 'She can't wait to get home.'

'I can imagine. Back to her beloved Fox Farm. Back to normal.'

'Not back to normal, though,' Alex pointed out. 'She's not up to that, is she?' He stopped pacing and fixed her with a disconcerting stare. 'Daisy, why didn't you tell me she offered you the studio permanently on Wednesday? You didn't say anything to me that night.' When Daisy said nothing, taken aback by the cold tone in his voice, he went on, 'Was it because you thought I wouldn't approve?'

'What? No!' Sebastian's suggestion of that very thing flitted through her mind, but she pushed it away. 'If anything, I would've thought you'd be pleased for me. For *us*.' She stressed 'us' because she didn't feel like there was much *us* in this conversation so far. 'I assumed Jean had already spoken to you about it. I *would* have told you, but it didn't feel like an appropriate time. You wanted to speak to me about you and me, and then... Well.'

'And in the morning?'

What is this, the Spanish Inquisition? 'Alex, we were both in a hurry after we... slept in. What's the problem?'

'Did you ask Jean for the studio?' he asked, his voice faltering. 'Was it your idea?'

'No!' Feeling at a disadvantage on her stool, Daisy stood. 'She phoned me, asking me to visit her at the hospital. Her offer came out of the blue. I was expecting to leave in the spring as planned. Naturally, I'm thrilled that I won't have to.'

'Yes, I can imagine.'

Daisy felt sick. 'What's that tone for?'

Alex seemed to weigh up his words before he spoke. 'You know Jean can't afford to give you this place rent-free. Why did you accept?'

'Whoa! Back up a minute.' Daisy held her hands in front of her. 'Have you spoken to Jean about this?'

'No. I was up to my eyes in physios and occupational therapists, and Aunt Jean was exhausted by the end of it all. Sebastian told me yesterday.'

'Sebastian.' Daisy felt unbelievably disappointed in Alex. 'He told you this rent-free rubbish?'

'I… Yes.'

'Then he's either got the wrong end of the stick or he's deliberately causing trouble, because that is *not* the arrangement.' Daisy toyed with telling him about Sebastian's visit yesterday – how he hadn't let her get a word in edgewise to clarify the arrangement – but she decided his accusations might be best left unsaid. What mattered was what Alex thought, not his cousin. 'I'm getting sick of people thinking I'm freeloading. I already told you I'll be paying Jean a percentage of my takings for this current year. And for your information, Jean *will* charge me rent from the spring – which I feel able to afford, now I'm better established. I wouldn't have allowed her to do it any other way. I thought you'd be happy for me *and* for Jean. Not changing artists each year is one less thing for her to worry about.'

Alex closed his eyes a moment. When he opened them, his expression was oddly lost. 'I'm sorry I misunderstood. Sebastian must have got his facts muddled.'

You're not entertaining the idea that he did it deliberately, then?

'But you and I need to have a confidential chat, Daisy.'

He sounded so serious, Daisy's heart beat erratically in her throat. 'Jean will be alright, won't she?' she asked.

'In the sense that you mean, yes. But Fox Farm…? I'm sorry she offered you the studio without asking me first. I know you'll be planning ahead, and that's the only reason I'm telling you this.'

'What? You're scaring me.'

'I'm going to persuade Aunt Jean to sell up.'

Daisy was so shocked, she swayed where she stood. 'I… I don't understand.'

'Oh, come on, Daisy, don't look so surprised.' Alex began to pace again. 'This whole thing's got out of hand. Aunt Jean can't run this place the way she did before. Now, the doctors say she has to avoid stress at all costs. How could it work?'

'But you can…'

'No, I can't! I have my own life! My own business!' he yelled. It was the first time Daisy had heard him raise his voice. 'Takings are already down at Riverside. Am I supposed to allow everything I've worked for to be squandered away for somebody else, no matter how much I love her?'

'No, but surely there are ways around it?'

'Like what? Feel free to throw any bright ideas my way, because my brain hurts, going round in circles.' The sarcasm was plain in his voice.

'Can't you get extra staff in at Riverside?'

'The budget won't stretch unless I expand – which I can't if I'm looking after this place,' he snapped.

'Maybe you could get someone in here, then?'

'I told you Fox Farm isn't making ends meet.'

'But the changes…'

'They're working, but they have to pay Aunt Jean back first, and not only for all the alterations we've made. She's been propping this damned place up with her savings for the past two years.'

Ah. No wonder Alex was so keen to improve income. 'But if it's working, then in the long term…'

'You're not listening to me. I don't *want* to look at the long term any more! She has to sell.'

'I can't believe what you're saying.'

Alex looked at her, shadows under his eyes and lines etched deep in his forehead. 'Then I suggest you try, because I'm telling you how it's got to be. I can't do this. When I look ahead, all I can see is hard work at Fox Farm, while Riverside and my own plans dribble away to nothing.' Tears formed in his eyes, alarming Daisy. 'I love Aunt Jean dearly, but I can't put aside everything I worked for to enable *her* dreams. Surely you can see how unfair that is?'

Daisy's heart jolted. She had so much sympathy for his situation, but this sudden turnaround had knocked her for six.

'But what about everything you've been doing around here?'

'I don't think it was time or money wasted. It's brought in plenty of revenue, and it'll continue to do that until we find a buyer.'

Daisy couldn't believe he was willing to throw it all away. 'But Jean's lifelong dream will be lost!'

'Aunt Jean's had her dream and watched it grow. Why does everyone think it's okay for me not to have that for myself, with Riverside? Why does everyone expect me to give up on my own life to live someone else's?'

'Jean's getting older, Alex, and she's been unwell. She only wants to see it go on a little longer.'

'Hardly! From beyond the grave, too. That's too much to ask of me.'

Daisy's blood ran cold. 'From beyond the grave? What are you talking about?'

'This isn't just about Aunt Jean wanting something to come back to *now*. It's about wanting to leave a legacy. About eliciting promises from me to keep Fox Farm going *ad infinitum*. I love her, but I can't promise that.'

Daisy should have kept quiet then. The raw frustration in his voice should have been enough to stop her. But she'd become too involved – with Fox Farm, with Jean. With *him*. She couldn't imagine coming this far and then the whole thing being snatched away from her.

'I didn't know that,' she said quietly. 'But I would've thought a Yorkshireman like you might have had more of a "where there's a will, there's a way" attitude. I don't see why you can't find a way to uphold Jean's wishes – a woman you say you love so dearly – without compromising your own.'

Alex looked at her, askance. 'You don't see why I'm not *superhuman*? I'm sorry to disappoint you!' He gave her a long look before shaking his head. 'This… this closeness that you and I have? I thought it was something special, but it seems I shouldn't have allowed myself to feel that way. Here I am, having the hardest time of my life, and the one person I hoped might understand is being so bloody judgemental.'

Daisy closed her eyes, hating the way he used the past tense. 'Sebastian.'

'What?'

'You've been listening to Sebastian, and he finally got his way.' After her encounter with Alex's cousin, she could imagine how that had happened. The man was insidiously persuasive. 'You're letting him bully you into this.'

'It's not bullying. It's talking sense – and me having the sense to listen.'

'That isn't what you said when he first started sticking his nose in.'

'A lot has happened since then – hard graft and sleepless nights that aren't sustainable. Have I listened to Sebastian? Yes. Am I going to persuade Aunt Jean that he's right, after all? Yes.'

Daisy bit back tears, the feeling of emptiness at what the future held overwhelming her. 'Oh, Alex. After everything we've been through to make things work. I'm so disappointed in you.'

He swallowed, his Adam's apple bobbing. 'Then that's what you'll have to be. I'm sorry if my personal and business battles are interfering with your designs on getting a foothold here – but for now, you're still a temporary tenant who doesn't pay her fair share of rent and therefore has no status, so your opinion about Fox Farm holds no sway with me. As for you and me? Perhaps we're just two people who were thrown together in adverse circumstances and allowed a little chemistry to get out of hand.' His expression was hard, turning Daisy's heart cold. 'Now, if you'll excuse me, I have things to get on with. Naturally, I'd ask you to say nothing about this to anyone. I'm not planning on shoving my traitorous dagger through Aunt Jean's soul until after Christmas.'

He stormed out, his tea untouched, leaving Daisy to stare at the door. How had everything she had come to hope for, everything she'd imagined might be hers – a permanent place to live and work, a budding relationship – come crashing down around her ears? What had she done to deserve that?

You dared hope. And look where that got you, Daisy Claybourne.

Chapter Twenty-Six

'I want to know what's going on, Alex. No prevaricating. Now!'

Alex had never heard his mother so angry. She had always been the peacemaker, the voice of reason, to make up for his father's temper.

He ran a hand over his face and took a glug of the whisky he'd poured to numb the guilt he felt over the way things had gone with Daisy. It didn't help. All it did was hit his empty stomach like liquid fire. He hadn't eaten much again today. That was becoming a bad habit.

'You look bloody awful.' His mother never swore. She also never insisted on a video call like she had tonight.

'Sorry if I don't pass muster. Why are you yelling at me?'

'I've been round at Eric's today for my weekly duty call. If I'd known how much that man irritates me, brother or no, I'd never have moved down here. I had no idea how much he was like his son. Anyway, that's my problem. *Your* problem is that Eric told me that Sebastian told him that he's persuaded you to persuade Jean to sell Fox Farm. Is that true? And don't you dare lie to me, young man, or there'll be trouble!'

In other circumstances, Alex would have smiled at that, but he was in no smiling mood. Sebastian had already got what he wanted. Why couldn't he leave well enough alone? What if this had got back to Aunt Jean before Alex could do it his way?

'It's true.' *No point in lying.*

'I can't believe it! Why?'

And so ensued a replica of the conversation he'd had with Daisy – the same explanations, the same recriminations.

'You were the one who told me not to let Aunt Jean's dream overtake mine, Mum. And it's not all selfishness. I'm thinking of her, too. Her gutters gave up the ghost this week, *and* Gary reckons the roof is shot. That'll be a huge expense. Aunt Jean expects me to convert the upstairs of the main house into holiday accommodation in the new year, but we're supposed to be preserving her savings, not squandering them. And…' He took another glug of whisky.

'What is it, love?'

'If Aunt Jean can't run the business properly now, what'll happen as she gets older? I'd be…'

'Lumbered?'

'Yeah. That about covers it. Then there's this wretched legacy idea…'

'What legacy?'

Alex explained, not caring whether it was supposed to be just between him and his aunt. He'd already told Daisy. And he couldn't handle the burden any longer.

'That *is* asking too much of you,' his mother agreed.

'Her will doesn't stipulate what we do with Fox Farm, so we could still sell. I'm sure Sebastian would insist on it. I can't promise her that I'll do as she's asked, knowing I most likely wouldn't. She can't stay under the misapprehension that all this can continue. She's already offered Daisy the studio permanently. The longer I avoid talking to her, the worse it'll be.'

'You can't *make* her sell, Alex. You can only advise. And please don't do it the minute she comes home. Let her have Christmas first.'

'I know that. What do you take me for?'

'I take you for an exhausted man at the end of his tether. And I wish I could take you in my arms and make it all right.' A tear ran down his mother's cheek. 'Oh, Alex, I'd give anything for a magic wand.'

'Don't be daft. You're a mother, not a fairy godmother.'

'Get some rest, won't you? I'll speak to you tomorrow.'

Get some rest? Chance would be a fine thing.

Alex grabbed a frozen pizza from the fridge, decided his stomach would hate him, and made eggs on toast. Unoriginal, but all he could face.

He tried watching a TV programme, but after half an hour he had no idea what was going on. All he could think about was how he had yelled at Daisy and accused her of trying to swindle Aunt Jean. And then the way she'd said she was disappointed in him… How *dare* she? He might take that from a wife or a long-term partner. He'd be damned if he'd take it from someone he'd known for just a few weeks, no matter how he'd thought he felt about her.

His phone pinged with an email – from Lisa.

Alex,

I heard from Angie today that Jean will be home next week. It would have been nice if you'd told me yourself. It's only common courtesy to keep me in the loop, but I feel this is the way things have been at Fox Farm – that I'm being pushed out and neglected, decisions made without me, my input not required.

Whilst it's good that the new gallery is so busy, it's been hard work for me, especially now I only have Jamie part-time. And when he leaves in September, I will have to train up yet another assistant. I have my family to think about, and this new arrangement is not what I signed up for.

I also wonder what will happen when Jean returns. I can't imagine Fox Farm will be what it was in terms of leadership.

With the above in mind, please accept this email as my official one month's notice. Apologies that I have to do this before Christmas, but I would like to start the new year in a more positive light.

Wishing you the best with your endeavours.
Lisa

Alex stared at his phone in disbelief.

What is this? Beat-Alex-over-the-head-with-a-stick week?

How Lisa had the cheek, he didn't know. She'd been lacklustre for weeks, ever since Jean's stroke and long before he'd moved the gallery space. She hadn't been pulling her weight, and yet apparently, she was hard done by? If she *had* been left out of the loop, it wasn't deliberate. He didn't have time to speak to everyone individually over every last little thing. And maybe he assumed she wasn't interested – she certainly gave that impression.

Now he would have to advertise for a new gallery supervisor, and a temporary one at that, assuming he convinced Aunt Jean of what was best. What if the other staff began to feel the same way? Sue was approaching retirement. All he needed was for Angie to follow Lisa's example, and Fox Farm would be up the proverbial creek with no paddle in sight.

Alex forwarded the email to his mother, saying:

See what I'm up against? And you wonder why I want Aunt Jean to sell up?

*

'Are you sure you can talk?' Daisy asked Grace. 'Aren't you flying first thing tomorrow?'

'I'm packing, but the phone's on speaker. What's up?'

Daisy promptly burst into tears.

'Hey, hey. You're not one to cry. What on earth…?' Grace tried to soothe.

In a rather incoherent manner, Daisy told Grace about Jean's offer – and about Alex's reaction to it, then his latest attitude to Jean and Fox Farm.

'Well, that's quite a turnabout,' Grace agreed. 'And terrible news for you, if they do decide to sell. Just when you thought you had somewhere permanent, too. But I can see his point of view about Fox Farm, Daisy.'

'I can too, although I said some mean things to him at the time. It was the accusation in his tone that did it – like I'd wormed my way into Jean's affections and engineered the offer of the studio. That hurt.'

'It must have,' Grace soothed. 'But I bet that dreadful cousin of his had something to do with *that*. Alex won't really believe it. He's a decent guy. He's just not thinking straight. He'll calm down and see sense.' When Daisy sniffled, Grace asked, 'What aren't you telling me?'

'I… Oh, Grace. You know last time we spoke, we said I could give Alex a get-out after we slept together that weekend of the Santa cabin thing? Tell him I knew it wasn't a proper relationship?'

'Ye-es,' Grace drawled. 'And as I recall, I didn't advise it. But you went ahead anyway, and you messaged me to say it was all okay. Did you lie to me, Daisy Claybourne?'

'I… I knew you were up against it with your commission and getting ready to go away, and I thought I could handle it.'

'Without your Auntie Grace? Idiot. What *actually* happened?'

'He accused me of making assumptions.'

'But you were only going on what he'd already told you about not wanting serious relationships.'

'That's what I said! But we had a row, and it seemed that was that. Then he came round the following night to tell me he had feelings for me. That he didn't feel so casual about *me*. And we made love again, only it was different.'

'Made love rather than had sex?'

'Yes.'

Grace whistled. 'And?'

'It was special, Grace. We fell asleep together, and he left in the morning. That was yesterday. Then I didn't hear from him until today, when he threw all that crap at me, and now it's a horrible mess.' She burst into tears again.

'Daisy, these tears are worrying me, so I'm going to ask you right out. Are you in love with him?'

'What? I… I hadn't even thought about it! After the way he spoke to me today? Huh!'

'I didn't ask whether you want to be or whether you think you should be,' Grace said gently. 'I asked you if you *are*.'

The certainty hit Daisy like a wave. 'I… Yes. Maybe for a while now. I hadn't recognised it. It's been so long since Eoin, and anyway, this is different.'

'More grown up?' Grace asked.

'I hope so. Although if this is what grown-up love is, you can keep it.' Daisy sniffled.

'Don't be like that. This is a bad patch for you all. Maybe you'll both pull through it. I hope so – I like the idea of you and him together.'

'Sebastian doesn't. He called in and made it quite clear that Alex isn't one for long-term relationships and I'm hardly likely to change that, even if I use sex as an incentive.'

Grace gaped. 'He said that?'

'Pretty much.'

'Ugh. If I ever meet that man, so help me, I'll… Well, I'm sure I'd think of something appropriate.'

'The thing is, Grace, he's probably right, isn't he? These feelings Alex thought he had for me… They were probably just the product of the terrible time he's been having. He's already saying he was mistaken.'

Grace sighed. 'Give Alex a chance. He can't see the wood for the trees. If he could find a solution for Fox Farm, he might be able to think clearer in other areas of his life. Can *you* think of anything that might help?'

'He's made it plain that he doesn't want my input.'

'That's because he's a man and he's floundering, and they do *not* like to ask for help. I'm not saying you can do it. Just that you could put your mind to it.'

'We'll see. It's late, and you need to finish packing.'

'I do. Keep me posted, my lovely.'

Grace clicked off, leaving Daisy staring desolately at her phone. Here she was in such a state, and the hundreds of miles that separated her from her best friend would soon be thousands.

That was what came of being so insular. She really should learn to make more effort with people. Perhaps that should be her New Year's resolution.

Yes, well, let's just get through Christmas in one piece, shall we?

*

On Saturday morning, Alex arrived early at the gallery to catch Lisa. He wasn't surprised that she turned up only five minutes before opening, or that Jamie was there ahead of her, making speaking to her alone more difficult. He had to insist she stay outside for a moment while Jamie set up, making the lad frown with curiosity.

'If you're here to change my mind, Alex, you're wasting your time,' Lisa said.

Alex had no intention of doing any such thing. He'd thought long and hard about it last night and come to the conclusion that Lisa had been a drain on everyone's goodwill for weeks now. He couldn't see that changing.

'I wasn't going to,' he retorted, feeling in a brutish mood and enjoying the look of surprise on her face. 'I was merely going to ask if you could keep it quiet until after Christmas, for Jean's sake.'

'I can't promise that. Unlike *some*, I like to tell people what I feel they should know.'

'Fine. I'll get Jean to send you a formal acknowledgement as soon as she's *well* enough to deal with it.'

Leaving Lisa with her mouth open at his unusual brusqueness, he turned on his heel and made his way across the farmyard to Aunt Jean's cottage, where the door stood open.

'Nigel. Can I give you a hand loading up?'

N.J. Giles looked up from stuffing his laptop into its case. 'That would be kind. Thank you.'

They loaded the writer's car in amicable silence, and when it was done, Nigel gazed around.

'You have quite a queue already, over at the Santa cabin,' he commented. 'I'm not surprised. It's so festive here, with the tree and lights and everything. I love what you did with the gallery.' He sighed wistfully. 'I'll miss this place. I'm London through and through, but it is nice up here. Shame I haven't had time to explore much beyond the odd stroll to get an idea of the surrounding countryside for my story.'

'Perhaps you could come back for a proper holiday. Rent a cottage nearby?'

'Hmmm. Maybe in the spring. Bring my wife.' Nigel shook Alex's hand. 'I hope your aunt makes a full recovery. She's built something wonderful here, and she's lucky to have you to help her. Goodbye.'

Despite the stab of guilt that Nigel's words caused – talk about rubbing his face in what a rotten thing he was about to do! – Alex waved him off with a sense of a job well done. The man was satisfied, and Aunt Jean's coffers had benefited.

He made a start on the cottage. Nigel was obviously a neat man who had kept up with the basics, thank goodness. Alex mopped the floors, cleaned the kitchen and bathroom, changed the bedding, then unlocked the spare room and took all Jean's personal effects and clothes out, putting them back to the best of his memory.

Next, he went to his truck and pulled out the small potted Christmas tree he'd brought from Riverside. He was amazed there was one left – it was as though it had known it would be needed. One set of lights, a small box of wicker angel ornaments… Sitting on a low table next to the sofa, it would serve its purpose. Aunt Jean wasn't one for a lot of glitter.

Throughout the day, he was conscious of the festive spirit outside as people crossed the farmyard between the gallery and café and Santa's cabin and Daisy's studio.

Daisy. Was it only a week since she had first dressed up as an elf? Less than that since they had first made love? It felt like longer. He'd had a restless night after speaking to her so badly yesterday, especially knowing he'd got his facts wrong about Aunt Jean's offer – or Sebastian had, blast him – but he hadn't liked *her* accusations, either. Every time he glanced over at her studio, he was reminded that he was about to take away the future she'd only just been offered.

When he'd finished at the cottage, he drove home for a well-deserved beer, but Fox Farm still dominated his thoughts. How could he possibly persuade Aunt Jean that selling up was best?

Saturday evenings should be spent at the pub with mates or on a date, but Alex spent his sitting at his kitchen table, scribbling ideas, screwing paper up and tossing it on the floor. He made bullet points of all the reasons that Sebastian had drummed home to him about why Aunt Jean would be better off out of her cottage and somewhere safer and less isolated. He had to make it about *her*, not about his inability to be everywhere at once for the next decade and more. He wouldn't talk to her about it till after Christmas, but at least he had got it clear in his mind.

That should have stopped him tossing and turning, but it didn't, and he was at Riverside by eight the next morning, trying to remind himself that this was what these difficult decisions, the painful conversations with Aunt Jean that lay ahead, were all about.

You could go and see Daisy.

Why? She doesn't want to see someone she's so disappointed *in. And what can I say? I'm still going to persuade Aunt Jean to sell. If Daisy can't accept that, we have no future together anyway.*

Alex stopped what he was doing. Had he foreseen a future with her? It all depended on what you meant by a future, didn't it? He wasn't the marrying type. And yet a future without Daisy felt suddenly bleak. A future without Daisy *and* Fox Farm? Even bleaker.

Jules expressed concern at his unshaven appearance and general demeanour when she arrived, but he growled at her to back off. They had just opened for Sunday business when his phone rang.

'Aunt Jean. Are you looking forward to coming home? The cottage is all sorted and…'

'Home? Huh! *That* won't be for long, will it? Not if you have anything to do with it!'

'Eh?'

'Don't play the innocent with me. You get your backside over to this hospital ASAP, Alex, do you understand me?'

Alex's heart sank. 'I… Okay, but it'll be a couple of hours.'

'I'll try not to give myself another stroke between now and then.' The phone went dead.

Crap. She knows.

Not wanting to annoy Jules, he finished what he'd started before telling her he had to go to the hospital.

'I thought Jean was coming home tomorrow?'

'She is. She wants to talk a few things through.'

Jules gave him a weary look. 'Whatever.'

His lunch consisted of an apple on the drive to the hospital. He would be amazed if he hadn't lost weight, but he couldn't eat when his stomach was constantly churning, and it was certainly churning now. How did Aunt Jean know? His mother wouldn't have said anything – she'd insisted he allow his aunt a Christmas without worry. Nor would Sebastian – he'd been adamant that it was Alex's job. The only other possibility was Uncle Eric, but surely Sebastian would have thought to tell him not to blab?

Alex entered his aunt's ward with dread. When he tried to kiss her on the cheek, she pushed him away.

'Sit down.'

He sat. 'What's all this about?'

'You know very well. How *dare* you plot and plan behind my back with that odious cousin of yours?' She was shaking.

Concerned, Alex said, 'Aunt Jean, please try to calm down.'

'Don't tell me to calm down! You're planning on selling my home, my entire life, out from under me!'

A physio helping a patient across the ward looked over in concern. Alex gave him a smile of reassurance and took his aunt's hand in a gentle but firm grip.

'Okay, Aunt Jean, I'm here now and we can do this. But you have to stay calm, or they'll kick me out and we'll be no further forward. I'll get us some tea from somewhere, shall I?'

'I have to make it myself,' she snapped. 'I'm supposed to practise.' She hoisted herself from her chair and used a stick to move halfway down the ward to a kettle station.

Alex followed, watching as she made two mugs, one only two thirds full so she didn't spill any on the way back.

'I can only manage mine. You'll have to carry your own.' She picked hers up and began the slow walk back to her bedside.

When they were seated, he said, 'So how…?'

'My own brother-in-law. Eric. All "How are you?" and "Lovely to hear you're coming home" and "So glad that you've seen sense and decided to sell, old girl".'

That idiot uncle of mine! Why didn't Sebastian warn him not to say anything?

He would deal with Sebastian later. He had enough problems right here. And his bullet point list, so painstakingly worked on last night, was sitting in his kitchen. Lucky it was still imprinted on his brain.

'Okay, Aunt Jean, here it is…'

His aunt listened with her lips pressed tightly together while he laid it out – the reasons, the logic, the financial sense. But what that list didn't cover was the *heart*.

'You think I'd be happier in a shoebox flat where I don't know anyone than in the cottage where I spent my entire married life?' she asked him.

'No,' he said honestly. 'But I do think it would be more sensible.'

'And what about my life's work?'

'We've been through that. It's a complex business. You can't manage it any more.'

'We definitely can't afford to hire someone?'

'Not at the salary someone would expect.'

'So, I'm supposed to give it all up. Just like that. All because of a stupid stroke.' Tears rolled down her face.

'Most people have retired by your age,' he tried.

'Fox Farm isn't a job, Alex. It's my life. It was supposed to be my legacy.'

'Aunt Jean, I can't look that far ahead. I have no idea what stage I'd be at in my *own* life.' He looked her in the eye. 'I can't make promises I may not be able to keep.'

'You're saying you'd sell when I'm gone.'

'It would take too much of my time to keep it going. And Sebastian wouldn't agree to it. He wouldn't want the liability. He's a busy man, living his own life.' *As I should be.*

'He put you up to this.'

'Yes and no. Sebastian's taken this line ever since you fell ill. I fought him at first, but as time's gone on, I can see that he's right. I'm sorry. I wouldn't have had this conversation with you until after Christmas.

Sebastian shouldn't have told Uncle Eric, and Uncle Eric shouldn't have said anything.'

'Can you *make* me sell, with that power of attorney?'

Alex looked horrified. 'Absolutely not. But you need to know that if you don't sell, I can't carry on doing what I've been doing.' He tried to lighten things up. 'Otherwise *I* might end up on a stroke ward!'

His quip was misguided. More tears fell. 'I asked too much.'

'Yes, you did.' No point in being anything other than truthful now. 'You know I would always have done what I've done so far. I love you, and I love Fox Farm. But in the long term? It's too much.'

'What will my life be without Fox Farm around me?' she murmured.

'You have a lot of life ahead of you. You can make new friends. Take up new hobbies. You might find the lack of stress and busyness a revelation. A freedom.'

But they both knew they were hollow words, and when Alex left her, she was still silently crying, a vision that haunted him on the long drive home.

When he finally pulled up outside his house, weary to the bone, his mother climbed out of her car.

'Mum! What are you doing here?'

'I had a *very* distressed call from Jean this morning, so I packed, got in the car and drove to where I'm needed. I'll be here till after Christmas.'

'What about your job?'

'I told my boss it's a family emergency.'

'Isn't this a busy time for a gift shop?'

'Yvonne pays me far too little for what I do, Alex. That's fine most of the time. But I don't feel guilty about taking time out for this. Are you going to let me in, or are we going to discuss it on the doorstep?'

Chapter Twenty-Seven

Daisy had spent the weekend in a miserable daze, despite the heavy footfall and cheering sales in her studio. Even the church carol-singers in the yard did nothing for her. The festive spirit that everyone else was experiencing was lost on her.

Christmas was generally a lonely time for Daisy. This year, she had hoped her present to herself would be planning all the ways she could move on with her business. She'd also dared imagine it would be spent partially in the presence – and the arms – of the man she had somehow fallen in love with.

How that had happened, she still wasn't sure, but once Grace had brought it to her attention, the notion had stuck and wouldn't shift.

Fat lot of use it is to me.

Angie came bustling over on Monday morning with another unordered mocha, this time accompanied by a melting snowman cupcake that had over-melted.

'Well, thanks, but…'

'Can I perch?'

'Nobody here yet.' Daisy indicated the stool. 'Seems a bit odd, opening today, closing the next two days as usual, then opening for Christmas Eve.'

'Jean would probably have asked us to open all week with Christmas coming up, but I didn't dare mention that to Alex,' Angie told her. 'He looked dreadful when he was waving Mr Giles off on Saturday. Have you noticed? Do you think it's tiredness, or is something else going on?'

'I haven't seen him since Friday,' Daisy said flatly.

The painful memories of the way he'd spoken to her, his accusations, his plans to get Jean to sell Fox Farm, flooded her head.

Angie frowned. 'Come to think of it, you don't look too good yourself. Are *you* alright?'

'It's been busy here.' Daisy forced a smile. 'Which is great.'

'Maybe Jean will keep you on next year. You never know.'

I do know. And it's not going to happen.

'I do know *one* reason why Alex might be looking miserable,' Angie went on. 'Lisa handed in her notice on Friday night. By email, if you please!'

Alex had quite a Friday, then, didn't he? Daisy pushed away a quick pang of sympathy. She refused to feel sorry for him.

'Why?' she asked.

'Oh, you know what Lisa's been like. Feels hard done to. Preferred the way it was before, toddling along without anything changing. I admit I felt the same way myself at first, but I appreciate that things have to move on, and if Alex felt it was needed, then it was. Between you and me, I wonder if Fox Farm was struggling a bit, financially. Otherwise, why go to all that trouble? Anyway, it's paid off so far. Trade will tail off in January, of course, but come the spring and summer? Fox Farm will be thriving for many a year to come, I reckon.'

There may not even be a spring and summer. And there certainly won't be many a year.

'Do you know what he's doing about replacing Lisa?' Daisy asked.

'No idea. I haven't spoken to Alex yet. It was Lisa who told me. Alex tried to silence her till after Christmas, she said, which I thought was fair enough for Jean's sake, but Lisa wouldn't have it, and now Jamie's panicking, poor lad.' Angie sighed. 'I've known Lisa a long while, but lately…? She's no sad loss, I'm afraid.'

'Does Jean know yet?'

'I'm not sure. Maybe Alex will get away with not bothering her about it till after Christmas. Still, it's small-fry in the scheme of things, isn't it?'

It certainly is.

Daisy spotted Alex's truck pull up at the roadside after lunchtime and watched him walk over to Jean's cottage. Soon after, the occupational therapists or assessors or whatever he'd called them followed him into the cottage. A while after that, another car crawled into the farmyard at a speed suitable for avoiding Christmas shoppers and café-goers, and Nicky got out then went around to the passenger door to help Jean.

Daisy hadn't known that Alex's mother was back up north. She must have wanted to welcome her sister-in-law home. Perhaps she would be in Yorkshire for Christmas?

An hour or so later, as she locked up, Daisy spotted Angie carrying a cake tin from the café to the cottage. That put her in a quandary. She would have to go and say hello to Jean sometime, but it felt so awkward – the atmosphere between her and Alex; knowing she couldn't have the studio but unable to say anything because Alex had said he wasn't going to talk to Jean about it till after Christmas; seeing Nicky again – the woman who, she now realised, had suspected Daisy was falling in love with her son and had been right.

And yet, living on the premises, Daisy had no excuse not to poke her head around the door. Perhaps it would be easier with the others there – two minutes, and then she had every excuse not to stay and clutter the place up.

Steeling herself, she walked across the empty farmyard and tapped lightly on the door before opening it and plastering a huge smile on her face, initially false but soon genuine as she saw her friend sitting on the sofa in her kitchen where she *belonged*.

'Jean. I'm so pleased you're back!' Doing her best not to catch Alex's or Nicky's eye, she crossed the kitchen to hug Jean.

'Daisy. Lovely to see you. Sit down. Have a cuppa.' Jean indicated the sofa next to her.

'No, thanks. You must be exhausted. I only came to welcome you home.'

'Tomorrow morning, then? Nicky and Alex are both busy.'

In the lamplight, Daisy noticed Jean's puffy eyes and unhappy face. No doubt she was overwhelmed by such an exhausting day.

'I'd love to catch up. See you tomorrow.'

Alex stood to one side as Daisy made her way back across the kitchen. They studiously avoided each other's gaze, and Daisy was sure she heard Nicky tutting.

Nicky followed her outside, closing the door behind her. 'What's with you two?'

'What do you mean?'

'Don't kid a kidder, Daisy. I've spent enough time in a rubbish relationship to know when two people have had a falling out.'

Daisy shuffled her feet on the stone path. 'It's a long story.'

'It usually is. Are you busy tomorrow afternoon?'

'I want to go for a walk. Clear my head.'

'Can I come with you?'

To interrogate me about me and Alex? Not likely! 'I don't know. I…'

Nicky read her mind. 'Don't worry. I'll drag *that* out of my son. No, I need to discuss Fox Farm with you. It's important.'

'With *me*?'

'You're the only one around here with a sensible head on their shoulders who I can trust. Please?'

'I… Well. If you want to.'

'I do. I'll come by about one thirty?'

'See you then.'

As Daisy walked back to her studio, her head felt as if it were filled with cotton wool. *I officially have no idea what's going on in my life any more.*

*

'What did you say to Daisy?' Alex asked his mother when they had left Aunt Jean in peace.

'I asked if I could join her on her walk tomorrow.'

'Why?'

'Because I enjoy her company, Alex. That's not against the law, is it?' She climbed into her car and started the engine, leaving Alex to follow in his truck.

Back home, his mother put the kettle on. 'I do wish Jean would let me stay with her, for tonight at least. I don't like her being there on her own.'

'I offered, too, but she wouldn't have it. Said there's no point in her being home if everyone's going to fuss around her. She has that fall alarm now – as long as she's not too stubborn to wear it. And they're sending a carer round first thing to help her get dressed, as a one-off. They checked she could do these things before they sent her home, Mum. I can't fight yet another battle. Please don't natter.'

'Alright, love. But talking of battles…' His mother passed him a mug of tea. He put it down and took a beer from the fridge instead. '… What's going on between you and Daisy? And don't tell me "nothing". I might take that from her, but I won't take it from you.'

Better get this over with, or she'll just keep on at me. Alex took a long swig of beer. 'I listened to your advice, that's what happened. I took that leap of faith you were harping on about and told her I had feelings for her. We made up. But then I found out from Sebastian that Aunt Jean had already offered her the studio on a permanent basis that day, and yet Daisy hadn't bothered to tell me.'

'Maybe she had other things on her mind, like a confirmed bachelor declaring his feelings for her… and whatever making up followed.'

Alex blushed like a schoolboy. 'Possibly. But Sebastian said Jean was giving it to her for free again. Fox Farm can't afford that. I was so mad that she'd accept it, and I got it in my head that she'd engineered it somehow.'

'You mean Sebastian *put* it in your head. You should know better than to listen to him. You were daft enough to accuse Daisy of this, were you?'

'It came out that way, yes. By the time she told me the arrangement would be different to this year, it was too late – I'd taken Sebastian at his word before establishing the facts and I'd made unpleasant accusations. Anyway, I told her it made no difference; that there won't be any Fox Farm.'

'She *knows*?'

'I'm not heartless, Mum. I didn't want her making plans when there was no chance of her seeing them through.'

'That must have upset her.'

'I imagine so.'

'I don't just mean about the studio. I mean about Fox Farm. Daisy feels that she belongs somewhere. You're taking that away from her.'

'I'm not doing anything! I'm simply trying to get it into everyone's heads that this is an impossible situation.'

'You and Daisy? Or Fox Farm?'

'Both.'

'Let's take Daisy first. Do you love her?'

Alex thrust his hands into already wild hair. '*What?*'

'It's a simple enough question.'

'It's not a simple answer.'

'It is. Ask your heart. Do it now. I can wait.'

Alex looked at his mother as if she'd lost her mind. 'I don't need you to wait! I don't need to ask my heart! It already knows! Yes, I love her. There. Are you happy now?'

'Of course. But you're not.' She placed a hand on his cheek. 'Don't fight it. Love is there to be enjoyed.'

'You didn't enjoy it.' Alex regretted the comment the moment he saw the hurt in his mother's eyes.

'No. But I was unlucky. Daisy's a woman to be cherished, Alex. Don't let her slip away.'

'I can't see a way around that. She's unlikely to forgive me for what I said, and I wouldn't blame her. She'll be ousted from the one place she thought she might call home, and that will be my fault. She'll have to move to wherever she can afford, and that could be anywhere. I can't see how that's a good basis for anything.'

'Then you have to overcome the obstacles. You could start by apologising for the way you spoke to her.'

'I *could* do that. But she said some awful things to me too.'

'Then she could apologise to you, as well. With that out of the way, you can tell her you love her.'

'What's the point?'

'She might tell you she loves you back.'

'But Mum, this thing with me and Daisy…? It all hinges around Fox Farm.'

'I know, which is why I told Jean that you and I will be busy tomorrow morning.'

'I assumed you wanted to sort out Christmas Day.'

'No. We are going to sit here and you are going to show me all the figures for Fox Farm. I want a complete overview. I want to satisfy myself that what you're trying to get Jean to do is the right thing.'

'You don't trust me?'

'Of course I trust you. But you're overwhelmed and overwrought. One morning. That's all I'm asking.' When he gave her a rebellious look, she said, 'My sister-in-law is heartbroken. If I have to reassure her, I should at least be sure myself.'

Alex stood. 'I could kill Sebastian! All this could have been avoided till after Christmas if he'd kept his mouth shut.'

'Have you spoken to him about that?'

'No. All I get is a message saying he's unobtainable, on business.'

'That's convenient.'

'Perhaps he knows I'll punch his lights out when I see him.'

His mother harrumphed. 'You'd have to beat me to it.'

*

Daisy waited at her door, togged up in warm clothing, trepidation running through her system.

She liked Nicky, but the woman was Alex's mother, and that made her nervous. Daisy was a private person, a consequence of her childhood – all those people involved in her life and her not having much say. She hoped Nicky wouldn't delve.

'Are you happy to stay local?' Nicky asked as she got out of her car.

'That's fine.' Daisy led Nicky along the footpath across the road from Fox Farm, from which they had a constant view of the fields and river below on their right. A tiny wren sang to them from a bare, spiky hedge until their footsteps made it flit away.

'Has your studio been busy?' Nicky asked.

'Yes. I've made actual money for the first time in my career.' Daisy made a scoffing noise. 'If I can call it a career.'

'Of course you can. You just had to find your feet and be given an opportunity. How was your visit with Jean this morning?'

'It was good to see her back at home,' Daisy said. 'And she loves the new gallery and café, but that's just made her sad about the idea of selling. She told me she'd spoken too soon about the studio and why, so I pretended Alex hadn't already said anything to me.'

Nicky nodded. 'Did she ask your opinion?'

'About selling? No. I wouldn't have offered it. It isn't my affair.'

'Isn't it?'

'Your son made it plain that it isn't.'

'My son is a placid man, Daisy. Hot-headed outbursts aren't his usual style. He's under a lot of pressure.'

Daisy thought about the quiet Alex she knew, the man with the mild sense of humour and calm, hazel eyes. The man who had made love to her so tenderly just a few nights ago.

'I know.'

'Besides,' Nicky went on, 'I wouldn't say it isn't your affair. You were hoping for a future at Fox Farm. You and Alex make quite a team. You and Jean are friends. Alex loves Fox Farm as much as he loves Riverside. It's all interconnected.'

'That doesn't alter the facts, though, does it? Alex wouldn't say there's no way around this if he didn't believe it.'

'Then it's up to us ladies.'

'What do you mean?'

'You. Me. Jean. We have to come up with a solution, fast, otherwise Christmas dinner will be an awfully miserable affair – to which, by the way, you're invited.'

'Oh, I… No, thanks.'

'No arguments. Jean wants you there.'

I'd prefer baked beans on toast in my room.

'I made Alex go through Fox Farm's accounts with me this morning,' Nicky said as they climbed over the stile to head downhill towards the river.

'Should you be talking to me about this?'

'I need a sounding board, Daisy, and Alex told me you're the only person besides family who knows the whole story.'

'Angie was beginning to guess,' Daisy said.

'I'm not surprised.' Nicky went on to tell Daisy what she'd learned that morning, finishing with, 'So, the changes are working, but Jean can't do as much, and the only way Fox Farm can keep going is if it has someone to oversee it, make decisions, pay bills, keep the accounts, deal with contracts and pay.'

'Fox Farm can't afford that?'

'No. Come up with something, Daisy, will you?'

'Fox Farm means that much to you?'

'It means a great deal to my sister-in-law. To my brother William's memory. To Alex. He *loves* that place. But he can't be expected to perform Jean's role indefinitely.'

Daisy's heart was beating faster than their walking pace merited. Nicky wanted to fix this. And if she did, if *they* did, Daisy could keep the studio.

They reached the river, Daisy's mind racing. She was impressed at how much Nicky had taken in about the workings of Fox Farm from just one morning with Alex – she was obviously a bright woman. And only one possibility presented itself.

Nicky allowed her the thinking space, but finally she could stand it no longer. 'Any ideas?' Seeing Daisy's hesitation, she grabbed her by the arm. 'You *do* have one, don't you?'

'I do, but it's presumptuous and possibly too personal. Alex doesn't like me crossing that line, Nicky, and I don't feel it's my place to—'

'I don't care. Run it by me.'

'Okay.' Daisy took a deep breath. 'How much do you like Devon? Living near your brother? Your job?'

Nicky stared at her, realisation dawning. 'You think *I* should take on Fox Farm?'

'Well, first off, you'd be perfect for Lisa's job. You've a real eye for presentation – we all saw that. But maybe you could take on some of Jean's role, too, when the gallery's quiet? It's not as though Jean worked on Fox Farm business eight hours a day. She did her pottery; enjoyed free time.' Daisy thought about it. 'You'd have to create a small office space in the gallery where you could concentrate on Fox Farm stuff when it's quiet and only needs one member of staff. When it's busy or a higher authority's needed, you'd be available. But you'd need Jamie full-time in there, so the café would need a part-timer.'

Nicky shrugged. 'That wouldn't cost much. I reckon Fox Farm could stretch to that, at least.'

'Only if *you* don't get a salary commensurate with the responsibilities you'd be taking on. You'd be doing Lisa's job *and* managing Fox Farm for the same pay.'

'I'm not worried about the money, Daisy. I'm comfortably enough off. I have savings from the payout after Keith's death, and a small widow's pension.'

'It would be hard work, taking on both roles at once.'

'Maybe, but the fact is, I've been coasting, the last few years. I could do with a challenge. It'd be good to stretch my wings before I think about retirement. Prove to myself I can do something new.'

'And maybe you wouldn't have to do it all,' Daisy pointed out. 'Jean needs *some* of her role back, or she'll feel useless – like everything's being taken away from her. Showing you the ropes would give her purpose, and after that, you could choose, between you, which tasks to share or keep, depending on how well she is.'

Nicky smiled as the idea took hold. 'It would mean Fox Farm could run with barely any input from Alex once I was settled in. The only cost would be the part-timer for the café. And Jean could continue to live there and take part as much as she feels able. Daisy, you are a genius!' Nicky grabbed her and hugged her.

Worried about being the cause of Nicky's runaway enthusiasm, Daisy decided to put on the brakes a little. She didn't want to be responsible for someone making such a huge life choice on a whim.

'It would mean leaving your home, Nicky. You're happy there. It's where you went to heal. Are you sure you want to move?'

Nicky gazed off into the distance. 'Devon's nice, and I'm glad I went. It gave me a chance to shake off old memories and become my own person. But Eric and I have nothing in common, even though I'd hoped we might. Jean and I, on the other hand, are close friends. I'd like to be nearer, to help her more. My friends in Devon... None are what I'd call bosom buddies. I can make more here.' She spread her hand out in front of her to encompass the scene before them – the frost-covered fields, the grey stone walls, the huddling sheep, the river shimmering in the winter light and trickling under the stone bridge at the village. 'They call this God's Own County for a reason. I was always in the suburbs – I've never lived in the Dales. I can afford to move, maybe to somewhere in the village where I can make friends easily. And I'm nowhere near ready to retire.' Her voice hitched. 'I'd like to be nearer my son. We have a lot of lost time to catch up on.'

Daisy swallowed down the lump in her throat. 'Do you think Alex will go for it?'

'Let's hope so.'

Daisy smiled, although she was aware that she had her own problems. Yes, she would keep her studio. But she and Alex were over. What would it be like to be a permanent fixture at Fox Farm, surrounded by his family, with him popping by all the time? Could she cope?

Nicky turned to head back up the hill. 'I'll need to speak to Jean before Alex. She'd have to be on board with it – Fox Farm is hers, not his. But Alex is still a deciding factor. I'm sixty. Eventually, some responsibility would come back to him. And one day, Fox Farm will be his and Sebastian's. If he'd rather be free of it all now – if he can only see it as an ongoing burden – then there's no point in all the upheaval.' Nicky linked her arm in Daisy's. 'As for you and him? If you two don't sort yourselves out, I shall have to bang your heads together!'

Chapter Twenty-Eight

Alex understood why his mother had stormed up to Yorkshire, and he was happy to have her staying with him and spending time with Jean. What he wasn't happy about was how much of his time she seemed determined to take up on the lost cause that was Fox Farm. Yesterday, she'd insisted on spending the entire morning looking at the accounts with him. He'd been impressed with how quickly she'd grasped what he was showing her... and she'd agreed with everything he'd said. She'd also insisted he'd be putting Jean in an early grave if he moved her away from her home to somewhere she didn't want to be.

Thanks, Mum.

Then she'd gone on a long walk with Daisy – effectively his ex-girlfriend. As if *that* wasn't weird.

'What are you doing today?' he asked her over breakfast.

'Spending the morning with Jean.'

'That's nice.'

'And the afternoon with *you* at Jean's. There are things to discuss.'

Uh-oh. 'About what?'

'Your favourite subject – Fox Farm.'

He sighed. 'Is there anything left to say?'

'One final discussion. You, me and Jean. I wouldn't ask if it weren't important. Meet me there at two. Are you going to Riverside this morning?'

'Yeah. No closing days this week, with the run-up to Christmas. Jules and I are like ships that pass in the night. Since I asked everyone else to do the overtime, the least I can do is show up for a while.'

His mother frowned. 'Do you sell much, so near to Christmas?'

'You'd be surprised. Last-minute poinsettias and Christmas cacti and potted hyacinths and narcissi are popular when people remember they still haven't got anything for Granny or Auntie Mabel. And there's an occasional Christmas tree disaster – climbing cats are good for those. We don't have any real trees left, but we stock a few artificial ones. It's worth our while to open.'

His mother nodded. 'Could you do something for me first?'

'What now?'

'Go and apologise to Daisy.'

Alex pushed his toast away and nursed his tea mug. 'What's the point? I said things I shouldn't. She said things she shouldn't.'

'That's what apologies are for. It's days since you had that awful row. Don't let it fester any longer, love. You two could at least be friends again.'

Daisy and I could never be just friends again. Whenever I look at her, I'll see the only woman I fell in love with.

'Besides,' his mother went on, 'I invited her to Christmas dinner, and we don't want an atmosphere.'

'You did *what?*'

'Jean won't let her sit on her own in that tiny room with a tin of soup, and you know it.' When he said nothing, her voice took on the warning tone he knew so well from childhood. 'I brought you up to be polite. Do the decent thing. For me.'

'Fine. You'll never give me any peace, otherwise.' Alex grabbed his jacket and slammed out of the house.

The drive to Fox Farm filled his stomach with butterflies. He'd been studiously avoiding Daisy for days. Seeing her on her two-minute visit to welcome Aunt Jean home had been hard enough. How he'd manage a conversation with her, he had no idea.

With any luck, she'll be out.

But Daisy was in her studio, painting. When she came to the door, reluctance was written plainly across her face.

'Alex.'

'Daisy.'

They stood, staring at each other, and he recognised hurt and sadness in her eyes.

'I came to apologise. I should have done it much sooner,' he managed.

'Did your mother send you?'

At that, he had to smile. 'Like a five-year-old. Yes.' When she moved aside, he stepped over the threshold. 'I said things I shouldn't have. I had the wrong facts, but that's no excuse. I know you better than to think you'd deliberately try to sway Aunt Jean into something she can't afford. I don't know what came over me.' That was true enough. Looking at her now, her face open and honest… How could he ever have doubted her?

'Sebastian got to you,' she stated simply. 'It was bound to happen. I said some hurtful things myself. I'm sorry. I shouldn't have added to the guilt and pressure you're already under.'

'You're not the only one. Mum's been on my case, too. I'm expected at Aunt Jean's this afternoon to "discuss" Fox Farm. Again. We've done the topic to death. I have no idea why she wants to keep on at it.'

'I know you've had enough of it all,' Daisy said, the sympathy clear in her voice. 'You've made your mind up about what's best. But you need to be *sure*. Fox Farm isn't just Jean's legacy, it's yours, too. It's a *part* of you. If it sells, and later you think of a way you could have prevented it, you'll never shake off the guilt, especially if Jean's unhappy.' She hesitated, seeming to toy with something. 'One more afternoon isn't much for them to ask. And…' She stopped, biting her lip.

That was quite a speech. Alex wasn't sure it made him feel any better, but it did remind him how well Daisy had come to know him. He could hear her out, couldn't he?

'And what, Daisy?'

'I'd be sticking my oar in again.'

'May as well. Everybody else does.'

'I think you should consider why Sebastian sounds so reasonable all of a sudden. The impression you've given me is that he doesn't get involved unless something's in it for him.'

She was right, of course, but Alex couldn't for the life of him see it this time.

'He's a busy man,' he said. 'Maybe he wants everything settled so he doesn't feel any responsibility for the situation.'

'You're a busy man, too. Besides, has Sebastian ever taken much responsibility for Jean in the past?'

'Not really. He paid lip service to it when William died, with the odd fleeting visit. He tried to get her to sell up then, too.'

'So, if the responsibility doesn't bother him – he knows it lies squarely with you – what else?'

'It's me who gains by selling, Daisy – the lack of responsibility, the freedom. The only gain for Sebastian, eventually, is that he's a beneficiary in Aunt Jean's will, but it's not as though he'll see any money if she sells now, is it? It's still hers until she's gone. Only then will he get half of whatever's left.' He saw it in her thoughtful brown eyes – the realisation. 'What is it?'

'You said it yourself – he gets half of whatever's *left*. Sebastian thinks Fox Farm is a drain on Jean's resources, costly to run, a liability in times of economic downturn or with bad investment decisions on your part. If she sells now, the money would be safely stashed away, and Jean would be in a small flat that costs little to buy and less to keep. And his inheritance would be maximised.'

Alex considered it. 'That's quite a gamble. The value of this property would only increase over the years. But…' *Could she be right?* 'Expensive repairs to the cottage are needed. Then there's the cost of converting the floor above the café into holiday accommodation…'

'Maybe he believes a bird in the hand is worth two in the bush.'

Alex sighed. 'You may well be right.'

'And I may well not be. But I do think you should consider the possibility when you have your meeting with Jean and Nicky this afternoon.' They stood in silence, awkward once again. 'Well. Thank you for coming.'

Alex hated the stilted atmosphere between them, despite their apologies. He didn't feel as if anything had been properly fixed. 'I gather you're joining us on Christmas Day?'

'Yes. I'm sorry. I tried to refuse.'

'Don't worry, I know what my mother's like. And Aunt Jean wants you there.' Realising he'd implied that his mother and aunt wanted her there but he didn't, Alex opened his mouth but closed it again. He didn't know what to say that wouldn't make it worse. 'See you then.'

'Yes. See you then.'

Alex couldn't swallow down the lump in his throat as he drove to Riverside. If this was what love was, you could keep it. Why people said that love made the world go round, he had no idea. This sort of thing would stop the globe in its tracks.

'You look like a wet weekend,' Jules commented when he arrived.

'Cheers. What do you need?'

'More bulbs somewhere in sight of the counter. The ones in the wicker baskets are selling like hot cakes.'

'Too many Auntie Mabels,' he muttered.

'What?'

'Nothing. Listen, Jules, I won't be here this afternoon. My mother's holding a conference at Jean's.'

'But you'll be in tomorrow? Christmas Eve, remember?'

'Of course.' Alex thought about the canvas he'd bought her for Christmas. Then he remembered the gift boxes of craft ale he'd decided on for Jim and Kieran but hadn't yet picked up from Skipton. He should do that before Aunt Jean's. 'I'll have to go at lunchtime. Sorry.'

With Jules' task list completed and the Skipton errand under his belt, Alex arrived at his aunt's with trepidation. The best he could expect was more upset from Aunt Jean, recrimination from her *and* his mother, and a further dollop of guilt to make his Christmas extra-festive.

But when he walked into the kitchen, it was filled with the aroma of mulled wine, and Aunt Jean and his mother were both smiling.

He took the mug his mother offered and sipped, recognising Angie's special recipe. 'What are you two so happy about?'

'We have an early Christmas present for you,' Aunt Jean declared.

'Oh?' Suspicion flowed through his veins quicker than the kick of alcohol. 'Is it a new bike? I asked Santa for a red racer.'

'Ha! Sit,' his mother told him.

He sat at the table, looking at their empty hands in confusion. 'What, then? Where is it?'

'It's to do with Fox Farm,' Aunt Jean told him. 'Alex, I realise I asked far too much of you, both now and in the future. I asked you to keep this place going even after I'm gone. That was the whim of a scared, ill woman, and it was unfair. I could hardly hold you to it, could I? I wouldn't come back to haunt you over it.'

Alex didn't like it when she talked about popping off, but he knew she'd been preoccupied by it lately. 'Aunt Jean—'

She cut him off. 'Anyway, let's deal with the here and now, shall we? Your mother and I have been talking.'

Alex listened to their proposal. He tried to find arguments against it but struggled to think of any. It would mean he might still have some responsibilities at Fox Farm – he didn't think his mother could manage it *all* – but it could work, or at least, he could find no reason not to give it a go. That in itself would satisfy his aunt.

And his mother would be living nearby. If she'd have suggested that a few months ago, he'd have been dubious. But the emotional distance between them had closed a remarkable amount recently. Wouldn't it be good to close the physical distance, too?

Alex thought about what Daisy had said earlier – that Fox Farm was a part of him; how terrible he would feel if he wasn't sure he'd done the right thing. Daisy, it seemed, was his conscience… and perhaps his saviour. He didn't *want* to let Fox Farm go. He'd simply believed he had no choice.

'I… I don't know what to say,' he managed. 'Thank you?'

'Actually, you have Daisy to thank,' his mother said. 'She and I had a long chat yesterday. This was all her idea.'

'Ah. I see.' Alex didn't like the idea that his mother might have felt coerced into this, to help everyone out.

She read his mind. 'I want to do it, Alex, and I'm grateful to Daisy for putting it in my head. I hope you'll say something to her.' She cast a furtive glance at Jean before asking him, 'You did what I asked this morning, didn't you?'

Jean was having none of it. 'Don't think I don't know those two are being idiots – and that some of it's my fault. If you let Daisy slip through your fingers, Alex Hirst, I *will* come back to haunt you, and I'll bring Uncle William with me.'

The idea alarmed Alex so much, he couldn't help but laugh. 'As long as I have to wait another twenty years for the privilege.'

She patted his hand. 'And that leads me neatly on to one more thing. I want to discuss my will. I *know* you don't like talking about it,' she said when he started to protest. 'But after this, it'll be a closed subject, I promise.'

'I'm holding you to that. What about it?'

Aunt Jean shook her head. 'We're waiting for Sebastian. It's only fair.'

'Oh, he's available all of a sudden, is he?'

'I made sure he was,' his mother said. 'He hadn't gone back to London, Alex. He was working from the B & B.'

'Laying low, more like,' Aunt Jean said crossly, 'until I told him I needed to discuss my will. Funny how he was available then.' They heard footsteps on the path. 'Talk of the devil.'

'Aunt Jean! How lovely to see you back in your own home.' Sebastian strode in, for all the world as though he hadn't caused so much heartache and trouble.

She accepted his kiss but said, 'I wouldn't be home for long, if you had anything to do with it, would I?'

'Now, Aunt Jean.' Sebastian turned on the charm. 'You know I only want what's best for you.'

'That's good, because that's what I'm getting. I'm staying in my cottage, Sebastian, and everyone around me has pulled together to work out a way to keep Fox Farm.'

At this, Sebastian turned to Alex. 'I thought you were at your wits' end. How on earth will you keep this place going?'

'That's none of your concern,' Aunt Jean said firmly. 'You haven't shown a blind bit of interest in Fox Farm over the years, not until I fell ill. Now I'm better, I don't see why that should change. Anyway, that's not why I asked you here. Sit down. Have some mulled wine. It might take the edge off.'

His face sulky at being told off in front of the others, Sebastian took the mug that Alex's mother handed him and sat. 'Take the edge off what?'

Alex felt as puzzled and suspicious as his cousin looked. What was their aunt up to? *Might as well ask right out.* 'What are you up to, Aunt Jean?'

Sebastian swivelled to look at him. 'You don't know?'

'I'm as much in the dark as you are.'

'When you two have quite finished…?' Aunt Jean gave them a steely glare. 'I'm changing my will. No ifs, no buts. The solicitor was kind enough to fit in a quick visit here this lunchtime. He'll draw up the new will after Christmas.'

'Change it in what way?' Sebastian asked, an edge of panic in his voice.

'Fox Farm will be left to Nicky and Alex,' Aunt Jean said, watching Sebastian carefully. 'Nicky's altering her will so that ultimately it will be left solely to Alex.'

Alex could only gape, his brain trying to process what she'd said.

Sebastian got there quicker. '*What?*' He stood, almost knocking over his wine.

'You heard.'

'I can't believe I heard right. What the hell…?'

Aunt Jean hoisted herself from her chair and stood facing him. Alex's concern that she was becoming stressed was soon replaced by the realisation that she simply wanted to make it plain to her nephew that she was sure of her own mind.

'You've never cared about Fox Farm, Sebastian. Your childhood memories aren't rooted here. Alex's are. Despite that, I've always done my best to treat you boys the same. But this is too important. I want Fox Farm to thrive, to offer opportunities to artists as it always has. To provide a watering hole to weary walkers and a surprise highlight to passing tourists, same as always. To act as a meeting place for locals, same as always. Alex and Nicky will keep it going for now, and Alex *may*' – she cast a knowing glance at Alex – 'carry on as and when I shuffle off this mortal coil. I take comfort in that. More comfort than I'd get from being "fair" and knowing it would be sold the minute I was in the ground, so you could line your pockets with money you have no need of.'

Sebastian's hands were shaking, Alex noticed… then he looked down at his own. They were the same.

'It's not about the money,' Sebastian protested.

'Then what is it about?' Aunt Jean asked him. 'Because for me, it's about my life's work. My legacy. My husband's memory. Can you honestly lay a claim to any of those things?'

'But… You can't! Alex and I are equal.'

'Not any more. Alex has devoted his adult life to me, Sebastian, uncomplaining and with unconditional love. You have a passing fondness for me at best. But this isn't about you. It's about what I want for Fox Farm when I'm gone. You can't and would never enable that. Alex can and would do his best.'

Still shocked, Alex looked across at his mother. She gave him a small, reassuring smile.

Sebastian caught it and wheeled on Alex. 'You *did* know about this.'

Alex's expression hardened. 'I had no idea.'

'I don't believe you.'

'I can't help that.'

'You're going to let her do it?'

'It's Aunt Jean's decision. She knows her own mind.'

Sebastian's eyes narrowed. 'Did Daisy have anything to do with this?'

'Daisy!' Alex gaped at him. 'Why would she?'

'I wouldn't put it past her. That woman doesn't have a penny. What better way to improve her state of affairs than to worm her way into this family and a relationship with you, so you inherit as a couple?'

'You leave Daisy out of it,' Jean snapped. 'She knows nothing about this. If you have nothing pleasant to say, Sebastian, feel free to leave.'

'Fine, but don't think you've heard the end of it,' Sebastian warned. 'I can contest a will. Alex and I have equal rights as your nephews.'

At this, Alex's mother spoke for the first time. 'The solicitor anticipated that. He suggested that that argument only tends to work with direct offspring – which you and Alex are not – and even then, with regard to someone who's dependent on the money… which you're not.'

Sebastian gave her a cold look. 'What about Aunt Jean's state of mind? The woman's had a major stroke. That would be grounds enough, if you ask me.'

Alex opened his mouth, his fist closing, but his mother placed a hand on his arm.

'The solicitor anticipated that, too,' she said mildly. 'He'll swear that Jean is of sound mind when she makes the new will. We'll ask Angie to do the same. We intend to ask the hospital consultant if she's willing, too. *And* Jean will be making a video – a living will – giving her reasons. He's covering every angle, Sebastian.'

Sebastian swung back to face Alex, almost nose to nose. 'You have no idea what's coming, Alex. However far down the line it may be, my solicitors will be waiting for you.'

Alex wanted to punch his cousin so hard, it took an iron will just to speak. 'I know I come across as a genial buffoon to you, pottering around with my flowers and plants, but don't mess with me. You may think you call the shots, that you have the best solicitors, and we all know you're so selfish, you'll go to any lengths to get what you want. But what you don't have – and can't begin to comprehend – is the love I have for Aunt Jean and Fox Farm. I will fight you tooth and nail. And you will get nowhere, because you will not find one single person to say that Aunt Jean was not of sound mind when she changed her will. She's making sure of that. You'd never win. I suggest you think about that when you've calmed down, and let it go.'

Alex could feel Sebastian's breath on his face, hot and angry. They stood like that for a long moment, Alex's pulse fast and strong.

It was Sebastian who broke it off. He stalked to the door, turning back as he yanked it open. 'You haven't heard the end of this.'

'I'm sure. But I'll be ready for you.'

The door shook the frame around it, and the three of them gave a collective sigh of relief.

'Well, that went better than I expected,' Jean said calmly, causing Alex and his mother to stare at her before breaking into peals of laughter.

'Oh, Jean.' Nicky hugged her. 'You were brilliant. So calm.'

Alex shook his head at the pair of them. 'Couldn't you two have given me a heads up?'

'That wouldn't have been fair,' Aunt Jean said. 'And I wanted him to see that you weren't in on it.'

'I'm not sure he *did* see that.'

'He'll know it, in his heart of hearts, when he calms down.' She sat again, looking exhausted.

Alex went to fill the kettle. 'Tea with sugar for you.'

'You're more in shock than I am.' Aunt Jean studied him. 'Are you okay with this, love?'

'I need to get used to the idea, that's all.'

'Then know this: No strings. No promises required. Just a hope on my part.'

He kissed her cheek. 'Thank you. That means a great deal.'

'And another thing.' Jean picked up a framed photo of herself and William, taken a couple of years before he died, and prodded at it. 'See that?'

'Ye-es…'

'You could have what we had. Don't be such a stubborn fool. Make up with that girl of yours.'

Alex took in the smiling face of his Uncle William, cheek to cheek with the woman he'd adored for over forty years. 'What if Daisy doesn't want me?'

'Why wouldn't she?' Jean looked at him with pride. 'You're the bee's knees, lad.'

Chapter Twenty-Nine

There was an air of excitement on Christmas Eve at Fox Farm, but Daisy felt immune to it. They were due to close at two today, thank goodness, and she went through the morning on automatic pilot. Dean Martin was doing nothing for her. Even Ella Fitzgerald failed to cheer her up.

Her studio was quiet. Jamie popped over to say the gallery was quiet, too, but the café was heaving with everyone out for a festive treat, so he'd been seconded by Angie for the day, much to Lisa's annoyance.

Daisy had spent the previous afternoon wondering how it was going between Alex, Jean and Nicky. It had been so awkward when Alex had called to see her, knowing what they were likely to discuss with him but not being able to admit to it. And despite their mutual apologies, things still felt damaged between them.

She'd seen Sebastian arrive at some point, too, no doubt to stick his oar in and try to complicate matters.

But when it was over, she'd heard nothing from Alex – she supposed he had much to consider. It was Nicky who had sent her a text in the early evening.

Daisy, you are brilliant. Alex went for it! Fox Farm is saved for as long as we can all make it work, and your studio is yours. See you at Christmas dinner (If I ever get to the end of this horrendous supermarket queue. Serves me right, trying to do the shopping the night before Christmas Eve). Nicky x

Relieved, Daisy had replied positively, but her melancholy had stayed with her all through the night and into the morning. She had her studio now, and she had her art… but it seemed that wasn't enough to feed her soul any more.

At two, she closed up and went over to the café, where it was tradition for the staff to enjoy a drink together before going home. They were all in high spirits, especially with Jean there.

'I'm not allowed alcohol yet,' Jean grumbled, holding up her glass. 'Bloomin' elderflower cordial.'

'Isn't Alex coming?' Lisa asked pointedly.

'He's finishing up at Riverside,' Jean said mildly. 'He wanted to see his *own* staff.'

Or he wanted to avoid me? Daisy wondered before deciding she should get over herself.

They exchanged little gifts. Daisy handed out small framed prints of her work; Angie gave home-baked spiced cookies; Sue had hand-stitched Christmas tree decorations in the shape of Christmas puddings; Jamie had bought organic goats' milk soap made in the Dales, and Lisa had managed grudging boxes of chocolates. Jean hadn't had time to get anything, of course, but Daisy knew the staff felt that having her back was enough of a gift.

As soon as she could get away, Daisy did so, claiming a headache. She wasn't feeling at all sociable, and she still had Christmas Day to face. Back in her studio, she was wrapping her special Christmas present for Jean when she got a text from Jules.

*Found your number on Alex's desk. Hope you don't mind. I wanted
to say thanks for hinting to Alex about the canvas. Can't wait to hang
it. He told me about your ideas for Fox Farm. Clever you! I thought
getting it sorted would make him feel better, but he's still like a bear
with a sore head. I'd hazard a guess that's to do with you. Can you
do something about it? Happy Christmas. Jules x*

'Huh! I doubt I can do much about *that*,' Daisy told her phone.

'Do much about what?'

Daisy spun round to find Alex standing in the doorway, a large
bunch of roses and gypsophila in one hand, and a package in the other.

He came towards her, holding out the flowers. 'For you.'

'Oh! Thank you. I'm not sure I have a vase.'

He held up the package. 'You do now.'

Daisy unwrapped it to find a rounded glass vase she recognised
from the gallery. 'It's beautiful.'

'The least I could do. Thank *you*. For your ideas. Your help. For
everything you've done for Fox Farm. I really appreciate it.'

They're just a thank-you, then. Ah, well. That's nice, I suppose. 'You're
welcome. It's all to my benefit, after all.'

'That isn't why you did it, though, is it? You did it for Fox Farm
and Aunt Jean and me. And Mum.'

Daisy began to arrange the flowers. They must have cost him a
fortune at this time of year, and he must have driven miles for them.

'Your mother texted to say you were going along with it,' she said,
trying not to sound hurt that it was his mother and not him who had
let her know.

But Alex wasn't fooled. 'I'm sorry I didn't get in touch. I had a lot
to think about.'

'I can imagine. I saw Sebastian arrive. I bet he wasn't pleased.'

'That's an understatement. Aunt Jean dropped quite a bombshell. She's cutting him out of her will. I didn't know myself until she announced it.'

Daisy's head snapped up, the flowers forgotten in her fingers. 'That's drastic!'

'But necessary. Sebastian hasn't done anything to reassure her that he's worthy of the inheritance. In fact, he's gone too far the other way. It'll come to me and Mum, and eventually me.'

'So that you can keep it going?'

'Only if that's possible. Aunt Jean promised not to haunt me if it doesn't work out.'

'Goodness! A lot *has* happened in the past few days.'

'Yes, it has.' Alex came closer and lifted her chin so that she had to look him in the eyes. 'But the most important thing is that I realised I love you.'

'What?' Daisy dropped the stem she was holding.

He gave her a tentative smile. 'You heard. But I'll say it again. I love you.'

'That's... But you...'

'I already told you that things had changed for me because of you, but I didn't know how *much*, and then all this crap blew up in our faces, and I couldn't see clearly. I can now.'

Daisy's heart thudded against her ribcage. Should she say it? Dare she?

Uncertainty clouded his eyes. 'I appreciate I've caught you by surprise, but I'd like to know how you feel about me. I *need* to know.'

'I miss being friends,' she admitted. 'That ease we had between us. The flirting and laughing.'

'I do as well. There are other things, too. You and I are so much alike, Daisy. We're not driven by material things or status. We want to achieve and do our best, but not hurt anyone else along the way.'

Daisy placed a hand on his cheek. 'If I tell you I love you, can we be friends again? The way we were?'

He held her gaze. 'Only if it's true.'

'Then I love you.' When his face broke into a relieved smile, she said, 'You have Grace to thank for that. I had no idea.'

'And you have Mum to thank. I had no idea either.'

His mouth met hers, their kiss an acknowledgement of what they had just said, their apologies for recent hurt, and hope for the future. When they broke off, Alex leaned his forehead against hers, his breathing unsteady.

Daisy placed a hand against his heart. 'Don't panic, Alex. We can take it slow. I'm not going to try to drag you up the aisle.'

'That's not why it's beating so fast.'

'Then why?'

'Why do you think?' In one swift movement, he lifted her off her feet, into his arms, and carried her through to her room, where he placed her none too delicately on the bed.

Daisy watched as he kicked off his boots, took off his shirt, impatiently tugged at his jeans, then lay beside her.

'You're at an unfair advantage,' she told him. 'I have too many clothes on.'

'You've been good at solving problems lately. Why don't you do something about it?'

Daisy did.

As they lay together afterwards, she wondered what they could eat. She had very little in. Then she figured they would be eating plenty tomorrow. What she needed now was his closeness. The knowledge that he felt the same way about her as she did about him was joyous. She turned to kiss him, to stroke his chest.

'Are you always this insatiable?' he asked.

'Never have been before. You must be a bad influence.'

'Happy to be.'

They made love again, then ate cheese and crackers, then slept together in the single bed, Daisy exhausted but finally at peace.

*

In the morning, Alex was the first to wake. 'We have to do something about this sleeping arrangement. I'm not designed for this,' he grumbled.

'Tea,' was all Daisy could say, smiling smugly when he obeyed and made her some. Whilst naked.

Now there's a novelty!

'Happy Christmas,' he murmured, kissing her lightly on the lips.

'Happy Christmas. I have something for you.' Daisy reached under the bed for the present she had wrapped for him after they had made up the first time.

Alex sat on the edge of the bed and unwrapped the flat package, then gasped. 'Daisy, it's beautiful.' He traced a finger over the original painting of himself, Jim and Kieran putting up the Christmas tree in the yard, Fox Farm's stone buildings in the background. 'Like you.' He kissed her, then peeped through her curtains. 'I have something for you, too. Come with me.'

He dragged her out of bed, allowing her to pull on a T-shirt and doing the same himself before taking her through to the studio where she could see through the large windows. Soft snowflakes fell onto the cobbles of the farmyard.

'A white Christmas!' she gasped. 'How did you know what to get me?'

'Lucky guess. I didn't have the chance to shop properly. But I do have this for you.' He went to his jacket pocket and pulled out a brown envelope.

Daisy opened it and took out some papers. 'A rental contract for the studio.' She flung her arms around his neck. 'Thank you.'

'Now all we have to do is find somewhere more suitable for you to live. And me. I don't like my house. I don't think I ever did or ever will. We should find something that suits us both. As a couple.'

Daisy's eyes grew wide. 'Are you saying you want us to move in together?'

'I'm sure as hell not sleeping here for the rest of my life.' He gave her a wicked look. 'It'll do for now, though.'

*

Daisy gazed around Jean's kitchen with a lump in her throat. Wonderful aromas of traditional food filled the room, the large pine table was set with textile placemats and mismatched china, and greenery was dotted wherever it could be dotted – a true farmhouse Christmas.

Daisy's painting of Fox Farm that she had given Jean for Christmas, the one with blue skies, hung in pride of place on the wall. She had given Alex's mother an original of Winterbridge, the view that had helped persuade Nicky to move to the Dales.

And Alex had given Daisy an extra gift – his first attempt at painting, the canvas of Jean's cottage garden, which was propped on the dresser for now so they could admire it.

Daisy had messaged Grace that morning to wish her a Happy Christmas and tell her that her world was perfect. Grace had replied with so many happy faces, Daisy couldn't count them.

Nicky and Alex bustled around, allowing Jean to boss them about even though they knew what they were doing.

A true *family* Christmas. And Daisy was a part of it.

Oh, she'd been a part of many family Christmases in her earlier years. Her foster families had always done their best to make sure she had a special time. But that feeling of not belonging had always been there, despite their efforts – the feeling that she was missing out, even though she wasn't sure what she was missing out on.

Now she knew. It had been *this*. Being with people who accepted her unconditionally and about whom she felt the same way, in a place she loved and felt could be her home for a long time to come.

Fox Farm.

Jean leaned towards her. 'You know more than anyone how temporary things can be, Daisy,' she said quietly. 'But I don't believe this is temporary for you. Fox Farm is your home. *Alex* is your home.'

'I know.'

'Then give yourself permission to *enjoy* it, love. Do what makes you happy. Your painting. Keeping this place going, if it's what you both want to do. Loving Alex. Having babies with him.' Jean's eyes misted over. 'I wasn't able to have my own. But I'd like to enjoy yours, so don't leave it *too* long, will you?'

'Jean Fox, you'll outlive us all! Besides, Alex and I aren't—'

'You're in love, and I have a good feeling about you two. Don't muck it up, or you'll have me to answer to. Promise?'

'I promise.'

'Turkey's ready,' Nicky called, supervising Alex as he lifted it, golden brown and fragrant, from the range.

They filled the table with steaming roast potatoes, glazed carrots, roasted parsnips, bread sauce, cranberry sauce, gravy… and, of course, Yorkshire puddings.

'You made those yourself?' Daisy asked, impressed.

'Absolutely. No frozen Yorkshire puds in my house!' Nicky declared.

'I remember that,' Alex said, helping himself. 'Every Sunday without fail. I loved those.'

'Then I'm glad I could make them for you again.' Nicky placed a hand over his. 'I'm glad I could make Christmas dinner for you again. *With* you,' she corrected, smiling. 'You had some pretty miserable Christmases, Alex, and I'm sorry for that. I hope you'll let me make up for them now.'

Alex took his mother's hand. 'You have nothing to make up for. You did your best. That's all anyone can ask. And you gave me the best Christmas ever *this* year. You got together with these two' – he jerked a thumb at Jean and Daisy – 'and had Daisy solving all our problems. You and Daisy have taken a massive weight off my shoulders, *and* you banged mine and Daisy's heads together. I couldn't ask for a better present.'

His mother swiped at a tear. 'Well, this is no good, all of us sitting here crying, whether they're happy tears or not.' She lifted her wine glass. 'To Jean, for taking care of my boy when he most needed it. For giving him a place where he felt he belonged. And to Daisy, for being the person he belongs here with now. Happy Christmas, all of you.'

They lifted their glasses in response. 'Happy Christmas!'

Daisy glanced over at Alex and smiled at the man she loved. This was the happiest Christmas of her life… so far.

Acknowledgements

As always, a huge thank you to my publisher Bookouture for helping me to bring my stories to life and get them out into the world. The entire team are hard-working and wonderful, but I would like to say a very special thank you to my editor Cara Chimirri for her gentle support and love of my stories. Thanks also to Peta Nightingale for her advice and patience, and to Kim Nash, Noelle Holten and Sarah Hardy for the publicity magic they weave.

I couldn't do any of this without the unswerving support of my family, especially my husband who has the patience of a saint and the ability to plug plot holes at three in the morning! My daughter's writerly understanding is invaluable on our lunchtime walks, and my son is appreciated for his much-needed shoulder massages!

To all those friends who follow my writing journey and enjoy my stories – thank you. Thank you also to my writing friends, Authors on the Edge. It's good to know we're all in it together, whatever 'it' is!

And last but definitely not least, a huge thank you to the book-loving community at large – fellow writers, bloggers, and of course all you readers out there. You make all the hard work worthwhile.

A Letter from Helen

Dear reader,

Thank you so much for choosing *Christmas at Fox Farm*. I hope you enjoyed reading about Daisy, Alex, Jean and her beloved Fox Farm as much as I enjoyed writing about them.

If you would like to keep up to date with all my latest releases, just sign up at the following link. Your email address will never be shared and you can unsubscribe at any time.

www.bookouture.com/helen-pollard

I was born and bred in Yorkshire, so where better to choose as a setting for a country Christmas story?

Fox Farm and the nearby village of Winterbridge are both entirely fictitious, but the nearby villages, towns and countryside are all very real. My mother adored the Yorkshire Dales and she passed that love on to me. She never had much desire to travel, and as soon as she returned from wherever my dad had taken her, she would make him drive her out from the suburbs into the countryside, encompass the scenery with widespread arms and say a heartfelt, 'My Dales!'

What I love most about writing is creating a story that readers can lose themselves in, to escape from their own lives for a while. The trouble is, I tend to lose myself in it, too, and my characters become so real in my head – their ups and downs, their worries, their good times – that I often have to remind myself they're imaginary!

I hope you loved *Christmas at Fox Farm*. If you did, I would be grateful if you could take the time to write a review. I'd love to hear what you think, and it makes such a difference helping new readers to discover one of my books for the first time.

I love hearing from my readers, and you can get in touch on my Facebook page or through Twitter.

Thank you,
Helen

HelenPollardWrites
helenpollard147

Made in the USA
Monee, IL
26 October 2021